THE C...

Kit B...

Anti-capitalist guerrillas unwitti... , forces when they kidnap a pregnant heiress, in a *Rosemary's Baby* for our conspiratorial 21st century.

From the Man Booker Prize longlisted author of *The Teleportation Accident* and Clarke Award winning author of *Venomous Lumpsucker*. Perfect for fans of Grady Hendrix and Joe Hill.

For months, Luke and his underground revolutionary group have been planning their biggest operation yet: kidnapping 23-year-old Adeline Woolsaw. They don't want a ransom—they want to expose the Woolsaw Group, the source of Adeline's parents' enormous wealth, a vast yet largely anonymous company that runs everything from military bases and mental hospitals to commuter trains, call centers, and prisons.

But the revolutionaries get a shock when they bundle Adeline into their van. She's about to go into labour. And she may not object to being kidnapped, if it allows her and the baby to escape her despotic parents.

It quickly becomes apparent that this is no ordinary child. He's capable of setting off deadly weather events and summoning plagues of vermin. And that's just the beginning. Luke discovers that Adeline's parents engineered the pregnancy as part of a dark bargain with an ancient evil of nearly limitless power. Now the Woolsaws and their henchmen will stop at nothing to get the infant back, so they can establish an infernal new kingdom on Earth with their grandchild on the throne.

9781835412015 | 30th Sept 2025 | Hardback & E-book £18.99 | 336pp

PRESS & PUBLICITY
Bahar Kutluk
bahar.kutluk@titanemail.com

These are uncorrected advance proofs bound for review purposes. All cover art, trim sizes, page counts, months of publication and prices should be considered tentative and subject to change without notice. Please check publication information and any quotations against the bound copy of the book. We urge this for the sake of editorial accuracy as well as for your legal protection and ours.

PRAISE FOR NED BEAUMAN

"Ned Beauman is a speculative genius."
ELVIA WILK, author of *Death by Landscape*

"[Beauman] has always had the curious knack of wrongfooting his readers with a beating heart where one has expected only cleverness."
NIKHIL KRISHNAN, *Daily Telegraph*

"Ned Beauman is a writer of unceasing invention."
Metro

"Full of fun and big ideas, [Beauman's] conceptually tricksy novels crackle with comic zip, alive to the past as well as the present... His mischievous intelligence can be felt everywhere."
Observer

THE CAPTIVE

KIT BURGOYNE

TITAN BOOKS

The Captive
Hardback edition ISBN: 9781835412015
E-book edition ISBN: 9781835412022

Published by Titan Books
A division of Titan Publishing Group Ltd
144 Southwark Street, London SE1 0UP
www.titanbooks.com

First edition: September 2025
10 9 8 7 6 5 4 3 2 1

This is a work of fiction. All of the characters, organizations, and events portrayed in this novel are either products of the author's imagination or are used fictitiously. Any resemblance to actual persons, living or dead (except for satirical purposes), is entirely coincidental.

© Kit Burgoyne 2025

Kit Burgoyne asserts the moral right to be identified as the author of this work.

No part of this publication may be reproduced, stored in a retrieval system, or transmitted, in any form or by any means without the prior written permission of the publisher, nor be otherwise circulated in any form of binding or cover other than that in which it is published and without a similar condition being imposed on the subsequent purchaser.

A CIP catalogue record for this title is available from the British Library.

EU RP (for authorities only)
eucomply OÜ, Pärnu mnt. 139b-14, 11317 Tallinn, Estonia
hello@eucompliancepartner.com, +3375690241

Typeset in Iowan Old Style.

Printed and bound by 4Edge in the UK

Chapter 1

Four paces. That's their window to take her. When she's coming down the front steps of the clinic, that's too early: the steps have cast-iron railings on either side, so they won't be able to get behind her. And once any part of her body is inside the Land Rover, that's too late: the open door will be in their way, and if she manages to hook herself onto some part of the interior, like maybe she wraps her arms around a headrest, then it's a tug of war. So all they have is the four paces between the steps and the kerb. It's no time at all. But if they miss that window, if she slips back into the building or the car drives away with her inside, they will never get another chance.

Across the road from the clinic, Luke is kneeling by his bicycle pretending to tighten the spokes with a wrench, and he's wearing the full kit – spandex trousers and jersey, gloves, helmet, sunglasses, anti-pollution mask – in the hope that anyone who sees him will think, 'Yeah, that looks like exactly the kind of nerd who would park up in the middle of Marylebone to tune his bike like it's a fucking viola.'

Also, the mask hides his face. The problem is, it's not ideal for taking deep calming breaths. He keeps telling himself that cyclists wear masks like this while they're huffing and puffing up hills, so objectively they can't be that bad, but all the same he feels like he's trying to breathe through a face full of cavity-wall insulation. The only way this could get worse would be if he puked into it before he could get it off, which unfortunately feels like a genuine possibility, because Luke is the most nervous he has ever been in his life. He cannot imagine any happier news right now, any more wonderful gift, than the operation suddenly being called off. Even though this is what they've been working towards for months.

It's 11:46 a.m. He glances up and down the street. On the outside, most of these posh Georgian townhouses look just how they must have the day they were built, but on the inside they have some of the most advanced medical technology in the world; apparently there's a surgeon here who will give you VR goggles when you come for your consultation so you can see what your breasts will look like after he's finished. What surprised Luke when he first came to Harley Street was that even the most exclusive clinics have their waiting rooms right at the front, in what would once have been the drawing rooms, so anybody can peer inside. In fact, the townhouse opposite is the only one on the whole row with frosted glass in its tall sash windows.

Since then he's been on several more scouting missions, so he knows the street's rhythms. The little half-hourly swells of patients arriving for their appointments. The couriers picking up blood and sperm samples. The delivery vans, like the one idling on a yellow line about four doors down – except that one isn't actually a delivery van . . .

He hears a door open. Looks up.

A bodyguard is coming out of the clinic. Bullet-headed in a grey suit.

And behind the bodyguard, there she is. Twenty-three-year-old Adeline Woolsaw, brown hair pinned up, grey leggings, baggy beige jumper. For months now this woman has been the centre of his universe but this is the first time he's ever seen her in the flesh. As if he's an adoring fan waiting at a stage door.

Four paces.

Luke rises, grabbing the flash-bang from the bike's pannier. With his free hand he wheels the bike at high speed towards the Land Rover, exactly as he's rehearsed a hundred times. A second, older woman is coming down the steps, Adeline's governess or chaperone or assistant or whatever she is, as the bodyguard opens the car door.

Luke pulls the pin of the flash-bang with his teeth and tosses it onto the pavement at Adeline Woolsaw's feet.

It looks like nothing much, just a white plastic cylinder the size of a can of deodorant. They sourced it from a guy who has blown up a lot of buildings: his day job is pyrotechnics at a VFX company. He warned them that a flash-bang isn't nearly as potent outdoors as it is in a confined space. But it doesn't need to burst anyone's eardrums. It just needs to buy a few seconds.

The bike clatters to the ground as Luke turns his back on the Land Rover, squeezing his eyes shut and clapping both hands over his ears, tight enough to make a seal.

But the detonation is still so loud that when he takes his hands away his ears are ringing and his guts are ringing too.

Adeline and the bodyguard and the assistant are all standing there like swatted flies, lolling, helpless. As the delivery van pulls up beside him, Luke lifts the bike up by the frame and pitches it with all his strength at the bodyguard. The bodyguard, who never saw it coming, is knocked over sideways.

The side door of the van slides open and out hops Rosa, who wears a surgical mask and a hoodie with the hood up. Together they grab Adeline Woolsaw, Rosa taking her by the left arm, Luke by the right – so he's touching her, he's actually touching her, this person who until now was only ever really an abstraction, a distant planet. As they drag her into the back of the van, she doesn't resist at all. In fact, she even ducks her head a little bit, as if to make it easier for them. Which has got to be the shock, Luke thinks. At the same time, he's starting to register that she's sort of the wrong shape –

But then, before they can slide the door shut, the assistant or governess or chaperone wraps both her arms around Adeline's left leg. Luke never imagined that instead of the bodyguard, who is only just getting up off the ground, their biggest obstacle would be this little middle-aged woman in a tweed suit. But she has a death grip on Adeline's calf, so for a moment it really is the tug of war they were determined to avoid.

'Just fucking punch her!' Rosa says.

The problem is, Luke has never in his life punched anyone in the face. His first kidnapping has come before his first proper fight. Which sounds ridiculous, but it's true. And so, presented with this woman who looks like somebody's mum, he hesitates.

Rosa handles it instead. She jabs the assistant right in the eye. The assistant staggers backward, releasing her hold on Adeline. At last Luke and Rosa are able to slide the van door shut.

And now Luke becomes aware of two things that he very much was not expecting.

The first is that Adeline Woolsaw is pregnant.

When she was coming down the stairs her midsection was hidden from view by the bodyguard in front, and during the struggle just now he was too busy to really clock it. But she is pregnant. Heavily pregnant, in fact. Huge under that baggy cashmere jumper.

And the second thing is that she's shouting, 'Go! Go! Come on! Go!' Urgency in her voice. Desperation.

As if she wants them to get away.

As if she doesn't realise she's being kidnapped.

As if she thinks she's being rescued.

Chapter 2

As Cam puts the van into reverse, Luke and Rosa force Adeline onto her knees, up against the side of the van, so they can zip-tie her wrists behind her back. They practised this over and over with Cam standing in for the target, but it's different with a big pregnant belly in the way. Luke tries not to be too rough, but Rosa doesn't hold back.

'Hey, you don't need to do that,' Adeline says. 'You don't need to – hey—'

It finally seems to dawn on her that she is not, after all, being rescued. And she starts to struggle. But it's too late. The zip tie is already tight around her wrists, and now Luke slips a black drawstring bag over her head. As Cam takes a corner at high speed, the three of them nearly topple over together, but Luke manages to grab one of the cargo straps hanging from the wall. As they reposition her, pulling her down onto her side, Luke isn't sure if they ought to be supporting her belly the same way they're supporting her head, and anyway he's hesitant to put his hands on it – though when he does he finds that Adeline's jumper is probably the softest object he's touched in his life, like a fleece sheared from the ghost of a goat. Lastly, they zip-tie her ankles as well, and Luke sees that one of her suede sandals must have come off during the scuffle.

The whole routine goes smoothly, or about as smoothly as you could hope for in the circumstances. But when Luke sees the result – a pregnant women curled up on the floor of the van, hood over her head, wrists and ankles bound – the image wallops him like that punch Rosa threw at the assistant. At that moment what he's feeling does not at all resemble triumph.

So he's not ready for it when Rosa pulls down her mask and pulls down his too and then kisses him, kisses him as if she wants to fuck right there in the van. He's so surprised he freezes up, and after a moment she detaches, frowning. They aren't supposed to talk too much in front of Adeline, but he wants to tell her that it's premature to celebrate, because it's not like they've got away yet. Not even close. And anyway his mind is racing, trying to work out what this development means for them.

Isn't this going to look terrible? Aren't people going to be horrified? Obviously the kidnapping was going to alienate a good chunk of the public no matter what, but what about the people in the middle, the people who are supposed to be shocked out of their complacency, the people who are supposed to come over to their side? How is this going to look to them? Taking an enemy prisoner is an act of war, but kidnapping a woman who's just about to have a baby – doesn't that feel a bit like a war crime?

'Who are you?' Adeline says, her voice muffled by the bag. 'What is this?'

'We're the Nail,' Luke says gently. 'We don't want to hurt you. Do as we say and in a few days we'll give you back to your family.'

'But I don't want that. I don't want to go back to my family.'

Rosa says, 'Where's your phone?'

'I haven't got a phone.'

'Don't lie.' With absolutely none of the reticence that Luke has been feeling about the softer parts of Adeline's body, Rosa starts frisking her from head to toe for electronics.

'I'm not. I haven't got a phone. I'm not allowed one.'

'GPS tracker? Panic button?'

'On my left wrist.'

Rosa unclasps from Rosa's wrist what looks like an expensive fitness tracker, with a shiny black face and a rose-gold strap. She passes it up to Cam in the driver's seat and he tosses out of the window.

'Is that everything?' Rosa says, still patting her down.

'Yes.'

'Anything you don't tell us about, I'll find it anyway. I don't care if it's up your fucking fanny, I'll find it. So give it up now, because if I find it and you haven't told me, there will be consequences.'

'That's everything, I promise you.'

The van's back windows are covered so it's only by feeling cobblestones under the tires that Luke knows they've pulled into the mews off Devonshire Street. Cam parks and gets out of the van. Luke hitches up the bottom of the black bag so that Rosa can put a strip of duct tape over Adeline's mouth, then pulls it back down and tightens the drawstring under her chin. As they're wrapping a big tartan blanket around her, Luke hears a garage door being hiked up. Then Cam bangs on the roof of the van: ready. Luke slides open the side door, then grabs Adeline under the armpits as Rosa takes her ankles. 'Don't squirm or we might drop you,' she says.

Along one side of the mews is a row of garages that have been in limbo for a long time because some developer bought them hoping to build houses but then Westminster Council wouldn't allow it. So they've been sitting there empty behind their garage in constant use signs, until last night, when Cam broke into one and left a second van inside. Like the first van, it has a fresh set of cloned plates, ordered from a company in Jersey where they don't ask too many questions.

The gap between one van and the other is just a few feet, and they're overlooked only by the spindly fire escape of a building on Weymouth Street, so there's nobody to see them transfer their big lumpy cargo. Also, there are no CCTV cameras in this mews, which is the reason they chose it.

However, the wider neighbourhood has plenty of them. It's so central, just a quarter mile south of Régent's Park, and as well as the clinics for the rich there are embassies around here, consulates, high commissions. It was mad, actually, to do this in W1. But they didn't have a choice. The Woolsaws so rarely come into the light. Even for four paces.

It means, though, that when the police comb through all the CCTV footage from the area, they'll probably be able to connect one van to the other. Meaning that this change of vans is not an escape, it's just a way to buy time. If they really want to cover their tracks, they'll have to go a lot farther afield.

So Cam takes them west.

By now Luke is not running on adrenaline so much as a slow-cooked stew of anxiety hormones, and periodically a skin forms over the stew when nothing happens for a little while, but then the van stops and the stew erupts again because Luke is absolutely certain they've been caught even though it's really just a red light. After several rounds of that, it's a relief when he feels the van decisively speed up, because that means they're past Marylebone Road and up onto the Westway. Cam hasn't said a word since well before the kidnapping. But that just means everything's going according to plan.

About twenty minutes later, the van comes down off the motorway. They must be in Park Royal. The largest warehouse district in Europe, a city-within-a-city here beside the railway sidings. Wholesalers of double glazing, wheelchairs, baklava. Lots of it perfectly respectable, but not all of it: squeezed into the smaller, odder-shaped lots, the little triangles and rhombuses, you find the more fly-by-night operations, the dodgy wrecking yards and the fake handbag importers.

There, you can nip up a ladder and disconnect the CCTV cameras, and nobody will notice for weeks. Which is exactly what Luke and Cam did two nights ago in a little patch of nothing-much between a warehouse and a body shop. And Park Royal has a constant flow of white vans just like this one, hundreds every hour.

If you switch vehicles in a blind spot, then you can just disappear into the herd.

So in this down-the-back-of-the-sofa zone with the dead hedge and the wheelie bins and the rotting stack of shipping pallets, they go through it all again: waiting until Cam gives them the all-clear, then carrying Adeline across to yet another van, this one silver and still decaled with the logo of the heating company it used to belong to. But they don't leave right away. Instead, they wait, nobody talking, Rosa holding Luke's hand, Cam still up in the driver's seat so he can keep lookout, Adeline lying there on her side. She must be wondering what's happening.

What's happening is that they're leaving a buffer. Yes, this corner might be a blind spot, but the police will be able to piece together a lot of footage from the cameras nearby, and you don't want them to be able to say 'At 11:31 a.m., this van entered Park Royal, and at 11:34 a.m., this other van left Park Royal.' That makes it easy for them. Instead you hold on as long as you think you can risk it. Every minute that goes by, that's more vehicles leaving Park Royal, more decoys, more chaff, more innocent catering vans the police will have to chase up before they ever get to you. In any other circumstances watching a clock makes time goes slower, but Luke finds the wait so unbearable that staring at his Casio actually *helps*, the seconds winking by a reassurance that the universe hasn't just completely ground to a halt—

Adeline groans through the duct tape.

Luke looks at Rosa. And Rosa shrugs to say they shouldn't pay any attention. All the same, he plucks at the fabric of the bag to make sure it's not blocking her nostrils.

Then they hear the helicopter.

It doesn't sound that far off. Once again, Luke looks at Rosa. And this time, she doesn't look as relaxed.

'Cam,' Luke says.

'Chill out,' Cam says. 'Nothing to do with us.'

'Should we get going anyway?'

'No. Parked is good. We're just another van. If they were looking. Which they aren't.'

But then, as if to express her disagreement, Adeline groans again. Luke sees her hands clench into fists – and sees, also, a dark patch on her leggings that wasn't there before.

The helicopter is definitely getting closer. Luke's bowels have been thrumming at various frequencies ever since Harley Street and this just adds one more. 'Cam,' he says again. But this time Cam doesn't answer.

Adeline is knocking on the floor of the van with the one sandal she still has on. Not thrashing around but knocking like she's trying to signal to them. Knock knock knock. Knock knock knock.

Luke can't take it any more. He goes to the back windows of the van and pulls back one corner of the blackout cover.

Right away he sees it. A flash of blue and green.

From here he has a view down the alley between two warehouses, and at the other end of the alley there's another access road, and that's where it was, just for a moment, about a hundred yards away. He's certain. That fluorescent chequerboard pattern on the side of police cars.

'Cam,' he says. 'Police.'

And at the same time he becomes aware of a smell inside the van, not strong but definitely new, a sort of sweet, bleachy smell.

Adeline's still doing it. Knock knock knock. Knock knock knock. So Luke loosens the drawstring of the bag again and pulls the tape off her mouth.

'What the fuck are you doing?' Rosa says to him.

Before he can answer, Adeline says, 'I'm fairly sure I'm going into labour.'

Chapter 3

'I thought you'd pissed yourself,' Luke says.

'I wish it were just that,' Adeline says.

'You're saying that's your waters breaking?' Rosa says. 'I thought it was like emptying a bucket out?'

'Sometimes it's more like a little leak in the bucket,' Adeline says. 'Look, this is my second time. I know what it feels like. It feels like *this*. I'm sorry if this isn't a good moment but it's really not up to me.'

Luke gets a bit claustrophobic any time a barber so much as drapes a hot towel over his eyes, yet somehow Adeline is conversing in a relatively normal way even with most of her face still covered by the bag. Luke doesn't understand how she can stay so calm. And on top of that, he's wondering what she means about this being her second time. Because it can't be, can it? She's only twenty-three, and in all their research on the Woolsaws, which has been pretty fucking thorough, there's never been any mention of a grandchild.

All Luke knows about the beginning of labour is something a friend once told him, a friend who had kids pretty young, about how for her it was like when you're just starting to come up on MDMA, not euphoric yet, just a whooshing change in your sense of everything as your brain is flooded with new chemicals.

He peeks out past the blackout covers again, and sees two more police cars whip by.

And then they hear a siren.

A siren is really, really, really bad. Because a siren means the police aren't even worried about tipping them off. It means they're confident of having them cornered. It means they're just trying to get more backup here as fast as they can. In hindsight all the worry Luke felt up until now *was* like a hot-towel wrap compared to the dread that swallows him at this moment.

Cam is exposed up at the front, so he now squeezes past the seats to join the others squatting beside Adeline in the back.

'How the fuck did they get here so quickly?' Rosa says. She gives Adeline a hard cuff on the arm. 'What didn't you tell us about?'

'There's nothing else. You saw the tracker. Where would I hide another one of those?'

'I don't know, maybe you have a chip in your ear like a fucking dog!'

'What I have is a surname which makes things happen quickly. Sometimes much more quickly than one would ever believe.'

Adeline could be right, Luke thinks. Maybe all it takes is the word 'Woolsaw' going out over the radio and instantly the entire policing apparatus of greater London converges like a single organism. Maybe somewhere near here there's a blood-spattered spree killer wearing only one handcuff because the arresting officers ran off halfway through. Cam was sure the Met couldn't react fast enough to track the vans in real time, and Luke trusted him, but what if every CCTV control room in London was drafted at once? Luke begins to wonder why they ever thought they could pull this off.

There are unmistakably at least two helicopters overhead. The van feels even smaller now that they're all here in the back together, foxes in a den as the hounds draw closer. Cam goes to the back windows to take a look himself.

'Cam, what are we going to do?' Luke says.

Adeline is doing what sound like breathing exercises, but she keeps losing the rhythm, the long, regular, serene breaths breaking down into short, shaky, grindy ones.

'I don't know,' Cam says. And to hear Cam say that is almost worse than the sirens. Those words are doom to Luke. Because Cam's been through everything several times over. Cam always, always knows what happens next.

'Can you see anything?'

'Yeah. There are guys getting out of a van. They've got guns.'

A noise on the roof of the van. A tapping. Rosa lets out a little whimper of surprise, then claps her hand over her mouth.

'That's just hail,' Cam says. 'It's started hailing.'

Which is odd, because even a few minutes ago, when they were switching vans, the sky was a perfect blue. But the tapping doesn't stop.

Luke watches Cam, wondering what's going through his mind. In the planning stages they talked about worst-case scenarios. About what they would do if it ended this way. And one point they agreed on was that they weren't going to bother with the Quebec thing.

The Quebec thing is saying to the police 'Put us on a plane to a nonextradition country or we'll kill the girl.' The reason they call it 'the Quebec thing' is because, as far as they can tell, that's the only time in history it's ever worked: Quebec in 1970, when five Quebecois separatists took the British trade commissioner hostage for two months. The night the police found their hideout, they tossed a note out through the window saying they'd murder the trade commissioner at the first sign of a raid and demanding that the Canadian government fly them to Cuba in exchange for his release. And the Canadians actually obliged. The next morning, a police escort accompanied the kidnappers and their hostage to an old World's Fair pavilion in Montreal, where they handed him over; then a Royal Canadian Airforce helicopter took the kidnappers to the airport; and from there an RCAF plane took them to Havana. The head negotiator apparently described the atmosphere on the flight as 'relaxed, quiet, and subdued.'

Maybe it could only have happened in Canada. Much more commonly, when people tried something like that, it was more like Munich two years later, the authorities just playing along until they could shoot the kidnappers dead on the runway.

So the Quebec thing was out. They weren't chumps. But what they would do instead – well, that they never entirely agreed on. A few weeks ago Rosa said that, hypothetically, if they ended up killing Adeline Woolsaw after everything went to shit, then at least they would have struck a blow. If they were going to prison for a long time anyway, at least it would show the world that you could fight back, tooth and claw. The bastards would feel fear after that, not just the Woolsaws but all the others of their kind.

Cam didn't say he agreed with her. But it didn't seem like he really disagreed either. Sometimes Luke thinks he should have walked away as soon as he found out that was on the table. But he didn't. He's here. And what is Cam thinking right now when he looks at Adeline?

The hail is getting louder. 'Can someone take my jumper off, please?' Adeline says, her cheeks flushed and sweaty. Luke hesitates, but then a wave seems to crash through Adeline, and she cries out, writhing on the nonslip mat. He has to do *something* for her, and the jumper is loose enough that even with her wrists behind her back he can pull it up off her torso, although he has to reach through it, her jaw moist against his wrist, to make sure he doesn't also pull off the bag as he's stretching the neckline over her head—

Rosa taps him and mouths, 'What the fuck are you doing?' Because there was never anything in the plan about keeping the hostage nice and comfortable.

All the same, he finishes pulling the jumper inside out around Adeline's shoulders until it's dangling off her by the sleeves, which is the furthest he can get with her wrists still tied. She has a white vest on underneath and Luke feels renewed amazement at how big her belly is. He realises he can bunch the jumper up like a pillow under her head, which has a pale grid down one side from being pressed into the mat –

The sound of glass smashing, outside the van, some distance away.

Luke thinks of a sniper on some high floor knocking through a window to make way for his rifle barrel.

But then they hear shouting too. A car alarm going off. Then another.

It has to be the hail, which isn't a tapping any more but a pummelling louder than the helicopters.

Cam is still at the back windows, so Luke pokes his head between the front seats, staying as low as he can, so he can get a look through the windscreen.

The clouds are so thick and dark it feels like dusk, and they're hurling polar quantities of ice at Park Royal. It's the most furious hailstorm he's ever seen.

And they aren't even getting the worst of it, here in the van. He can see broken windscreens, creased bonnets, dangling wing mirrors. One of the cameras they so carefully disabled has been torn off its bracket. At the edge of the scrapyard there's a skip heaped with bulging waste bags, and the waste bags are quivering around and spurting out their insides like somebody getting shot to pieces with a chain gun.

He sees a lot of police – some in full tactical gear with carbines slung across their chests, others in the normal black vests and white shirtsleeves – but none of them are even looking at the van any more, they're all just huddled in whatever shelter they can find, one beneath the open lid of a wheelie bin, another in the cab of a forklift. Out in the road, two of them are carrying a third to one of their vehicles as if she's a battlefield casualty.

There's a continuous shattering sound of ice breaking on the asphalt, and it's difficult to make out any individual hailstone amid the glinting shingle, but where Luke can, he sees there's something strange about these hailstones. They're not round, like any hailstone he's seen before. They're long and pointed. Like icicles. Or daggers.

A flash of movement in the sky. He looks up.

It's one of the helicopters. Falling.

'Oh fuck—' he hears himself say. 'Oh fuck—'

It twirls as it falls, and even just the twirling is sickening to see, knowing there are passengers inside that cockpit as it spins on its axis like some unspeakable fairground ride. But, even worse, the helicopter is skidding through the air on a long diagonal towards the roof of a warehouse – and now, as Luke watches, it crashes straight through. Out of sight. So he doesn't see it hit the ground, but he hears it, a thunderous impact with a fading aftersound as the steel walls of the warehouse reverberate over the hail.

Immediately, several cops come sprinting out of their shelters, heading for the warehouse. Luke cannot imagine there could possibly be any survivors, but clearly they feel they have to check. Behind him Adeline lets out a guttural wail.

Then Luke sees blood. A spray of it from the neck of one of the sprinting policemen. And he sprawls forward onto the icy ground, carried along by his own momentum.

For a moment Luke wonders if it was a hailstone – but no, that's crazy, a hailstone can't do that to someone, it had to have been a bullet – there are plenty of guns around, so maybe in all the confusion—

But then a second guy drops. And this time there's no denying what happened, because as he lies prone you can see the hailstone sticking out of him, a chisel of ice in his calf.

Before long, the entire rescue party is on the ground, punctured in one place or another by hailstones. And of course it doesn't stop when they're down. The storm keeps hitting them, chewing at their bodies like the needle of a sewing machine, spike after spike.

By this point Luke can see only two cops still alive. One is dragging herself back towards the shelter of a loading dock, but then an enormous hailstone, eight or ten inches long, plunges straight through the small of her back. She goes limp.

And another, less than a hundred feet from the van, is shielding himself under a metal signboard that the hail has knocked loose from a fence, big orange letters advertising mot testing. He's trying to curl himself up as small as he can, but the sign isn't big enough to protect him properly.

'There's a guy out there,' Luke says. 'We could help him.'

'What guy?' Rosa says.

'A cop.'

'Are you taking the piss?'

She's got a point. They are, after all, in the middle of a kidnapping. But even if they don't want to pull him inside the van, Luke thinks they could just drive over there, nose the front bumper carefully over the cop so that he could crawl underneath.

The keys are still in the ignition. He could just get into the driver's seat and do it. Instead of sitting here and watching while the storm hacks at this guy's extremities.

But before he can make up his mind, it's too late.

Because, impossibly, the blitz gets even heavier. For a few seconds the hail comes down so hard you can't see anything else, just a staticky boil of ice unbroken in any direction, the roar of its impact drowning out all thought. How can the atmosphere even manufacture this much solid matter? By now the windscreen of the van ought to be in smithereens, but they must be parked right in the eye of the storm, because it's almost as if the hail is avoiding them.

Then the crescendo ends. Rapidly the storm begins to ease. The hailstones are diminishing both in size and in number, so that before long the sound is once again a clatter of individual impacts rather than an undifferentiated hiss. Until it's coming down on the roof no faster than the tapping that startled them all at the beginning.

What's left, afterwards, is an apocalypse. An eroded, punished landscape. Broken windows, fallen drainpipes, limbless trees. Garage doors and car panels pitted and gouged. The canopy of a bus stop has collapsed onto the people sheltering under it. They lie there motionless, blood pooling on the ground, which is as crystal white as fresh snow but with a much bumpier surface, like a billion packing peanuts spilled out of a box.

The mot testing guy is lying on his back, the signboard resting halfway across him. His face and hands look like raw meat. There is a long spike protruding from his eye socket.

Luke realises he can smell vomit. He turns to see that Adeline has thrown up on the mat. Good thing they took the duct tape off, although a little bit got on her hair and on the drawstring of the bag. She's not twisting around or gritting her teeth any more. 'Adeline, are you . . .' He doesn't know what question to ask. 'Is it still . . .'

'The contractions have just calmed down for a bit,' she answers. 'They'll come back. May I please have some water?'

They have a couple of litre bottles in the corner. He props her head up so she can drink. He wants to wipe the vomit from the corner of her mouth, but there's nothing at hand to do it with, so in the end he uses the hem of her cashmere jumper. The world's most expensive puke rag.

'We should get going,' Cam says, climbing back into the driver's seat.

At first the words hardly mean anything to Luke. The idea of escaping feels like something from another life.

But Cam is a pragmatist. Always. So it doesn't matter that they're all still gaping at what they've just been through. It doesn't matter that the plan collided with something utterly inexplicable. All that matters is what's next.

'She's right,' Cam says, nodding at Adeline. 'When it's the Woolsaws, they don't hold anything back. They would have sent everyone they had from miles around. And I don't know if any of them survived that. Plus every camera's in bits. If we get going now, we could be well away before the second wave arrives.'

So they reverse out of the yard, tires crunching over the hailstones. And nobody stops them. Because there's nobody left.

Chapter 4

At Greenford Roundabout they come off the motorway so they can swap vans one last time at a smaller industrial estate that straddles the canal. No more surprises, thank God. Then back on the A40 until they're almost at the RAF base. It's all very green and spacious out here but it's not countryside, just golf courses and cricket clubs and shooting ranges – hobbyland. Down the West End Road, turn right at the tire shop, and they're home. Cam parks the van round the back, then they carry Adeline into the school.

Ruislip School for Blind and Partially Sighted Children, closed since 2011. In squatter terms, it's a paradise. Just like those garages off Devonshire Street, it's in indefinite stasis, dead-stopped by overoptimistic capital flows. After the council ran out of money to keep it open, they sold the property to an investment trust in the British Virgin Islands. Maybe there was once a plan to turn it into something, a hotel or a private rehab centre, but in twelve years it hasn't been touched. Sheets still on the beds, crockery still in the cupboards. The electricity was cut off, but Cam knows a bloke from UK Power Networks who came in and turned it back on for them, no metre, no bills. And the water was never disconnected in the first place. No gas, which means no hot water or central heating, and there's mould in the walls. But they get by with hot plates and kettles and space heaters and one dodgy electric shower unit that hasn't fried anybody yet but probably will someday.

Other than the textured mats at the top of every staircase and the Braille signs outside every door, there's little to distinguish it from any other school building. It's ludicrously oversized for just three tenants, but at least they have all the space they could ever need, and it's far enough from the road that they never get any unwelcome attention (plus they've put up a sign outside that says this property is protected by live-in guardians, just in case anyone ever does get close enough to see that it's inhabited). Luke sometimes wonders if the people who own it even remember that they own it.

A bedroom – which is to say a cell – has already been made up for Adeline, one of the rooms with an en suite on Corridor B. It still has its beige carpets and pine furniture from back when the school took boarders, but it's been modified pretty extensively for its new purpose. The door handle has been replaced with a privacy knob, like on a bathroom door, except it only locks from the outside; a peephole has been cut into the door, with a cover hanging off a nail; the actual bathroom door has been replaced with a curtain; wooden boards have been nailed up over the window; and every fitting that she could possibly use to hurt herself or anyone else – desk chair, wardrobe rail, bedside lamp, bathroom mirror, shower door, toilet-tank lid – has been taken out.

If they wanted, they could have her chained to a radiator and shitting in a pail. But even apart from how that would sound to the public if Adeline ever told her story, Cam says it would be a bad idea for them, the captors. Especially first-timers like Luke and Rosa. When you're fighting a war you do whatever's necessary, Cam says, even if it turns your stomach. But once you go beyond what's necessary, once it becomes cruelty, that's different. A lot of people seem to think that indulging in a bit of collective sadism can be a bonding exercise, good for morale. And it can, Cam says, but it's a quick, cheap hit, and you come down from it fast, and very soon you need to do it again. You start to look at one another differently, you start to treat one another differently. Cam's speaking from experience.

Once she's on the bed, Cam snips the zip ties at her wrists and ankles and pulls the black bag off her head. He has his two-foot wheel wrench to hand, just in case she tries anything, even though that seems extremely unlikely while she's in the middle of having a baby. This is the first time since the fracas that Luke has seen her whole face, and the sudden unveiling makes her grey eyes seem even brighter.

Adeline is now finally able to pull the jumper the rest of the way off, and as she flexes the feeling back into her arms she takes in her new situation. The room. The three of them still in their masks and hoods. The wheel wrench. She can probably guess that they wouldn't have taken the restraints off her unless she was going to be here for the foreseeable future. And Luke hears, for the first time, unchecked panic in her voice as she says, 'So are you just going to stand there and watch me while I—'

'A doctor's coming,' Cam says.

Sure enough, not long afterwards, they hear the car pulling off the road. Luke goes to meet Shirley at the door.

By day, Shirley's an NHS doctor, working at a hospital somewhere in London; Luke doesn't know which one. Shirley Drain, his nom de guerre, is the name of a tube that sucks blood out of a wound, but it was also the stage name of a drummer in some post-punk band from the 1980s, and that drummer was male too, which is why Shirley thought of it. Even though Cam doesn't really approve of aliases that are too colourful.

Shirley was warned beforehand that he might be needed at some point: the children of the megarich can be delicate flowers, and there was no knowing what boutique medical conditions Adeline might have, what exclusive psychopharmaceuticals she might be dependent upon. But there was absolutely no suggestion that they might be dealing with what they are now dealing with. His arrival is an enormous relief to Luke, who was on the verge of looking up how-to videos on YouTube.

'Cam said it was urgent,' Shirley says, toting his gym bag full of doctor's stuff, 'so I thought someone had got hurt.'

'Not us,' Luke says.

'I heard a lot of sirens on the way here. A hell of a lot, around Hanger Lane. Was that anything to do with you?'

'Some of them, probably, yeah. But not all of them. There was a storm. A big one.'

Shirley puts on a surgical mask and cap before he goes into Adeline's room. Obviously they weren't prepping for the Miracle of Life to take place in there, but he says he can make it work.

While Shirley is ministering to his new patient, the others go into the common room across the landing, where they take off their masks and hoods. To be back here, in these familiar surroundings, together, free, the whole thing behind them – for the first time it hits Luke that it actually worked, they actually did it, and there's part of him that wants to be revelling like they just won the World Cup. But it doesn't feel right yet with so much unresolved.

'What the fuck happened out there?' Rosa says.

'We got lucky,' Luke says. 'Insanely lucky. Freak weather. Freak weather saved us.'

But even as he's saying it, he's not sure he believes it. And Cam shakes his head. 'No. Mate. You know as well as I do. You saw it. That wasn't natural.'

'Then what was it?' Rosa says. And Luke is hopeful that Cam can settle this question like he settles so many questions, that somewhere in the deep hinterlands of his experience an answer can be found. Luke, at twenty-five, and Rosa, at twenty-eight, are both rookies. But Cam, at forty-eight, is a veteran. Back in the early '90s, he took one of the more roundabout routes into activism that Luke has ever heard of. Growing up on an estate in Salford, his two older brothers were wannabe gangsters who ran security and sold drugs for acid house parties. Cam, already a pretty formidable physical presence even as a teenager, would sometimes come along to lend a hand. His brothers had nothing but contempt for the ravers, but Cam couldn't help making friends. By 1993, he was helping to run a sound system for the anti-eviction protests in northeast London. By 2001, an old hand at only twenty-five, he was in Genoa rioting against the G8 summit. But he was already losing faith in his fellow activists, and the wimpy response to the police brutality in Genoa convinced him that they were never going to accomplish anything serious.

So he went underground. Unfortunately, leaving behind his old comrades didn't mean he could escape the fecklessness and self-sabotage that has dogged every leftist movement since the beginning of time. Today he will sometimes compare the three types of outlaws he mixed with as a young man. 'My brothers and their mates, when they were selling pills, they were the best organised. Then the people who put on the raves, they were in the middle. And then the people who put on the protests, they were dead last. They were the most fucking inept, easily. Which is saying a lot, if you know anything about the first two.' The history of his efforts over the last twenty years has been a history of failure – that's a sadness he carries openly – and he blames his allies, and himself, as much as he blames his enemies. But his determination hasn't faltered. Luke has never been able to piece together anything resembling a chronology of Cam's activities. But even though he's not *that* old, he seems to have been everywhere, done everything. You can hear it in the way he talks, or rather doesn't talk: it's almost as if, once he's said a given sentence once in his life, he never feels the need to say it again, so by now what's worth opening his mouth for? For Cam, there's not much new under the sun.

Except today is new. Even for him. 'I don't know what it was,' he says. 'I really don't know. What I do know is that the CIA have done a lot of research into weather modification. Cloud seeding. They used to do it with salt, but now they have these little diamond balloons. You use them as an area-denial weapon. You fog the whole place up, then you send in the guys with infrared goggles, and they're the only ones who can see.'

'But it wasn't fog, it was hail,' Luke says. 'And it didn't hurt us, it hurt them.'

'Maybe it's still experimental. Maybe it went wrong. Happens all the time. Look at Waco, look at the Moscow theatre. And this is the Woolsaws, right? They're going to pull out all the stops. Someone at the top is probably shouting down the phone, "Well if you've got this thing, you'd better use it. I don't care if it's supposed to be secret. I don't care if it's not ready." The point is, we made it. We've got her.'

'And she's having a baby,' Luke says. 'All that planning and we didn't even know she was having a baby.'

'It's a good thing,' Rosa says. 'Two hostages for the price of one.'

Cam goes outside to bring in a few more things from the van. Adeline cries out so loud it carries down the corridor and through the fire doors.

Rosa smirks. 'Bet she thought she'd be having it in a nice comfy hospital, off her face on painkillers.'

There's a pitter-patter at the window. Luke and Rosa freeze.

Like the van, the windows of the school are covered with black privacy film, so that nobody will see from a distance that the lights are on at night. But it also means they can't see out.

'Is that . . .' Rosa says.

'It's probably just rain,' Luke says.

'But if it's the hail again – and if Cam's right—'

'They wouldn't use it a second time. After what happened.'

'Yeah, but still—'

Adeline lets out another yowl.

Luke goes to the window, which looks out onto the overgrown field behind the main building. As on the door to Adeline's room, there's a square of cardboard that can be pushed to one side to peek out through a gap in the privacy film.

Just as he thought, it's not hail, it's heavy rain. But this isn't like any rain he's ever seen.

The droplets are thick and gluey, leaving snail trails down the glass. Yellowish white with twists of red or pink inside. It so blears the air that you can hardly make out the spruce trees a quarter mile from the school. If you were driving in this your windscreen wipers would manage about three wipes before they had heart attacks from the exertion.

Cam comes back into the common room, breathing hard. After just a minute outside, he looks like he's been dipped in batter. And he reeks. It's a strange, unplaceable reek, like if you took one of those nostril-numbing chemistry-lab smells and left it to rot in a dark place.

And unless Luke's imagining it, he can also detect a hint of that sweetish smell from when Adeline's waters broke in the van.

Okay, so when police used their prototype area-denial weapon, that caused some anomalous pressure system in the atmosphere which sucked up industrial runoff from a reservoir somewhere and is now scattering it across west London . . .

Any rational explanation just crumbles in his hands, no matter how hard he tries to hold it together.

Cam warned them once that very large concentrations of wealth are like deformations in space-time; they warp reality around them. The closer you get to a family like the Woolsaws, the more you depart from any recognisable everyday logic. But surely he didn't mean *this*.

'Are you okay?' he says to Cam.

'I need a fucking shower.'

But then Shirley shouts from Corridor B: 'Hey, I need you in here. Two of you. Cam and somebody else.'

Cam grabs a blanket so he can towel himself off on the way. Luke follows him to the door of Adeline's bedroom, where Shirley raises his eyebrows at Cam's bedragglement. He wants to talk to Cam alone, meaning Luke will be guarding Adeline. So Luke puts on his balaclava. Not the old-fashioned type with three separate holes – surely nobody buys those any more unless they're dressing up as a burglar for Halloween – but the athletic type with just one big opening for the eyes.

He feels awkward going into Adeline's room. Nervous, even. But when Adeline glances up, face redder than ever, hair pasted to her forehead, it's without interest, as if on her priority list the fact of his existence comes way, way below what's currently going on in her body. He has the urge to give her a look of apology. He didn't get into this so he could force a twenty-three-year-old girl to have her baby in a cell surrounded by strangers in masks. But he stops himself. If he were really that sorry, he could do something about it, couldn't he? But he's not going to.

'The clinic you took her from,' he hears Shirley say to Cam out in the corridor. 'What exactly were they treating her for?'

'No clue,' Cam says. 'Like I said, we didn't even know she was pregnant. We only got access to the appointments calendar, not the medical notes.'

'So you know which doctor she was seeing?'

'Yeah, but we couldn't find out anything about him. You look him up online, there's nothing there. What's the issue?'

Shirley shuts the door and slides the cover over the peephole.

But Luke wants to hear this. So he presses his ear against the wood. He feels weaselly, even more so because Adeline can see him doing it. Not that he should care what she thinks.

'This isn't a straightforward pregnancy,' he hears Shirley say. 'I can tell you that much already. But that's about all I can tell you.'

'How bad is it?'

'I don't know. And I don't have what I'd need to find out. I'm mystified, to be honest with you. The point is, I can't make any guarantees about this delivery. Not with what I have to work with here – and anyway, I've assisted with a few deliveries but I'm not an obstetrician. If this were happening on the ward, I'd call a consultant.'

'What are you saying? Are you saying we could lose her?'

'More likely the baby. But as I said, I can't make any guarantees. Sometimes you lose both. Not often, but it does still happen, and it's almost always when they haven't made it to a hospital. Cam, I think we should put her in an ambulance.'

'You want to call an ambulance? Here?'

'No, obviously not. I mean we could blindfold her again, dump her in the park, call an ambulance to pick her up.'

'She'd know she hadn't gone far. She'd tell them that and they'd have an area to search. Unless we knocked her out.'

'In the middle of labour?'

'You're telling me things *could* go wrong. But you don't know that. It could be fine.'

'Well, yeah, but—'

'Then I think you'd better do the best you can, and the rest of us had better hope. We didn't come this far to just give her back.'

'What are they saying about me?' Adeline says.

And it's lucky she does, because Luke jolts at the sound of her voice, pulling his ear from the door while he searches for a response – which means he doesn't get caught eavesdropping when Shirley comes back in.

'If we're really going to do this here, I strongly suggest we put something waterproof under her,' Shirley says. 'Otherwise you'll be stuck with a mattress that looks like someone got murdered on top of it.'

Cam tells Luke to go and forage a couple of shower curtains from bathrooms down the corridor. When he returns, Shirley examines them and says, 'That's mildew.'

Cam gives him a look like he's running out of patience, and Shirley takes the point. 'I will need a change of sheets as well.'

'In the wardrobe.'

So Luke leaves the bedroom without ever answering Adeline's question, and it feels wrong, when you've just heard that someone could die or lose their baby, to walk away like that. But what could he possibly say? 'Good luck! Hang in there! We're all rooting for you!'

Back in the common room, he at least wants to say something to Cam. He's on Shirley's side. He doesn't want Adeline's life to end in that room, or her baby's, any more than he wanted it to end in the van as the police closed in.

Anyway – to take the pragmatic view, the Cam view – it wouldn't be good for the Nail. In PR terms, kidnapping a pregnant woman is already bad enough. But if that were followed by tragic news about a botched delivery . . .

But once again he doesn't say anything. Because he's already scared that Rosa and Cam think he's weak. He didn't lamp the assistant when he had the chance, and then he was so solicitous with Adeline in the van, and then he wanted to rescue that cop during the storm. There's something about the way Rosa has looked at him since then. As if she's reassessing. And certainly Cam will have picked up on it all too, even if he's given no sign yet.

This operation was supposed to be Luke's chance to prove himself. Well, he did, didn't he? They got her. But is he proving, also, that he doesn't really have the temperament for this? That he's fundamentally an amateur, a liability?

Shirley still has a life outside the Nail, but Luke doesn't. He gave up everything else. He hasn't talked to anyone from his old life in over a year. The Nail is his only home now. If Cam decided he wasn't up to it, sent him away, he has no idea where he would go.

So he holds his peace. And this is weakness too. Not having the balls to speak up when it matters. But at least it's a private weakness.

Back in the common room, Rosa has the TV on and she's flicking back and forth between the BBC and Sky News. Coverage is about equally divided between the abduction of Adeline Woolsaw and the extraordinarily destructive hailstorm in northwest London. A phone video from an upstairs window in Park Royal shows people sheltering under the canopy in front of a supermarket until the canopy glass starts cracking over their heads. Regarding the kidnapping, there's no CCTV footage from Harley Street yet, just a couple of pictures of Adeline released to the media by the family. The public are asked to be on the lookout for a woman meeting her description. Rosa snorts at this: 'Uh-oh, I guess we shouldn't take her out for Nando's tonight like we were planning.' Luke notices that there's no mention of any pregnancy.

Then Cam turns the TV off. After all, the only thing that's operationally relevant at this point is how much the police know, and it's too early to glean anything about that from the media. Later, when he notices Rosa refreshing a news website on her phone, he scolds her. 'No more of that. Doesn't help. Time like this, you stay in reality, you don't watch them watching you.'

So they just sit there in silence and wait.

Chapter 5

Cam made a video about the Woolsaws that you can still watch on YouTube. It's pretty rough around the edges – Cam has an extremely broad skill set but documentary filmmaking is not really part of it, nor is voice-over work. Still, it gets the point across in five minutes and twenty-two seconds.

'You probably haven't heard of the Woolsaw Group,' Cam says on the video. 'Or what I mean is, you probably *have* heard of them, but you don't remember the name. Think about drain covers in the street. A drain cover is stamped with the name of the company that made it. Maybe you've walked past a hundred thousand drain covers in your life. Right now, off the top of your head, can you remember even one of those names on a drain cover? Woolsaw is like that. People see that name over and over again, but it just doesn't stick.

'Part of the problem is that the Woolsaw Group does so many different things that you can't really sum up what it is – except that it's "the largest public service outsourcing company in the UK", which is so boring your brain just switches off. Which is good for the Woolsaw Group. The Woolsaw Group doesn't want you to remember its name. But you *should* remember the name. Because the Woolsaw Group runs your life.

'It runs hospitals and GP surgeries. It runs commuter trains and passenger ferries. It runs rubbish collection and recycling. It runs swimming pools and leisure centres. It runs prisons and mental hospitals. It runs immigration detention centres and deportation flights. It runs educational authorities and school inspections. It runs air traffic control and motorway speed cameras. It runs armed forces recruitment and military academies. It runs the maintenance at missile silos and the catering at submarine bases. It runs the call centres for child benefit and the assessments for jobseekers' allowance. During Covid it was running the contact tracing and the PPE procurement. It runs fucking *everything*, all paid for by your taxes. And the people at the top have enough blood on their hands to fill the Queen Mary Reservoir.

'There have been campaigns against the Woolsaw Group. Of course there have. There have been legal cases against the Woolsaw Group. There have been exposés of the Woolsaw Group. But none of it ever gets any traction, because people see "the largest public service outsourcing company in the UK" and they just fall asleep.

'Not everyone falls asleep, though. There are some people who remember the name Woolsaw. They remember it and they'll never, ever forget it. As long as they live. Because of something that happened to someone they love.

'Maybe someone they love died of a heart attack at work, after some Woolsaw Group computer program decided they couldn't go on disability because they were healthy enough to take that warehouse job.

'Or died of heatstroke, locked up in a transfer van, which was sitting in traffic for hours and hours on the way to one of the Woolsaw Group's immigration detention centres.

'Or died from smoke inhalation in the middle of an English lesson, after an electrical fault set fire to the cheap shitty insulation in a primary school the Woolsaw Group built.

'Or got run down at a pedestrian crossing by the driver of a Woolsaw Group lorry, because the driver was barely awake after they gave him a choice between working a double shift or losing his job.

'Or hung themselves in their garden shed after their family business went tits up, because the Woolsaw Group used some kind of legal fuckery to avoid paying a year's worth of invoices, just because it could.'

Luke gets tearful every time he watches this part of the video. Because although his own story – which is to say, his sister Holly's story – is not a part of Cam's litany, it easily could be.

When he first came across the video, before he joined the Nail, it only had about nine hundred views. Even today, it hasn't passed twenty thousand. You post a video announcing that the sky is a hologram or that crude oil is made from human corpses and you get a hundred thousand views easy, but you try to alert people to an actual blight on their lives and they don't listen. People just aren't interested in the Woolsaws.

But they will be now. When they hear the news about the kidnapping of Adeline Woolsaw, the only child of Conrad and Silvia Woolsaw, billionaire founders of the Woolsaw Group. Brought up at Cyneburne, the Woolsaws' sixty-five-room mansion in Highgate, the third largest private home in all of London.

This is why Luke joined the Nail. This is why he believes in what they're doing. Because when people find out who the Woolsaws are, surely, *surely* they'll start asking questions. Surely, *surely* things will have to change.

So he will put his qualms aside and fight. Because it's all he can do for Holly now.

And yet as he sits there in the common room, five hours already gone by – five hours in which none of them have felt inclined to talk or eat or do anything in particular except just hold on grimly for Shirley to give them some news – he wonders whether his sister would really want this.

Whether she would want him to sit here, complicit, passive, as Adeline Woolsaw fights for her life and the life of her child, in circumstances no less nightmarish than one of those women giving birth in a Woolsaw-run prison.

Whether Holly would think this is justice, or something quite unlike justice.

But then he hears a baby cry.

Chapter 6

It's a relief, obviously, but it's also disconcerting in its own way. Because this isn't the place for a newborn. Not here, not with them.

What happens right afterwards is almost funny, though, the way they all jump up at once, as if they're expectant relatives. Luke follows the other two from the common room to Corridor B, and Cam knocks on the door.

'Not yet!' Shirley shouts from inside. So they hang around there for a while longer until Shirley comes out of the bedroom carrying a black bin bag. There are blotches of blood on his T-shirt. Once the door is shut behind him, he takes off his mask and cap and drops them into the bag, then his gloves as well, doing that thing doctors do where they invert the second glove around the bunched-up first one so they can cleanly shed a single wad of nitrile.

Without the mask, he looks about as hollowed out as Luke has ever seen a human being look. Like he's ready to be dumped into a landfill himself.

'Was it okay?' Luke says. 'Are they okay?'

'They're fine,' Shirley says. Then, after a moment, he adds: 'Did you really not know anything about . . . I mean was there no indication at all that . . .' He can't seem to formulate the end of the question. Luke sees that his free hand, the one that's not clenched tight around the neck of the bin bag, is trembling at his side.

'What happened in there?' Cam says.

'Five hours isn't that long for this, right?' Luke says. 'So it must have gone all right?'

Instead of an answer, Shirley just gives him a long, distant look. Then he says, 'I've cleaned them both up a bit. She'll need pads for the bleeding. Ice packs. Painkillers. Obviously the baby will need a place to sleep. Nappies. They'll both need something to wear. Also, she says she's hungry.'

'So just the normal stuff?'

At this point he lets out a totally mirthless sound that you could just about take for a laugh. '"The normal stuff." Yes. As far as I am able to tell you, the normal stuff. Do you have any petrol?'

'Why would she need that?' Luke says, confused.

'This is medical waste,' Shirley says, holding up the bag. 'I'm not just going to put it in a bin. Normally I'd just use rubbing alcohol but there are shower curtains in here, they won't burn easily.'

'Rosa, you remember where that can of engine oil is?'

She nods, and goes off with Shirley to show him.

'Shirley!' Cam calls after them. 'Is it a boy or a girl?'

'A boy.'

Cam turns back to Luke. 'Time to do the video.'

'Isn't it a bit soon?'

'If they find us before we go public, everyone's just going to assume we did it for the money. You know that. So we need to put a video out now.'

'Cam, give her a couple of hours. Just to, you know . . .hang out with the baby.'

'That's a couple of hours we could regret later.'

They both put balaclavas on and go into the bedroom. Once again there's a faintly ridiculous feeling to it like they're extended family shuffling into a maternity ward. When Adeline looks up from the unbelievably tiny person cradled in her arms, it's with a steady expression, no fear, no submission. Softened only by some combination of endorphins and extreme fatigue.

Luke can't stop staring at the baby. He's never seen one this new in real life. It's so red. Shirley has already changed Adeline's sheets, and the baby is nestled in a fresh towel, but there's blood on Adeline's vest, a bit more trodden into the carpet, and even a smear on the wall beside the bed.

'I'm glad you both came out of it all right,' Cam says. 'Now we need to film you.'

'Why?' Adeline says.

'We want your family to know you're okay, yes? So we're going to film you and we just need you to say that you're all right and the baby's all right and you really hope you can get back to them soon. Same things you'd say if you had them on the phone.'

'But I told you before – I don't want to go back to them.'

'Okay, but we need you to say that you do.'

'If I say that, my family will know I'm lying.'

This is one complication they were not expecting. 'Luke, I think Adeline and I are going to need to talk about this more.'

It takes Luke a second to realise that Cam is telling him to leave. 'Oh, okay, um—'

'We still need quite a bit of shopping done, don't we?'

'Right. Yes. We do.' Before he leaves the room, he takes one last look at the baby, searching for an outward sign of whatever so rattled Shirley. But he can find nothing out of the ordinary, other than the basic marvel of its newness.

After changing out of his cycling costume, Luke takes the old Corsa from the garage. Outside, where the tarmac is still tacky from the rain of ooze, he passes Shirley kneeling to light his little bonfire. The school's closest neighbour to the east, across the Ruislip Road, is a driving range with high walls of netting, and the wind is pushing black ruffles across them, a slow glide left to right like readings on an oscilloscope.

Luke's shopping list is a combination of what Shirley already mentioned and whatever else he can find by googling 'postpartum care kit'. He goes to four different shops, all of them spread out at least three or four miles from home, so it takes him a while. It feels completely insane to be walking down a bakery aisle like a normal person after everything that's happened today. The only disguise he wears is a baseball cap. When he or Rosa is out in public doing something innocuous, Cam insists that they don't overdo it: after all, nobody is hunting for a person who looks like Luke. Not yet.

But at the last shop, a woman smiles at him knowingly as he's taking nappies off the shelf. 'You've got that look,' she says.

Luke's heart starts pounding in his chest. 'Sorry?' he says. His first thought is, Does she know something? Is she on to me somehow?

'Shell-shocked. You're still thinking, "Oh God, what have I got myself into?"'

'Um—'

'Don't worry, it gets easier. I mean, it gets harder in some ways, but it gets easier in others.'

Luke finally realises what she means, and he comes very close to blurting out 'I don't have a baby,' because his reflex is to deny everything – no kidnapping, no baby, not me – but he stops himself in time. Why else would he be buying nappies? But he's too rattled to come up with anything to say instead, so he just smiles vacantly back at her, and eventually the woman says, 'Well, good luck,' and turns away.

By the time he gets back to the school it's dusk, and his headlights pick out a mound on the tarmac. The remains of Shirley's bonfire. It must have gone out before it fully burned through, because there's a lot more left of it than just ash. Luke gets out of the car to check. He can see the scorched fingers of a surgical glove, the melted edges of a shower curtain. Wondering if he ought to light it on fire again to finish the job, he pokes at the mound with a toe.

There's something else there, something with a texture he doesn't recognise, half-hidden under a bloody, cindery bedsheet.

He thinks about that look on Shirley's face, that terrible pressure of things he couldn't bring himself to say. And his white-knuckle grip on the neck of the bin bag.

Luke goes back to the car and empties out one of the plastic carrier bags from the pharmacy. Puts his hand inside the bag and pincers his fingers to make a clumsy glove. Then he squats down and excavates the thing from the mound, using the torch on his phone to get a clearer look.

It's a membrane of some kind, ragged and floppy and pale. But unlike the surgical glove or the shower curtain, it is unmistakably biological. This isn't the placenta, which he knows looks like raw liver. It has to be the amniotic sac. Part of him recoils, not in disgust, exactly, but more because he feels like you're not supposed to poke around in someone else's body parts without their permission. Yes, this thing is now as separate from Adeline as a pile of hair clippings, but it looks so *internal* still.

All the same, he peers closer. He thought it would be smooth, but he finds instead that it has these rows of very tiny slits, almost like gills, and alongside the slits are very tiny tendrils, not quite like hairs, more like the little polyps you'd see on a coral.

Chapter 1

Cam volunteers to take the overnight shift guarding Adeline's cell. Which leaves Luke and Rosa alone together for the first time since early this morning. Their bedroom is the old art room, nice and spacious, although they did have to put blankets down over the winter because the vinyl floors got so cold underfoot. This long, long day has left Luke feeling mostly just drained, but for Rosa it's the opposite – the adrenaline of the kidnapping, the bewilderment of the aftermath, the long wait during the delivery – she's banked up all that pressure like a gas cylinder and now she's finally ready for release. They've barely said a word to each other – nothing about the uncanny rains, nothing about what Luke found in the ashes outside – before her mouth is on his mouth and her hand is on his cock.

'That was the weirdest day of my life,' he says when she lets him have some air.

'That was the best day of my life,' she says. She tugs on the waistband of his jeans, which is the signal for him to undress. Rosa is completely uninterested in the incremental timeline of layer-shedding that was customary with all the girls he knew before her. Most of the time she's naked while he's still fumbling with buttons, and so it is today as she pulls him down impatiently onto the bed.

They met seven months ago, both as newcomers to the Nail, Luke arriving a few weeks after Rosa. It was a period of upheaval. One member of the cell had got deported back to Turkey, and another had dematerialised for reasons Luke still doesn't know. Then, in April, they lost Rani and Emmy, a middle-aged lesbian couple, after Emmy finally persuaded Rani that it was time for them to return to some kind of normality. That left just the three of them, Cam and two complete novices, practically work-experience kids. But by that point Cam was well into the planning of the Adeline Woolsaw op, and he didn't know how much longer she'd be going to that clinic on Harley Street, so he couldn't put it off until he had a stronger bench.

The larger organisational structure of the Nail remains extremely murky to Luke. He knows there are some people, like Cam's friend from UK Power Networks, who just do an occasional favour; others, like Shirley, who lead double lives, helping however they can while keeping one foot in the surface world; and then a core of members like Cam and Rosa and himself who have relinquished everything but this. Of that latter category, he has no idea how many there might be in London. *Are* there any others here, or are they the only ones? And how many allies do they have, all told? Dozens? Thousands? For that matter, who started the Nail, and when? Is there anyone out there with a higher 'security clearance' than Cam?

Luke does know, at least, that there is some Nail presence in the Midlands and in Scotland, and not everyone is as fixated on the Woolsaws as Cam and his cell. But the basic point everyone in the Nail agrees on is that it's an obscenity for a country like the UK to be so stinking rich and yet leave such a mass of people in such wretched circumstances, and that you're dreaming if you think the fuckers who designed this state of affairs, and who do very nicely from it, will ever allow themselves to be dislodged by anything resembling conventional politics. As to what things should look like instead, the Nail does not have a dogmatic view. In the short term the goal is to get the boot off the throat. Once that's done, there'll be plenty of time to talk about the future.

Because Luke's own motives are so personal, he sometimes feels a bit at sea with the revolutionary side of it. Not Rosa, though. Her convictions are ironclad. For most people, joining an organisation like the Nail means cutting ties with your past, but not for Rosa, who hardly had any ties to cut. She once told him that she came into the universe alone so that nothing could hold her back. Orphaned as a baby, grew up in a foster home, ran away at fifteen, off the grid ever since. And yet she could out-argue anybody with a PhD. She says the squats she used to live in down on the south coat very often used to have some sort of professorial older bloke, a benign fossil who knew his Marx and his Gramsci, and with these guys she would have long arguments and seminars, and they would tell her what books to steal and read.

Even when they first met, she was committed. But over the last several months, her commitment has grown even more ferocious, roughly in proportion to the spread of stick-'n'-poke tattoos all over her body. For instance, there's the questions of guns.

Cam's long-held position is that it's better to avoid guns if you possibly can. If the police know you have a gun, he says, they can do whatever they want. Open season for the armed response units. They could shoot your limbs off and cut your tongue out as a trophy and leave your body for the crows and most people in this country would still think they treated you too leniently. If you hope to wave a gun around and still be a hero to even a fraction of the public, you pretty much have to time travel back to Northern Ireland in the 1970s. Maybe if the public understood how they are being bled by the Woolsaws, they would see the need for real warfare. But they don't. Not yet.

And all of this is before you even fire the thing. When bystanders start getting killed in the middle of an operation because you gave a gun to somebody with no proper training, it's game over.

Whereas if you never touch a gun, it becomes a lot more awkward for the state to kill you. They can still do it, of course – in fact they quite often do – but at least there'll be some kind of stink in the press.

Luke is certain that Cam would know how to get hold of guns if he wanted to. In fact, Luke wouldn't be that surprised if there were a few buried somewhere on the school grounds. But Cam will not allow them on an op unless there's absolutely no other way of accomplishing what they need to accomplish.

Rosa is constantly tussling with him about this. If you're not armed, she says, you're not a resistance, you're just a protest movement, you might as well be circulating a petition. And it's not just guns she wants. Bombs too. We ought to enact out in the open a tiny particle of the savagery that the state is constantly enacting behind closed doors – that's how she puts it. She has a special fixation on the Woolsaw summer party, the expensive shindig Conrad and Silvia throw in Regent's Park every year to lubricate their enablers in the British political establishment. She has vivid fantasies of setting off nail bombs halfway through the speeches, getting it done in one fell swoop, decapitating the entire power structure at an industrial scale like one of those machines that cut the heads off tulips.

And it freaks Luke out to hear her talk about it. Because it feels vindictive sometimes, obsessive, almost libidinal. She doesn't just want revolution, she wants punishment. And this extends not just to the Woolsaws but to everyone she deems complicit. Which is a lot of people. To put all of them up against the wall you'd need a wall you could see from space.

Yes, Luke would like to see the Woolsaw family reduced to scrubbing toilets for a living. But he doesn't take any particular pleasure in the thought of heads on pikes. Not like Rosa. Even Cam, who has clearly done some harrowing shit in his time, doesn't yearn for it the way she seems to.

Yet, in another way, all of this just redoubles Luke's attraction to Rosa. He's never been with anyone like her, anyone so fierce and scalding and determined, and it's like gaining entry to a new, more potent version of life, even as the actual reality of joining the Nail has mostly involved a lot of waiting and hiding and rehearsals and chores.

He's just about to push inside her, there on the bed which is really two single beds brought together to make a double, when she says to him, 'Do you have the bag?'

'What bag?'

'The one we put over her head.'

It's still in the pocket of the spandex cycling trousers that he changed out of earlier. 'What about it?'

'Put it on me.'

He's taken aback for a moment. They've done a bit of this kind of thing before, but never with an actual item of Nail paraphernalia. Never with a bag that a woman struggled to breathe through as she was torn away from everything she knew.

'Come on,' Rosa says. And she's smiling so mischievously as she says it that it's impossible for him to say no.

He retrieves the bag from the trousers and puts it over her head. Faceless, Rosa lies back. 'Hold my wrists,' she says.

So he holds her wrists over her head as he fucks her, and she comes about as fast as he's ever known her to come. Then, after she stops trembling, she pushes him over onto his back, and the businesslike way she handles him makes him think of how they moved Adeline around this morning. But she still doesn't take the bag off her head, even once she's astride him.

He has no idea any more what scenario Rosa is playing out here, and it's so much stranger from this position, the black bag looming over him like an executioner's mask. But right away she starts making that urgent rocking motion with her hips, which does what it always does, draws out of him a climax he couldn't resist even if he wanted to.

Yes, life in the Nail has involved a lot of waiting, but in that waiting there's been time for a lot of sex. A gluttonous amount, in fact, month after month. Which has been good for a number of reasons. One is that, during sex, they meet as equals, and he doesn't have to feel so much like a sidekick rushing to keep with her. Another is that, although they have lived in the same building since the day they met – they have no lives of their own, no friends to complain about each other to – any vexation or resentment is washed away within hours by the inrushing tide of their desire for each other.

Later, Cam knocks on the door to wake them. 'Luke, you're up,' Cam says.

Luke dresses quickly and goes outside. It's nearly 5 a.m. 'How's she doing?' he says.

'Didn't hear much from her.'

'You put out the video?'

'Yeah.'

Luke settles down in the chair outside Adeline's room. Cam has left the wheel wrench for him. Outside, it's raining hard, but when he peels back the corner of the privacy film on the window, it looks like perfectly normal rain this time, a proper release after several humid June days.

He hears the baby crying through the door as he takes out his phone to look at the news. There it is. 'Anti-Capitalist Group Release Video of Kidnapped Woman.' Adeline's face framed against the white bedroom wall. Cam never did get her to say that she wanted to be reunited with her family. In the video she says only that she's had a baby boy.

The infuriating thing is that a lot of the stories just ignore what Cam added in his voice-over.

'We aren't interested in money. We will release Adeline unharmed as soon as the Woolsaw Group puts out a full audit of its service-user databases. We just want to know what it's got on everyone.'

Whether that ever actually happens, Cam says, doesn't matter so much. What matters is that people will find out these databases *exist*. Every man, woman, or child in the UK who comes into contact with any of the Group's services, no matter whether it's a skating rink or halfway house, gets an entry which will follow them for the rest of their life. The tech companies who track our internet searches might know us pretty well, but even they would kill for parts of the Woolsaw data hoard, because when you're filling out a form at a clinic or a job centre or a prison, you will answer questions of tremendous intimacy. You're not worried about privacy because you're reassured by your institutional surroundings: they need to check this stuff, everyone does it, it's no different from taking your trousers off in a doctor's office . . .What you don't realise, perhaps, is that they don't just check. They retain. They collate. All of this with a seamless technological efficiency that would be unimaginable for an actual government, as opposed to a business empire in government costume. Nobody knows exactly what uses the Group makes of this trove of knowledge, but when the public is finally confronted with its existence, maybe they'll start questioning why this one completely unaccountable company should be woven so deeply into the fabric of daily existence.

But of course the news stories don't get into any of that. Not yet.

Browsing more of the coverage, seeing those screengrabs from the hostage video repeated again and again, he thinks about what Adeline said to Cam. 'I don't want to go back to them. If I say that, my family will know I'm lying.' And that moment on Harley Street, when it seemed liked she was climbing willingly into the van. Lots of rich kids think they hate their parents, of course. Lots of rich kids think they want to run away from it all. But he's pretty sure 99 percent of them would be howling for Mum and Dad if what happened to Adeline happened to them. Clearly there's more to this than just your basic squirming against the bonds of privilege. She means it. So what is going on up there in Highgate?

He's still wondering about this when he begins to perceive a very faint sound through the door.

A sound like wood splitting.

Chapter 8

She's afraid to turn on the overhead light in case they can see that from out in the corridor, so all she has to work with is the glow coming through the bedsheet they've tacked up in place of a bathroom door. Which is why she doesn't see it until the third time she looks under the bed. In the far corner, next to the skirting board. The tiniest glint.

To stretch her arm that far she has to flatten her head and shoulders against the carpet, which means she can't look at it and reach for it at the same time. But eventually one groping fingertip brushes the coin. After that she inches it towards her, or rather fraction-of-an-inches it towards her, until she can grab it in her hand.

Her heart leaps. It's a penny. The most valuable penny in the world. If it does what she's hoping it'll do. She gets to her feet, wincing. She heard somewhere that postpartum yoga is great for your core, but probably not twelve hours after giving birth.

They've taken most of the fittings out of the room, but they didn't take the wardrobe door handles, which are metal, about ten inches long. Each handle is fixed to its door by two screws and the heads of the screws are exposed on the insides of the doors. She jams the penny into the groove of the left-hand handle's upper screw. Turns it counterclockwise. The penny slips out of the groove. But she tries again, pushing harder, and this time she feels the screw give.

Her plan is to use the door handle like a crowbar. Earlier she tried pulling the wooden boards off the window with her bare hands, but that was a complete nonstarter. With a bit of leverage, though, she might be able to pry them off. Then break the glass and get out.

If she escaped from Cyneburne, then she can escape from here. She keeps telling herself that.

She carries on working away with the coin. It keeps slipping, but she's making incremental progress. Until the screw is far enough out of the wood that she can turn it with her fingers. It pulls free, and she lets it fall to the carpet. Easy. Now she just has to do that three more times. And the first paragraph of the first subsection of the first chapter of her escape plan will be complete.

Except that the screw below simply will not turn. No matter how hard she twists, she cannot make it budge.

She tries the other door handle. And it's exactly the same. She can get the first screw out, but not the second one. Whoever assembled this wardrobe, maybe they gave the upper screws a few extra turns to make sure the handles were solid, but didn't bother with the lower ones.

But now both handles are loose. And she's pretty sure she could get one off the wardrobe by just yanking. It's crappy fibreboard, not real wood. When you're brought up at a place like Cyneburne you eventually discover that life outside is quite different – in innumerable ways it is quite different, but one of them is the basic physical fabric of it; even as a girl she remembers thinking that most things out in the real world felt unaccountably flimsy and thin. At Cyneburne, you would never be able get a metal fitting off a piece of furniture. But supposing you did, it would be so heavy you could use it as a wrecking bar.

She knows that pulling the handle off the door will make a noise. So she goes over to the baby — they haven't brought a cot yet, so she's made a little nest for him against the wall at the side of the bed — and turns him over onto his front. Mia always used to cry like she was being burned at the stake whenever she ended up on her front.

She waits.

He registers no objection whatsoever.

So she turns him over onto his back again. Gets the plastic tumbler full of water from the bedside table. Flicks water into his face a few times.

Now he starts grizzling. But not screaming. Not even close.

Of course. The one time you really want your baby to scream, he won't.

She isn't prepared to do anything that will actually hurt him. So she pours some of the water between his legs so he'll think he needs to be changed.

The crying gets louder. Still not nearly as loud as she wanted. But maybe this is the best she's going to get. She remembers that Mia was like this, actually, at the very beginning. Cried a lot later on. But for those first twenty-four hours, the instrument was still in its case.

She goes back over to the wardrobe. When she tugs on the left-hand handle, trying to rip the bottom screw out of the wood, the pain catches her off guard. You'd think her arms would be in okay shape compared to the rest of her. But then that was one of the things that surprised her about having Mia: that you push the baby out with your back and your knees and your jaw and pretty much every part of you in addition to the obvious one.

At least she didn't need any stitches this time round. So she persists. And she can feel the screw start to give. But as it does, the fibreboard makes a creaking, splintering sound. She freezes.

They won't hear that through the bedroom door. Surely. Not over the baby. She just has to get it over with fast. If she can't even do this, then what hope does she have of prying the boards off the window?

So she pulls again – and this time the handle comes loose from the door – but at the very same moment the baby falls silent, so there's nothing to mask the sound of the wood breaking.

The handle feels disappointingly light in her hand. More like a piece of cutlery than a crowbar.

She hears a scrape from outside. Someone getting up from a chair.

More adjustment to the world outside Cyneburne. Back there, a door was three soundproof inches of oak.

A small circle of light appears in the door as the peephole cover is moved aside. 'Adeline?' It's the younger guy, she heard one of the others call him Luke, although unless they're very careless that presumably is not his real name. He's the one who chucked the bicycle at her driver, yet here at the school his body language always seems a bit timid. 'I heard something,' he says. 'What are you doing?'

Her body is between the peephole and the wardrobe, so he won't be able to see that a handle is missing. 'I was just going to the loo,' she says.

'I'm going to come in, okay?' She hears him unlocking the door.

Quickly she drops the handle and kicks it under the bed. The door opens. He's wearing his balaclava, and he's carrying that long metal tool – some kind of tire thing, maybe. He flips on the overhead light.

You'd think she would be good at this. Innocent body language. The number of times her parents walked in while she was doing something she wasn't meant to be doing. Stealing sherry from the drinks cabinet. Vandalising an antique out of boredom. If she doesn't want to look guilty, she should meet his eye. Or at least that would usually be the case, but does it still apply here? As a hostage, isn't she supposed to be scared of him? Would it be more realistic to bow her head in fear?

She doesn't see any burning suspicion in his eyes. But then the baby starts wailing. Finally, just a bit too late to be helpful, the baby starts really wailing.

And she is the baby's mother, so what's expected of her now is to go over and soothe him. But she's afraid to move, because if she moves that will reveal the wardrobe door with the missing handle. Will he notice? Yes, he probably will. If both handles were gone maybe it would be all right, but people see right away when things aren't symmetrical.

'Can I . . .?' she says, nodding towards the baby. To make it seem like the reason she isn't moving is that she isn't sure if she's allowed to.

'Of course.'

But she still doesn't move. Instead she says, 'Thank you, I'm fine,' with a small grateful smile and an our-interaction-is-now-concluded-to-the-satisfaction-of-all-involved sort of tone. Maybe that will make him feel like he's done his job. Maybe he'll just leave.

But he doesn't. Instead, something in his eyes does finally shift. He's starting to wonder if something is up.

It's only a wardrobe handle, she thinks. It's not like she started digging a tunnel. Maybe she could say it just came off. Sometimes things just come off, in this insubstantial world beyond Cyneburne.

'All right, sweetheart!' she says as brightly as possible, bustling over to the bed. 'It's all right! Mummy's here!' She's trying to make the whole thing into a big performance. Draw his attention. The way you'd jiggle something in front of a dog.

She keeps her eyes on the baby, so she has no idea if it's worked—

Until Luke says, 'What happened to the wardrobe?'

Chapter 9

'The handle came off,' she says, like it's nothing. Still not looking up. By this point the baby is letting loose with one of those absolutely razor-edged screams.

'Where is it?'

If the handle just came off, she thinks, why would it now be under the bed, unless she were trying to hide it? Also, what if he finds the screws on the carpet? Screws don't just unscrew themselves. God, she was so stupid to go with 'It came off.'

'I don't know,' she says. 'I put it down somewhere.'

There were moments in the van when she wondered: are they going to rape me, are they going to torture me, are they going to murder me? By this point, eighteen hours later, she's almost sure they won't go as far as killing her. She's much more valuable to them alive, and Cam, the leader, seems like a rational agent, at least as terrorists go. But what if they realise what she was planning with the handle? Will they punish her? Make her regret trying to get away, just like her mother did?

'Adeline, I need to know where the handle is,' Luke says. Maybe he's thinking she might have stashed it somewhere to use as a weapon. Which it probably wouldn't be any good for. Unless you could really jam it into someone's softer parts.

'I think maybe it's under the bed.'

'Okay. Can you stand facing the wall, please?'

She does as he says, head down, hands in the pockets of the grey sweatpants they gave her. But as soon as she moves away from the baby, the screaming gets even louder. And the scream sounds more and more off-key: yes, any baby's cry is grating, that's the whole idea, that's all they've got to negotiate with, but Mia never used to sound like this . . .It's as if one of his little vocal cords has been *mistuned* somehow, so the scream comes to you at the wrong angle, makes your eardrums tingle like a thwacked nerve. It's rather sickening.

But not nearly as sickening as what happens next.

'Jesus,' Luke says, with real shock in his voice.

She turns to look. And sees something moving on the carpet.

In fact, dozens of somethings. All slithering in one direction. Out from underneath the bed. Towards where Luke stands. They look like caterpillars, each about the size of her little finger, covered in long hairs. Their colours are mottled, chameleonic, partly black but also partly the beige of the carpet beneath them, and even in places the rust red of the dried blood on that carpet. They're moving surprisingly fast.

'Jesus Christ,' Luke says. 'What the fuck?'

She hurries over to the baby. Picks him up.

'Are there any on him?' Luke says.

'No,' she says, surprised that he would care.

'Jesus Christ, there are so fucking many!'

One of the caterpillars is on the toe of Luke's right trainer. He lifts the foot and jiggles it. But the caterpillar clings on. And by now they're swarming around his other shoe as well. All the while, ranks of them continue to march out from the shadows under the bed – and not only the bed, she sees, but also the ventilation grate in the wall. There aren't just dozens now, there are hundreds, converging on Luke like he's food.

'Fuck! Fuck!' Luke reaches down and tries to brush them off his trouser legs. But there are too many, and a few of them cling on to his hand. As the fallen caterpillars regroup on the carpet, she notices that they have no discernible heads or tails, meaning they never have to turn around, they just lead with whichever end happens to be facing the way they want to go. Which is always towards Luke.

He yelps in pain. Dropping the tire thing, he covers that hand with the other hand as if he's been stung. Even more of the caterpillars are hiking up the rise of his trainers and disappearing inside his trouser legs. He bends over, scraping at his legs, slapping them, shaking them. Then he cries out in pain again, and wobbles, losing his balance. He puts one hand on the carpet to steady himself – but that means the caterpillars can climb up onto him that way too.

Desperate, he glances at the door. 'Hey—' he shouts. But then she sees him stiffen. He coughs. Retches.

One of them must have got under his balaclava and into his mouth.

When he shouted just now, was that loud enough, over the screaming of the baby, for any of the others to hear him? She listens, but she can't hear anyone coming down the corridor.

Luke is sitting down on the carpet looking like he's having a seizure. His eyes are squeezed shut and he's jerking around and clawing at himself. The exposed part of his face is completely aswarm, and below that she can see the fabric of the balaclava rippling from all the movement underneath. Just the sight of it makes her own skin tingle in horror, but the caterpillars don't seem interested in her at all.

Experimentally she bends down and reaches for the tire thing.

He doesn't seem to notice. Just carries on squirming and moaning as the caterpillars invade every inch of him.

She closes her fingers around the tire thing. Straightens up. Still cradling the baby with her other arm.

And then she simply walks out through the door. Shuts it behind her. Leaving Luke to the caterpillars.

She tries the door of the next bedroom down. It's unlocked. The room inside is presumably just the pre-hostage-refurbishment version of hers: same layout, same everything, except it still has the bathroom door and a desk chair and a bedside lamp. And a window with no boards nailed over it.

She tries the window. But that *is* locked. Whatever sort of institution this used to be, maybe they didn't want any hijinks at night. Outside it's dark but through the rain there's a faint wash of light pollution in the distance.

She puts the baby down on the bed. Draws the sheet over him in case of splinters. Then she swings the tire thing at the glass. But not hard enough, because she just makes a big crack, and the rest of the window goes icy.

The second time, holding the tire thing with both hands, she knocks half a pane of glass out. So she swings a third time, and a fourth. Now most of it's gone, and she can feel flecks of rain on her face. Knowing that she is now very much on a time limit if anybody heard the window shatter, she uses the tire thing to snap the remaining glass teeth off the edges of the frame. She pulls the desk chair over to the window. Picks up the baby from the bed. Crouching on the chair, she grips the sill to steady herself, and swings a leg through—

A thought strikes her just in time. She retreats. Puts the baby down. Picks up the pillow from the bed and drops it on the other side. She hears a faint click of broken glass where it lands. That would have been her bare feet.

Through all this the baby is still howling. And for the first time she wonders how she's supposed to get away from her kidnappers if she has this distress beacon leading them to her.

Something inside her says: just leave it. Leave the baby. You didn't want it. You don't owe it anything. It's an evil thing. Didn't those caterpillars prove that, if you didn't already know? So let your parents be the ones to grieve if something happens to it.

But instead she scoops up the baby yet again. All the way through the window this time, hunching as tight as she can in case she missed any more glass – and though her rear still grazes the frame, she doesn't get cut. Outside, she tries to shelter the wrinkly little impediment under her arm. The rain will probably just make him cry harder.

But then—

It always feels like a small miracle when your baby suddenly stops crying. But especially this time.

Silence.

Adeline takes off running into the night.

Chapter 10

Running is agony. If somebody were beating her pelvis and lower back with that tire thing, it wouldn't hurt one-tenth as much. Obviously she doesn't want to shake the baby around too much as she runs, so to avoid jouncing him up and down she's attempting a sort of high-speed glide, like something you'd learn in a deportment class, but that means tensing various muscles in unnatural ways that just make them hurt even more. She can't go on like this.

But then, from back at the school, she hears a screech, like a fire-exit door scraping on tarmac. And she speeds up.

She hasn't the slightest idea where she's going. This is some kind of open space, flat, bare, wet grass underfoot. She's already soaked to the skin.

After a hundred metres or so she comes to a hedgerow. She pushes through the first gap she finds, shielding the baby from the twigs that scratch at her elbows. On the other side, more open space. And beyond that, streetlights along a road. She doesn't think they were in the van long enough to get all the way out of London, so maybe she's somewhere in the suburbs.

She hears a car coming.

She rushes across the second field. Out to the road. Bright cones of rainfall beneath the streetlights. She waves desperately to the driver – for an instant they make eye contact – a guy with long hair and a beard—

Who just sails on past.

If anyone is following, she'll be easily visible here under the streetlights. With the car gone, the road is dead quiet. Semi-detached houses on the other side. She crosses the road, picks a house at random, goes up the paved driveway. A security light clicks on, and she rings the doorbell. Immediately a dog starts yapping furiously inside. But there's no other sign of life. She waits. What if they catch up to her while she's standing in the driveway? Drag her away before anyone realises that she was ever here? She's about to move to next house down—

But then she sees another light come on inside. Through the window in the front door she can see into the little vestibule that protrudes from the front of the house, and beyond that there's another door, and through the frosted glass of that other door she can make out a human-shaped blob. When the inner door opens she's relieved to see it's a woman. A middle-aged woman in a fuzzy dressing gown with a black Pomeranian raising hell at her feet.

The woman studies her through the front door window, and Adeline sees the shock mounting in her expression like a gauge ticking up. Because Adeline herself must look a state, tearful and panting and drenched – and then the woman notices the newborn in her arms – and then the woman notices . . .Well, she's staring straight at Adeline's crotch in a way that people don't tend to do, so Adeline looks down herself, and realises for the first time that she is bleeding quite profusely through the heather-grey sweatpants.

'Please,' Adeline says through the window glass of the door. 'I need help. There are people chasing me. Please.'

Adeline has led a pretty sheltered life, but she still has an idea of how things work in big cities: on the whole, the more operatically wretched someone looks, the more likely it is that they're trying to scam you. Maybe that's why the woman's first instinct is to say no. Adeline can see it in her face.

Or maybe she's just thinking that whether or not it's a scam, this is more than anyone can reasonably be expected to take on in the middle of the night. Maybe she's thinking about how wonderful it would be to just go back to bed and pretend this never happened.

But then she scoops up the dog. Unlatches the front door. And when it opens, they're like comical reflections of each other: two barefoot woman holding tiny creatures in their arms.

'Come in, love,' she says.

For the first time in her life Adeline learns that gratitude is an emotion you can feel every bit as viscerally and all-consumingly as any of the more celebrated passions. The woman locks the door after her, sets down the dog, and guides her into the living room. 'It's okay,' she says. 'You're okay. Do you need, um . . .Well, why don't you sit down, first of all.' She gestures towards the cream-coloured sofa – and then hurriedly converts the gesture into a stop-and-wait. 'Just a sec, love,' she says. With an apologetic smile she grabs a blanket from the armchair and puts it down on the sofa.

Now Adeline does sit down. The dog starts running laps around the sofa – probably thinking, 'By what possible standards of fairness is this creature allowed on the furniture when I'm not?'

'Jim!' the woman shouts. But there's no response from upstairs. 'He'll sleep through anything! Now, um – can I call someone for you?'

If that video got released, Adeline thinks, then her face must have been on the news by now. But the woman gives no sign of recognising her. 'No.'

'Are you hurt? Is the little one hurt?'

Adeline shakes her head. 'He's fine. I'm fine.'

But they are both acutely conscious of the blood still wet on her sweatpants.

'Pretty new arrival, is he?' the woman says.

'About twelve hours.'

'Blimey. I think I've got some pads upstairs. Let me get you one. And wake Jim.'

She pauses for a moment in the doorway, probably wondering

if it's a good idea to leave this complete stranger unattended in the house. But she goes anyway. The dog rushes off after her.

Even in London, Adeline thinks, people can still be so trusting, it almost defies belief. She looks around. She's never actually set foot in a house like this before. A normal person's house full of normal-person things. It's not just the sofa that's cream-coloured, it's practically everything in the room. Maybe in other circumstances she'd think it was ugly, but right now it feels the ninth sphere of paradise.

After a couple of minutes the woman comes back down. 'I'm really sorry, love. Couldn't find any pads after all.' She passes Adeline two white towels, a big one and a small one. 'Better than nothing?'

'I don't want to ruin them.'

'Don't worry about that. Jim'll be down in his own good time. His mobility's not the best at the moment. Why don't I put the kettle on?'

She goes out again. Adeline mops herself up as best she can. Afterwards, she doesn't want to put the bloody towel down on the furniture, so she just rests it on her knee. The woman comes back with two cups of tea. She pushes one across the coffee table to Adeline, then sits down opposite. 'Is this your first?' she says, nodding at the baby.

'No.'

'Oh . . .' She looks worried again. Which is reasonable. The news that this vagrant girl who was skeltering barefoot through the street twelve hours after giving birth *already has a kid somewhere* has probably made the whole situation seem that much more catastrophic.

'She's with my family,' Adeline says.

This fact is the most awful fact there is. But she says it to reassure the woman. Because the woman won't know why it's awful.

'Your family.'

Adeline nods.

'You really don't want me to get in touch with them for you?'

'No.'

'You're sure?'

Adeline hears a car on the road outside. And sees a gleam of blue light slide across the wall.

'Blimey, that was fast,' the woman says, looking past her. 'You keep hearing about how they take hours and hours to get round to anything these days but, well . . .'

Adeline turns to look out through the net curtains.

A police car. Lights flashing as it pulls into the drive.

'Did you call them?' she says, horrified.

'Jim did.'

'Why?'

'You said there were people chasing you. I thought . . .'

Adeline gets up from the sofa, heart pounding. The Woolsaw Group runs the Met Police's databases. It runs the command and control systems. It manages the police stations. It even supplies the helmets. If the police find her here, they'll deliver her back to Cyneburne. Back to her parents' warm embrace.

Chapter 11

'It's okay, love,' the woman says, 'they'll help you.'

'Do you have a back door?'

The woman hesitates. 'In the kitchen, but—'

'Please. Tell them this was a false alarm.'

'I can't just—'

'Yes, you can. Tell them it was a false alarm. Nothing happened. And don't tell *anyone* you saw me. Please. Don't tell anyone, ever, *no matter what*. And make sure your husband doesn't tell anyone either.'

The doorbell rings. The dog starts barking again. Charges off towards the vestibule.

'Please,' she goes on. 'Promise me. For my sake. For the baby's sake.' But right away she regrets saying that, because if you really care about the baby, what are you going to do? Listen to the mental case who doesn't want any help from the authorities? Let her just stagger back out into the night?

But then the woman nods. Ruefully, like she's reproaching herself even as she's doing it. 'All right, love. I promise.'

Adeline picks up the baby and rushes to the kitchen, where she finds the key to the back door already in the lock. Then out into the garden, she makes out a male voice from the other side of the house. The woman must already be talking to the police at the front door.

She emerges through the back gate into some kind of close.

More red-brick terraces with a row of garages at the end. Birds are chirping and the sky is beginning to brighten behind the rain clouds. She doesn't know if the police will really be persuaded that they came all the way out here for nothing; maybe they'll take a look around the neighbourhood just in case. She has to get as far away from here as possible.

But as soon as she tries to pick up her pace, she finds herself groaning in pain. Yes, she managed the sprint from the school across the fields – but it's as if, while she was sitting on the sofa just now, all her ravaged tissues had time to swell up, boil over, levy a very punitive toll. They are not going to let her do that twice in succession. No way. In fact, she feels like her legs could give out at any time.

She staggers along, following the curve of the road. She has an almost delirious moment when she becomes vividly, absorbingly aware of the warmth of the baby against her damp chest. It's a relief from everything else, but she knows she can't let her awareness shrink down like that, she can't let the iris tighten and shut. Perhaps it's fortunate that the aches soon come back to slap her awake.

More houses. Useless. People will be waking up, opening their curtains, but she can't knock on another door, not knowing if they'll take her in or give her up, and she can't let them see her out of the window.

Then, down a lane on her left, she sees a crack in the texture of things. It looks almost like a shantytown, here in the middle of the suburbs. Shacks, tarpaulins, chain-link fencing, unpaved paths. She heads in that direction, because it seems like the kind of place you could hide. And then she realises what she's looking at. It's not a favela, it's allotments. Some plots are junky and overgrown, others as immaculate as anything on Cyneburne's grounds.

The first shed she tries is padlocked. So is the second. But the third door creaks open. She goes inside and pulls it shut it behind her.

It's musty in here, but at least she's out of the rain. She can't stay on her feet for another second, but there isn't really anywhere to sit amongst the flowerpots and storage tubs and watering cans and garden tools and bicycle parts, all feebly illuminated by the daybreak filtering through the grubby window. In the end she lowers herself onto a bag of fertiliser.

She's grateful that the baby has been quiet this long, but now he starts to grumble again. Maybe he wants his little sip of colostrum. She lifts up her T-shirt to see if he'll feed, and sure enough, that's what he was after. He latches on, eyes closed, planting one little hand on the slope of her breast. And it makes her feel a tiny bit better, the sense that at least while she cowers in this shed she is doing something worthwhile for someone.

But she's hungry herself, and exhausted, and sodden, and bleeding again. She can't stay here forever, but she has nowhere else to go. Nowhere in the world. And she's so far away from Mia.

She looks down at the baby's downy head. For the first time in his short life, she talks to him. 'What on earth are we going to do?' she says. His eyes open, and he blinks up at her, no help at all.

Chapter 12

The knock on the door comes early, but Douglas is ready for it. Last night, as soon as he saw the news about the kidnapping, he knew he'd be getting visitors today. So he's been up and dressed since 5 a.m., because the police like to catch you off guard, and he doesn't want to give them the satisfaction.

Except, when he goes to the aft doors and pulls back the curtain for a look, it's not the police. Or he doesn't think so, anyway. First of all, it's just one guy, and cops don't come on their own. Second, he's wearing a grey three-piece suit, not flashy but still expensive-looking, and cops don't dress like that.

Douglas is prepared for a few journalists to turn up eventually, but journalists don't dress like that either, and anyway there's no way they would have tracked him down so fast. You really have to do some digging to find out he used to be part of the Nail. Outside of police files, the only place it's ever been documented is the court transcripts from 2009, and you have to apply specially to read those. It was never in the papers. So he doesn't just pop up on Google.

And even once you have his name, you have to find out that he lives aboard the *Hinayana*, and once you know *that*, you have to find out where the *Hinayana*'s moored this week. No reporter could have managed all that overnight.

He opens the doors.

'Mr. Bromet?' The guy is in his late forties, with thinning greyish hair trimmed neatly to the scalp, and he's carrying a leather briefcase, the old-fashioned kind with the hard sides.

Douglas nods.

'I'm very sorry to disturb you so early, Mr. Bromet. My name is Alexander Fennig. I work for the Woolsaw family.'

Oh. That explains the suit. And maybe it explains how they found him so fast. If you're one of those people who are really paranoid about the Woolsaws. Which Douglas certainly is.

'I know what this is about, obviously,' Douglas says. 'But I'm sorry. I can't help you.'

'I'm quite anxious that you don't misinterpret the nature of this visit, Mr. Bromet. I'm not here to stamp around accusing you of things or making demands or causing any unpleasantness at all. I'm well aware that I'm standing here on your property and you don't owe me or my employers the time of day. But I hope you can understand that in the circumstances I had no choice but to visit you. And really all I'm here to say, Mr. Bonnet, is . . .Well, perhaps I could explain in private?'

Douglas's first instinct is to say no. The Woolsaws are the enemy. Fennig's manner is so deferential, so self-effacing, so apologetic, you feel like he'd hang himself if you told him he'd run your bath too cold – which is just what the very wealthy look for in their staff. All the same, that doesn't mean he wants to invite a Woolsaw flunky into his home.

Then again, the towpath is starting to wake up. The first joggers, the first cyclists, and of course his neighbours, the other houseboat owners, who tend to get up very early if they don't get up very late. Up and down the canal, the familiar sound of engines coming on to charge up battery banks for the day.

There's going to be a spotlight on him over the next few weeks. He's resigned to that already. But there's no point making it worse than it has to be, by standing here, out in the open, and having a conversation about his links to a high-profile kidnapping case.

So he gestures into the cabin, then follows Fennig inside, closing the doors after him. This is very much not a make-yourself-at-home situation, so instead they just stand there by the galley counter, and Fennig sets the briefcase down at his feet.

'You have an exceedingly handsome boat, Mr. Bromet.'

This is said without apparent condescension, but all the same Douglas doesn't acknowledge the compliment. He doesn't need some butler from a mansion on a hill to tell him that his boat is nice. He's lived on the *Hinayana* ever since he got out of jail. The name is a word from Indian Buddhism meaning 'small and deficient vehicle' – more conventionally applied to certain disfavoured forms of the religion. At first, it seemed funny. By now, it doesn't seem that funny any more. Those fucking pumps. He still loves her, though.

'Well, I'll try not to take up any more of your time than I absolutely have to,' Fennig says. 'As I'm sure you can imagine, Mr. and Mrs. Woolsaw are worried out of their minds. Not only is Adeline their only daughter, but she has just delivered – in conditions we hardly dare imagine – their only grandchild. And one of the most upsetting aspects of what's happening is that there aren't any lines of communication open. Mr. and Mrs. Woolsaw are extremely keen to talk to Adeline's captors – and they assume that at some point Adeline's captors will want to talk to them – but there isn't yet any means for this to happen. Now, once again I must emphasise that when I say what I'm about to say, I am implying nothing, I am imputing nothing – but Mr. Bromet, I have no choice but to ask—'

Douglas interrupts him. 'I'm not in touch with any of that lot any more. I haven't been for years.'

Which is a lie. But there's no way anyone could prove that. Not even if they went through his phone.

'But could you think of any means of getting in touch with them? Anything at all that could be tried? Of course the police wouldn't need to hear even a whisper. Or at least they would only need to know that such a means had been found. They wouldn't need to know *how* it had been found. I can assure you the Woolsaws are quite capable of maintaining complete secrecy even in the face of vigorous official pleading.'

'Like I said, I can't help you.'

'Mr. and Mrs. Woolsaw would happily pay you, of course. An unconditional fee, by which I mean not resting on the success of any efforts. You could name your price.'

Douglas is losing his patience. 'Given what you must know about me, do you really think I'm after Woolsaw money?'

'Mr. Bromet, I'm not entreating you to undermine in any way the plans of these . . .May I call them your former associates? This is just so that two parents – two grandparents, as of yesterday – can have some peace of mind.'

'Look, I'm only having this conversation so you'll go back and tell them not to bother sending anyone else. So why don't you get on and do that?'

He's about to open the doors to usher Fennig back out—

When Fennig grabs him by the hair and slams his face into the rim of the galley counter.

It's so fast he hasn't even quite worked out what's happening by the time Fennig jerks his head back again and does it a second time.

Douglas slides to the floor. His senses are blank except for the explosion of pain in his nose. But it's nowhere near as bad as what comes next.

Fennig picks up the kitchen stool by the legs. It's that old bistro kind, sheet metal, pretty rusty by now because it's even older than the boat. He steps on Douglas's right ankle, holding his leg in place. Then he swings the stool down.

The edge of the seat meets Douglas's shin. Douglas feels the bone break.

Somehow Fennig's hand is over Douglas's mouth before the scream can escape him. Fennig keeps it there until the first wave of reaction has finished quaking through Douglas's body. 'Please try to be quiet, Mr. Bromet, or I'll do the same to the other one.' When he takes his hand away, Douglas is so terrified that he does as he's told, gritting his teeth to stop the whimpering in his throat from spilling over.

Fennig clicks open the catches of his briefcase, and through the blur of tears and the fog of pain Douglas is aware that what happens next is quite remarkable. Fingers moving expertly, as if he's done this a thousand times, Fennig performs an operation that looks almost like a gimmick from a magic act. The briefcase doesn't just open, it practically flips inside out, the lid hinging almost 360 degrees around to the other side. Then the handle telescopes out and a set of legs folds down from the back. The result is an A-frame that stands up solidly with the interior of the briefcase on full display.

And the interior is quite remarkable, too. Instead of any space to carry things, there is a mass of what looks like dark wood, intricately carved, widening out from top to bottom. Douglas can't make out what if anything the carvings might depict, but overall it looks almost like someone cut out a chunk of an old Gothic church and turned it into something you could check in at an airline counter. Fennig wasn't carrying it like it was heavy, but it must weight a hell of a lot.

'What was the last contact you had with the Nail?' Fennig says. From the other side of the briefcase, the side Douglas can't see, he produces a candle, and from his inner jacket pocket he produces a small silver cylinder.

'Cam gives me a bell a couple of times a year,' Douglas says, his voice hoarse with agony and stifled by his broken nose. 'That's it. Mostly just for old times' sake. I'm not relevant any more.'

The silver cylinder turns out to be a cigarette lighter, with which Fennig lights the candle. 'And how would you contact him if you needed to?'

'I couldn't. He never calls me from his actual number.'

'But if it was an emergency?'

'I still couldn't. I promise you. I'd just have to wait.'

Now, from the briefcase, Fennig produces a knife. The blade is pearlescent, uneven, microfaceted, like quartz.

Mingled with his terror, Douglas feels, paradoxically, a sort of relief. Because it's one hundred percent true, what he told Fennig. He would have no way of setting up a meeting with Cam. No way of even saying hi. Which means that he doesn't have to make a hard choice. Fennig can't make him choose between betraying his friend or dying. There have been times when he's felt mildly resentful that, after all they went through back in the day, Cam won't even trust him with a phone number or an email address. But now he's grateful for it.

Once again, Fennig takes him by the hair. Out of pure panic, Douglas starts shouting, flailing his arms, trying to bat Fennig away. But then Fennig puts the toe of one polished black shoe on Douglas's leg, right where the break is, pushing lightly, just enough for Douglas to feel it. And Douglas freezes.

But pain comes anyway, because Fennig proceeds to pull him over to the briefcase, his leg dragging along behind him. Then Fennig positions him so that he's twisted on his side with his neck resting on top of the wood. The way an executioner would rest someone's neck on a block for the axe.

'When was the last time you conducted any substantial business with Cam? More than just for old times' sake?'

'About a year ago. I sent a girl to him.'

'Who?'

'She went by Rosa.'

Douglas never stopped being an activist. Not at HMP Brixton and not afterwards. But he's an activist of a different kind now. He's taken up Buddhism, and also, more importantly, he doesn't ever want to go back inside. Pathetic, some might say, that he called himself a guerrilla and then the very first time he got arrested he found it triggered some sort of confinement phobia, previously unsuspected but severe enough to grip him every single day he was in prison. But that's what happened. So it's all nonviolent these days. Vigils, sit-ins, hunger strikes. He tells himself it's the better way. (Although with these new laws they're bringing in, even the mild stuff isn't that safe any more.)

But even if he's soft now – and perhaps he always was soft – he still longs for it sometimes. Real action. Fire and blood. And when he got to know Rosa, it was obvious to him that real action was what she was meant for. She was fire and blood in the shape of a girl. At the time she joined his group, she didn't know anything about the Nail. She didn't know anything about his history. And it was several months before he began to sound her out, even in an oblique, tentative way. But when he did, he began to feel a vicarious thrill just thinking about what she might be capable of. The battles she could fight and win.

So he waited to hear from Cam again. And the next time they spoke, he told Cam, 'I think I might have someone for you.' He vouched for her as far as he could, but he also knew that Cam had his own ways of testing people. Well, she must have passed, because a few weeks after that she dropped off the face of the earth.

'Who was she really?' Fennig said. 'Where did she come from?'

Once again, Douglas feels relief. He can't give Fennig any intel, because he doesn't have any. 'I only ever knew her as Rosa. She came from all over the place. She hardly told me anything about her past. And even what she did tell me I could never get straight.'

A sharpness at his neck. That pale blade. Finally, they're being tested, all these years of meditation and study, of contemplating impermanence, of learning to let go of the self: is he facing death with complete serenity?

No, of course he fucking isn't. He's so, so scared.

But not as scared as he would have been otherwise. So it helps. It does help. That's something.

'This is exactly why we do things how we do things,' he says. 'I can't tell you what I don't know.'

'We'll see about that,' Fennig says. Then he mutters something in a language that isn't English. But it sounds solemn, liturgical.

The blade pushes down.

❖

While the blood is still trickling down the channels of the altar, Fennig turns Douglas over and lifts his T-shirt to expose his belly. He cuts from sternum down to navel and then from navel across to left hip, creating a curtain of skin that he can peel back to expose Douglas's insides.

He reaches in and finds the liver. One by one he severs the tubes and tendons that hold it in place, until he is able to lift it free of the abdomen, the smooth purple organ bound in the middle by a ligament like a loop of butcher's twine.

Immediately he senses that Douglas was telling the truth. He didn't know anything else useful about 'Rosa.'

Which is to say he didn't *remember* anything useful. But as he turns the liver over in his hands, Fennig can feel something else there. A memory, lost but recoverable. 'Rosa' must have slipped up at least once. Because Douglas heard, or read, another name. A name connected to her. It must not have seemed important at the time, because afterwards Douglas forgot it ever happened.

What the name is, though, Fennig cannot bring into focus. He is skilled in hepatomancy, but not *that* skilled. So he seals the liver in a clear plastic specimen bag. Blows out the candle. Folds the altar back into the briefcase, placing the bag, the candle, and the dagger into their appropriate niches within.

He will arrange things here. Set a fire in the boat that will spread very quickly. Make it look as if Douglas were smoking a joint in bed. As if he'd dozed off and the mattress caught light. Then he will drive back to Cyneburne as fast as he can. So that the liver will be as fresh as possible when he presents it to Mrs. Woolsaw. She will have no difficulty reading the name.

Chapter 13

Luke was only barely conscious of Adeline leaving with the baby. He was too busy trying to defend himself against those caterpillars or whatever the fuck they were. But as the sound of the crying baby dwindled, the assault on him seemed to dwindle too. And when he opened his eyes, still curled up on the carpet, face slick with vomit beneath the balaclava, there were only a few left under him, as if all the others had retreated back into the shadows. When he got up, several more fell out of his clothes, but instead of trying to climb back onto him they just lay there waggling lethargically.

He pulls up his balaclava to wipe his face on a bedsheet, then goes out to Corridor B, where he sees that the door to the next bedroom down is ajar. He checks inside. The window is broken. The wheel wrench lies on the carpet below. Swearing under his breath, he goes to look out through the window. But he can't see any movement outside. They're long gone.

As he comes back out into the corridor, Cam arrives. 'What happened? I heard glass breaking.'

'She got out.'

'With the baby?'

Luke nods.

'What happened to your face?'

The stings are still hot with pain, but he doesn't know how

to answer Cam's question. 'I got stung.' That doesn't seem like enough. 'I got stung by . . .' What? A plague of insects that appeared from nowhere? The hail he could just about rationalise if he really tried, and the rain, and the amniotic sac – 'This isn't a straightforward pregnancy,' Shirley told Cam, and who is Luke to say what an amniotic sac is supposed to look like? – but if his sense of reality was already under almost unbearable strain, it has now definitively popped. Those insects weren't CIA and they weren't freak summer weather.

'Go,' Cam says. 'I'll wake up Rosa.'

'Which way?'

'You try the road. I'll head up towards the lorry-hire place. Rosa can try the woods.'

'What if we can't find her?'

But Cam doesn't answer. And Luke doesn't need him to. If they don't find Adeline before Adeline finds help, they're fucked. It's over. He knows that.

He goes back into the bedroom, the one with the broken window, and climbs out into the rain the same way Adeline must have. Dropping onto the pillow that covers the window glass, he looks out across the open field and tries to imagine which way he would have gone if he were her. Run straight across towards the streetlights on Old Ruislip Road, or stick by the hedgerows where she'd be harder to see?

The hedgerows, probably. So that's the direction he goes. He's running fast, but still pacing himself a little bit, because if he sees her he'll need enough energy to chase her down. One of his ankles hurts from when he banged it on the leg of the bed while he was thrashing around on the floor.

He gets as far as the road without seeing any sign that Adeline has been this way. Then again, what sign is he hoping to see, exactly? Big footprints like she's the Abominable Snowman? He wonders how long they have. At a certain point, they will simply have to assume the worst: that she's with the police, telling them where she came from. Before that happens, they need to scatter. Abandon the school. Abandon everything. Because Luke let her get away. Because Luke, the complete moron, not only opened her cell door for her but really went that extra mile by bringing her a tool to break a window.

So what's the window of time to recapture her? Twenty minutes? Ten? And how far could she have got already? Maybe a kilometre? Okay, so the search area is a circle two kilometres in diameter, widening every second, and there are only three of them. They have to run her to ground without anybody seeing, whereas all she has to do is flag down a car, knock on a door, scream until somebody hears her. This is a game they can't win.

North or south on the Old Ruislip Road? Another arbitrary decision. He turns south –

And sees a police car come around the curve. It carries on straight past him, blue lights flashing.

That's it. It's over. He has to call Cam right now. Tell him they're blown. He reaches for the phone in his pocket.

But he doesn't want to. God, he doesn't want to. All those months of preparation. The thrilling, unbelievable success of the operation yesterday. All wasted. The Nail will be a laughing stock when the world finds out they couldn't hold on to Adeline for even twenty-four hours. He doesn't know which will be worse: Cam's disappointment, which will be a disappointment without even a particle of real surprise, because so many people have failed him before, and Luke is just the latest, or Rosa's contempt, which unlike Cam's will be searing and incredulous. Neither of them will ever forgive him.

He has to make the call. But it's so hard to go through with it.

The police car pulls into the drive of one of the semis farther down the road.

He scuttles in that direction, just far enough to see what's going on, staying as far as possible from the pools of light under the streetlights, even though there's enough grey dawn in the sky now that he's probably pretty visible anyway. Two cops get out of the car and ring the doorbell. From this angle Luke can't really see who opens the door, just a flash of what might be dressing gown.

He waits for them to go inside. Adeline must have found refuge in this house. Once they call it in, the whole Met will descend upon this road, a chorus of sirens like at Park Royal.

And a feeling wells up in him that he wasn't expecting. That it's good. That it's a relief. It's better that Adeline and her baby are safe in that house than locked up in a derelict school for the blind.

But the police don't go inside. They just carry on the conversation on the doorstep. And then, after a couple of minutes, they walk back to their car. Is it his imagination, or when one of them shakes his head at the other one, is there a scornful quality to it, like they're pissed off with the person they were talking to?

When the car drives off, the lights aren't even flashing. And the road settles back into its sleepy drizzly silence.

Adeline isn't in that house.

So either the call had nothing to do with Adeline, or it *did* have to do with Adeline, but only in some glancing way – like maybe someone noticed a distressed-looking woman with a baby in the street, but didn't recognise her from the news, and didn't see where she went, so the police have no reason to pursue it.

If that's the case, Adeline was right here, not that long ago. He knows that, and the police don't.

He tries to be stern with himself. Probably this is one of those moments when you make up a fantasy scenario where everything's going to be fine because you can't bring yourself to admit that the worst has happened. He should still just call Cam.

Instead, he sets off again, north this time, because the police came from the south and clearly didn't pass her on the way. He pulls the balaclava back down over his face. It's sweaty and snotty and pukey and it rubs on his stings, but if by some miracle he does find her, he'll need it. And if anyone else sees him – well, supposing you were the sort of masochist who went on dawn jogs in terrible weather, this is probably the type you'd wear.

He can't understand why Adeline wouldn't just pick a house. Hammer on the door. Collapse into the arms of an astonished suburbanite. Was she too spooked, too traumatised? Did she want to hide somewhere absolutely nobody could find her?

He passes a building site. New flats going up. He stands up on tiptoe to look over the fence, then he tries round the back. Jesus Christ, this is what serial killers do, isn't it? He's literally hunting a woman down . . .He sees waste ground, wheelie bins, overgrown bushes, not totally unpromising as a place to stay out of sight, but there's no sign of her. Only a fox, one of the biggest he's seen around here even with its coat wet down. It stares straight into his eyes for a moment before darting under the wheelie bins.

And at that moment he hears it. Very faintly. If the rain weren't letting up he probably couldn't have made it out.

A baby crying.

And sure, Adeline's baby isn't the only baby in Ruislip. But the cry feels familiar somehow. Inwardly, nauseatingly familiar. Like when you get food poisoning, and the next day when you're taking the rubbish out you get a whiff of the scraps, and instantly you know, your body knows, exactly what it was that poisoned you. He swivels his head, trying to situate the sound.

Is it coming from over there? The allotments on the other side of the playground? He thinks about those lost-cat posters you see. *Please check your sheds . . .*

He walks across to the allotment. Homes in on the crying. It sounds like it's coming from the most rickety-looking of the nearby sheds.

His phone vibrates in his pocket. Cam calling him. He realises he ought to send an update, otherwise Cam might think he's been arrested or something. Quickly he dismisses the call and types a text. *Think we might be OK*.

But when he presses his ear to the side of the shed, he hears nothing.

He goes around to the door. Still treading as lightly as he can. Pulls it open—

And right away a pair of garden shears is in his face.

Adeline holds them in front of her, two-handed, blades open. 'Get away from me!'

So he steps back. But he's pretty sure he could take her. The shears are big, unwieldy, more like loppers than pruners. The blades aren't even that pointy at the ends and she hasn't got a hand free to defend herself. Dodge them just once and he could throw a knee or a fist into her stomach. He notices that her sweatpants are dark with blood. Behind her, he can see the baby, set down on a bag of fertiliser. The phone buzzes in his pocket again.

What he says next, he has no idea he's about to say until the words are out of his mouth.

'Adeline, it's okay. If you don't want to go back, I won't take you back.'

Chapter 14

She doesn't know whether to believe him.

'Are the others coming?' she says.

'No. Not yet.'

There's a silence. She doesn't lower the shears. Neither of them seems to know what to do.

'Why didn't you just go into a house or something?' he says.

She's about to tell him that she did. But she stops herself. He probably won't be happy to hear that she was sitting in a stranger's living room not that long ago. That might trigger some drastic measures. So it feels safer to give him a different answer. 'I don't want the police to come for me.'

But immediately she realises that wasn't safer at all. If he knows she has nowhere to turn, that gives him the upper hand, doesn't it? Brainwashing your captive into thinking the authorities can't help her, that's probably number one on every kidnapper's wish list. And she's just given it to him for free.

'Why not?' he says.

She doesn't answer.

'Because you don't want to go back to your parents?'

She doesn't answer.

'You could just tell the police . . .' And here he looks down like *he's* saying something he isn't supposed to. 'You could just tell them you don't want to go back. You're an adult. They won't take you back there if you don't want them to.'

Still she doesn't answer. Her arms are already aching from holding the sheers up.

'Unless you think you can't trust the police when your parents are involved,' he says.

She nods. She can't help it.

Because when she looks at this man, she feels fear and rage. Of course she does. He trussed her up and hauled her around and made her give birth in a cell.

But that's not all she feels. Because the first time she heard about the existence of the Nail, a year or two ago, she was so excited. Even if it was all futile, someone was actually fighting back against her parents. Everyone else sees the Woolsaws as just a couple of run-of-the-mill rich arseholes – you may not like them but you'd still probably go to one of their summer parties if you got invited. Whereas even if her kidnappers don't know what her parents really are, at least they understand that they're the enemy.

Even those simple questions he was asking just now roused in her an almost irresistible yearning to talk. This is only the second time in living memory that anybody has talked to her about her situation. The first was that doctor last year. But she couldn't tell him anything. Nobody out there would understand if she said she was afraid of the police. Just an addled posh girl off her meds – that's what they'd think. Whereas Luke got it without her even having to say it out loud.

But also he fucking kidnapped her.

So this is the choice now? Her parents or the Nail? She's like one of those hapless little villages that get caught in the middle of a war. It's totally up to you: would you prefer it to be the resistance partisans who raze you to the ground, or the fascist regime?

'So what is . . .' Hesitating as if he isn't sure how to formulate the question. 'What is all this stuff that's been going on? All this completely insane stuff. Like the caterpillars. And the hail at Park

Royal. Cam thinks that was some kind of technology, but, like . . .' He trails off.

'You wouldn't believe me if I told you.'

The sound of tires. They both look over. A car is pulling up at the edge of the allotments.

Will the driver know that the two of them don't belong here? Maybe even call the police about a couple of drug addicts trampling on somebody's carrots? Urgently Luke meets her eye. If they don't want to be seen, they have only a few seconds.

She lowers the shears and gestures with her head for Luke to come into the shed with her.

Is she the most gullible girl on the planet? Behaving like she's more afraid of some stranger in a family hatchback – about whom she definitively knows one thing, which is that to date they haven't kidnapped her – than of the man who just hunted her down?

Maybe it's because of that exchange she overheard in the van. When he wanted to save a policeman from a hailstorm. There's some kind of gap between him and the others.

As he pulls the door shut, she tells herself that she's not making a binding commitment. She still has the shears.

Unless he takes this opportunity to wrestle them out of her hands and pummel her unconscious.

But he doesn't. Or not right away. Instead, they just wait silently for a little while. With all the clutter in the shed, it was cramped even before Luke came in, and now she has no choice but to sit down on the bag of fertiliser again with the baby on her lap, because it's the only way they can both fit in here without pressing up against each other. She's conscious, and no doubt he is too, that if their luck is really bad, the driver of that car could turn out to be the owner of this plot.

But they don't hear any movement nearby. And Adeline has started to wonder how exactly she is supposed to answer Luke's question. What is all this stuff that's been going on?

'My parents are evil people,' she says after a while, keeping her voice to a murmur.

'We know that.'

'No, you don't. They're evil in a way that you aren't acquainted with. You and your friends are fighting something you don't remotely understand.'

'Well, yeah, I can't argue with that. Listen, if you come back, that doesn't mean you have to stay with us forever. We could get you out.'

'What do you mean?'

'I mean an escape,' Luke says. 'A permanent one. For you and the baby. Somewhere a million miles from your family. I'm pretty sure Cam has been involved in that kind of thing before. When people were in trouble and they couldn't just go underground like he did. Obviously that wasn't what we had in mind when we took you. But the point was always to strike a blow against the Woolsaws – I mean your parents, not you – and that would definitely be striking a blow. If we were the ones to get you out. They would hate that, right?'

'Did the video get released?' she says.

Luke nods.

'Is it all over the news?'

Luke nods.

'Well, maybe forty-eight hours ago that notion wouldn't have been quite as ridiculous. There weren't all that many people who knew what I looked like. But you've just made me extremely recognisable. Even if I wasn't, my family would find me.'

'You don't know Cam. The connections he has—'

'No, that's right, I don't know Cam. But *you* don't know my parents. The resources they have. The *methods* they have. As I said, you have no idea whom you're fighting. Anyway, this is all academic. I can't just run away.'

'Why not?'

'I have two children. One of them is on my lap. The other one is with my parents. I can't just leave her behind.'

Except she *has* left Mia behind. She left Mia behind as soon as she fled through the back garden of that house. If she hadn't – if she'd just let herself be scooped up by the police – she could be with her. Not today, maybe, but soon. Her mother promised that Mia would be brought home to Cyneburne as soon as the baby was delivered safe and healthy.

In that moment, back in that cream-coloured living room, when the police pulled into the drive, she lost her head. All she could think about was freedom. Her own freedom. Just like on Harley Street when she thought they were rescuing her. But in this context 'freedom' is only another way of saying 'Mia doesn't get her mother back.' Did she make a mistake? Did she do an unspeakably selfish thing? Her eyes well up when she thinks about how Mia has no idea that any of this is happening. No idea that Mummy has abandoned her.

'Where is she? Your daughter?'

'I don't know. I haven't seen her in six months. They took her away from me.'

'Why?'

She glances down at her baby. 'Because I tried to have this little fellow aborted.'

Chapter 15

'You didn't want the baby?' Luke says. He stands side-on to her so as not to have his back to the door. Some early attempts at leaning were soon abandoned because you can't so much as glance at the walls without something clattering on its hook or sliding off its shelf.

'No. And I didn't want Mia either. I tried to get rid of her too.'

'How old were you, the first time?'

'Sixteen. A teenage single mother, like people are always so disapproving of. That's why, officially, Mia is not my daughter, she's my cousin.'

'So how did . . .Um . . .'

'You want to know why I can't seem to stop getting knocked up?'

Luke nods.

'I suppose you're wondering if it was my father. After all, I did tell you that my parents are evil people.' For her own amusement she leaves him hanging for a moment. 'No. My father has never shown any tendencies in that direction. The dark secret of the House of Woolsaw is nothing so banal as incest. I was artificially inseminated. Straight into the uterus, under sedation, both times.'

'So whose . . .you know . . .contribution was it?'

'The Long-Before. That's what my parents call him. Or Him, I should say. You can hear the capital letter in their voices. I can tell you that His "contribution", as you put it, was very complicated to obtain, but I can't tell you very much else. That first time, once it had sunk in that it was really happening, I threw myself down a flight of stairs. Like Gene Tierney in *Leave Her to Heaven*. But it didn't have the desired effect. And I was seen doing it. I said it was an accident, but my mother immediately knew what I'd been trying to do – what she didn't know was that it was the third time I'd tried it. I was already forbidden from leaving the house, but after that I was watched over, every moment, night and day, in case I tried again. To all intents and purposes I was on suicide watch, except it wasn't my own life I was interested in taking. Well, actually, sometimes it was. I did think of that too.

'But after a few weeks under surveillance, I was taken for my first ultrasound. And after that it all just stopped. Nobody followed me around any more.'

'What happened?' Luke says.

'It was a girl. And they needed a boy. I believe they'd taken various measures at the clinic to increase the chances I'd have one, but those measures hadn't worked. A girl was no use to them, so after that it didn't matter any more. I could fish her out with a coat hanger for all they cared.'

'What do you mean, they needed a boy?'

'These things you've seen happen since he was born,' she says, nodding at the baby, 'none of that ever happened with Mia. She's just a normal little girl, because evidently certain qualities pass down only to the boys. My parents want an heir to their kingdom and it has to be a male. I know that may sound rather old-fashioned and patriarchal, but I assure you that's the absolute least of it.

'Well, I was a teenager, and I reacted to that in a perfectly teenage way. This baby that I hadn't wanted at all – as soon as I found out that my *parents* didn't want it, it became the most precious thing in the world to me. I was incredibly worried that I might have damaged her with my reckless behaviour early on. I had nightmares about what she might look like. But she came out undented. A perfect, beautiful little girl. And I called her Mia because it means "mine." She's mine, and she's hers, and she's not my parents'. If that sounds a bit trite now, remember I was sixteen.'

For the next seven years, she explains, the only times she was ever allowed to leave Cyneburne were for holidays at her parents' other residences. Until then, she'd been attending North London Collegiate in Edgware. She'd had a large number of friends. She'd kissed a small number of boys. Not any more. No school, no friends, no boys, no days out, no contact with anyone other than her parents and the Woolsaws' trusted staff. No phone, no email, no internet. Whether any of her old friends from school had ever enquired after her, and if so what they were told, she had no idea.

'Have you seen pictures of Cyneburne?' she asks.

'Satellite pictures. And a few old black-and-white ones of the inside. But there's nothing recent out there.'

'No, my parents wouldn't want there to be.'

Cyneburne, she tells him, was a very luxurious prison. Built in 1909 for the shipping magnate Samuel Holyoake, the house was famous for its entrance hall, where the sun shone down through an enormous glass dome – 'As the saying goes, no man is so rich that he can own the rays of the sun,' wrote GK Chesterton after visiting Cyneburne for lunch, 'but Holyoake's dome is probably as close as anyone has ever come to buying a controlling share' – though more spectacular still was the seventy-foot ballroom, with its intricate parquet of mahogany, tulipwood, amaranth, palisander, palm, walnut, maple and birch. There were sixty-five rooms above ground, and, since the excavation of the basement during Adeline's childhood, almost as many below, so many that for simplicity's sake the entire third floor was kept more or less shuttered. The grounds, too, were enormous, eleven acres of ponds and tennis courts and pavilions and outbuildings, all this less than five miles from the centre of London, with the 214 bus going past the front gate. Dotted across these grounds were monumental outdoor sculptures, one part of a treasure hoard of art and antiques and relics that few museums in the world could equal. The only thing about Cyneburne that wasn't grotesquely oversized was the staff roster, since the Woolsaws preferred to minimise the number of outsiders who came through the gates. But it was only compared to the oligarchs on the Bishops Avenue that you could say the Woolsaws were thrifty in this respect. There was still a brigade of servants, including the two most trusted of all: Hattie, who had been Adeline's nanny since she was born, and who stayed on as her governess even as Adeline passed into adulthood, and Fennig, her parents' factotum and right-hand man.

'I was so unbelievably lonely there,' Adeline says. 'So bored. So bitter about my situation. The only thing that kept me going was Mia. So you can imagine I had complicated feelings last summer when they got me pregnant again. By the same method as before. Except this time the ultrasound gave the desired result. It was a boy.

'As I said, Mia was the only source of happiness in my life. So I can't pretend that the thought of a second Mia was *completely* unappealing. Especially considering that the chances of my ever being allowed to have a child in the normal way – you know, with somebody I loved – seemed very, very remote.

'But there were two things that made up my mind. The first was that I wasn't livestock. If I just calmly submitted to this a second time, who would I be? What would be left of me, as a human being? And the second was that by then I'd gained a much better understanding of why my parents were doing it. Of why they were so happy when they found out it was a boy this time. So I became determined to snuff this one out.

'This time I decided no half measures. No more DIY. I'd scared myself too much the first time, thinking about what might become of the baby if it survived one of my assassination attempts. And also the stakes were just too high. I decided I had to get it done professionally. Unfortunately, all I knew about abortion clinics was what I'd been able to find out from the fridge.'

'The fridge?' Luke says.

In December the previous year, she explains, a new fridge was delivered to Cyneburne's kitchen. Everything at Cyneburne tends to be, by default, the most expensive possible version of that thing, and this fridge is so high-end that, preposterously, it has a touchscreen and an internet connection and a web browser. The day it was installed, though her morning sickness was as bad as it had ever been and even the smell from the coffee machine made her want to throw up, she hung around the kitchen until she could get a few minutes in front of the fridge with nobody else paying attention.

The first thing she tried to do was set up an email address so she could contact somebody on the outside. But it didn't work. She wasn't sure whether that was because this was the first time she'd been on the internet in seven years and she didn't know what she was doing, or because the smart fridge wasn't really designed for anything so advanced, or some combination of the two. In the end, knowing that her time was short, she gave up on email. Instead, she started trawling for information on women's health clinics in London. Her heart was in her mouth the whole time, and she thought to herself, God, if you're this nervous just fiddling with the white goods, how are you ever going to manage the rest of it?

She wasn't sure whether she would be able to get out of Cyneburne even once. But she *was* sure that she wouldn't be able to get out twice. Which meant she would have to have the consultation and the termination on the same day. From her hurried research, she learned that each clinic had its own rules about this, along with rules about which procedures they were willing to perform at which stage of the pregnancy. For instance, it looked as if you could only get a vacuum aspiration, which didn't require a second visit or an overnight stay, if you were less than fourteen weeks along. She was already at thirteen weeks. If she waited much longer there might not be a single viable option in London.

She had only just memorised the names of a few promising clinics when one of the cooks came back into the kitchen. Adeline closed the web browser as fast as she could. The following day, when she tried again, she found that the fridge had been disconnected from the internet.

She considered, and rejected, a dozen different schemes to get out of Cyneburne. Starting a fire. Causing a flood. Hiding in the boot of a car before it drove out through the gates. Stealing a key to the third floor, climbing out onto the roof, and then . . .Well, like all these plans, at least half the steps were a bit undefined.

The number one problem was that she was being watched at every moment, just like when she was pregnant the first time. And the machinery of Cyneburne was just too robust and well oiled for anything as trivial as a small fire to really interfere. Furthermore, she had no allies against her parents. Hattie was her ally in some things, but certainly not in this.

But what about Mia? Wasn't Mia her ally?

She had deep misgivings about enlisting her daughter. But she thought of a way of creating a sufficiently serious breach in Cyneburne's smooth routines. And she needed Mia to do it.

The tall red-brick wall around Cyneburne had two gates onto Highgate West Hill, one at the east end of the grounds, one at the southwest end. The drive from the southwest gate led past a pond, and over this pond loomed a bronze Henry Moore, one of his famous 'large spindles' – large in this case meaning over three metres high, all curves and spikes and hollows, adding up to something resembling a huge melted knuckle-duster on a plinth. One of Adeline's earliest memories was this sculpture being lowered into place by a crane, and the pond was one of her favourite places within Cyneburne's walls.

She had started taking Mia on strolls around the grounds before breakfast, ostensibly because the fresh air helped with her nausea. Often, because these walks were so early, it wasn't Hattie who accompanied her and Mia, but someone else from the staff. Sure enough, on the morning she escaped, it was Jeff, one of the security men, who trudged along behind the two of them.

They reached the pond. As usual, Mia started looking around for the ducks. Adeline kept Jeff in her peripheral vision. Waited for his attention to be distracted just for a moment.

What would he hear? A heavy splash. A scream. 'Mia!'

What would he see? Adeline running over to the water's edge. Ripples on the water. And no sign of the six year old.

Jeff stopped her before she could jump in herself. 'No, ma'am. Let me.' The pond wasn't really deep enough for an adult to drown in, but all the same it was a winter day and the water was cold and things could go wrong. He threw off his black overcoat and rushed into the water.

She stood on the shore still screaming Mia's name, and as the seconds ticked by, and Jeff still couldn't find the drowning girl, her screams grew louder and more ragged, so that anyone hearing them would recognise that some unspeakable calamity was in progress.

They were only a stone's throw from the southwest gatehouse, which Stuart was manning that day. Adeline knew that if you were on duty there you weren't supposed to abandon your post even in an emergency. There could be Messerschmitts strafing Highgate West Hill and you still didn't take your eye off that gate. But Stuart heard those screams and came sprinting over. Adeline, seeing him, stammered and moaned as if she couldn't get the words out to explain what happened. But she didn't have to. He put it together at once.

Stuart followed Jeff into the pond, and together they searched the murky water with increasing desperation. Both of them no doubt conscious that Mia might very well be dead by now, and Jeff, in particular, no doubt thinking about what his employers would do to him if their granddaughter drowned on his watch.

So neither of them were watching as Adeline took a step back from the pond.

Then another step. She turned. Ran.

Chapter 16

In the gatehouse, Stuart's tea was still steaming on the desk. She pressed the button to open the gates.

But nothing happened. She didn't hear that familiar creak as they sprang into life.

She pressed it again and again. Still nothing was happening. Clearly there was more to it than just the button. But there wasn't time to work out what.

Instead, she grabbed the office chair from behind the desk and wheeled it out of the gatehouse, castors crunching on the gravel. Catching sight of Stuart now looking in her direction, she pushed the chair up against the wooden gates. Climbed up onto the seat.

Stuart shouted at her. She hooked both her arms over the top of the gate. Pulled herself higher, lifting one foot up high enough to push against the backrest. Then the other foot. She felt the chair slide away beneath her.

But she didn't fall. She had just enough purchase to hurl one leg over the top of the gate.

Maybe it might still have been possible, in theory, to get over the gate with some measure of grace and control, but she saw Stuart running straight for her, dripping pond water. So instead she just lurched sideways, fell, and landed on the pavement on the other side. Hard enough to hurt but probably not hard enough to render the whole outing redundant.

The first thing she saw was a black cab.

Like a gift from the gods. Yet later she would feel a perverse twinge of regret about it. Because it meant that within a few seconds she was ensconced in its interior. That very familiar feeling of being driven around. And the cab took her straight to the clinic in Camden Town. Meaning she never actually experienced what it might have been like to walk around the city, alone, unobserved, free, which she hadn't done even once in her life. Of course, that was a mere fantasy in any case. If she hadn't found the cab so fast, Stuart would have caught up with her and wrestled her back through the gates. But still.

What about after the clinic? She wasn't allowing herself to think about that. She was so certain that her family would catch up with her before the day was over. All that mattered was taking care of business before they did.

What preoccupied her much more, as the cab descended the hill, was Mia.

'When you don't hear Mummy shouting any more, just wait a bit longer. Count to twenty. And then it's safe to come out.' Out of that womb-like hollow in the Henry Moore sculpture. They had practised the week before, quite openly, in front of Hattie, since there was no reason why Hattie should report a game of hide-and-seek to the security staff. That was also when Adeline had strategically positioned the urn that she would push into the pond to cause the splash. And this morning she'd made sure that Mia was wearing her mittens so the cold bronze wouldn't sting her hands.

What pained her most was that she had promised Mia she would get an enormous prize for being the ultimate hide-and-seek champion of the universe. Instead everyone would be angry with her when they realised what had happened. And Mummy wouldn't even be there.

But it had to be done. It was Mia's future too.

Out of curiosity, she said to the driver, 'May I ask you something?

Have you ever heard of the Woolsaw family?'

'I don't think so.'

'The Woolsaw Group?'

'Sorry, love. Should I have?'

They arrived on Camden Street and she paid him with cash she'd swiped from the house. It felt silly, or funny, or ironic, or something, that even though she was from one of the richest families in the country, she went to an NHS-funded clinic. According to her research on the fridge, it was actually easier to get a same-day procedure here than it was at one of the private ones, she supposed because this kind was a bit more industrial in scale.

All the websites she'd looked at had been written in such gentle, caring tones, yet somehow not a single one of them had bothered to mention the most salient fact about the whole racket, which a nurse had to explain to her during her assessment: you couldn't have an abortion just because you wanted one – in fact an abortion was still against the law unless two doctors could agree that either, one, the pregnancy was a risk to your 'physical and mental health' or, two, the eventual baby would be born unspeakably handicapped. For a moment Adeline thought she'd have to make up some elaborate lie about her medical history, but then, to her relief, it became clear that she could just sort of waffle about the mental health question and that would get the necessary box ticked.

Unfortunately there were more hurdles to come. They took her blood pressure, extracted some blood, offered her an STD check – 'I'm still a virgin so that would be rather a waste of effort,' Adeline wanted to reply – and then it was time for the ultrasound. She was apprehensive about this, because all her other ultrasounds had taken place at the clinic on Harley Street where they understood exactly what they were dealing with. However, although she did notice the doctor frown at the image, he did not, apparently, detect anything so out of the ordinary that it would entail further questions.

Then, just when she thought she'd finally got through all this palaver, he told her she'd have to come back another day.

'I can't,' Adeline said.

'I'm sorry, but you will have to.'

'Please. If it doesn't happen today it can't happen at all.'

'Again, I'm sorry, but—'

'What if I'd already had a miscarriage and it was going septic inside me? Then wouldn't you do it today?'

'Well—'

'Please!' She begged, rather incoherently, because she wasn't sure how much to say. Obviously she couldn't tell the doctor the whole truth about her family, otherwise he would think she was delusional, unfit to make her own decisions. So she tried to give some vague sense of it, intimating that her home was abusive, cultlike, carceral, yet she had to be careful even going that far, because she didn't want to say anything that would oblige the doctor to alert the police.

Finally he did relent.

This was a bit ironic too. She knew that. One notorious quality of the services the Woolsaw Group ran was that nobody would ever make allowances, bend the rules, be reasonable, be human, even if it would save somebody's life. They would be sacked if they did. So this was the last thing that she, the Woolsaw heiress, deserved: special treatment from a sympathetic person.

But she got it. A procedure at the very end of the day. She took the pill that would make her cervix open. Then five hours in the waiting room, self-conscious about not having a phone to look down at like all the other women. She was so curious about them, about what kind of lives they led, and though she was careful not to stare, she did strain to eavesdrop on any calls they made – not wholly out of nosiness but also because it was just so stimulating to hear a person she didn't know having a conversation that didn't pertain to her, something almost unobtainable at Cyneburne. A distraction from her hunger, which mounted as the hours passed because she'd known not to have breakfast this morning. And from her fear, as she watched the door, waiting for Fennig.

But he didn't come. Finally it was time to change into a hospital gown. The staff here were much kinder to her than the staff at the clinic on Harley Street, even though the latter was the medical equivalent of a royal suite in a luxury hotel. There, they might have been polite to her, but fundamentally they were working for her parents, the same way that a vet is working for the owner, not the animal. Here, it actually felt like they were working for *her*, no matter that she wasn't even paying.

Slipping the needle into the back of her hand, the nurse said more or less what they'd said to her the first time she was sedated for insemination: 'You won't be fully asleep, but you may not remember very much afterwards.'

And she didn't. In fact, the next thing she remembered was waking up at home. In her bedroom. With her mother standing by the bed.

'What happened?' Adeline said. She felt sore between her legs. That meant the surgery must have happened.

So she'd done it. She'd actually beaten them for once.

But then she noticed fresh flowers in the vase behind her mother. Drowsy as she was, she knew that wasn't right. In the old days, whenever she used to get in trouble at school or at friends' houses, no matter what punishment was to follow, her mother would always put fresh flowers in her room. This didn't seem to Adeline like a conciliatory gesture so much as a way of saying 'This is trivial. You're trivial. I'm not angry, because you're beneath my anger.' Surely if the baby were dead—

'The doctor will be arriving soon to look at you,' her mother said. 'But the important thing is, the child seems to be all right. I listened to the heartbeat myself just now.'

'What?'

'You don't remember, then? The procedure was interrupted before the worst could happen, thank goodness. Adeline, I've come to tell you that you won't be seeing Mia for a while. She'll be living elsewhere until you prove you can be a responsible mother.'

'What? What are you talking about?'

'Once you deliver a healthy baby boy, Mia will come back to Cyneburne.'

'No – no – you can't . . .' She wanted to rage at her mother – she wanted to get up out of bed and throttle her – but she didn't have the strength.

'Darling, it's long past time for you to learn that your actions have consequences. For all sorts of people. A doctor and a nurse are dead because of what you did today. Fennig saw the aftermath. He said it was terribly untidy.'

Afterwards, Hattie came in, and Adeline refused to look at her, but she could tell from Hattie's voice as she fussed around the room that she was upset. 'We'll all get through this together,' Hattie kept saying, 'and Mia will be back here with us before we know it,' as if the separation were a misfortune beyond anyone's control, rather than a decree by the people who paid her salary.

For the most part, Adeline had given up feeling disappointed in Hattie at moments like this. If she hadn't done anything when Adeline was inseminated against her will, she certainly wasn't going to do anything now. She simply wasn't capable of it. She was not only frightened of her employers – which was reasonable – she was deferential and timid by nature, a footstool upholstered in tweed. Adeline sometimes told herself that if anything she should be thankful for even the very minor moments when Hattie took her side, conspired with her against her parents, because for a woman as spineless as Hattie these were feats of heroic courage.

But broad-mindedness was for another time. For the next few weeks she refused to say a single word to Hattie, and spent most of that time in bed, sleeping and crying. And it was just on the edge of sleep, usually, that she got flashes of what had happened at the clinic while she was under sedation.

Lying there on the padded chair. The cannula inside her. A hurricane inside the room. The doctor and the nurse pinned against the wall. The skin lifting off their faces.

Chapter 17

'He didn't want to die,' she says to Luke, nodding down at the baby, 'so he didn't let them kill him. It's natural enough, in a way. But I felt defeated. Like I'd had whatever the opposite of a miscarriage is. So after that I just gave up. No more adventures. Until this one. Did you know that Isabella of Portugal asked for a veil during childbirth so that nobody would witness her agony? I wonder how she would have felt about going into labour with a bag over her head.'

'I'm sorry about all that stuff,' Luke says. 'I'm sorry we did that to you.' And then: 'Come back to the school with me.'

'What?'

'We're on the same side. We're hiding from the same people. You *should* be with us. You'll be safer. And you won't be a prisoner any more. You can leave whenever you want. And we can help you get your daughter back,' he says.

'From my parents? Be serious.'

'We kidnapped *you*, didn't we?'

She allows him a small smile. 'Yes, point taken. Even though I think there was a lot of good luck involved.'

'Do you have any idea where Mia is?'

'Probably at one of my parents' other houses. They have a place in the Cotswolds. Another in Scotland. I don't think they would have taken her out of the country, although I can't be sure. They haven't even let me speak to her on the phone. Not once in six months.'

'We'll get to her. We will.'

'Before my parents get to you?'

'We know what we're doing.' Half true, because Cam does, even if Luke doesn't.

'And is this an official offer? From all three of you?'

'No, I haven't talked to the others yet. But they'll be okay with it. You'll be treated well. By everybody.' He tries to say this with the same boundless confidence, but privately he wonders if he has any business making that promise. Regardless, just talking to her like this is an incredible relief after the day before. He hadn't realised until now how much shame he had been feeling about it all.

'But wouldn't I be mad? Absolutely raving mad? To get myself kidnapped, and then escape, and then go back *voluntarily*?'

So Luke pulls off his balaclava.

This, too, is a relief. But Adeline's first reaction is horror. 'My God, is all that from the caterpillars?'

'You know what I look like now,' Luke says. 'If you wanted, you could go to the police and give them a description. I can't take this back.'

'Except by killing me.'

'I swear to you, I'd rather turn myself in than do that.'

Adeline holds his gaze. Gives a long sigh. Shakes her head . . .But then says, 'Fine. Because you're right about one thing. I don't have a better option.'

He texts Cam, and they wait about ten minutes, silent except for the baby, Adeline tight-mouthed as if she's having second thoughts. An old friend of Luke's used to make deliveries for a posh florist, and he was adamant that the very rich were already genetically engineering their offspring, because there was no other explanation for how frequently two average-looking rich people ended up with a good-looking kid. What about diet, Luke countered, plastic surgery, Korean skincare, all that stuff, but his friend wasn't swayed. 'You can see it when you get close to them,' he said, 'they're just *different*, it's in their *cells*.' Now that Luke is inches from Adeline and she isn't in the middle of having a baby, this is his first chance to really assess that. But he's not sure. If he knew nothing else about her, certainly he'd say she was beautiful, but he wouldn't recognise her straight off as some rarefied species.

Cam texts him back a thumbs up, meaning he's arrived with the van and the coast is clear. Luke sees Adeline wince as she's rising from the fertiliser sacks, so he helps her up. She starts to pat the topmost sack like a sofa cushion to smooth out the little depression she's left in it, then rolls her eyes at the pointlessness of the gesture and follows him out the door. They cross the plots, past some Bronze Age–looking pea frames, and out through the gate to the road. Climb into the back of the van, where Rosa is waiting.

'What the fuck do you think you're doing?' Rosa hisses. 'Why have you let her see your face?' She's wearing a balaclava, Cam a Covid mask and a hood.

'First things first,' Cam says from the front seat. 'Did you talk to anyone while you were out here? Did anyone recognise you?'

'No,' says Adeline. 'Nobody.'

'Grab the baby off her,' Rosa says to Luke, taking zip ties out of her pocket.

Luke shakes his head. 'No. We're not doing that any more.'

Rosa gives him an incredulous look. 'Well, obviously at least we're going to put the hood on her.'

'No.'

'She'll see the HQ.'

'She's already seen it, remember? On the way out.'

'Luke, what the actual fuck is going on here?'

From then on, Rosa keeps looking furiously at Adeline, and when they get back to the school she takes her by the arm to march her like a convict from the van to the door. Luke wants nothing more than to make his case, get the others to see it his way, but they wait until they're back in the common room to have the conversation.

And he finds himself stumbling through a lot of it, partly because he's never had to advocate like this before, and partly because there are such fundamental aspects of Adeline's situation that are still a mystery to him. It's like he's trying to sell the other two a house when he doesn't know what those noises are coming from the attic. 'If we could get Mia back – Mia, her daughter – and then we could get all three of them out of the country together . . .I think that would be a huge victory. Massive. It would humiliate the Woolsaws and it would show everybody what monsters they are – I mean, if even their daughter wants to get away from them, with the grandchildren . . .'

'It's all a bit personal,' Cam says. 'Family strife. It doesn't have anything to do with the larger structures. It doesn't have anything to do with what they're doing to this country.'

'Well, it does a bit,' Adeline says. Rosa and Cam are still wearing their masks for this conversation, and Adeline's gaze is wary when she looks at them, but there is also just the faintest shade of amusement in it – an acknowledgement, perhaps, of how strange it is, this cordial chat they're all having. 'My parents had a purpose for Mia. If she had been a boy. And they have a purpose for this one.'

'What do you mean?'

'When he's older there will be a kind of coronation. That's what they've been working towards ever since they met. It's when their business stops being just a business and starts being . . .well.'

'What?'

'When it starts being everything.'

'It already is. The whole fabric of this country – '

'No. I'm talking about something quite different. I promise you. Those databases you're so concerned about – that's why they've been building them up all this time. To make the transition, and what comes after, as efficient as possible.'

'So what's the kid got to do with it?' Rosa says. While the others sit on the sofas, Rosa is perched on the windowsill, just out of Adeline's eyeline, so Adeline has to turn her head to return Rosa's sceptical gaze.

'He has a rather crucial role. Or he's supposed to. Seven years after his conception, that's when it can start. If Mia had been a boy, it would have happened last year, and I can assure you we wouldn't all be sitting here having such a pleasant conversation.'

'How crucial can he be if he'll still be at primary school when it happens?'

'I assure you, he'll be at the centre of it all.'

'This is all really fucking vague,' Rosa says.

'Yes, I know it's all a bit incomplete, but you have to realise, even this much took me years to piece together. My parents never talked about it in front of me. Very occasionally, when they were careless, I would overhear a conversation, or one side of a phone call.'

'Why should we believe you?'

'Rosa,' Luke says. 'The hailstorm. The gungy rain. You didn't see the caterpillars, but look at my face. And Shirley – you remember the way he was looking after the delivery. All of that just in the last twenty-four hours. She told me we have no idea what we're dealing with, and, like . . .that has to be true, right?'

This doesn't feel like selling a house so much as selling the whole parish, but Luke can't back down from the role he's taken on, even as his own mind is on fire trying to absorb it all. His mother is a Catholic. She rarely goes to church but she believes in God. In fact she's felt God with her at times, and she's felt the devil too, and she's seen two ghosts, and she's never seen a banshee herself but when she was growing up she knew people who had and she doesn't doubt their stories. Luke believed in a lot of that as a boy but he doesn't any more. And it's funny how that seemingly unbridgeable gulf, between one person who believes the world is fundamentally magical and one person who doesn't, in practice never really gets in the way. But it helps that she has quite an elastic point of view on it all. And that would certainly be useful here, the elastic point of view. What makes it so hard to get your head around is how these revelations are on every different scale all at once, from the tickle of a caterpillar leg on his skin to the vast, intangible, inconceivable power of the Woolsaws. One narky banshee would be child's play in comparison.

Rosa shoots Cam a frown that says: surely we're not supposed to just take all this in stride? Cam looks thoughtful for a moment, then breaks his silence.

'When I was in Brazil,' he says, 'we spent a lot of time making maps. The people I was with down there were getting squeezed out by the soy plantations. And we worked out a few new ways to fuck up a farm truck. But after a while I realised, that wasn't getting to the root of it. The root of it was, they weren't on any government maps, so they didn't officially exist. One day we were out on the river and I said, "Who lives north of here?" Because there was a big blank space on the map we were making. And my friend said, "The Exoaladi used to have all of this"' – Cam sweeps his arm wide – '"but then they went away." And I said, "What do you mean, they went way?" And he said his grandma could tell me the story. So when we got back to the village I asked her. And she said, "In *my* grandma's time, the Exoaladi wanted power. So they got a new *patrão*." That means, like, "master" or "boss." "And for a while we were all afraid of them. But then they made their *patrão* angry, and they disappeared. And we don't go to that part of the forest. And the wolves and the jaguars don't go either. And you certainly shouldn't go. And I hope to God the soy farmers take it, because that way they'll get what's coming to them." That made her crack up laughing. And I couldn't get much else out of her.'

'So did you ever find out what it was all about?' Rosa says.

'No. But I can think of a few different stories like that over the years, from a few different places. You put them all together, and . . . Well, I never drew any conclusions. Except that there's a lot of different kinds of darkness in the world that we don't know much about. That's for absolutely fucking sure.'

'You were the one saying the hail was a secret government weapon.'

'That's one kind of darkness. But I can believe there are other kinds.'

Rosa joins Luke on the sofa, which he chose because it felt like a neutral umpiring position in the room, except that Rosa plants herself on the arm closest to Adeline, almost leaning over her as she speaks. 'All right,' Rosa says, 'say the Woolsaws do have all these big spooky plans. She says they need the baby for it, and the baby's here. So we've got nothing to worry about, do we?' Though her mouth is hidden Luke can tell she's giving Adeline an obnoxious smile.

'That doesn't mean the fight's over,' Cam says.

'No, obviously it doesn't, but why do we need to help her get the other kid back, if this is the one that matters? I agree with Cam – it's all soap opera stuff. It's not revolution. It's not war. Look, at the end of the day, she's a Woolsaw. Her big day out at the abortion clinic, are we supposed to believe that was the first chance she ever had to run away? Seems like she didn't really mind living in that massive house. Spending all that money. She's a parasite on the rest of us just as much as they are. And now we're supposed to drop everything for her just because she says she's pissed off with Mum and Dad and she misses her little miniparasite?'

'You're not thinking about how useful she could be,' Luke says. 'You just heard – she knows stuff about her family that nobody else knows. Whatever we do next, she can be our secret weapon.'

Cam looks at Adeline. 'Is that right?'

'How do you mean?'

'We have more actions against your family planned. Are you willing to be part of that?'

'I can tell you anything I know about them that might be useful.'

'I said, are you willing to be *part* of it? Are you willing to go out there with us and show the world that you've come over to our side?'

'What kind of "actions" are we talking about? More kidnappings?'

'Whatever it is,' Cam says. 'Are you willing to be a soldier?'

'Even if I hadn't given birth about two minutes ago,' Adeline says, 'I can't do things like that. I'm not violent. As has been so astutely noted, I've lived a rather pampered life.'

'You were pretty convincing earlier with the shears,' Luke says.

'Yes, well, I was backed into a corner. That's not really who I am. Anyway, even though I agree with you that my parents are enemies worth fighting, I don't know if I agree with your tactics. All this chaos in the streets, I can't help feeling it plays right into their hands.'

'You're going to have to change your thinking on that if you want us to get your daughter back,' Cam says. 'We aren't putting our lives on the line for you unless you put your life on the line for us.'

'To start with, why don't I record another video?' Adeline says. 'With a bit more feeling this time. I'll tell the whole truth about my parents. That should cover my room and board for at least a night, shouldn't it?'

'The thing is, if you tell the whole truth,' Luke says, 'with all the really weird stuff, and that just comes out of nowhere – I mean, *we* believe it, obviously—'

'Do we?' Rosa says.

'I'll sound like I've lost my mind,' Adeline says. 'That's true. But I can say that my parents are power-hungry, evil people with a lot of blood on their hands. I can say that I've borne two children against my will and my parents wouldn't let me see my daughter for months. I can say that I'm afraid to go to the police because the police would send me back to my abusive home. I don't think any of that is too baroque to be believable.'

'That could do nicely, yeah,' Cam says. He takes out one of his phones. 'We can film it right now.'

'When I looked in a mirror just now I saw something pretty ghastly staring back. I haven't slept in about twenty-four hours. Don't you think in terms of image-making it might be helpful if I wasn't looking quite so haggard?'

'Fine. We'll find you a new bedroom.'

'None of the others have locks on the doors,' Rosa says.

'We're not going to lock her up any more,' Luke says.

'Are you taking the piss?' Rosa says. 'That's the plan? We used to have a hostage and now we have a fucking duchess? This is just a hotel for her now? And as soon as she gets bored she can just walk out the door again and put us all in jail?'

'I'm not going to do that,' Adeline says.

'Why should we believe you?'

'Because Luke is right. We're on the same side. And I have nowhere else to go. That's why I agreed to come back here.'

'"Agreed"?'

Adeline's eyes flicker towards Luke, as she realises, perhaps, that she shouldn't have put it like that. 'What I mean is, I wasn't exactly kicking and screaming.'

Cam brings the conversation to an end by getting to his feet. Adeline gets up too, the baby in her arms, and Luke sees her steel herself just for a moment before she follows Cam out of the common room. Now that the two of them are alone, Rosa fixes Luke with a glare. 'You texted Cam "I think we might be okay" around six a.m.,' she says. 'That must have been when you found her?'

'Yeah.'

'But you didn't text him to come and pick you up until closer to seven.'

'So?'

'What happened in between?'

'She told me about her family.'

'So you were just in that shed having a heart-to-heart?' Rosa says. 'While me and Cam didn't have a fucking clue what was going on? You know we almost cut the painter?' 'Cut the painter' being Cam's old-fashioned phrase for abandoning a hideout for good before the police can arrive.

'The only way I was able to persuade her to come back was by talking it through with her.'

'What's this about "persuade,", Luke? What's this about "I agreed to come back here"?' With a mocking imitation of Adeline's upper-class accent.

'Obviously I was going to bring her back either way—'

'Were you?'

He feels like he's in court. 'Yes. Of course.'

'So what were you going to do if she said no?'

'I would have made her come with me.'

'How? Tell me.'

'I would have hit her or something.' Luke tries his best to make this sound sincere. While she had the garden shears in his face, he thinks he could have done it. But not while she was telling him her life story with her baby on her knee.

'Would you? You couldn't hit that bitch on Harley Street.'

'Yeah, I would have.'

'In that case I don't know why you didn't just do that in the first place. I would have thought you'd want to. After she made you look like an idiot, getting away like that.'

'Don't you think it's better this way? Now she's not just a hostage. She's an ally.'

'No, I don't think it's better,' Rosa says. She picks up the towel that Adeline had under her and tosses it into his lap. 'We kidnapped her, remember? I know she's good-looking and everything, but *we're* supposed be the ones breaking *her* down psychologically. Okay, Luke? Not the other way round.'

Chapter 18

In the early afternoon, Luke hauls a stepladder into the corridor outside Adeline's new bedroom, then knocks on the door. 'Adeline? Are you awake?'

'Yes.'

When he opens the door, Adeline is sitting up in bed, breastfeeding the baby, so he keeps his eyes on the floor. The stings on his face have started to fade, although he has a few on his legs that are still intermittently aching and leaking fluid, and that aching has a kind of nauseous knife-scrape quality that isn't like any pain he's experienced before.

'Cam said to come and get you. We need to do the video now if it's going to get on the evening news shows.' Bad phone signal combined with an anonymised proxy connection means they have to budget an extra half hour just to upload the file.

'What's that for?' she says, meaning the stepladder.

'While you're busy with Cam, I'm going to try and build you a bassinet.' Obviously it's not going to be some whimsical macramé creation like the pictures he found on the internet; it's going to be a plastic storage tub he found in the kitchen which he'll line with foam and hang from the ceiling off a hook. His mum often had him doing DIY when he was a teenager, and he's done plenty more since moving into the school, but for all that practice he's still not particularly good at it.

'That's very kind of you.'

'Have you given him a name yet?'

'Well, I'd been putting it off. Because when I look at him, there's still a very tiny part of me . . .I shouldn't say that. Not in his earshot. But also it's a bit like stamping a document, isn't it? Making it official. The last couple of days really happened. The last nine months really happened. You can't deny that any more, when he's got a name.'

'So you haven't decided?'

'No, I have. I'm going to call him Percy.'

'Oh, that's nice,' Luke says, even though he doesn't like it.

'I know it's a bit outmoded – or maybe it's fashionable again, I don't know – but, all the same . . .As I told you, my parents have plans for him. These incredibly grand, ominous plans. But it's impossible for me to imagine anyone called Percy – or Percival, the long version – at the centre of anything grand or ominous. It's silly. But so many tiny things determine a person's destiny and I thought maybe that could be one of them.'

'It's not silly. I mean, you *can* change things. That's why I think you should join us for real. You'd be great. That story about how you got out of your parents' house . . .That was clever. That was brave. Most people couldn't do that.'

'Thank you. But no. As I said, I'm not a terrorist. No offence.'

'Well, like I said, Cam wants to do the video.'

'I'll be along in five minutes.'

Luke is on his way back to the common room when he comes upon Rosa. And it startles him to see her. She looks grim, pale, desperate, and he's so used to the brightness in her face, the high voltage, that when the current is cut it's like looking at a different person, a person he doesn't even recognise.

'What's wrong?' he says.

'Douglas is dead,' she says. And he wants to react sympathetically but the problem is it takes him a second to remember who

Douglas is.

The guy who first introduced Rosa to Cam. He used to be a member of the Nail back in the day, but an op went wrong and he ended up in jail. That's about all Luke knows.

'What happened?'

'Cam got word just now. There was a fire on his boat. He burned up in there before anyone could do anything. They killed him!'

'Who?'

'Who do you fucking think?'

Luke tries to catch up. 'Are we – I mean, are we sure?'

'Of course we're sure! One day after we finally hit the Woolsaws where it hurts. What, you think it's just a coincidence?'

For a long time Luke has thought of the Woolsaws as murderers. But their murders are indirect. At a distance. Licit. Fundamentally they're just managers, rentiers, grey suits. To him, there are no greater villains in the world than the Woolsaws, but it would still be a big adjustment to believe that they could just . . .what? Take out a hit on someone?

And yet he knows now – Adeline has made it very clear – that his old picture of the Woolsaws was not at all adequate.

'It's so fucking scary,' Rosa says. Luke doesn't remember ever hearing Rosa describe *anything* as 'scary' before. And he realises that, whatever grief she may be feeling about Douglas's death, it's not grief that's made her like this. It's fear. As he puts his arms around her, stroking her back, trying to calm her down, he can feel her shaking.

'Douglas was living out in the open, wasn't he?'

She jerks back from him. 'Oh, so he was asking for it?'

'No, that's not what I'm saying! I just mean it would have been a lot easier for the Woolsaws to get to him than it would be for them to get to us.'

'But what if he talked to them?'

'What do you mean?'

'I mean what if they questioned him or interrogated him or whatever?' Rosa says. 'Douglas was my way in to all of this. You know that.'

'Did he have any pictures of you?'

'I don't know. I don't think so. He wasn't stupid about stuff like that.'

'Okay, and Cam was probably keeping Douglas at arm's length, right? He wouldn't have known how to find us. Which means, no matter what he told them, they don't either.' It's good to say all this out loud, because it helps him believe it. 'At worst they might have a description of you. Which also matches thousands and thousands of other women in London.'

'Yeah, but . . .'

She gulps back a sob.

'Hey. It's okay.'

He takes her arm and leads her to their bedroom. There, they lie down in bed and he spoons her, breathing slowly to help her get her own shuddering breaths under control. This is a role reversal: normally she's the one telling him not to worry, telling him to embrace the danger of it all. He'd be lying if he said there wasn't a small part of him that quite liked it. It makes him feel needed. Useful.

Speaking of being useful, he remembers the bassinet he'd supposed to be building. That will have to wait. Even if there have been some dicey moments over the last few months – moments when Rosa has shown a cruelty or a bloodlust that has alarmed him – she's still his girlfriend. Waking up next to her every morning is still one of the defining facts of his life. He'll stay with her as long as she needs.

After a while, he finds himself getting an erection, for no reason except the pressure of her against him. He moves away because it's not remotely what's called for.

But then he feels her shift in that familiar way. Suddenly she seems impatient for it, furiously impatient. This time they barely undress, only what's necessary, and she fucks him like she's trying to escape from something, her tears cool against his skin as she presses her face into his neck.

Chapter 19

It's surreal for Adeline to see her face on the news. After all those years of hardly leaving Cyneburne, there she is on the television screen, broadcast to millions of people. It's almost like a continuation of her escape, as if she's a gas that has leaked from its sealed container and then expanded to fill the whole atmosphere. She doesn't even care that she looks almost as bad here as she did in the previous video – the lighting is harsh and she still has her lingering pregnancy acne – because the exhilaration she feels watching it in the common room matches the exhilaration she felt recording the video. This afternoon, as Cam set up a phone on a tripod, her hands were trembling, and she was worried that she wouldn't be able to get through it, or that they'd need to do endless takes. But in fact, it only took one, no notes, no rehearsals. She didn't hesitate, didn't falter, as if she'd known these words by heart all her life. And now it's out there, what the newsreader calls 'an astonishing development in the kidnapping of Adeline Woolsaw.' When it's over, Cam says to her, 'You did good,' and although she's not particularly interested in praise from him, she believes he's right. She did good. Her voice is out there now, calling her parents monsters, and there is absolutely nothing they can do about it.

Or so she thinks.

But the next night, there's another video on the news.

Once again, they watch it together, all four of them – five, counting Percy – in the common room, with bowls of dal and rice in their laps. It's extraordinary, Adeline thinks, how the act of eating together, watching television together, can make almost any situation – even this one – feel homely for a moment. Of course, there are certain parts of her new existence that didn't take any getting used to at all. The confinement, the lack of any real privacy, the sense of being observed and evaluated. All of that is familiar from Cyneburne.

The newsreader is teeing up one of the reporters.

'And what can you tell us about this footage, Louise?'

'Well, Michael, it was recorded some time in 2005, but it hasn't been seen publicly until now. Back then, if you remember, online video sharing was not as widespread as it is today, and so the people who recorded it tried to distribute it by emailing copies to various news programmes, including, actually, this one. However, the Met Police asked broadcasters *not* to air the footage. The kidnapping of the woman seen here, Eve Denton, had not yet been reported, and investigators believed her chances would be better if her alleged kidnappers – the organisation calling themselves the Nail – were not able to get the publicity they wanted.'

'Thank you, Louise. Now, just a warning that this footage may be distressing to some viewers.'

A woman filmed from the shoulders up against a white wall. It all looks very 2005, not only the layered cut of her blond hair, but also the washed-out image itself, which brings to Adeline's mind a word that she is almost surprised to find that she knows, a word she's definitely never said out loud, a word so dead it might as well be a thousand years old: 'camcorder.'

'My name is Eve Denton,' the woman says. 'Three days ago I was kidnapped by the Nail. I didn't choose to go with them, but I am now choosing to stay with them, because they're the only people I can trust. If you knew who my parents really are, I promise you would understand. For years and years I've been a captive in their house, and they won't even let me see my son. They are evil people, and I'm afraid to involve the authorities in any way because my parents have so much power in this country. I don't know how this is going to end but I just hope it forces people to pay attention.'

It's not word for word what Adeline said yesterday but it's pretty close. The big difference is how she looks. Adeline knows she spoke with conviction, but this woman is unmistakably frightened and exhausted. From time to time her eyes dart off camera.

She talks for a little bit longer, still along the same lines as Adeline, then the footage cuts to an interview. It has a much more institutional feel, like an evaluation or a deposition. This time the woman is seated at a desk in a well-lit room, with a glass of water and a box of tissues in front of her, and she's a bit more composed, although her eyes still look haunted.

'They raped me again and again,' she says. 'It just didn't stop. They wouldn't let me sleep. They shouted at me about how I was a bourgeois pig and my parents were bourgeois pigs. I think they were trying to brainwash me. I told myself that it couldn't last forever. When I was recording the videos, they gave me a script, but they said I should put it in my own words. But they kept making me start from the beginning because it wasn't good enough. He had a gun pointed at me while I was filming – '

'Who are you referring to?' a female voice interrupts.

'The others called him Cam.'

The footage cuts to another point in the interview. 'When they knew the police were closing in, I thought they were going to kill me,' the woman says. 'But then they said that in war it's better to wound than to kill. Because then you're a . . .' As she tries to get this out her voice cracks for the first time. 'Then you're a burden on the enemy.' Until now, her hands have been hidden below the table, but she lifts them up to show the camera –

And in fact she has no hands. Her arms end in bandaged stumps.

Cam isn't usually an easy man to read but there's a rage in his eyes fit to crack the TV screen.

Part of Adeline is feeling genuine curiosity about how her parents managed to put this together so fast. The woman is a really good actress. She wonders whether they actually cast somebody with both her hands missing, or whether it's a special effect. And she wonders, also, how many people at the television channel had to be complicit for this to happen, and what they are getting in return.

Regardless, it's a masterstroke. People must be waiting for her parents to give a press conference, but she knows they'd do absolutely anything to avoid stepping into the spotlight, even in such extraordinary circumstances. Instead, they've released a few photos of her at Cyneburne – photos where she looks misleadingly happy – and this all-too-believable video. Which is going to be more effective than any rote press conference would have been.

And that's why the other part of her is furious, just as furious as Cam. The conviction she spoke with in her own video – seen in this new light, what is it going to look like? Numbness? Trauma? A desperation to perform well so that the ordeal can be over? It's pointless to make any more videos now, because anything she says will just be more evidence that she's being coerced.

The one chance she's ever had to tell the truth about her life. The incredible catharsis of it. And her parents have made sure that nobody will listen. Nobody will take it seriously.

She remembers being a little girl and having tantrums at mealtimes when there were grown-ups trying to eat. 'Go to your room,' her mother used to say to her, 'and you can cry as much as you like.' It's as if she were still no more than a naughty child.

Maybe she shouldn't be surprised. This is so like her parents – her mother especially. To come up with something that is at once so brilliantly deft and so piercingly cruel.

When the segment ends, Luke and Rosa both erupt. The way they're talking, it's as if they're innocent bystanders whose spotless reputations have been outrageously tarred on national television, and she's tempted to remind them 'Hey, you *did* kidnap me, you *did* tie me up, you *did* pressure me into recording that first video on

Monday.'

But that's not what she says. Because, for the most part, she shares their indignation. This cannot stand. She will not let it stand.

'I'll do it,' she says. But they're in such a furore they don't even hear her. So she has to repeat herself. 'I said I'll do it.'

This time Luke breaks off and looks at her. 'Do what?'

'I'll be part of it. For real. I'll fight. Whatever you want. I'll do it.'

Chapter 20

'You mean that?' Cam says.
'Yes.'
'What happened to "I'm not violent"?' Rosa says.
'I'm not. But you're not asking me to gouge out any eyeballs. I mean, are you?'
'Would you do to someone else what we did to you?' Cam says.
Luke sees Adeline hesitate. 'One thing at a time,' he interjects.
'It would certainly depend on who it was,' Adeline says.
'Why don't we tell her what the next action is going to be?' Luke says. 'She could be part of that.'
'What, we're just going to spill everything?' Rosa says. 'What if she changes her mind again?'
Adeline explains her decision. She tells them that with this new video her parents have stifled her. Infantilised her. Outplayed her. She has to make herself heard again and there's only one way to do it. When she's finished, even Rosa seems convinced, at least for the time being.
So, as Luke tidies up the dinner bowls, Cam tells her about the security-van thing.
Say you're visiting a detainee at a Woolsaw Group–managed immigration detention centre and you want to buy them a coffee. The coffee machine won't take cash, it will only take cards. If you

can't use your credit or debit card – because you don't have a bank account, or you do but it's too overdrawn, or it's not overdrawn but your card gets rejected for inscrutable security reasons – you have to use ReadyPay, which is the Woolsaw Group's proprietary payment card.

Every Woolsaw Group–managed site, whether a swimming pool or a hospital or a prison, will have a ReadyPay machine, where you can top up your ReadyPay card with coins and notes. ReadyPay machines charge a 12 percent service fee on all top-ups, and they don't give change. Although you have to give a lot of personal details to get issued your ReadyPay card in the first place, there's no way to convert your ReadyPay balance back into real money, and there's no way to get a refund if you lose the card. It goes without saying that anyone who's ever used ReadyPay loathes it.

But from the Woolsaw Group's point of view, ReadyPay is great, because it means none of the support staff at these sites have to handle cash, and the Woolsaw Group's security vans can very efficiently collect the takings from a dozen or more ReadyPay machines a day.

So the plan is to rob one of these vans.

This is partly because the Nail wants to draw attention to all the heartless and petty ways the Woolsaw Group squeezes money out of the British public. But it's also partly because they're a bit broke.

Day to day, they don't have many expenses – they live on lentils and stolen electricity. But the ops need proper support. Even Adeline's kidnapping, which was such a straightforward, no-frills scheme, needed three clean vehicles. Sometimes they can source what they need for free from other members of the network, but not always. So Cam maintains a modest reserve of funds, and like a ReadyPay card it has to be topped up once in a while.

'You won't get much,' Adeline says.

'One of those vans at the end of the day?' Rosa says. 'Yes, we will. Those ReadyPay machines are fucking goldmines.'

'Maybe they were goldmines once, with the service fees and

so on, but not so much any more. I remember hearing my father complaining about it once. The number of people without a debit card keeps shrinking, and also too many people have got wise to what a rip-off it is.'

'It's not just about the money,' Luke says. 'It's about the symbolism too.'

'But is the symbolism quite right? When you made me record that first video so promptly, wasn't it because above all you wanted people to understand that you weren't looking for a ransom? Because it wasn't about the money? Well, how's it going to look if the next thing you do is rob a van full of loose change? I hesitate to use a word like "tawdry", but all the same . . .'

Luke wonders if she's right. It's true that they came up with this plan before the Woolsaws' latest gambit with the fake video. Right now everybody out there is thinking of them as lowlifes.

'Do you have a better idea?' Rosa says.

'I have an idea,' Adeline says. 'I don't know if it's better, but it's an idea.'

'Let's hear it,' Cam says.

'What about if you could steal something from my parents worth a few million pounds?'

'What are you talking about?'

'As you know, my parents have a very extensive art collection.'

'You mean at the house in Highgate?' Luke says. 'We'd never get in there.'

'If we ever *did* get in there, it wouldn't be for the art,' Rosa says darkly.

'No,' Adeline says, 'not at Cyneburne. What you have to understand is, although my parents are very devoted to their business, they also feel it's slightly beneath them. My mother more than my father. Whenever she actually has to visit one of the corporate offices, she finds it distasteful. All those banal people and their banal spreadsheets about banal matters. So my mother does a few little things to make herself feel better about it . . .'

Here she tails off because a rumble is getting louder and louder. You might think that after Park Royal Luke would be twitchy about rotors, but this vibration is deeper than those police choppers, and so familiar he could sleep through it. 'Don't worry,' he says, 'it's one of the Chinooks from the air force base.' The runway at RAF Northolt runs east–west, so they don't get planes right overhead, just helicopters. It's absurd, in a way, that they are almost next-door neighbours with this citadel of British state power, where the Woolsaw Group probably does the maintenance. But the reality is, the building-control department at Hillingdon Council represents a more immediate threat than any number of fighter jets on training runs.

Adeline looks relieved, but there's no way to convey the all-clear to Percy, who's whimpering, and she has to bounce him around as she continues. 'One of the little things my mother does is put a painting in the lobby of the headquarters on St Ann's Street. It changes every three months. It's never one of her real favourites, it's normally just something good enough that she hopes it will be improving to all those sad little drones filing in and out every day. At the moment it's a painting from the 1960s called *Hampstead* by Frank Auerbach. My mother was never particularly fond if it – we had it in an upstairs bathroom – but I've always liked it, so I noticed straight away when it wasn't there. The last Auerbach of that type that came up for sale went for almost two million at Sotheby's. I know because it was my parents who bought it.'

'The security must be crazy, then,' Luke says, as the Chinook's throb dies away to the south.

'Only what's required for the insurance. I imagine there will be an alarm, and a guard or two, but no more than they normally post in the lobby to harass the couriers. After all, the building isn't open to the public and the painting isn't visible from the street. It's actually rather surprising, or at least it always has been to me, how many very valuable things there are lying around in various central-London buildings just on the assumption that nobody is going to have the cheek to take them.'

'And how much would we get for it on the black market?' Rosa says.

'Nothing,' Adeline says. 'Because there is no black market. Not really. Not like in films. Perhaps there are a handful of people in the world who might be willing to pay for a stolen Auerbach, but unless you already know one of those people, there is no realistic way of finding them. If you stole one of my parents' Henry Moores you might at least be able to get a few thousand for the scrap metal, but those weigh two tonnes each.'

'So why bother?'

'Isn't the point of a hostage that she has no value to you, she only has value to the people you took her from? This is the same. If you take this painting, you are making my parents poorer, but you are not making yourselves any richer. That gives it a sort of purity, don't you think?'

'Yeah, look,' Rosa says, 'I know the downside of the van thing is that it makes us look like we want money. But also the upside of the van thing is that we actually *do* want money.'

'Why don't we do both?' Luke says. 'First this. Then the van.'

Before the kidnapping, he would never have voiced such a bold idea. And even now he's prepared for Cam to slap him down—

But instead Cam says, 'Luke's right. We'll do both. And we don't wait. We don't give things time to settle down. We start right away.'

Chapter 21

After he finishes examining Adeline, Shirley moves on to the baby. By the end of Monday's delivery he was so shaken he hardly knew what he was doing, and he can't even remember what checks he did. So now, as if for the first time, he listens to the baby's heartbeat. Palpates his chest. Looks at his hips, his spine, his anus, his genitals.

'Everything looks fine. You both look fine.'

To remember the last time he really felt awkward around a patient he has to think back to medical school. Hospital shifts just beat that out of you. Well, you get the occasional mad old divorcée who basically tries to drag you into bed with her, which can make things a bit uncomfortable during the examination, but apart from that there's no conceivable development either medical or interpersonal that would cause him to meet the patient's eye with anything less than perfect steadiness.

But he does feel awkward around Adeline now. Because they spent all those hours in that room together, they're the only two people alive who saw everything that happened, yet they've never really exchanged a word about it.

He doesn't know whether she feels the same. Maybe not. After all, that delivery was the most nightmarish and baffling event of his entire life. But for her it must have been just one chapter of a much longer story.

'All right, well, if you want to see me again for any reason at all, ask them to send for me. Normally, you'd have another check-up in about six weeks, but . . .'

Again Shirley tails off. Is she still going to be here in six weeks? She doesn't seem to be a prisoner any more, but she's still at the school, so what is her part in all this now? Cam hasn't told him much, and neither has Adeline, although a minute ago, when he was asking about her health, she did intimate that the last seventy-two hours haven't exactly been the unbroken expanse of blissful recuperation that new mothers are entitled to.

Back in the common room he finds Rosa and Cam. Neither of them is wearing their balaclavas, which leaves Shirley as the only one still disguising his face around Adeline. Evidently he must be pertinent to whatever they're talking about, because Cam gestures to him as he enters.

'Couldn't Shirley have brought you some?' Cam says. 'You knew he was coming.'

'Is this about the diphenhydramine?' Shirley says.

Rosa gets nasty skin rashes sometimes, probably aggravated by the damp at the school, and she treats them with a 2 percent antihistamine cream that you can only get on prescription. So twice before Shirley has prescribed diphenhydramine to himself, picked it up from the hospital pharmacy, and brought it here for Rosa. He would never write a prescription for Rosa to pick up herself, because in that case a very diligent investigator could theoretically connect his real name on the form to CCTV footage of her at the pharmacy.

'You can't have finished that last tube already,' Shirley says.

'I don't know where it's gone. Shit timing for me to lose it. I was going to use it on Luke's stings as well.'

'Well, it's a bit late for his stings.' Those stings: another mystery. 'I'll just bring you some next time?'

'I couldn't sleep last night. It's my knees and my elbows again.'

She does look tired, and Shirley is sympathetic to this, even more than normal, because he's hardly been able to sleep himself since the delivery. 'Are they worse?' he says. 'Can I have a look?'

Rosa waves him off, impatient. 'I'm just going to head up to the place in Edgware.'

The place in Edgware is a pharmacy where the owners, an uncle and nephew, will sell you pretty much anything you ask for regardless of whether you have a prescription. Diazepam, temazepam, liquid morphine, Viagra. Shirley once referred Cam there when somebody urgently needed amoxicillin – he still doesn't know who, or why – and Shirley wasn't available to deal with it himself.

Shirley can understand why Cam might be reluctant for Rosa to drive all the way to Edgware, to visit a shop that the police probably have at least an incipient curiosity about, just for an itch.

But in the end Cam doesn't stop her. 'I think the Corsa needs filling up,' he says.

Rosa goes out, leaving Shirley to update Cam about Adeline. 'They're both okay,' he says. 'Just carry on giving her whatever she asks for and call me if you're not sure about anything.' He adds, 'I saw the video. And then . . . the other video.'

As expected, Cam offers no comment.

'So is she with us now? I mean really with us?'

Again, nothing. Military secrecy as usual. Of course. Why should they tell Shirley anything? He's only the guy who went to the abyss and back delivering the fucking baby. So he just says goodbye and heads out to his car.

He missed lunch, so he nearly pulls into the nearest service station to buy something to munch on while he's driving. But then he remembers the rule: never go into a shop within a mile of the hideout. He carries on to the next one, five minutes farther down Western Avenue.

He parks on the forecourt, opposite the self-storage place. And he's about to get out of the car when he sees the grey Corsa. The one from the school. He's caught up with Rosa without meaning to. She must be inside paying for her petrol.

He'll sit in his car until she's finished. Goes without saying, if they ever crossed paths in public, they wouldn't acknowledge each other. But it's better if they don't cross paths at all. Again, you have to think about the CCTV: what if it's hoovered up by some Met Police algorithm that's good at making connections? Ideally he shouldn't even have parked at the same service station, but it's too late now.

As he waits, he wonders what she's doing here. To get to Edgware, she should have gone north up the West End Road. There's no possible configuration of traffic or roadworks that would send you east down Western Avenue.

Well, maybe she's got some other errand to run on the way.

But then his mind goes back to the conversation they had in the common room. He has no special talent for spotting liars. Not as a general rule. But he does have a lot of experience with people trying to blag prescriptions they don't really need.

It didn't stand out at the time. The context was so different. But now, when he thinks back to her demeanour, it *did* have a certain familiar quality. And people claiming they've mislaid their medications – the ones they insist they can't live without – is very often a hint.

Rosa comes out of the petrol station. Her gaze passes across his car for a moment, but she doesn't seem to recognise it. So he is able to watch closely as she gets into the Corsa. And is it just his imagination, or does she look furtive? Preoccupied?

Of course, in the circumstances, it's not unreasonable for her to be furtive and preoccupied. She's being hunted. All of them are. The heir to one of the most powerful families in Europe is stashed a couple of miles up the road.

And yet what she's supposedly doing now – driving out to pick up supplies – is a matter of routine. She does it all the time. She shouldn't feel like she's taking her life in her hands.

The Corsa pulls out of the forecourt.

Shirley is exhausted. He just wants to get home. He doesn't have any shifts at the hospital until Friday and a little white sleeping pill is calling out to him from the horizon like the most beautiful moon that ever shone. Maybe with the pill's help he'll finally be able to put his head down without the birth playing out again and again behind his eyelids. In any case, there's probably some innocent explanation for what Rosa is up to. He's never liked her that much, but that's all the more reason to ignore his suspicions, because he knows he's biased.

At the same time, though, he knows Cam's military secrecy has a purpose. Any kind of leak or breach could take down every single one of them, including him. He may be a peripheral member of the network, but he's vulnerable, just like the others.

Which means he has a responsibility, just like the others.

He gives it a few more seconds, then he follows the Corsa east.

Chapter 22

'When did you first notice that something weird was going on?' Luke says.

Rosa has gone to Edgware to buy her rash cream and Cam has gone to Westminster to scope out the Woolsaw Group head office, so he and Adeline have the school to themselves. The place feels very big and quiet at times like this, although the hum of the A40 is always there in the background. The two of them are sitting in her room, Luke on a chair and Adeline cross-legged on her bed, plus Percy in his bassinet, which finally got built yesterday and has not yet fallen down. So far Luke has been quite surprised by how much a newborn can be at once an enormous hassle (always crying and shitting itself) and no hassle at all (it is basically just a lump that you can put down anywhere and it won't move).

'I had a brother,' Adeline says. 'Alston. He was two years younger than me. He died when he was four. Obviously at the time I was too young to understand very much, but when I got older, that was when it dawned on me that something was really amiss in our house.'

'How did he die?' Luke says.

'An accident. Supposedly. I wasn't there when it happened. When I was around ten or eleven, I started to ask about him more. No matter whom I asked – my mother or my father or my nanny – well, of course you'd expect people to clam up a bit, it still would have been quite raw . . .But even at that age I think I could sense that it wasn't just that. It wasn't just grief. They would look at me with such intensity. As if there was something they couldn't say to me. As if they hated the questions because of the pressure of this thing they couldn't say. Hattie, my nanny, especially. She looked so tortured whenever it came up. Tortured about some unspeakable thing. And she said something once. Let something slip. About how it was merciful, really, that I didn't know.'

'So what do you think really happened?'

'You know Isaac and Abraham? "Take your son, your only son Isaac, who you love, and give him to me as a burnt offering." In the Bible, Abraham just ends up killing a goat instead. But that's a cleaned-up version of a much older story where Abraham *does* kill his son because God asks for it.'

'You think your parents killed Alston?'

'There's a phrase I heard my father use once. *Carissimum sacrificium*. The sacrifice of the most beloved thing. That's the most valuable sacrifice of all. And I know my parents have killed other people at the house.'

Luke gapes at her. 'What?'

'In the basement, they have a chapel. And in the chapel, there's an altar. An enormous thing carved out of black stone. I only ever laid eyes on it once, during some building work. They spend hours down there, both of them. And so does Fennig. He helps with all that when he's not on some mission overseas.'

'These "sacrifices", this altar, it's . . .'

'It's all for the Long-Before. The thing they believe in.' Her tone is scornful without quite going so far as to suggest they're mistaken for believing in it. 'That's why they do it all. As a sick sort of worship. I think that altar is where Alston died. And afterwards my parents had the audacity to plant a garden for him – Alston's Garden, they call it. As if they would ever be that sentimental unless they had something to hide. But if there's the tiniest silver lining – sometimes I wonder, if he'd lived, and we'd all been a happy family together, and my parents had gradually lifted the veil, telling me about these special things we knew that other people didn't know, and this extraordinary power we had that other people didn't have – if they'd got me at the right time, is it possible I would have been seduced? After all, most people rebel a little bit, but after they rebel they more or less end up with their parents' politics, don't they? But because I had this sense very early on that there was some connection between my brother's death and my parents' private pursuits, that was absolutely out of the question.' She sighs. 'I was so young when Alston died, but I did love him. And I still love him now. When people used to talk to me about what he was like – I mean when they weren't just clamming up about his death – it sounded to me like he was a bit of an odd little boy. I wish I could have known him properly. I still have dreams about him sometimes. Or nightmares, really. I see him falling away from me.'

'I, um . . .'

'What?'

Luke shakes his head, dismissing the thought. But Adeline won't let him off that easily. 'What were you going to say?' she says.

'I was going to say . . . I had a younger sister. And the way I've always seen it is, your parents killed her too. But that's stupid. It's not the same.'

'Tell me about her.'

'Her name was Holly. She was . . . amazing. She was one of the coolest, most amazing people I've ever known in my whole life. Just unbelievably clever and funny. So, so funny. But she also had really serious bipolar I. A lot of the time she was fine, and when she wasn't, we took care of her – my dad lives in Spain so it was just me and my mum. Sometimes when she had a mild episode, all she needed was for someone to look her in the eyes and have a normal conversation with her. Even a stranger. Once we found her talking to this homeless guy in a park and he'd pulled her right out of it without even realising what he was doing.

'But when she was seventeen she had a really bad one and she ran away from home. And we couldn't find her for almost a week. We still have no idea where she was all that time. And then one night she turned up on the Old Kent Road, and she was ranting and screaming, and she had a bit of pipe in her hand, and she was, like . . .The traffic was pretty slow so apparently she was just wandering around in the road, smashing people's wing mirrors and stuff. And the police came and they sectioned her. And she got taken to Hazelwood. Did you ever hear about Hazelwood?'

Adeline shakes her head.

'It was a mental health unit run by the Woolsaw Group.'

'Ah.' She purses her lips, bracing herself, the way you do when you're about to hear something awful a family member has done.

'There had already been loads of problems there. Someone at the local hospital had already blown the whistle on it – they said, "We keep getting people admitted from Hazelwood with severe malnutrition or dehydration, what the fuck is going on over there?" It turned out there just weren't enough staff. And the ones they did have, most of them didn't have the right training. So they weren't even checking if people were eating or drinking. And apparently all the food was horrible anyway. Sometimes it was mouldy, literally mouldy. Not fit for animals. Of course the patients didn't want to eat. And there were supposed to be therapy sessions and gym sessions and stuff like that, but none of it ever actually happened because there weren't enough staff, so the patients just sat around. Rotting away in there.

'The NHS were paying the Woolsaw Group one hundred and fifty million pounds a year to run these mental health units. So they tried to cancel the contract, after it all came out about the malnutrition. And the Woolsaw Group fought them. Fought them really hard with their fucking armies of lawyers. They said, "Legally, you don't have grounds to cancel. If you want to get out of the contract, you have to pay a penalty of—" I can't remember how much, but it was some insane amount. So the NHS backed down. And Hazelwood stayed open.

'Holly was sectioned for a minimum of twenty-eight days. And they wouldn't let us visit her. Afterwards it turned out that was a mistake, the rules said we should have been allowed to, but at the time we couldn't get in. And after twenty-three days she hung herself in her room with a bedsheet.'

'God, I'm sorry,' Adeline says.

'Her room was supposed to have all the special fittings that you can't hang yourself from. But some of them were the wrong kind, so she could still sling the sheet up there.' Without Luke thinking about it, his finger is scratching at the sheet under Adeline, more institutional linen. 'And afterwards the NHS looked into it and apparently one of the other patients said . . .' He can't stop himself from crying now. 'She said that before Holly died, she'd been screaming for help. For hours. Maybe four or five hours. She just wanted someone to come and talk to her. But there were no staff on the ward the entire time. I don't think Holly actually wanted to die. Even during her episodes she never talked about wanting to die. But she was in hell – inside her head, but also inside that place – and all she needed was for someone to talk her down, just one person to come along and treat her like a human being and talk her down, but . . .'

He can't go any further. Adeline scoots far enough forward on the bed to put a hand on his shoulder. When he recovers his voice, he says, 'Nobody has any figures from inside the Woolsaw Group, so we don't know exactly how much profit it was making, but if it fought that hard to hold on to the contract . . .'

'Believe me,' Adeline says, 'the margins in that sector are really good. Especially if you skimp on the staff. I've heard my father talk about it. You're right. My parents killed your sister. They killed her just as much as they killed Alston.'

'It's not the same. There must have been so many layers of people between them and Hazelwood—'

'Nevertheless. All that money my parents saved on those mental health units? That's probably a Francis Bacon for my mother, or a few antique Pateks for my father. They're culpable. They did kill her.'

'Back when it happened I didn't know anything about the Woolsaw Group,' Luke says. 'But when I started to really look around – I couldn't believe it. It was everywhere. There were so many stories like this. And yet somehow it wasn't even famous. People didn't recognise the name. At the start I felt like I was just this lone crazy voice trying to talk about this, but then I realised there were others. Not many of us, but some. And eventually I found the Nail.'

'And you started kidnapping pregnant women.' She fixes him with an unblinking look.

After a moment Luke has to look away from her. He knows by now that she's one of those people who find it funny when you get flustered, so he should take this in that spirit. She's not really trying to flay him with her gaze. All the same, he feels new shame rising in him. He can't believe she put her hand on his shoulder just now. The hostage comforting her abductor. It's obscene, really.

After a while she says, 'That was a joke.'

'I know.' He looks at her again, hoping that at least she understands his choices better now. 'I believe in what we're doing. I do. It's just there are times . . .' He tails off. 'And also, it means I can't see my mum any more. I mean, after what happened with Holly, she moved back to Ireland, where her family are from. She just couldn't hack it any more. London. She had to go home. So I wasn't seeing her that much anyway. But now I can't even risk talking to her on the phone. And sometimes I think . . . She already lost one of her kids, and now is it like she's lost the other one too?'

The door opens. It's Rosa.

There's no good reason for Luke to feel like he's been caught doing something he shouldn't. He was just sitting here talking to Adeline. They're in her bedroom only so that she can be within easy reach of all her baby paraphernalia.

All the same, he finds himself jerking back in his chair, away from Adeline, and it's as difficult to meet Rosa's eye now as it was to meet Adeline's a moment ago. His whole face is hot.

Rosa holds up a tube. 'I was at the chemist anyway so I got you some lanolin,' Rosa says. 'You know, for your nipples. Because Luke forgot it the last time.' Her voice is as taut as a garrotte.

'Thank you, Rosa,' Adeline says, accepting the tube.

'Do you want Luke to stay and put it on for you, or . . .?'

With one last sheepish glance at Adeline, Luke gets up and walks out of the room.

Chapter 23

'Come in here for a moment, please, Fennig.

'Here, you see, I was just doing a bit of work on this codex you brought back from Yerevan. It's a lovely thing, isn't it, although I fear it may be too far gone for a re-hinging.

'Have you seen much of my wife today? No? Do you think you'll be with her later?

'No doubt you already know that she's not speaking to me at the moment. She blames me for what happened. She never thought Adeline should have been going to Harley Street, and I was the one who insisted. But I just wanted the best for Adeline. You can get very good treatment at home but there are a few things that need to be taken care of in the proper place. I simply felt we ought to be scrupulous about it, after what Adeline nearly did to the baby.

'My wife is beside herself, of course. The impudence of it all. And that video. Our daughter lashing out like that. In front of the whole world.

'But I know Adeline didn't mean what she was saying. She's still our daughter. We're still her parents. The foundation is firm. She's just feeling raw at the moment because of what we've asked of her lately. And in a sense it's understandable. You know, Fennig, when you look at your baby and you know that it was fathered by . . .Well, I mean, when someone muscles in like that . . .It can put you out of sorts.

'But in the long run she'll see that she was wrong to make such a fuss. No mother could watch her son rise to that kind of eminence and not look back gratefully on everything that got him there. That's what being a mother is.

. . .

'No, no, Fennig, it's all right. I'm all right. Just pour me a brandy, will you? A small one. How long was I gone for?

'Oh, that's good. I can never quite tell. You know, it's not so bad in the privacy of one's home, but when it happens in the middle of a board meeting . . .To glaze over like that in front of everyone – and my wife has told me I make a sound, a rather pathetic sound out of my mouth . . .That's why I started wearing the cuff. Most of the time the cuff stops it from happening.

'It makes you think about penitents, doesn't it, Fennig? You know, the whipping, the hair shirts, the spiked garters. To put the body in its place, that's why we're told they were doing it. But I have my suspicions, now I know how helpful a bit of pain can be, I mean in terms of keeping you in the here and now. Those mystics, they'd probably seen things, hadn't they? Just like I have. So perhaps they had the same difficulty I do. Perhaps the things they'd seen kept interrupting. Whereas if you have sores on your shoulders and they're niggling you all day, it's harder for your mind to wander. Perhaps it wasn't really about getting closer to the numinous. Perhaps it was about keeping the numinous at bay.

'At first I thought it would be enough to have it on all the time. The cuff, I mean. Just a mild electric current. The problem is, you can get used to that. After a while I realised it has to be intermittent. Random. That works much better. That keeps you from drifting away. Although sometimes I wonder whether in the long run the shocks won't drive me almost as loopy as . . .Well.

'Do you ever have this problem, Fennig? No, I didn't think you would. My wife doesn't seem to either. According to her, it shows I've gone soft – exhibit 101! It's hard to believe now, but when I met her, she was the soft one and I was the hard one. After all, I was the one brought up with all this. It had been in my family for generations. She was just an initiate. I wasn't even sure she'd be strong enough at first. That's rather funny to think of now.

'I was fearless back then. As a young man. I really was. I went further, I think, than anybody ever has, at least in modern times. Well, does that make me soft, if I wasn't entirely prepared for . . .I mean, if a man has the courage to set out into uncharted places and he quite naturally comes home with a few scars must we then blame him for his . . .

'. . .

'. . .

'Oh, thank you, Fennig. No, I'm all right, I'm all right. I'm sorry, I must have spilled it. Yes, if you wouldn't mind. Thank you. I was remembering, you see. It's a mistake, sometimes, to remember. I'd better turn up the voltage.

'I won't keep you any longer, Fennig, but if you see my wife, do try to convey . . .I just mean I don't see any reason why at this moment of all moments we should turn away from each other. As I said, we're still a family. The foundation is firm. Even if things have been tricky from time to time, ever since . . .

'Well, frankly, since Alston. That was when it all started to go . . .Not off the rails, that would be overstating it, but . . .

'All marriages have their ups and downs. "She loves her art collection more than she loves you." That's what Adeline said to me once, in an especially heated moment. But that just isn't true. My wife isn't hard-hearted – even if she might look it sometimes. Have you heard she doesn't even want to cancel the summer party? I think if we don't it will make us look callous. But she thinks if we do it will make us look weak. And anyway, she doesn't think we can afford to take even one year off. Without the party, things might start to fray at the edges.

'Of course she's quite right that it's always been pretty pivotal. In terms of maintaining things. Consolidating things. When we started it, I had no inkling of quite how fruitful it would be – after all it's just a few cocktails in a park, really – but my wife understood from the very beginning.

'She has such a genius for that kind of thing. She understands power better than anyone. Earthly power. You know, I shouldn't say this – not at such a fraught moment, not after all this talk about solidarity – but I sometimes I ask myself if my wife hasn't become rather . . .I mean she's always had power so squarely in her sights that I wonder if it hasn't come at the cost of real piety.

'Forgive me, Fennig. I shouldn't say these things to you. I don't mean to put you in the middle. It must be awkward for you. But at the end of the day, piety's the thing, isn't it? Devotion. The devotion for which we ask no reward. I know you agree with me there.

'That's why I never have to think twice about your loyalties. Because I know where your highest loyalty is. Not to me, and not to my wife either. Your highest loyalty is exactly where it should be.'

❆

Fennig is a patient man by nature and his work has made him more patient still. No virtue contributes more to his effectiveness and so he has cultivated it to its highest flourishing. Which is why it wouldn't be true to say that Mr. Woolsaw's monologue tests his patience. He has listened attentively to hundreds of these fitful, circular monologues over the years. All the same, the knowledge of what awaits him in the basement does produce in him a certain physical tightness, one hand squeezing the colour out of the other as he stands there with them clasped behind his back. Until the monologue finally sputters out, Mr. Woolsaw releases him, and he is able to hurry to the lift.

Three days ago, when he brought home the liver for Mrs. Woolsaw to read, it yielded exactly what they had hoped for. Another name connected to the terrorist who calls herself Rosa.

Douglas Bromet had forgotten all about it. At least consciously. But it was still there in the depths of his memory. The Woolsaws have a number of scholars in their permanent employ, and some years ago these scholars used X-rays to decipher the text of 1,200-year-old parchment palimpsest that Fennig had recovered from a site outside Damascus, but no X-ray machine ever built will have the reach and precision of Mrs. Woolsaw studying a bowl of entrails. In her mastery, she was able to dredge up the name, and further investigation of this name has just produced some very interesting results.

But the delivery of this news isn't the only reason Fennig is in such a hurry.

When he comes into the chapel, he finds her standing naked at the altar. Her face and breasts are slick with blood, which shines almost black in the candlelight, and runs in rivulets down her thighs. She still has the chalcedony dagger in her hand. 'You're late, Fennig.'

A body lies crumpled at the base of the altar. The girl from the video. They needed somebody who wouldn't be recognised and wouldn't be missed, so they trawled the service-user database until they found a suitable candidate in a mental health unit down in Eastbourne. Her acting talents were not so important. The drugs took care of that. They ensured that she would utterly believe every line she was reciting. Just as they ensured that she would still be able to perform for the camera even after they cut off her hands. It all had to be done very quickly to get the video out in time. The doctor had barely finished bandaging the stumps before hair and makeup took over.

Behind the altar stands the reredos. Fifteen feet of black meteoric rock, the lower part intricately carved, the upper part still as raw as the day it crashed to Earth. In 2004 he supervised its transport from Tierra del Fuego, and it was lifted into the house with a crane, like one of Mrs. Woolsaw's Henry Moores, while the basement was still under construction. The walls, floor, and ceiling of the chapel had to be panelled in weathering steel, the better to survive such proximity to the reredos. According to Mr. Woolsaw's research, even marble would eventually crack. Resin would bubble. Certain extinct hardwoods were reported to be fit for purpose but proved impossible to source in sufficient quantities, even for the Woolsaws, who seriously investigated the possibility of salvaging a shipwreck. So instead they resorted to cladding the place in this rather industrial fashion.

To be in a room with the reredos is to feel its hunger. Its hunger is a deafening drone, an inescapable gravity.

'I'm very sorry, Mrs. Woolsaw. I was speaking to your husband and I couldn't get away. But I have some news—'

'If this news can wait for my husband to finish rambling, Fennig, then it can certainly wait for the ritual to come to a proper close.' She sets the dagger back in its niche in the altar.

'Yes, of course, Mrs. Woolsaw. I apologise.'

She leans back against the altar, parts her legs slightly, looks him straight in the eye while she waits for him to come to her. Mr. Woolsaw was right, in a way. It's not pious, the way she turns away from it, rests on it, uses it like a piece of furniture. And yet Fennig does not disapprove. Because for all her casualness, she is still feeding the altar. The altar is always hungry and nobody can feed it like Mrs. Woolsaw can.

Fennig disrobes under her gaze. He carefully hangs up his clothes. His suits are exquisitely made, every buttonhole handsewn – anything less would be out of place at Cyneburne – and although he is well practised at not getting mess on him, it would be a shame to risk a stubborn stain.

He kneels down before Mrs. Woolsaw, the metal floor chilly against his knees, and begins to lick the blood from her feet. He prefers to work his way up slowly, making sure every inch is spotless, but she won't always let him take his time.

Chapter 24

After dinner, Cam asks Luke to give him a hand with the van. Earlier, he says, when he was out doing recon, a guy passing him on a bike shouted something about his lights. So Luke follows him out to the back of the school so he can look for any dead bulbs while Cam blinks everything on and off.

Except when they get to the van, it turns out that's not really why Cam brought him out here.

'A few hours ago I got a call from Shirley.'

'About what?' Luke says. On this side of the school there's nothing but meadows and fairways for a couple of miles out to Hillingdon. During the day you can sometimes make out a very faint plume of smoke from the pet crematorium on Sharvel Lane, but in the evenings, with the sky pink behind the oaks, you really feel like you're in the countryside.

'He told me Rosa didn't go to Edgware when she said she was going to Edgware. He followed her. She went east. To a café in Acton. Sat down at a table with two people. Shirley waited in his car so he could watch her through the window. He says they talked for a long time.'

'Who were they?'

'One man, one woman,' Cam says.

'Have you asked her about it?'

'Not yet. She doesn't know I know. But Shirley thinks they might have been handlers. He thinks they had that look.'

'*Handlers?*' Luke says, incredulous. 'Meaning she's – you think she's been turned?'

'Or she's been undercover all along.'

'Oh, come on!' Luke says, struggling to keep his voice under control. About a dozen different reasons why this is the most ridiculous thing he's ever heard are swirling around in his head. Cam might as well have told him that Rosa is secretly a Greek Orthodox nun. 'If one of us was a rat – how are we still here talking about it? We kidnapped Adeline. She's been here three days. Nothing's happened.'

'That's true.'

'And Rosa? Of all people? She's so hardcore! She's, like . . . *psychotically* hardcore. Rosa's the one who's always trying to get us to use bombs or guns or whatever. If she was working for the police, why would she . . .'

All it takes is a look from Cam to make him realise what he's saying. Of course if she were working for the police she would try to goad them into more serious crimes. That's the whole game.

'But she got scoped out, right?' Luke says. 'Just like I did.'

Quite early in Luke's acquaintance with Cam, around the fifth or sixth time they met, Cam drove him all the way out to a lay-by on the M3. Then he got out of the car without a word. It was late at night and Luke had no idea what was going on.

The driver's-side door opened again and another guy got in to replace Cam. He was stocky and he wore a balaclava and he carried a plastic bag. Luke's heart was thumping. But then the guy offered Luke a can of lager from the bag. There are not a lot of people who can slide into a car with a total stranger while wearing a black balaclava and still make the other person feel immediately at ease, but that was how warm and natural this guy's manner was. They talked for about an hour, sitting there in the greyish slant of the nearest motorway light, a pleasant, meandering conversation that barely touched on the Nail or Luke's reasons for being in that car at that moment. At last the guy said goodbye and got out of the car. About ten minutes went by. Then Cam returned and drove a bemused Luke back into London.

Later, Luke found out that the guy in the balaclava was a Nail member known as Shanker, and Shanker had been evaluating him to see whether he might be an undercover police officer trying to infiltrate the network. Shanker was well qualified to carry out this evaluation because he had been an undercover police officer himself.

Shanker, Cam explained, had spent several years worming his way into the animal rights movement as an agent of the National Public Order Intelligence Unit, using some dead little boy's identity just like they all did back then. Ultimately he became so trusted that he was put in charge of the finances for a group that was planning arson attacks on battery-farm lorries. Meanwhile, he had a number of unwitting girlfriends. One of them fell in love with him and wanted to have his baby. And he just went along with it. With no intention of ever telling her that, like Adeline Woolsaw, she was carrying an enemy's child.

But then she had the baby. He looked into the newborn's eyes for the first time. And he couldn't go on any longer. He told his girlfriend everything. He didn't ask her to forgive him because he knew he didn't deserve it. She told him to leave and he never saw her or his daughter again.

These days, Shanker helps activists and dissidents protect themselves against infiltration. His conversation with Luke in the car was a test that he calls Plate Number Nine. It's named after one of the Ishihara tests for colour blindness, the circles of multicoloured blobs that have numbers hidden in them. The first eight Ishihara tests work in a straightforward way: if you can find the number, that means you aren't colour blind. But the nineth test introduces a new twist: it's only if you *are* colour blind that you *can* find the number. It's a bit cruel, really: a colour-blind child, wanting desperately to pass, will cry out their answer – 'I can see it, it's a two!' – feeling relief that they've escaped their fate, when in fact they've just confirmed the diagnosis. Knowing what he knows about what it's like to do his old job, Shanker has invented his own version of Plate Number Nine. Exactly how it translates to rooting out double agents, Luke isn't sure, and when he thinks back over that conversation in the car, he can never work out what parts of it might have been significant. But Cam has always seemed confident in Shanker's method. Right up until now.

'Yes, he tested her,' Cam says. 'But I called him today. And he was telling me about the Long-Term Monitoring Unit.'

'What's that?'

'After they had to shut down the NPOIU because of all the bad publicity – because of all those guys like Shanker who were having sex with the women they were spying on – they didn't want to just call it quits. So they started the Long-Term Monitoring Unit. It's much smaller. Much more secretive. Even Shanker doesn't know much about it. But he told me it's different. The whole way they operate is different. From what he's been hearing lately, it's about choosing your targets and going really, really, really deep. A cop might only do one of these assignments in their whole career.

'So, because of that – and also because the Unit isn't really supposed to exist – they won't prosecute unless it's worth it for them. None of that "conspiracy to commit aggravated trespass" or whatever the fuck. It means proper scalps. Life sentences. Good PR. The public baying for blood. Wanting a crackdown. Wanting more surveillance. Anything less than that, they'll just bide their time.'

'So you think Rosa's just waiting?' Luke says. 'Kidnapping isn't enough? Cam, this is crazy.'

'We took a girl from a posh family who won't even show their faces on TV to say they want her back. Then she put out a video where she said she was pretty much fine with it. And she definitely won't testify in court that we mistreated her. Yeah, maybe it's not enough. Maybe they want us to kill some civilians. Then we look like a real threat. You know the government thinks long-term just like we do.'

'If the police knew where Adeline was, that would mean the Woolsaws would hear about it, right? And the Woolsaws would say, "Fuck your long-term." If they did kill Douglas trying to get to us, well, clearly they're not just sitting back patiently.'

'That's conjecture. It's all conjecture. Except that Rosa is getting debriefed by someone on the outside and not telling us about it. *That* we know.'

'But . . .'

'But I've slept beside her every night for months,' Luke wants to say. 'I've listened to her sing to herself while she's dreaming. I know every different sound she makes when she comes.'

Except all of that feels too intimate, too sentimental, so instead he says, 'But what about her tattoos?' And even as it comes out of his mouth he's cringing at how lame it sounds.

'Like I said. Only one of these assignments, then they're finished. So they'll go a lot further than tattoos if they have to.'

'But she didn't seek you out. Not like I did. When she started hanging around with Douglas, she hadn't even heard of the Nail.'

'So she said. But the cops know Douglas is linked to me. That's in the databases. So maybe she decided to use him. Get close to him. Say the right things. So that eventually he'd lead her to me. If she was clever enough to fool Shanker, then she certainly would have been clever enough to fool Douglas. There are traces out there and we're vulnerable that way. Doesn't make me happy to admit it but it's true.'

'No. Cam. There's no way. Why don't we just ask her? Ask her who those people were that she was meeting with?'

Cam shakes his head. 'If she *is* undercover – as soon as she finds out we suspect something, that's it. She'll have them pull her out. And the rest of us get picked up before we can scatter.'

'So what are you going to do?'

'I'm going to watch her. And so are you. We pretend everything's normal.'

'We'll have to call off the Auerbach thing, right?' Luke says. 'How are we going to explain that to her?'

'No. That still goes ahead. Tomorrow night.'

'Without her?'

'No. Like I said, we pretend everything's normal.'

'Cam, this makes no sense. You think she might be undercover, and you still want to bring her along on a burglary?'

'Look, either she's undercover or she's not. If she's not, we're all right. If she is, we don't have anything to lose, do we? We're already fucked. We were fucked as soon as she got here. It makes no difference whether we bring her. Actually, it's *better* if we bring her. We can watch her. It might be our best chance to find out for sure.'

'And if something happens that makes up your mind – I mean if it really looks like she *is* a rat . . .'

Over the past two days, as he's learned more about the Woolsaws, Luke has had a sense of another universe beginning to intersect with his own, something vast and light-absorbing and unknowable, like a kraken passing beneath your fishing boat. But there are moments like that with Cam, too, when you hear an implication of his past. And Cam's world doesn't defy logic like the Woolsaws,' but it can chill you just as much when he's standing there giving you a hard look. 'Then we make sure her handlers never hear from her again,' Cam says. 'We make sure she doesn't have a chance to call for help.'

Luke's stomach drops. 'Fucking hell. No. I can't go along with this.'

'Well, the only other option is, we do the safe thing. Which is cut the painter. I mean tonight. In the next hour. We send Rosa out on an errand, then you and I pack our bags, disappear, never see each other again. Is that what you want to do?'

Is it?

Once again, Luke thinks back over his last few months with Rosa. And he tries to keep in mind that even as Shanker's girlfriend was squeezing his hand during her contractions, she still had no idea who he really was. If somebody had come to her and told her she shouldn't trust Shanker, she probably would have told them to get fucked. That ought to be a warning. You can never know for certain.

And yet he *does* know. It can't all be fake. It just can't. The passion they feel for each other is as obviously real to him as the ground under his feet. The sex, the rows, the political debates, even those long boring days of just hanging around together in the lead-up to Adeline's kidnapping. The way she visibly relaxes sometimes when she breathes in his smell. The way she burrowed into him when she was sobbing over Douglas's death. The way she tells him she wishes she could have met Holly, and always says Holly's name with a kind of reverence. In those moments he is seeing a person. Not an act. Not a cover story, a 'legend,' as the spy cops call it. He is seeing through a transparent shell into a human heart. He's as sure of that as he's ever been sure of anything.

'No,' he says. 'I don't want to just leave.'

'All right, well, I came to you with this because I trust you. You're not going to fuck us over, Luke? You're not going to let yourself get pulled in two directions?'

'No, Cam, I would never.'

But as they go back inside – Cam, ever scrupulous, reminds him that if anyone asks, the lights on the van were fine after all – Luke turns it all over in his head. The verdict he came to and the promise he made. Yes, what he has with Rosa is real, and no, he won't let himself get pulled in two directions.

If that's true, though – if Rosa means so much to him, if she's one of the only fixed points left in a world that's feeling increasingly strange and unsolid – then what's his excuse for the way he's been thinking about Adeline? Why does he look forward to every chance he gets to be alone with her? Why has he allowed the little glimpses he's had of her bare body to imprint themselves on his mind? What is wrong with him?

When he gets back to the common room, they're both there. Rosa and Adeline. And it's clear from the brittle quality of the silence that he's walked in on something.

Rosa looks up at him. After his conversation with Cam, he can't think what to say that will sound casual and normal. In fact he so profoundly can't think what to say that it feels like he'll never be able to utter a word to her again. He wouldn't be very good undercover.

She gets up. Nods towards the door. So he follows her to their bedroom. As he enters, his gaze falls upon the full tube of antihistamine cream on the nightstand. She really came back with it, so doesn't that mean . . .

No, dummy, that doesn't mean anything. She didn't go to Edgware, she went to Acton. Shirley saw that with his own eyes. She could have arranged for her 'handlers' to give it to her, so it would look like she'd been to the pharmacy.

'I've had it with her,' Rosa says.

'What happened?'

'She doesn't want to bring the baby.'

'Bring him where?'

'Tomorrow night.'

It takes Luke a moment to catch up with what Rosa is talking about. The Auerbach thing. 'Yeah, Cam was talking about having Shirley come over to look after him—'

'That's fucking stupid. She should be bringing him.'

'To steal a painting?' Luke says. 'How? In a papoose?'

'I don't mean bring him into the building. I just mean we should bring him in the car. If it's all true – if we're all living in some kind of fucking spooky witch world now and everything that happened at Park Royal is because of that little shitbag – he's the best weapon we have. We wouldn't have got away if he hadn't been there. What if something goes wrong tomorrow night? What if they catch up with us again? What if it's just like Park Royal – except this time we don't have the baby? Plus, Cam is always talking about how bringing guns or Molotovs or whatever is just asking for trouble – well, a baby's kind of perfect, isn't it? Nobody's going to tell a sniper to take a kill shot just because you're near a small baby.'

And of course, to Luke, every word of this sounds different from how it would have before. Could she be working an angle here? Say she told her handlers about the burglary. Say the police are planning to catch them in the act. Wouldn't they prefer to scoop up Adeline and her baby all at once?

He keeps telling himself to act normal. The instruction repeats over and over again in his head, completely drowning out everything else. All he can think of to say is 'I understand why she doesn't want to bring him.'

'Oh, right. Of course you fucking do.' Rosa grabs his arm. 'Luke—'

And he goes rigid at her touch. In a way he never normally would. Not even in the middle of an argument.

He doesn't know if it's because he's feeling paranoid about Rosa or because he's feeling guilty about Adeline. But he can tell she notices.

He's expecting rage. But instead, her shoulders slump, and what he sees on her face is more like fear or anguish. It's another unmistakable glimpse into her core.

'Luke,' she says again, quieter this time, blinking away tears. Still holding his arm, she takes his other hand in hers. 'I love you. Okay? I don't want to lose you. Not now. Sweetheart. Please. Not now.'

Chapter 25

Adeline makes the others promise not to damage the painting. Not to burn it on camera, or spray-paint fuck the woolsaws on it, or anything like that. And she feels bashful about speaking up, in case it confirms their worst expectations of her as a decadent heiress who cares more about fine art than people.

But really the whole subject is a bit fraught for her. For years she's watched her mother funnel Woolsaw Group profits into Cyneburne's art collection. And at least part of that is about image. The collection reassures everybody that the Woolsaws are humane, educated, decent people. How else could they have such a sincere appreciation for Hepworth and Freud? And they support new work too, very generously. The Woolsaw Foundation funds a mentoring scheme for early-career artists. Her parents have a full-time publicist, which is funny, considering they shun all publicity, but the art stuff is the one thing that the publicist is actually allowed to tip off the press about. 'Friends of Silvia Woolsaw say she has a lifelong passion for modern and contemporary art . . .She is well known for championing artists from outside the white male canon, such as the British Tanzanian painter Lubaina Himid . . .' (More of that kind of thing lately.)

But Adeline thinks her mother's very particular interest in twentieth-century British masterworks may have a deeper explanation, beyond PR, and beyond aesthetics too. Adeline's suspicion is that, for her mother, these pieces capture something about the country, a sort of vital essence, and this is her way of sucking it out, bottling it up. She seems to take a special satisfaction in buying work at auction from local authorities. During the budget cuts of the austerity years, struggling councils all over the country resorted to selling art off the walls of their museums and public buildings, and lots of it ended up at Cyneburne. Silvia Woolsaw picked up a particularly beautiful Solomon J. Solomon nude from Ealing Council (the same council who are trapped in a long-term maintenance contract with Woolsaw Group's building services division where they have to pay eight grand every time they want a window blind replaced in a council house).

So maybe Adeline ought to feel contempt for the whole subject. And yet she can't bring herself to do so. Her mother – reluctant as Adeline might be to admit it – has a good eye. A lot of the art at Cyneburne is wonderful. And even before Adeline learned to appreciate it for its formal qualities, it represented a kind of escape to her. A purer air to breathe. That's one of the reasons she loves *Hampstead*, the Auerbach, so much. In its bright expressionist colours it shows the neighbourhood she grew up in as a lively, benign place. Not merely the outskirts of Cyneburne.

At times, she even dreamed of going to Courtauld or Saint Martins to study art history or curating. She knew it was a cliché, practically a pipeline, for a girl with her background, and also she wondered what the other students would think of her when they found out who her parents were. Then again, maybe nobody would care. She'd read an article once about a girl studying fashion at Saint Martins whose father was on trial at the Hague.

Regardless, it was just a fantasy. Maybe if she'd spent every single second of her life demonstrating that she was completely obedient, complicit, brainwashed, her parents might have been persuaded to consider the possibility. Short of that, no way.

So now, instead, she's getting a different sort of education.

As 3:59 a.m. ticks over to 4 they're driving up Victoria Street into Westminster, past that huge new office building with its glass front all seamed and angled so it multiplies the streetlights like a cracked mirror. The four them in a black Toyota Prius, acquired specially for the occasion because it's the most common car for Uber drivers in London, so Westminster is full of them at all hours. She's nervous, more nervous, even, than when she broke out of Cyneburne. Because this is all so completely new, and there are people here with her who will be let down if she fails, and she is performing on a very public stage.

She's barefoot, and she's wearing the same grey sweatpants she was given that first night at the school. She got so much blood on them that they were beyond washing – indeed, the intention had been to burn them like evidence – but nobody ever got round to that, which is fortunate, because now they're her costume.

'Almost there,' Cam says. And so she starts trying to summon up tears, with the same technique she's heard that actors use. Just as she did when she escaped from Cyneburne, she's exploiting Mia as a tool. It still feels wrong. But what else in the world could wreck her as efficiently as the thought of Mia, alone, confused, wanting her mother? So that's what she focuses on. And very soon she's crying.

Like Marylebone, where the Nail kidnapped her, Westminster has a lot of embassies and consulates. But Westminster also has the machinery of government, which is why her parents chose to base the company here. The Woolsaw Group building is literally around the corner from the Department of Education and the Department for Health and Social Care. Five minutes from the Conservative Campaign Headquarters, five minutes from the Labour Party Head Office.

However, for a borough with the highest concentration of terror targets in the country, in the most surveilled city in the world outside China, Westminster doesn't have *quite* as much CCTV coverage as you might expect – partly for the extremely English reason that the heritage protection laws limit which buildings you can put cameras on. St Ann's Street does have a few, but yesterday Cam identified a blind spot where Old Pye Street comes up to meet it.

So the Prius isn't going to drive right up to the Woolsaw Group building. Instead, they'll park halfway down Old Pye Street, with Adeline and Cam covering the last forty metres on foot. That way, there will be no good CCTV coverage of them jumping into the getaway car. Which may, with any luck, help them avoid a repeat of Park Royal, when the police were able to trace them while they were still on the road.

Turning onto Old Pye Street takes them abruptly back in time, with its cobblestones and its black iron railings and its handsome red-brick housing estate dating back to when that notion was still pretty novel; as Rosa parks the car, the Woolsaw Group office, tall and narrow, six storeys with a glass-fronted lobby, is the only really modern building in view. It has one of those set-ups where there's a revolving door for visitors with a normal hinged door right next to it for when you can't fit something through the other one.

'Ready?' Cam says.

She glances at Luke. He nods, encouragingly, telling her she can do this. He's wearing a cycling helmet, just like he was for her kidnapping, except this time he also has on a shiny windbreaker in what will apparently be recognisable to any normal person as the colours of a ubiquitous food-delivery service (recognisable to any normal person, but not to Adeline, who sometimes feels she might as well have been living on Jupiter for the last six years). Luke finishes off his disguise by pulling a pollution mask up over his mouth and then he, Cam, and Adeline get out of the car.

The pavement is cold under her bare feet, just like when she fled the school. And her calves still ache when she walks, although not quite as badly as they did back then. She speeds up her breathing, not hyperventilating so much that she'll feel dizzy, but enough so that maybe she'll look flushed and shaky on top of the tears already running down her cheeks. Of course, it's not a bravura feat of acting to present herself as something other than completely cool and collected right now.

On past the estate, with its flues and drainpipes and telephone wires clinging like epiphytes to the old brick walls that weren't designed for them. As they come up on the Woolsaw Group building, Luke peels off, heading south down St. Ann's Street to stand lookout. Cam murmurs into his earpiece, double-checking the connection with Luke and Rosa, then he gives Adeline a final nod and peels off himself, moving to one side so he won't be visible from the lobby. She's on her own now.

The lobby is decorated in a corporate style that she happens to know her mother finds repugnant in its every detail, but the stately old grandeur of Cyneburne wouldn't be very appropriate for the vibrant, forward-looking Woolsaw Group. Behind the polygonal white reception desk sits the lone security guard, head down like he's staring at his phone.

She allows herself one last deep breath, then she hurls herself against the glass of the nonrevolving door.

'Help me! Help me! Please! Help me!' She shouts until her lungs are empty and then gulps raggedly for breath, all the while banging on the door with an open hand.

The guard gets up from his chair with an expression like he was having a nice quiet shift and this is a nuisance he doesn't want to deal with. He comes out from behind the desk, moving at a not particularly urgent pace –

And then he recognises her through the glass. She can see it in his face. He stops dead.

But maybe he still doesn't quite believe what he's seeing. So for a moment he just stands there, staring at her.

If she helps him along, she doesn't think that will be laying it on too thick . . .

'I'm Adeline Woolsaw!' she screams through the glass.

She sees the guard's eyes widen. It's really her. The girl from those videos on the news. The daughter of his boss's boss's boss's boss.

Weeping, barefoot, in blood-stained clothes. She has just escaped from some dank basement near the coach station, and she has staggered here, to the only place she could think of in her panic, the only place she knew would be safe. An hour from now, maybe she can be reunited with her parents. Maybe she can be home.

The guard rushes over to open the door.

'Oh my God, thank you! Thank you! Oh my God, I didn't know if . . . I didn't . . .' Sobbing and babbling. Trying to channel how she felt four nights ago when the woman with the Pomeranian let her into the house.

'You're all right, love. It's all right. You're safe.'

But instead of coming inside the lobby and letting the door swing shut behind her, she holds it ajar.

'Come on, love, let's get that shut—'

'No, no, she might still be coming!'

The guard frowns. 'Who?'

'There was another girl down there with me. We got out at the same time. We were running and – and we had to split up but she knows to come here, I told her to come here . . .' She makes sure to gabble the words. If he feels like he can hardly keep up, all the better.

'Well, if she does, we can open up for her, but in the meantime—'

'She could be almost here!'

Adeline turns back and leans out of the door, as if she's searching the street. She's very aware that this is the trickiest part of the whole plan. If it does go wrong, she has a can of pepper spray in the pocket of her sweatpants. It's hair spray–sized, rather than the dinky little key ring type – imported illegally from the Czech Republic, Cam said – and it's supposed to have a ten-foot range.

But there are two reasons why she doesn't want to use it. The first reason – the self-interested one – is that any release of pepper spray in the lobby could make the remaining part of this operation quite unpleasant.

The second reason – the decisive one – is that the guard doesn't deserve it. She'd willingly do much worse to the security guys at Cyneburne; they have a pretty good idea of what they're involved in, so as far as she's concerned, they're asking for it. But not this guy. Yes, he's nominally a security guard, but her parents probably pay him some piddling wage, so it wouldn't be any different to assaulting a cleaner or a tea lady. This is why she flat-out refused an earlier suggestion for how to do this next bit, which was to ask the guard to phone her parents, wait for him to turn away from her, and then simply bash him in the side of the head with a cosh. This isn't a cartoon and she's not going to risk giving anyone a brain injury.

So instead she has to carry off something rather more delicate.

'There she is!' she yelps. 'There! Look!' Pointing north up St. Ann's Street.

The guard steps forward, just across the threshold, so he can peer in the same direction.

Don't even glance back, they told her. Because if you do, he will too. So Adeline keeps her eyes fixed on her completely imaginary fellow escapee. But even so, it's extraordinary how Cam, big as he is, seems to pop into existence out of nowhere. She doesn't hear so much as a tread before all of a sudden he's there, hooking his arm around the security guard's neck.

Her only job, now, is to grab the guard's wrists, in case he goes for a panic button or anything like that. But she doesn't get the chance, because of course if someone puts you in a chokehold your first instinct is to try to peel their arm away. And that's what the guard does, in vain, because Cam's grip is like steel as he slowly drags the two of them down to a kneeling position and then a sitting position with Cam's back against the frame of the door. Adeline squats down with them too, even though she'd rather look away because it feels like she shouldn't be watching this raw transaction between the two men – she's never seen anything like it up close, never been eye to eye with such a horrible vein-popping grimace – until finally the guard's arms and legs begin to slacken, and at the first sign of this Cam uncurls his arms from the guard's neck.

'It's perfectly safe,' Cam insisted to her, 'as long as you know how to stop at the right time.' As if it were no more complicated than taking a béarnaise off the heat. Even if that's true, it's still violence against an innocent person, the exact thing she swore to them she wouldn't do. And how long ago was that? Less than three days? Has she really made it so easy for them? Seduced by her own abusers and now pouring out their savagery on whoever is at hand.

But as Cam drags the unconscious guard into the lobby, she has to put all that out of her mind. Because it's time to steal a painting.

There it is, hung on a pillar in between the glass panels of the lobby's front. Facing inwards, so it won't announce its presence to the street and it won't get any direct sunlight. A little label beside it so you can find out what you're walking past every day. '*Hampstead*, Frank Auerbach, 1967, oil on wood.' Houses as dauby blue lines against a yellow sky.

A part of her inheritance, come to her early.

One long-simmering argument between her parents is that her father wants the most expensive artworks at Cyneburne – anything worth more than a few million pounds – fitted with anti-theft devices, and her mother feels this is a pointless inconvenience. In a sense, Adeline agrees with her mother: it's very difficult to imagine a burglar getting a painting out of Cyneburne without getting caught by the security team (and then probably taken down to the basement, never to be heard of again). In any event, one summer afternoon a couple of years ago, Adeline's mother decided that she absolutely had to rehang one of her Lucian Freuds and it absolutely couldn't wait until tomorrow. She lifted it off the wall – with bare hands, because gloves are just for conservators and handlers – and an alarm started blaring loud enough to wake the dead in Highgate Cemetery. She'd forgotten about the anti-theft device on the back.

The type in use at Cyneburne looks a bit like a white plastic smoke alarm with a groove at the top to take a picture wire. You arm it by pulling a little tag out of the bottom, after which it will go off if it detects a change in the tension on the wire. And you disarm it by reinserting the tag. On this particular day, the box containing the tags could not be located in Adeline's mother's study, and the conservator who had most recently dealt with the anti-theft devices could not be reached on the phone. Everyone was flapping around, the alarm giving a sort of hysterical air-raid feeling even though nothing had really happened.

Until finally Jock, one of Cyneburne's handymen, tried shoving a screwdriver into the slot where the tag was supposed to go. And the alarm stopped.

Afterwards, Adeline overheard Jock talking to one of the other staff. 'Oh yeah, very bloody secure!' he said. 'And you know that's the same type they use in the offices as well?' But Silvia Woolsaw, who never wanted them in the first place, had no reason to demand that they should be replaced by radio frequency chips or some other technology that would make reshuffling her collection even more of a hassle.

Now, in the lobby, Cam produces from the pocket of his cargo trousers a plastic case containing several screwdrivers of different sizes. Specifically, they're electrician's screwdrivers, because apparently these tend to have slimmer handles designed for tighter spaces. Then he holds the bottom of *Hampstead*'s frame just a few centimetres away from the wall so that Adeline can reach up behind it with one of the screwdrivers from the case. There's hardly any room back there and she's working blind as she jiggles the tip of the tool against the plastic casing of the anti-theft device, searching for the slot.

Then she feels it. The tip of the screwdriver catching on the edge of the slot. But the tip won't fit all the way in. So Cam passes her the next size down.

Somehow finding the slot is no quicker the second time. But when she finally does, she is able to push the tip of the screwdriver up inside. It just barely fits. And when she loosens her grip on the handle, the screwdriver doesn't slip. It's jammed.

Of course, they don't know for certain that this trick will work.

But although it would be very much preferable if the alarm didn't go off, the plan isn't sunk if it does. Their getaway car is only down the road.

Cam leaves her to do the honours. Biting her lip, she lifts the painting –

And it barely moves.

That's all right. They prepared for this too. When they researched the anti-theft devices online, they found out that you can clip them to the picture wire for extra protection. But that isn't really supposed to stop a determined thief, only someone trying to make off with the thing on a lark. So Cam gives her a pair of long-handled pliers and once again she reaches behind the painting, scrabbling around until she feels the pliers catch a wire in their jaws, close enough to the device that it has to be the security cord, not the main picture wire.

She snips it.

Now, a second time, she lifts the painting. And nothing interferes. Including the alarm. The lobby is silent as she holds *Hampstead* in her hands. It worked. She breathes out. Time to make a run for the car—

But then Cam holds up a hand. She can tell from his eyes that he's listening to his earpiece.

'Luke says he sees a police car coming down St. Ann's Street.'

Adeline feels like someone's just put her guts in one of those chokeholds. But Cam's voice is steady. 'Not too fast, Luke says. No sirens. Not like they're responding to a call. Remember what I said.' Cam has already warned that, for obvious reasons, this neighbourhood has a higher than average number of patrols. And because he made it pretty clear in that first video that the Nail planned to strike the Woolsaws again very soon, it's possible that orders might have been issued to cruise past the Woolsaw Group headquarters every once in a while. In other words, a police car coming down St. Ann's Street doesn't mean anyone knows they're here. 'We're okay,' Cam adds, holding eye contact with her. 'We just stay exactly where we are.' From where they're standing, they won't be visible from the street, and neither will the unconscious guard, who Cam has propped against a wall.

The seconds tick by, Adeline barely breathing, fingers gripping tight on *Hampstead*'s plain wooden frame. They hear a car approach. The universe is showing real sadism, she thinks, to put a woman four days out from childbirth in a situation which could not be better designed to make her piss herself.

But then the car passes by. The sound of the engine recedes up the street.

If Cam is as drunk with relief as she is, he doesn't show it. 'Now we wait. A good few minutes. Until Luke and Rosa tell us the coast is clear.'

Adeline nods. And for the first time she notices a security camera up in the corner. They're directly in its gaze. But that doesn't matter, because nobody's watching. Yet.

Seized by a whim, she hoists the painting up like a trophy and looks straight into the lens with a big grin on her face. Hello Mum and Dad.

But at that moment two sounds shatter the silence in the lobby.

The first is a clattering on the floor. But that one's brief, and only barely audible under the second. Which is the howling of the alarm from the anti-theft device.

She looks over and sees that the screwdriver has fallen out of the slot.

Chapter 26

The idea is that Luke will look like a Deliveroo driver trying to work out which of the Abbey Orchard Street Estate's entrances he needs to present himself at to deliver a 4 a.m. kebab order. So when the police car rolls past, he doesn't hide, he just paces around and talks on his earpiece. But what he's saying is 'Cam, police car, coming from the north.' And what he's thinking is, Is this really just a coincidence? Yes, like Cam said, there's every reason to expect a heavy police presence around here. But these guys arrived at the perfect moment to catch Cam and Adeline in the act. Almost like they were up the road waiting for a signal. A signal from, say, an undercover operative sitting on her own in a black Prius.

But then the police car sails past the Woolsaw Group building as blithely as it sailed past Luke. And already he's scolding himself for ever doubting Rosa –

Until the alarm goes off.

The police car stops. Makes a quick three-point turn at the junction with Great Peter Street and then drives back down towards the Woolsaw Group building. 'Cam,' Luke says frantically, 'Cam, what's going on? Cam?' But the sound of the alarm over the earpiece drowns out everything else. Which means right now neither of them can communicate with Rosa, either, because they're all on the same channel.

The police car parks and two cops get out. Luke is rushing straight for them, thinking maybe he can cause a distraction, but he still has about fifty metres to cover when he sees both of them draw guns. Those Glock sidearms that some Met Police are allowed to carry now. And the shock of it is like a barrier slamming down in front of him. He falters. Stops.

'Fuck,' he says under his breath. 'Fuck, fuck, fuck.' Maybe this is what you get for trying to pull off a robbery a quarter mile south of 10 Downing Street and a quarter mile west of the Houses of Parliament. Anywhere else, you'd probably just be dealing with a baton and a Taser. So what happens now? Cam and Adeline under siege in that lobby? Park Royal again but this time no infernal hail to save them?

But at that same moment, Adeline and Cam come out through the door. Adeline is holding the painting in front of her, and Cam is holding Adeline in front of *him*. Like a hostage or a human shield.

The two cops are shouting, guns raised. Cam is shouting too. Adeline is screaming. But Luke can't make out any of it over the alarm.

Then Adeline drops the painting. Jerks free of Cam's grip. And hurls herself towards the cops as if this is her last bid for freedom.

In that instant, Luke doesn't know what to think. Is this real? When they saw those guns, did Cam and Adeline both rapidly recalculate their roles in all of this? Did Cam decide that threatening Adeline's life was his only way out? Did Adeline decide that finding refuge with the police was *her* only way out?

But then, as she reaches them – as one of them is about to pull her in to safety – she goes into what looks almost like a ballet dancer's twirl. Something is in her hand. And right away both cops are recoiling, scowling, covering their eyes. But so is Adeline.

The pepper spray.

Luke realises what has just happened. The cops let their guard down long enough for Adeline to turn herself into a sort of capsaicin dervish. She misted the two of them like one of those spinning lawn sprinklers. But she's been caught in the cloud herself.

Now Cam has pulled those long-handled pliers out of his pocket and he's whaling on the cops. He alternates between them, bouncing the pliers back and forth, first one head, then the other, keeping them both off balance, until he can force them down onto the pavement.

Cam picks up the painting. Presses it on Adeline. She takes it blindly. Then he grabs her arm and together they start trotting up the street towards the Prius.

They're getting away. They're actually getting away. Which means Luke needs to peg it in that direction if he wants to get away too.

But then one of the cops rises. There's a trickle of blood on his forehead and he doesn't seem to have his pistol any more. Wobbly, leaning on the car with one hand, he goes around to open the boot. From the direction of Old Pye Street, Luke hears tires squeal. That's got to be Rosa in the Prius. He assumes she's racing to scoop up Cam and Adeline. But in fact Cam has to yank Adeline up to the kerb, because the Prius isn't slowing. Instead, it's heading at top speed for the cop still rummaging in the police car's boot.

The cop glances behind him and sees the Prius bearing down. At the last moment Rosa brakes so she doesn't crash straight into the police car, and the cop scrambles out of the way. But he's not fast enough. The front bumper clips him and he spins halfway around before he hits the pavement.

Jesus Christ, did she kill him? Luke doesn't think so – the impact didn't look as bad as that – but he can't be sure. No alarm system could be louder than the panic now blaring in his head.

Rosa puts the car into reverse. Glides right back up to where Adeline and Cam are waiting. Luke is close enough that he can hop into the passenger seat just after they get in the back with the painting. Adeline's eyes are red and streaming, like a parody of the weepy performance she was planning to put on for the security guard, and he can smell the acrid oil on her clothes. He looks past her through the back window. No movement near the police car.

'Why the fuck did you do that?' he says to Rosa.

'What is it?' Adeline says. 'What happened? I couldn't see anything.'

Rosa ignores her. 'He was going for the boot.'

'So?'

A black cat darts out of the way as Rosa backs up towards Strutton Ground. They won't even start to feel safe until they can melt into the traffic on Victoria Street.

'Those armed response cars,' Rosa says, 'the boot is where they keep the rest of the hardware. The MP5s and all that shit.'

'Maybe he was just getting something for his eyes.'

'He was going for a bigger gun. If I hadn't stopped him, Cam would either be dead or in cuffs by now.'

Luke sits there, stricken, as the windows of the housing estate spool endlessly past. Maybe he *is* too squeamish for all this.

Regardless, it makes one thing clear. Rosa just ran down a cop. She is definitely not working for them.

Chapter 21

With the sun rising behind them they drive home through sparse Saturday-morning traffic (swapping cars twice on the way) and Luke can't help but be reminded of a drug comedown after a night out. Because he feels totally exhausted and totally wired at the same time; because normality is all around him but also unreachably distant; but above all because he's slipping back and forth between euphoria and dread. Different images rolling around inside him like ball bearings or air bubbles so that every time he shifts in his seat his whole mood changes.

'Anyone injured?' says Shirley when they get home. Of course he's only asking about the four of them, but instinctively Luke glances at Rosa, who pretends not to notice. 'No,' she says, 'nothing serious.' Adeline's eyes are still stinging, though, and Shirley warns her to shower before she touches the baby (who didn't sleep much, he reports, but seemed to take to formula okay). 'Don't run the water too hot, and keep your underwear on.'

'Why?'

'Because when you're rinsing that stuff off, some of it can run down between your legs.'

'Ah,' Adeline says. 'Just what I need. More genital trauma.'

Even *Hampstead* proves to be more or less uninjured when they take it out of the bin bag Cam wrapped it in for the car journey.

There's a conspicuous scratch on the wooden frame where Adeline dropped it, but the canvas itself didn't touch the pavement. While Adeline is in the shower, Shirley examines it. 'So this is a priceless masterpiece, is it?'

'Yeah, apparently,' Luke says.

'I'm not sure I would have known that if you hadn't told me.'

'Right, yeah, I know what you mean,' Luke says, regarding *Hampstead*'s bright colours and thick lines.

'What I would probably have said is "This looks like when they get a nice, cheerful painting by a 'local artist' to put up in the geriatric care ward."'

'It's worth about two mil, though.'

'I see.'

And the painting isn't the only bounty they've brought home with them from Westminster. Because Cam turns out to have swiped one of those Glocks from the police. The sight of it startles Luke almost as much here as it did back there. Cam says he would have taken the other one too but he thinks maybe in the chaos it got kicked under the police car.

After Shirley goes home, they all get some sleep. To escape talking to Rosa as they're getting into bed, he makes a show of being too wiped out to form a sentence. Maybe they could be celebrating right now, even fucking like they did after the kidnapping, if he could put aside all thought of the cop she ran down. But he can't. And maybe she can sense that, but she clearly has no interest in justifying herself to him. As he shuts his eyes, he's thinking about how tomorrow – or really later today – they'll find out whether the guy survived.

Yet, when they rise, the latest developments are so exciting that actually for a while he *is* able to ignore everything else.

It's everywhere. The still from the CCTV camera in the lobby. Adeline holding up the painting with a smile that's triumphant, mischievous, even slightly manic.

Adeline tells them she's certain that her parents would never have released it voluntarily. Which means it must have been leaked, either by somebody inside the Woolsaw Group or by somebody inside the police. Whoever it was, Rosa thinks they could have sold it to a newspaper for five figures if they were smart. The Woolsaws are going to be apoplectic.

Yes, those two video testimonials caught people's attention. But it was nothing like this. You can't spend a minute on social media without seeing the photo a dozen times. Only half a day has passed but somehow it feels historic already, Adeline in the pantheon next to Marilyn Monroe holding her dress down and Buzz Aldrin walking on the moon. The fact that they actually have *Hampstead* in their possession seems almost irrelevant compared to that one unplanned gesture – and of course it doesn't hurt that Adeline is pretty. 'Sometimes it's just about one good image,' Cam says. 'Sometimes an army can't do as much as one good image.' Inevitably, it becomes a meme as well. People are photoshopping other things inside the frame of the painting that Adeline is holding. Kittens, spicy chicken sandwiches, Danny DeVito. 'If I'm going to be seeing this picture for the rest of my life,' Adeline says, 'I do slightly wish I hadn't been wearing filthy jogging bottoms.'

Maybe the Woolsaws did make everyone believe that Adeline was at gunpoint when she recorded her video. But plainly she wasn't at gunpoint when she cracked that smile. Some people are still convinced it's brainwashing or Stockholm syndrome. But others are pointing out the Nail has only had her for five days; short of inventing some kind of hypno-ray, it would be a pretty tall order to completely mentally demolish and rebuild someone in less than the time it takes to get over jet lag.

Most importantly, the question is being asked – the question they've been trying to get people to ask all along:

So who *are* the Woolsaw family?

It's incredible. It's everything they've been working towards. In every corner of the planet, people are talking about this, all because of the four of them now cooped up in a squat on the outskirts of

Northolt. They all eat toast for lunch because nobody wants to tear themself away from the TV for long enough to cook anything proper.

Yet eventually the other side of it does come crashing back in.

The security guard seems to be fine. There's footage of him going into the block of flats where he lives, repeating 'I have no comment on the incident', very much as if someone has told him to say that.

One of the cops, the news says, was released from hospital after being treated for head injuries.

But the other – the one Rosa ran down – is in a coma.

As they're watching the news reports about this, Rosa acts like it doesn't bother her in the least. The police are basically just the Woolsaw Group's private army, so why should they worry about casualties of war? All Cops Are Bastards, like she has tattooed on her arm, right between the sunburst flag of the PKK's all-female brigades and a somewhat botched werewolf. Firearms officers, in particular, are notoriously card-carrying members of the English Defence League, the whole lot of them. At one point she makes a joke about how maybe she should have finished him off.

And yet Luke can see the cracks in this performance. She has misgivings that she's trying to stifle. He senses that she would really like someone else to reassure her that what she did is okay. The nearest she gets is Cam, who isn't gloating like she is but doesn't seem particularly troubled either.

Luke goes back and forth. At times he almost finds himself agreeing with Rosa. What the fuck is the point of joining an underground revolutionary group if you're going to sit around moping about a cop getting hurt? After all, how many activists and protesters have been beaten, choked, blinded by the opposing side? Not to mention raped by deception, impregnated, traumatised, in the case of Shanker's old colleagues in the undercover units. And these guys don't sign up to carry a Glock unless they're willing to go into battle. Plus, this is nothing compared to what happened at Park Royal.

On the other hand, he joined the Nail to fight tyrants like the Woolsaws. But Damon Cowans, thirty-seven years old, two kids, isn't that. And when the news programmes start showing photos of him they've pulled off social media, that really undermines Rosa's English Defence League thing, because he looks mixed race.

Still, the next time he finds himself alone with Adeline, it's exhilaration that surges in him once again. She's coming back from the toilet as he fills a glass of water in the kitchen, and rather clownishly he steps out into the corridor in an imitation of her pose from the photo. She chuckles. 'I wasn't smiling like *that*.'

'You know, it was amazing, what you did. I mean, I know it all got really messy, but that wasn't your fault. When we took you, we thought you were just going to be collateral . . .'

'Meat in a cashmere jumper.'

'Yeah. Basically. But now you're really part of it.'

'Well, I hate to disappoint, but I didn't like it. I didn't like the violence.'

'I know,' Luke says. 'But it's means to an end. And I think it's working. A week ago, it still seemed like nothing could touch your parents. And now . . .'

'They're vulnerable.'

Just how vulnerable, they find out the next day.

Chapter 28

Adeline doesn't recognise the room on the TV, but it's probably somewhere inside the offices she just burgled. The press conference has five participants, seated along a table with microphones and bottled water in front of them.

Her mother.

Her father.

Hattie, her nanny.

And two functionaries in suits, lawyers presumably, an older one who acts as a compere, and a younger one who must have visited Cyneburne at some point because Adeline is certain she recognises him.

Adeline remembers her father once repeating something that *his* father said to him, which is that some of the finest men of his generation achieved very great things and yet only ever had their names in a newspaper three times: their birth announcements, their wedding announcements, and their death announcements. People of their class aren't supposed to want fame, and if Adeline's parents were ever to learn of the thrill she felt upon seeing her face on the news, they would deride it as beneath her. Combine that general attitude with the Woolsaws' specific endeavours, which thrive in deepest shadow, and you get a very strong preference for privacy. As far as Adeline knows, no picture of her parents has ever appeared in the press. A few years ago it looked as if her father might be called to appear before a parliamentary committee, but he fought back until the idea was dropped. And it just so happens that the Labour MP who initially demanded it has had quite a number of misfortunes since then, not just politically but also personally and even medically.

So it is astonishing to see them lined up in front of TV cameras. The press conference is being shown live on Sky News, and Adeline is delighted that as they take their seats they look visibly uncomfortable.

It must have been the picture that did it. The smile heard round the world. Up until then, they could maintain their silence. An anguished family trying to hold on to their privacy in the worst moment of their lives. They weren't hiding anything, they just had strict advice from the authorities not to weaken their negotiating position with the terrorists.

But the picture tipped the balance. The picture, and also the policeman in a coma because of the crime their daughter was part of. At this point, it will leave too much of a void if they say nothing.

Everything they do say is rote. They love her, they miss her, they so desperately want her to come back safely, they're looking forward to meeting their grandson, etc. etc. 'Whatever you've been forced to do,' her mother says to the camera, 'whatever you've had to go along with, we understand. We know how strong you are, darling, and we know you're just trying to get through this.' She does succeed in producing a few tears, and Adeline wonders what technique she used. The same one Adeline herself used the other night? It makes her realise how little she really knows her mother. If her mother needed to think about something heartbreakingly sad from her life, what would she choose? What, if anything, has ever affected her like that? Adeline couldn't even venture a guess. Maybe her mother cheated and used glycerin drops. Anyway, Adeline's review would be that overall it's an adequate performance in which Silvia Woolsaw mostly manages not to look too much like she's being held hostage herself. When she's not talking, the camera sometimes catches her wringing her hands, which Adeline recognises as a sign of irritation, but anyone who doesn't know her will probably mistake for grief.

Next, her mother hands over to the younger lawyer.

Except it turns out he isn't a lawyer.

'My name is Jasper Brownlow,' he says. 'I am Adeline's husband of sixteen months, and the father of her child. I realise that our relationship has not been widely known until now. We never wanted to hide anything, we just...Well, the Woolsaws are a family who really value their privacy and my own family do too, to be quite honest.'

Now Adeline remembers why she recognises this guy. About two years ago, her parents invited him to Cyneburne for tea. It was a strange episode. And not only because this was the first time she had really socialised as an adult.

All he did, over scones and jam, was ask her about the art she liked. Presumably he'd been warned in advance that it would be tactless to pose the usual getting-to-know-you questions to a girl being held captive by her parents ('So where did you go on your gap year?') At first, Adeline was so taken aback by the whole charade that she found herself giving earnest answers about Auerbach and Hepworth. But slowly it dawned on her that her parents wouldn't have contrived this visit unless they had something very specific in mind for the two youngsters. Jasper's father, it emerged, was an earl who sat in the House of Lords. Jasper himself had been educated at Winchester and Oxford, and he was now learning the ropes at the company that administered the family's extensive land and property holdings.

A perfect husband for a girl like her.

After that realisation, Adeline let her responses grow clipped and sardonic. Until eventually the whole occasion ground to a halt, despite her mother's repeated attempts to get it going again.

But afterwards, Adeline was ashamed to find herself thinking about Jasper quite a lot. After all, he *was* pretty handsome. Repellent in almost every way, of course, and not at all her type, but undeniably pretty handsome. Charismatic, too, with beautiful manners. And she was just so starved of male attention. Indeed, it was a bit absurd to think of herself as even having a type, considering she'd never had a boyfriend before. As a teenager she'd been reduced to developing crushes on the younger members of Cyneburne's security staff.

Jasper had never come back to Cyneburne. And Adeline thought her parents might have shelved the whole idea.

But now the world knows that she's a mother, because she mentioned it in that first video she recorded with Cam. And her parents clearly felt that required a dignified cover story. Adeline wonders what Jasper's getting in return for this. After all, it has a cost. Now that he's gone on TV and announced he's her husband, that will rule him out for any other dynastic marriages.

Have her parents promised that when they recapture her, she'll be given to him?

Have they promised that when their kingdom is established, he will take his place in the power structure?

'You never said you were married,' Luke says dryly.

Jasper offers nothing else of substance before handing back over to Adeline's mother. Who in turn introduces Hattie.

'Now, Hattie is not a Woolsaw,' she says, 'but she is very much a member of our family. She's been Adeline's nanny and teacher and companion and very dear friend since my daughter was learning to walk – indeed, she risked her own life trying to protect Adeline on Monday – and she has felt as much heartbreak as any of us over these last few days. So it may be a bit unconventional, but we thought she ought to have the chance to speak to you today as well.'

As the camera turns to Hattie, Adeline can see right away that she's holding back tears. Real ones, otherwise she wouldn't be holding them back, would she? She'd be shaking them out of herself like the last drops of water from a dry canteen, as the woman next to her just did. But on the contrary, everything she says sounds heartfelt. 'Adeline, we all love you so much,' she says, and these words are just as banal as everyone else's, yet Adeline now finds herself holding back tears too, because it's different hearing them from Hattie. She knows it's true. Hattie does love her. And Adeline loves her back.

And yet isn't it ridiculous to be moved by the sight of her? Obscene? Humiliating? To get all soppy about this woman who was just as much one of her captors as anyone else at Cyneburne? All those people online chattering about Stockholm syndrome – well, if they really want to see Stockholm syndrome, they should take a look at Hattie, who's been on both ends of it. Twenty years as a tireless servant to the Woolsaws even though they treat her like a kitchen drudge. Twenty years as a loyal accomplice in the imprisonment of the girl she's supposedly devoted her life to. And meanwhile that girl still can't stop missing her. Can't stop making excuses for her. Because once again Adeline is turning over in her head the old question: is there any point resenting Hattie for the qualities she doesn't have? Hattie will never stand up for herself and neither will a garden earthworm, and if you hate either of them for that you're wasting your energy.

Even on top of her earnestness – and her swollen eyelid from when Rosa punched her on Monday – another reason Hattie comes across quite sympathetically on TV is that, compared to the Woolsaws, she seems almost like a normal person. The reality is, nobody who has spent that long at Cyneburne could ever be normal. She was trained at Norland, the academy in Somerset where they teach you how to nanny for oligarchs and royalty, and she had only a couple of other clients between that and the Woolsaws. The Woolsaw family has been almost her whole adult life. All that time in their palace of blood, well aware of what's happening there. Not normal at all. But on television she does seem normal in comparison.

Hattie talks for no more than a couple of minutes. And it's only at the very end that she says it. The thing that makes Adeline's heart hammer in her chest.

'. . . And I just keep running through my favourite memories of you. Like when you were little and on Sundays I used to take you swimming and you loved it so much. I know you're a bit big for it now but I just hope we can go swimming again. Really soon.'

'Oh my God,' Adeline says.

'What?' Luke says.

'She's talking to me. She wants to meet.'

Chapter 29

The thing about growing up at Cyneburne, she explains to the others, was that there were two layers of aberrance stacked on top of each other. There were the secrets, the portents, the altar in the basement. The Long-Before. But that isn't to say if you took all that away you would be left with a totally average family. After all, her parents were both of aristocratic stock, and had been brought up in big houses in the countryside where the clocks were set back somewhere between twenty and a thousand years compared to the rest of England. Though not quite as constrained and unusual as Adeline's, their childhoods had been constrained and unusual all the same. So they had neuroses and obsessions quite unrelated to the monstrous thing they'd devoted their lives to, and Adeline had to endure those as well.

One example of this – one of the more benign and manageable examples – was that her father had an unshakeable conviction that a well-brought-up young woman ought to be an elegant swimmer. Yes, there were other ladylike modes of exercise, such as tennis, but really that was just a nice summer hobby, whereas your form in the water was a basic function of your being, like your smile or your speaking voice.

Unfortunately, when Adeline was twelve, the swimming pool in Cyneburne's basement was out of use for nearly two years.

Her parents claimed it was some complicated structural problem, but later Adeline wondered if it had to with the swimming pool's location. Directly above the chapel.

As a consequence, her father insisted that Hattie took her to the Connaught hotel every Sunday so she could practice her swimming in the pool there. It was a half-hour drive into Mayfair, when they could have just walked down to Hampstead Ponds in no time at all, but of course it was out of the question for Adeline to swim anywhere so plebeian.

The trips to the Connaught turned out to have an upside, however. Because pretty soon they stopped going to the pool.

Instead, Hattie would leave her GPS panic button in a changing room locker. Then they would leave the hotel by a different exit, to make sure they weren't spotted by the security man who'd driven them there.

They would hurry along Mount Street and down through Berkeley Square to the McDonald's in the southwest corner. Hattie would buy her whatever she wanted and they would linger there until it was time to go back to the Connaught.

She loved the food. Of course she did. She had the palette of a twelve-year-old whose parents never let her eat junk.

She also loved the deception. Before they left the Connaught the second time, they would both wet their hair in the showers. Later on, if either of her parents asked her how their outing was, she and Hattie would exchange a little look. The conspiracy gave Adeline such joy, even more so because it seemed to have a real edge of danger: for that hour, without the panic button or the security man, they would have no way of summoning help if anything happened.

But, most of all, she loved feeling normal for a little while. Sitting there in a normal place where normal people went, eating normal food that normal people ate. Surrounded by real Londoners (and some tourists) who didn't know or care who she was. Occasionally, as an alternative, they'd walk north to Oxford Street, so that Adeline could try on cheap clothes surrounded by girls her own age.

Later, as an older teenager, she began to find it pathetic in hindsight. How independent she had felt in those moments – even though she was with her nanny. How fearless she had felt – even though it was Mayfair in the middle of the day. But today she would give a lot for another moment like that. The closest she'd come in several years was the waiting room at the family-planning clinic. And that morning she hadn't been in much of a state to enjoy it.

❀

After Adeline tells the others how she knows that Hattie wants to meet this Sunday, Rosa says, 'Sounds like a bit of a reach.'

'No, it isn't. Why else would she bring up swimming? Why else would she make a point of saying I loved it? It's the only way for her to send me a message, in front of everybody, that nobody else but me and her could possibly understand. She wants me to be at the McDonald's on Berkeley Square – well, assuming it's still there; can someone check? – tomorrow, Sunday, around eleven-thirty a.m..'

'I agree that the message is clear,' Cam says. 'I also think it's probably a trap.'

As gratifying as it was to observe her parents' desperation, Adeline is relieved that the TV's off and they're out of the room. And without that distraction, she only feels more certain. 'I've known Hattie almost as long as I've been alive. Sometimes she's being herself and sometimes she's being my parents' hand puppet and I can always tell the difference. That was real, just now. That was between her and me.'

'Even if we knew that for sure – which we can't – it's out of the question.'

'The McDonald's is still there,' Luke says, looking at his phone.

'Out of the question,' Cam says again. 'You can't go out in broad daylight in the middle of London.'

'It's worth it,' Adeline says. 'I can turn her.'

Chapter 30

'You told us she never had enough of a spine to help you,' Rosa says. 'Not help you like buy you a secret Happy Meal, I mean really help you. Because at the end of the day she's just another toady. So why would that change now?'

'You three believe in revolution, right? I mean, presumably you do?' Adeline looks from Rosa to Cam to Luke. 'So why haven't we had one, if everyone's so unhappy with the way things are? Because they simply can't believe that another world is possible – correct? They can't imagine things getting better. So they just cling to the status quo, even though they detest it. Because it's familiar, and it makes sense to them, and anyway it feels completely impregnable. Isn't that what people like you think?'

Luke sees Rosa bristle at those last few words. But in Adeline's voice there was only mild archness, not any real derision.

'It's a little bit more complicated than that,' Cam says. 'But yeah, all right – what's your point?'

'Well, that's Hattie. She always wanted the best for me. She honestly did. But that was always limited by what she thought was safe and realistic, for me, and for her. Which was very, very narrow. She was never going to be the one to chuck the first Molotov. But then came this week. A very *un*safe, *un*realistic thing has already happened. I'm out of Cyneburne. So now that the horizon of possibility has been rather brutally expanded, she must have realised that she has an opportunity to pick a side and it will actually matter. That's why she said what she said at the press conference. It's the bravest thing I've ever seen her do, even if it might not impress the likes of you very much.'

'This is a whole lot of speculation about what's going on inside the head of one specific middle-aged woman,' Cam says.

'Every op's a dice roll, right? And we have to save our dice rolls for when it really matters. Like the ReadyPay van.' Rosa turns to Adeline. 'I think you just want to talk to her because you're hoping she can tell you where your other kid is.'

Adeline nods calmly. 'Yes, that's true, I am hoping she can tell me where Mia is. I want my daughter back. But that's just the start. This caper with the ReadyPay van – it will make news, I'm sure, but do you think it will really hurt my parents? I mean, really *wound* them? It's just money. Whereas if we had someone on the inside at Cyneburne – someone that close to my mother and father – someone they've trusted for twenty years? We could carve them into pieces.'

Although Luke isn't one hundred percent on board himself, he can't help feeling some admiration for how good Adeline is at salesmanship, and how well she knows her audience. Sure enough, Cam makes a major concession, which is that he will scope out the McDonald's in Berkeley Square, first online and then maybe even in person. Decide whether the operation would be remotely feasible.

The baby starts crying, so Adeline takes him back to her room, and Luke goes into the kitchen to do some washing up. Crazy as it might sound, that press conference was the first time he's ever seen the faces of Conrad and Silvia Woolsaw. Up until now they've just been sinister blanks to him, just as he must be a sinister blank to them. He thinks back to his conversation with Adeline about whether it's fair to say her parents murdered his sister. Finally seeing them embodied as human beings, fidgeting, swallowing, shedding a few tears, has that in any way blunted his desire for revenge upon them? Or has it only sharpened it?

He's still reflecting on this when Rosa comes rushing into the kitchen. And if Luke thought she looked bad after she found out Douglas died, well, that was a picture of serenity compared to this. That day she had an expression as if she'd seen something awful pass in front of her. Whereas now she has an expression as if she can feel something far worse right behind her. Her eyes alone almost make him drop the bowl he's drying.

'You have to come with me,' she says.

'Where? Jesus Christ, Rosa, what's wrong?'

'We have to take the car. Don't say anything to Cam. Cam doesn't need to know. Just come with me. Now.'

Chapter 31

Rosa peels the Corsa out of the driveway before Luke even has his door shut. Obviously, Cam is going to hear them leaving, so when she said he didn't need to know about this, what she must have really meant was that she didn't want him to find out in time to stop them.

'What the fuck is going on?' Luke says.

'There are some people in danger and we need to help them,' Rosa says, her voice halting and toneless.

'What people?'

She yanks the gearstick around like she's trying to snap it out of its housing.

'Rosa, what people? I mean, is this – are they Nail people?'

She hesitates. 'Yes.'

'Then why aren't we talking to Cam about this?' He feels his phone vibrate. Glances at it. 'It's Cam.'

'Don't answer.'

White Hart Roundabout is notorious for accidents, and Rosa is driving very much as if she wants to do her bit for the stats, so Luke is relieved when they swing off it unscathed – but now she's taking them south down Parkway, and for a wild moment he wonders if they're making for Heathrow Airport. 'Why not?'

'He won't get it. He won't want us to do this, but – but we just have to. Put your phone in the bag.' She means the foil bag under the seat, which is where they stow their phones during an operation to make sure the cops can't pick up their trail from phone mast pings. So is that what this is? An op?

'Rosa, I love you but unless you tell me what's really going on—'

'It's my parents!' She shouts this even though he's sitting right next to her. 'It's my fucking parents, all right?'

'Your foster parents?' Luke says, confused. 'I didn't think you were in touch with them any more.'

'Not my foster parents. My real parents. I think they're in danger. They live in Wimbledon. We have to go there and make sure they're okay.'

'I thought you never knew your real parents.'

She just stares at the road ahead of her.

'Rosa—'

'That was a lie.'

'So were you – I mean, how well do you know them?'

'I fucking grew up with them! I was never in foster care. That was just something I made up.'

The realisation falls upon him like someone has picked up Ruislip School for Blind and Partially Sighted Children and dropped it on his head. 'It was a cover story.'

Rosa nods.

'You're undercover,' Luke says, and she nods again. The impossible is possible, he thinks. Insects can condense out of shadow and the woman he loves was never really there. Only two days ago, Cam gave him the clearest possible warning, and he still didn't believe it. What a fucking idiot he's been. 'But you nearly killed that cop.'

'Luke, you don't understand – I was undercover at the *beginning*. But then I found out all about the Woolsaws and I saw what Cam was doing and I fell in love with you and it all made so much more sense than who I was before. I got turned or brainwashed or born again or whatever you want to call it. I'm part of it now. I'm really part of it. The Nail is my life. There's nothing else any more. But I couldn't tell you the truth. I was hoping I could just leave it in the past and you'd never have to find out.'

Luke is reeling. Yet this does explain a lot. When she was pushing so hard for more violence, more blood, it wasn't because she was trying to entrap them. It was the zealotry of the recent convert, kindling a flame hot enough to annihilate her old self.

'At the beginning – were you informing on us?'

'"Informing"? No. I took some notes, but that's it.'

'So you never told them anything?'

'Told who?'

'The Long-Term Monitoring Unit. Or whoever you work for.'

'What the fuck is the Long-Term Monitoring Unit?'

'The undercover squad. The new one. Cam said . . .'

Rosa's mouth gapes for a moment. And then she laughs. A grim, panicky laugh. 'Jesus Christ, Luke, I'm not a cop! I'm a fucking journalist! I was writing a book!'

As shattering as this conversation has been up until now, at least Luke was on some level prepared for it. But what she's just said is so impossible for him to process that he doesn't even really have an emotional response. He stares at her like she's just told him she's a tangerine or an interest rate. 'What?'

So Rosa tells him how she found the Nail.

Her journalism career wasn't going anywhere. She couldn't get a staff job. She had trained as an investigative reporter but she was paying her bills writing web articles with headlines like 'The Surprising Truth About *Too Hot to Handle*'s Most Controversial Kiss.' All she wanted was a chance to make her name.

She decided she was going to go undercover in the climate protest movement. Work her way deeper inside until she met the militants planning to blow up oil pipelines and burn down SUV dealerships. A year or so hanging around with them was guaranteed to make a pretty juicy book.

But after she'd already invested several months of evenings and weekends in her new persona, she came to the conclusion that although the climate movement did have a lot of people talking about the necessity for sabotage, it didn't have many people actually doing it. The real bomb throwers were still where they'd always been: among the anarchists, the insurrectionists, the accelerationists. For them the end of fossil fuels wasn't the big prize, it was just a bonus that was going to come with the end of capitalism.

So she went looking for those people instead. But she still got nowhere. Increasingly she felt as if she were wasting her time physically turning up to meetings and protests. She would have met more extremists in chat rooms (and she could have done that in the other tab while she was knocking out 'The Eight Most Scandalous *Love Island* Outfits Ever to Enter the Villa')

Until finally, searching for a shortcut, she started looking into past prosecutions of left-wing activists. Including Douglas Bromet. The records of his trial at the Old Bailey were the only place she had ever set eyes on any solid evidence of the semi-mythical organisation known as the Nail. In his testimony, Douglas Bromet had admitted to being a member. And now he was out of prison again. What were the chances he'd really cut ties for good?

So she joined a meditation class he was helping to run. Started going along to the vigils and sit-ins that he organised. Got to know him better and better. But she never once asked him about the Nail. Never even directed the conversation towards his past, even when it was incredibly tempting. To ensure he wouldn't have the faintest suspicion that she wanted something from him.

By this point she was fully inhabiting her cover story as 'Rosa'. It was fun, sometimes, filling out the little details of Rosa's past, almost like writing a novel (another ambition she'd never fulfilled). She always knew exactly how Rosa would react, what Rosa would say. There was just one time she slipped up.

They were up in Lincolnshire, Rosa and Douglas and about a dozen others, staging a week-long sit-down protest outside the immigration removal centre in Morton Hall. They couldn't camp there overnight because the police would clear them out, but

Douglas knew a farmer nearby who was letting them sleep in his barn. For morning showers they were allowed to use the bathroom in the house, but for everything else there was a portacabin outside.

The first night, Douglas came out of the portacabin and said to Rosa, 'Who's Sophie Meade?'

She froze.

'Your rash stuff,' he said. 'Sophie Meade.'

She still got her diphenhydramine on prescription. And the dispensing label from the chemist's had her real name on it. So she always made sure to get rid of the box before she put the cream in her washbag.

Except this time she must have forgotten. All he'd need to do was google the name on his phone and he would see her photo next to her byline. She tried very hard to hold her voice steady. 'Nosy,' she said.

'It was on the counter.'

She shrugged. 'I have to get that stuff online. Off these fucking sketchy websites. Sometimes they send you somebody else's prescription.'

Any shortcuts or innovations of off-grid life, Douglas always had an appreciation for, and sure enough he smiled. 'Well, whoever Sophie Meade is, I hope her rash cleared up all right.'

❧

Luke already knew, of course, that Rosa was a false name. Yet somehow this makes it seem *more* false. Not just pseudonymous but fraudulent. He's so disoriented he can hardly focus on anything else, but he does notice that Rosa is well over the speed limit. 'Slow down,' he says. 'There are tons of cameras here.' The M4 is snaking over Brentford, chain hotels and car dealerships and electronic billboards, that part of the city which doesn't feel so much like London as a space on the map where an algorithm has been asked to generate vaguely city-like filler.

She gives a tight shake of the head. 'We'll just swap the plates again when we get home.'

'Okay but what if we get pulled over?'

'They never pull you over in London.'

Luke doesn't even want to contemplate how Cam would react if he knew they were being this reckless. 'Rosa, you have to tell me, what is so urgent?'

She takes a long breath. 'Douglas never brought up the diphenhydramine thing again. I thought he must have forgotten about it. I mean, why would you remember something like that, unless you were already suspicious? And I know he wasn't suspicious because a few months after that he introduced me to Cam for the first time. So I stopped worrying about it. But then Douglas got killed and suddenly I was thinking, "Fuck, what if he didn't totally forget? What if he still remembered 'Sophie Meade' and they got it out of him somehow before they finished him off?" Because if the Woolsaws have that . . .'

Another long, ragged breath before she goes on. 'Up until then I wasn't in touch with my parents. Back when I started at the Nail I was still texting them and stuff, but then when I got serious, I stopped. But after Douglas I had to warn them. Because anyone who knows my real name could find them easily. I said, "Things are getting really scary, and I need you to get out of the UK for a while, so you'll be safer." But they were like "No, we haven't seen you in months, we don't know if you're in some cult situation or something, we're worried maybe you've lost touch with reality and we just want you to come back to us. We're not going anywhere." So then I was like "Jesus, okay, I'll fucking see you, I'll explain it to your face, if that's what it takes to make you understand that I am talking to you rationally and you are in actual danger because of me."'

'That's who you were meeting when you said you were going to Edgware.' Not her 'handlers.' Her parents. He thinks bitterly about how much he'd love to talk to *his* mother, even on the phone, even for a minute. But he's never broken that rule.

'Yeah, that was when I saw them.' Rosa frowns at him. 'You said that like you already knew.'

'Shirley followed you. He told Cam and Cam told me.'

'What the fuck?'

'Cam was worried that – you know . . . He was thinking police. But he asked me and I said to him, "No way."'

'But you didn't say anything to *me*?'

Luke cannot believe that Rosa has managed to flip this conversation around so that now *he* is the one being forced to justify his deception. 'Cam told me not to.'

'I'm your girlfriend, Luke!'

'Yeah, but—'

'I fucking knew it. I knew I was losing you. Ever since that bitch arrived. There's been this gap between us.'

'Would you have told me the truth? If I'd come out and asked you, before all this?'

Rosa sighs, then shakes her head, conceding. 'No. Look, I know it's all a fucking mess, and we can talk about it later, but right now, I just need you to help me, okay? When I saw my parents, I still couldn't convince them to leave, but I said to them, "If you feel like anything weird is going on, just text me right away." I think my mum believed me more than my dad did. And just now I got this text from my mum saying "There's this guy outside. I think he might be watching the house. Your dad thinks it's nothing but I'm not sure." And I texted, "Get out of the house without him seeing you." But then my mum texted . . .' Rosa swallows. 'She texted, "Your dad is going to go out and talk to the guy just to check." And that's the last thing I heard. Neither of them are answering their phones.'

'So you think—'

'What if it's the same guy who killed Douglas?'

'Okay, and if it is, what are we going to—'

Rosa nods towards the glove box. 'I brought the gun.'

'What?'

'The one Cam picked up last night. I swiped it.'

Luke opens the glove box, and sure enough, there it is, glinting like a scorpion in its burrow. 'Jesus, Rosa, I've never shot a gun. Have you?'

'It can't be that difficult. Cops do it all the time.'

Chapter 32

Rosa told him that for a while she lived in a mansion, a derelict old place on Pevensey Bay that was on the point of collapsing into the sea. She also told him that for a while she shared an abandoned train carriage outside Woodingdean with a family of foxes. But the house she drives up to is neither a mansion nor a train carriage. It's just a house. A nice three-storey house with box hedges in the front garden and ornamental lions flanking the portico. Obviously there are more important things to be worrying about right now, but part of Luke is still just goggling at the revelation that this is where Rosa really grew up.

They drive slowly past the house, but from that distance nothing looks out of the ordinary. So they park at the end of the road and Rosa tucks the gun into her jeans as they get out of the car into the early evening drizzle. As they make for the house, she almost breaks into a jog, but he murmurs 'Steady,' because they shouldn't be calling attention to themselves. Before they try the front door Rosa peers in through the living room windows.

'Anything?' He's still holding on to the hope that all that's about to happen is a very awkward meeting with his girlfriend's parents.

'No.'

She takes from her pocket a key Luke has never seen before. Unlocks the front door. They step into the house, and for a moment they just stand in the hall, listening. But the house is silent.

'Should we just shout?' Luke whispers. 'See if they're here?'

Rosa eases the front door shut so it locks without a sound, one-handed and not even looking, a well-practised motion. 'We don't know who else could be here.'

Moving quietly, they check every room on the ground floor. Living room, kitchen, utility room, bathroom, study. Empty. After so many months breathing mildew at the school it's strange to be enveloped in the soft domestic atmosphere of someone else's house, like burying your face in a stranger's hair. Here and there he sees photos of Rosa at different ages. In one of them she's standing with several other girls in front of a projection screen that reads *South London Schools Debating Competition 2009*. She *has* always been good at debating.

They move up the stairs. Stepping carefully so the boards don't creak. The gun in Rosa's hand. Two flights up to the first floor, with a doorway coming into view at the head of the stairs –

Rosa stops dead. Luke, a couple of steps below her, has to get up on tiptoes to see what she sees.

Someone's feet, in pale blue socks, sticking out sideways past the edge of the doorway. That's all that's visible from this angle.

Rosa takes another step up. Another. Then a terrible wail rises out of her, and she rushes into the bedroom, stealth completely forgotten, Luke following behind.

The two bodies are positioned almost symmetrically. Imagine a man and a woman who have crawled towards each other on all fours until they are close enough to whisper in each other's ears – that's what it looks like. Except their wrists are tied behind their backs. And their heads are propped up cheek to cheek on some kind of trestle. And their throats are cut, so the stand is slick with blood, and the carpet beneath is swamped, and there is a smell of iron in the air.

Rosa kneels beside them, howling. Drops the gun and puts her arms around what must be her mother. Hauls her sideways, off the stand, so that the body flops onto the soggy carpet. Does the same with her father. When Luke gets a better look at Rosa's father's face, he sees that the nose has been completely stoved in. As he stands there more or less paralysed, somewhere in his mind it registers that the trestle is quite a mysterious object: with its spindly legs and top hinge, it reminds him of a double-sided art easel that he and Holly had when they were kids, except instead of wipe-clean drawing surfaces it presents some sort of ridged black convexity.

With Rosa crouched over her parents' two bodies as if she's trying to gather them up into herself, it suddenly strikes Luke that the person who did this could still be in the house—

And at that moment he hears a very soft footstep on the landing outside the bedroom. He turns.

A man stands there in the doorway of the bedroom. Middle-aged, thinning hair, grey suit.

Luke snatches up the gun from where it lies on the carpet. He points it at the man, who is only a couple of strides distant. He's never even held one in his hand before and he has no idea if he's going to look convincing. But a gun is a gun. 'Who the fuck are you?' he says.

The man raises his hands, not panicking at the sight of the gun, just making a don't-want-any-trouble gesture. 'I'm Detective Inspector John Deakin, I'm with the Met Police. Please put the gun down.'

'Why should we believe you're police?' Rosa says, looking up at Deakin with smears of her parents' blood on her face.

'Show us your badge,' Luke says.

Deakin gives a small smile. 'That's more of an American practice. In this country we don't actually carry badges. If you'll just put the gun down—'

'Get on the floor,' Rosa says.

'I'm not going to do that. I recognise you from the photos downstairs, so I know these must be your parents. I'm extremely sorry we weren't here in time to prevent this from happening, but the two men who did it are now in custody.'

'Do it,' Luke says. 'Get on the floor.'

What happens next is so fast that Luke's finger doesn't even have time to twitch on the trigger. In fact the electrical impulse probably hasn't even got all the way across his brain before both of Deakin's hands are on Luke's right hand. Wrenching it around so that for an instant the gun is pointing straight down at the ground – then locking his whole arm so this lunge that initially just seemed directed at the gun is now forcing Luke down onto his back, all in the same flash of movement—

Luke finds himself on the floor, inches from Rosa's parents' bodies, watching as Deakin, or whoever he really is, raises the gun he just snatched—

But then he hears Rosa cry out in rage, and something comes rushing through the air over his head, smashing into Deakin. It's the easel, swung by its legs the way you'd wallop someone with a chair in a pub fight. Except the easel looks a hell of a lot heavier than a chair, and Deakin lurches backwards, losing his footing at the head of the stairs and then toppling what sounds like most of the way down the top flight.

Luke gets to his feet, wondering if Deakin dropped the gun when he fell—

But then two gunshots come from the half landing below. And Luke hears Rosa grunt in pain.

Luke slams the bedroom door shut. There's no lock, but maybe it will buy them a quarter of a second. Rosa is clutching her shoulder. Her grabs her by the arm and pulls her past the bed and over to the window. 'Come on.'

'No!'

And Luke doesn't know if she just doesn't want to leave her parents, or if, insanely, she wants to stay and fight. He lifts the sash, just high enough to climb out. Then pushes Rosa on ahead of him, practically cramming her through the window.

Because she's taken her hand away from her shoulder, he gets his first good look at where she got hit. High, above the clavicle. The trickle from the wound mixes with the blood already smudged on her hoodie.

Out onto the leaded roof over the ground-floor bay window. They just need to drop down into the hedges, then they can make a run for the car. From back inside he hears the bedroom door open.

Chapter 33

The first Adeline hears about Luke and Rosa absconding is when she emerges from her bedroom hoping someone might have cooked dinner. Breastfeeding makes her ravenously hungry. Loathe as she is to admit it, she misses the food at Cyneburne; in theory she'd choose righteous dal over corrupt lobster any day, but in practice your body doesn't care about the moral angle. Nobody's around but Cam, and she remembers hearing a car drive off some time ago, so she assumes the others have gone to run some errand. But when she asks Cam where they are, he replies, 'I don't know.'

'You don't know?'

'You should get ready. If I don't get word from them in the next' – he glances at his watch – 'thirty-five minutes, we're leaving.'

'Leaving for . . .where?'

'Another safe house.'

'And that's it? We never come back?'

Cam nods.

It's not as if Adeline can pack a bag: she doesn't have anything. But she takes a shower, in case it's her last chance for a while. Then she brings Percy into the common room so they can wait with Cam, because she wants to know as soon as he knows. 'Do we have any idea where they *might* be?' she says, and he doesn't answer. An unwelcome thought enters her head: is it possible that

Luke convinced Rosa to bow out of this completely, and they ran off together, as a couple? Eloped, as it were? Without Luke even saying goodbye first?

There's absolutely no reason why she should feel hurt by that prospect. She's known him only five days, and anyway, he has every right to make a discreet exit from a dangerous business. That's what she tells herself.

Obviously she doesn't voice any of that to Cam, so nothing more is said until he passes her his phone so she can look at an article he's just read in the diary column of the *Evening Standard*.

> Conrad and Silvia Woolsaw's summer party is known as the high point of the Westminster social calendar, the Met Gala for people who know what 'hypothecated taxation' means. But it was widely assumed that this year's bash would be called off, since less than a week has gone by since Adeline Woolsaw's kidnapping by Maoist paramilitary group the Nail. Needless to say, the political set have been overflowing with sympathy, but they were also starting to worry about how they were going to meet their schmoozing quotas for the season. Well, they can rest easy: it has been confirmed that the party will be going ahead on Monday, now rejigged as a charitable fundraiser to benefit a cause close to Adeline's heart. 'Conrad and Juliet won't be in attendance themselves, of course, but they're determined that it should still happen,' said a source close to the family. 'They're confident that they're going to get Adeline back safe and sound, and the last thing they want is for all their friends to go into premature mourning. That would be letting the terrorists win.'

She gives him the phone back.

'What do you think about that?' he says.

'About the paper describing you as Maoists? That must be very irritating.'

'No, about – '

She smiles. 'I know. About the party. It's comforting, in a way.'

'What do you mean?'

'To see that my mother is capable of making a strategic blunder. I expect my father wanted to cancel but my mother overruled him. You wouldn't think it would matter that much, would you? A party. But it does. It's extraordinary how much it matters. Everyone goes, every single year. The fact is – the horrendous fact is – it's become part of the fabric of how this country is run. Important things happen at that party. Historic things. And many of those things don't even have anything to do with my parents. But in some way they still contribute to my parents' power. Because they're happening under my parents' auspices.

'So of course my mother would do *anything* rather than cancel. It's true what they say in the article – if she did, then in some sense you'd be winning. Not dismantling the machine, but at least interfering with its upkeep. And she must have thought, "Well, so what if the timing makes us look a bit cold-blooded? So what if people make jokes about how we didn't want to lose the deposit on the marquee? Everyone will still come." And everyone *will* still come. But clearly she hasn't thought enough about how it will look to the wider world. Because she's never really had to think about that sort of thing before. She's so new to being in the public eye.'

'There's been talk, sometimes, about that party,' Cam says.

'I'd forget about it, if I were you. They brought me along a few times when I was younger and I remember the security was very, very, very heavy. I mean, it has to be – the whole Cabinet goes. I'd say you're much better off with oil paintings and pregnant women.'

The article has been a nice distraction, but at this point it comes back to her that they are still in the middle of a crisis. Not long to go until Cam's deadline. Adeline tries to imagine what might come next. Will they find refuge with some other cell? How different will things be without Luke here to advocate for her? What if the other cell is a whole snarling pack of Rosas instead of just one? Will she once again be just a commodity, a chess piece? Is this her very last chance to reconsider her options?

But then Cam's phone rings. Even as he's answering he's up on his feet. And then on his way out.

After the van drives away, it's the first time Adeline has ever been left alone in the school – well, alone but for Percy, whose periodic whimpering is the only sound in the whole place. Home was often silent, but it was the silence of servants creeping around on the other side of a door, whereas this silence is pure and echoey and a little bit unsettling. Yes, she reminds herself, this may be an abandoned school for the blind, but it would actually be quite offensive to suggest that blind kids are inherently spookier than any other kind, particularly because these weren't the sort of blind kids who wear ragged hessian bandages tied over their empty sockets like in a horror film, they were just normal blind kids, who vanished because of a funding cut, not because of some long-forgotten tragedy . . . Plus it is truly ridiculous for a person who grew up at Cyneburne to worry about a place as mundane as this.

All the same, she finds herself turning on the TV for comfort. At home she'd watch whatever would annoy her parents, which on tonight's schedule is everything: football (beneath her), soap opera (beneath her), documentary about the Royal Family (absolute tosh, her mother would complain, no matter if it was positive or negative, because she always knew the real gossip). She settles with pleasure into *Casualty*, but when she hears the van, about an hour later, she jumps to her feet even faster than Cam did.

When Rosa comes in, she looks like someone who's been pulled from the rubble a week after an earthquake. There's blood all over her face and torso; Cam and Luke are on either side of her, helping her falteringly along the corridor; and her eyes are as derelict, as shuttered, as the school she's just come home to. The worst-case scenario for Luke and Rosa going AWOL was supposed to be that they might get picked up by the police. But whatever has happened here seems grimmer still.

Yet Adeline can't even find out exactly what it is, not right away, because Luke stays with Rosa in their room, and Cam just shakes his head when she asks. It's not until a couple of hours later, when Shirley arrives to examine Rosa, taking Luke's place, that Adeline has a chance to talk to him.

'Her parents are dead,' Luke says. 'She got shot in the shoulder herself. We only barely made it out.'

'Her parents? I thought she was an orphan.'

'No, actually she . . .' He hesitates. 'There are various things she wasn't. It's a long story. But one of them is she wasn't an orphan. I mean, until today.'

'God, the poor thing.'

'Adeline, it was . . .horrible. Really fucking horrible. The guy who did it – who killed them and then shot her – he was a white guy, late forties. Maybe a few inches taller than me. Balding. Posh accent. He was wearing a grey suit, sort of old-school-looking, expensive-looking?'

The description makes Adeline go cold. 'That must have been Fennig. The man who does my parents' dirty work.'

'Jesus, I'm so fucking stupid. He told us he was police and for a second I thought maybe he was telling the truth.'

'No rebukes. I don't know where Fennig came from or where my parents found him. But I do know he never disappoints them. Never. Yet you got out alive. That's enough of an accomplishment.'

'Yeah, well, that's not how Cam sees it,' Luke says.

'I can imagine.'

'The fact that Rosa took the gun and then lost it is only, like, fifth place on his shit list. Mainly it's that Rosa was still in touch with her parents, still meeting up with them in person . . .But what's he going to do? It's not like he can . . .sack her. Or me. He has to roll with it.'

'I suppose tomorrow is out of the question, then.' Meaning the meeting with Hattie.

'No, tomorrow's happening, one hundred percent. Cam's angry about what Rosa did. But he's a fuck of a lot angrier about what your parents have just done to her. I think until now, he wasn't sure about tomorrow. But like you said – this could be a chance to carve them into pieces.'

Chapter 34

The Berkeley Square McDonald's has got to be the most incongruous McDonald's in London, looking out across the gardens at a bunch of swanky restaurants with £150 tasting menus. Tucked into the commercial unit at the bottom of a big grey office block, it's where the paparazzi eat after they've spent a few hours staking out the celebrities at the Asian-fusion seafood place.

The Nail arrived at 10:30 a.m., and they've spent the past half hour scanning the square for anybody who might be staking out *them*. Luke is sitting on a bench at the north end of the gardens, pretending to read a book, while Cam has parked the van nearby, in the shade of one of the towering plane trees. If there's a surveillance operation underway here, there's been no sign of it so far. But although Luke has discreetly checked every parked car, it's not as if he can check all those hundreds of windows overlooking the square. Back at the school, Shirley is looking after Percy, and looking after Rosa too.

Cam wouldn't let Adeline see daylight before it was absolutely necessary, so a few minutes before eleven, when he says 'That's her, right?', she has to scramble forward in the van and poke her head between the front seats. Sure enough, Hattie is coming around the corner of Fitzmaurice Place. She glances around anxiously before she goes into the McDonald's – but is that the lonely anxiety of somebody taking a dreadful risk all by herself, or is it the stage fright of somebody with a radio earpiece and a lot of people relying on her to perform? Adeline tells herself that it's unmistakably the former – and tells herself, also, that *she* shouldn't be anxious, because she would only be anxious if she wasn't sure of Hattie, but she's told the others a hundred times that she *is* sure, so she must be, mustn't she? Regardless, she wants to get it over with, but Cam insists they wait another half hour, keep watching the square for anyone moving into position. You can't eliminate the risks of an operation like this. You can only chip away at them.

Finally, at eleven-thirty, Cam gives her the nod, and she gets out of the van. She's wearing a black hijab along with oversized sunglasses that look a bit like they could be Gucci but actually cost twenty quid. Normally this would break the Nail's rule about laying it on too thick in the disguise department. But in fact there are plenty of women around here who dress like this, and she won't stand out (except in the sense that she doesn't have the complexion to be Lebanese).

They've remodelled the Berkeley Square McDonald's since she was last here a decade ago. But the basic layout is the same, the smell, the ambient clamour, and she still gets a rush of nostalgia. Out of all the places on Earth, this is not the one she would have chosen to occupy a formative and indelible place in her heart, but there's not much she can do about that now.

There are only four tables occupied. A mum with two kids; a teenage couple; a guy on his own; and Hattie, in the far corner.

She looks up. Sees Adeline. The disguise doesn't confuse her even for a second.

Adeline walks over, heart pounding. 'Do you mind if we sit over there?' she says to Hattie. 'By the window?'

Hattie carries her tray over to the table Adeline picked out. Hattie never liked McDonald's but she would always get a meal anyway to keep Adeline company, and she's done the same today, an untouched burger, fries, and drink. They both sit down, Hattie with her back to the window, Adeline facing out at the square.

'Are we not a bit . . .visible?' Hattie says.

'My friend is in a vehicle outside. If I start to feel like I'm in trouble, I'll give a signal, and he'll drive it straight through that window. Your body will be my shield, for the van and for all the broken glass.'

Adeline rehearsed this speech in her head, but she never anticipated how hard it would be to say to Hattie's face. As a teenager, during the angriest moments of her long confinement, she would scream at Hattie, call her a bitch or a cunt, 'I hope you get cancer' or 'I hope you get raped.' But that was all pantomime, really. Whereas this is serious. And she can't stop herself from adding, 'Sorry. I have to say that.'

'I know,' Hattie says. 'I understand.'

Of course she does. She's always such a bloody martyr. Yet Adeline reminds herself that, when Hattie is so exasperatingly forgiving and obliging, it's not just because she's a weak person. It's also because she truly loves Adeline, and she doesn't have anyone else. She never started a family of her own. It's just her and the Woolsaws. Not a captive, exactly, because she could have fled if she'd wanted to; more like one of those merchant sailors who have barely seen dry land in twenty years. A human sacrifice herself, and a willing one.

'I promise, no one else knows about this,' Hattie says.

'And you're sure no one followed you?'

Hattie nods earnestly. 'I took the Tube all over the place, I got off and on and off and on. And I didn't see any of the same faces.'

'That doesn't prove anything. They can do it like a relay.'

'I know. I did my best, but – oh, Addie, I'm sorry if this was stupid – I never would have—'

'It's okay. We're here now. And – it's nice to see you.' She means that.

'It's wonderful to see you, sweetheart. Just wonderful. Everyone's been so worried.'

'I'm fine. It's been fine, mostly.'

'And the baby . . .?'

'He's fine too. I'm calling him Percy.'

'Percy.'

'Yeah.'

'Your mother and father will hate that,' Hattie says.

'I know.'

They both laugh.

'Are my parents . . .I mean, what's happening at the house?'

'It's been very, very tense and difficult. Of course it has. Your parents were devastated when it happened. They still are. At the moment they're not really talking to each other.'

That Adeline feels happy to see her old nanny is merely embarrassing. That she feels upset to hear her parents are at odds is absolutely humiliating, even if it's only a tiny part of her. It should be great news, like finding out that Hitler isn't talking to Göring, yet inside her there is still some uncauterised vestige of mindless comfort-seeking daughterly emotion. Will she at some level always be five years old?

'And I was devastated too,' Hattie says. 'At first.'

'At first?'

'We didn't know if they might kill you, or . . .' Hattie's voice cracks. 'And even after that video came out, the first one, and we knew you were alive – I still couldn't bear to think of you going through it all on your own.' A tear runs down her cheek. Adeline reaches across the laminate tabletop and takes her hand. 'But then the second video came out,' Hattie goes on, 'and I was just so thrilled.'

Adeline smiles. 'Really?'

'It was so wonderful to see you speaking in your own voice. To everyone. Your mother and father were livid, of course – especially after what happened at the offices – but to me you seemed so strong and so brave and so much yourself. And it made me realise – it's better this way. These people that you're with now, Addie, they're not who I would ever have . . .Well, you know. But the point is, you're a grown woman. I never wanted you to be stuck in that house for the rest of your life.'

As Hattie says this, Adeline feels such a surge of elation that she gets tearful herself. Maybe she's been unfair to Hattie all this time. Hattie does have a spine, it was just scrunched up so tight you couldn't see it. 'So you'll help?'

'Of course, sweetheart. That's why I'm here. I want to help. However I can.'

'There are so many things. But the first one is—'

'Mia.'

Adeline knows she can't take the sunglasses off even for an instant, so she has to poke a finger behind them to wipe her eyes. 'Will you help me get her back?'

'Yes. Of course I will. When I think of you and Mia, just a happy little family again, somewhere far away from your mother and father – I'll miss you, sweetheart, I'll miss you so, so terribly, but I know that's how it should be.'

All of this is almost too much for Adeline to take. The relief she feels, the optimism. Like it or not, chicken nuggets have always smelled like freedom to her, but never so profoundly as today. 'Where is she? Is she okay? Have you heard anything?'

'She's absolutely fine. She's at home.'

'What do you mean?'

'She's at Cyneburne.'

'They brought her back?'

Hattie shakes her head. 'That's where she's always been.'

'But my mother sent her away.'

'No, sweetheart, she didn't. She just kept you separated. Mia has been living on the third floor.'

Sixty-five rooms above ground, even more below. Thick doors. Thick walls.

Adeline feels rage rising in her. 'So all that time she was right there? She was just at the top of the fucking house? I could have got to her if I'd just . . .' And is this exactly why her mother arranged it like that? So that Adeline would feel as stupid as possible if she ever found out?

But as much as it hurts, Adeline tells herself to focus on what matters.

Mia is in London. Mia is reachable.

'We can get her out,' she says. 'You and me can get her out.'

Hattie squeezes her hand. 'And there needn't be any violence. Nothing that would upset Mia, or, God forbid, put her in danger. And afterwards the two of you won't have anything to worry about ever again.'

'Yes, I will. No matter where I go, I'll always be looking over my shoulder. At least for as long as my parents are still alive. As long they still have power.'

'No, sweetheart, you won't. Not if we settle it all in advance.'

'What do you mean, settle it?'

'Addie, what I'm about to say – you might not like it very much at first, but I just want you to listen, and think it over, because you know that all I care about is what's best for you, don't you? Now, nobody knows I'm here. I told you that. Your mother and father don't know. But I did sound your mother out a bit. It was all roundabout and abstract and hypothetical. I promise I didn't let her see that I had anything in mind. But I came away from it absolutely certain that they would be reasonable about this, and we could come to an arrangement.'

'What are you talking about?'

'A swap. You give them the baby, and in exchange they give you Mia.'

What Adeline would like to do is pick up that tray and slam it into Hattie's face hard enough to break her nose. But she knows she can't draw any attention.

So instead – and the act is too quiet, too controlled, to be truly satisfying, but it's better than nothing – she picks up Hattie's drink, takes off the cap, and dumps it into Hattie's lap.

Hattie winces. But she doesn't move and doesn't make a sound. Even though the Diet Coke and melted ice must be soaking right through her underwear.

Liquid can be heard spattering onto the floor. But nobody else in the restaurant seems to have noticed.

And Hattie continues talking as if nothing has happened. 'Adeline, I want you to really think about this. Mia misses you so much, and I know how much you must miss her. This way, you would have her back. Right away. And it would all be completely safe, and afterwards you could go wherever you wanted, and you would never have to worry about your parents again.'

For a moment Adeline does think about it.

She never asked for a baby. She's just a surrogate. A womb on legs. A breeding cow.

She has only known the child for six days. She didn't want him and she doesn't love him. Any fondness she does already feel for him, any maternal protective instinct, that's just programming. She knows that. She could have popped out a ferret and she'd probably feel the same way. Whatever marvellous and distinctive qualities a child may have, absolutely none of them show themselves in the first week, and that little prune is no exception.

Compare that to Mia. Next to her daughter everything else in the universe is just hair clippings and pencil shavings. She would walk into hell to save Mia from scraping her knee.

And the baby is a derangement, an abomination, a Chernobyl in nappies. Think about the hail. Think about the caterpillars. And that's just in the first few days. What unspeakable miracles might he wreak as he gets older? Whereas Mia is a normal little girl.

Give Percy up, get Mia back, run a very long way away. If she's honest with herself, of all the ways this could realistically work out, isn't that pretty near the top? By that accounting, it's a very good deal indeed.

But she won't take it.

'You think I'd send my son back to Cyneburne?' Adeline says.

'You think I'd do that to him?'

So that her parents could raise him as their heir. Put him at the head of their empire. Just because she doesn't really love him yet, that doesn't mean she'd condemn him to that. Him, and everyone else who'd have to live on this earth after her parents had triumphed.

'Just think it over—'

'You are never, ever going to change, are you? I was an idiot to think that you could. You actually *like* being my parents' dried-up little spinster slave. I mean, after what happened to Alston – if even *that* couldn't unstick you, then how on earth could anything else? God, you're pathetic.'

Hattie cringes. 'Oh, sweetheart, if you really knew what happened to Alston—'

'I do know. They killed him. Don't tell me we're back to "It was just an accident."'

'There's a reason – I swear on my life, Addie, there's a very good reason your parents couldn't tell you the truth—'

'Still defending them. Jesus Christ.' Adeline gets up from her seat. 'Look, clearly I'm never going to see you again and this is a complete waste of time, but I told the others I'd do it, so . . .' She takes a slip of paper out of her pocket and tosses it onto Hattie's tray. 'If you ever come to your senses, call that number. Not from your mobile, obviously. From another phone. Someone will answer and tell you what to do. Either that, or you live out the rest of your life at Cyneburne, and eventually you die there. Maybe in your bed, or maybe on the altar.'

※

Back in the van, after they pick up Luke in a side street, she's too angry to explain what happened. She just shakes her head. On the drive back to the school, she thinks about how foolish she was to get her hopes up.

As they're getting out of the van, Shirley rushes out to meet them, looking frantic. He has a fresh bruise on his cheekbone.

'I couldn't call you,' he says, 'she took my phone.'

'Who did?' Cam says, and then, incredulously, 'Rosa?'

'She's gone.' He gestures back into the school with one flailing hand. 'She's gone and she took the baby.'

Chapter 35

At first, Luke doesn't believe it. Refuses to believe it. And when Shirley mentions that the bruise is from when his face hit the kitchen counter, because the blow to the head came from behind, Luke starts gabbling. Doesn't that mean the attacker could have been someone else entirely, who took Rosa *and* Percy? Even as Shirley is explaining that no, there was nobody in the room with him but Rosa, he's absolutely sure of it, Luke is rushing to the old art room, hoping to find some indication that Rosa never expected to leave the school . . .

But what he actually finds is the opposite. Her go bag – the rucksack she keeps packed in case they ever have to cut the painter – is gone. And so is that tube of diphenhydramine.

Rosa wants revenge on the Woolsaws. He remembers what she said before the *Hampstead* op, that they should bring the baby with them as a weapon. But the *Hampstead* op is behind them now, and surely she's not planning to raid a ReadyPay van all by herself. So how does she mean to use him?

He's on his way back to report all this to the others when he passes the open door to Adeline's room, and she's just standing there in a helpless posture that reminds him more than anything of those few seconds after he let the flash-bang off at her feet. But when she looks up and sees Luke, she rounds on him, fury in her eyes.

'I didn't have to come back, you know. I chose to. Because you persuaded me. You said it would be fine. You said I'd be "safer." Do you understand, Luke, that if I'd let the police take me – if I'd just gone home to my parents – I would be with *both* my children now? Instead of neither. My son is gone because your girlfriend took her. And my daughter – if I ever want to see her again, either I have to go up to Highgate and knock on my parents' door, or I have to rely on . . .What? Some squatters who got fooled by an undercover journalist with a personality disorder?'

'Adeline, I'm so sorry.' He's never felt so useless. Is there *anyone* he hasn't let down over the past week?

'You're an amateur and an idiot,' she says, and turns away. He reaches out to touch her arm, but his hand falters and then it's too late.

Back in the common room he finds Cam, who says to him, 'We have to assume Rosa's going to get picked up. Probably in the next few hours. So you need to be ready to leave. Tell Adeline too.'

Yesterday Adeline told him she was surprised by Cam's seemingly rather leisurely response to this prospect. Instead of rushing around making preparations to flee, he just sat with her in the common room. Luke explained that Cam would regard it as a serious personal failure if there were anything left to do at that moment. The point is to remain in an immaculate state of readiness at all times. And sure enough, Cam is just sitting there with three phones in front of him, still as a meditator.

'Rosa's clever,' Luke says. 'She wouldn't have done this if she didn't think she could survive out there.'

'Yes, she's clever. Most of the time. But right now she's not thinking rationally.'

Luke knows what Cam means, of course. All of this is demented. Even beyond the act of stealing a fucking baby, Rosa has just betrayed her only allies and abandoned her only refuge.

Okay, so she was broken by grief. But that doesn't really explain it.

Okay, so she was not only broken by grief, but *shattered* by finding her parents bound and executed in their home, her home. But that *still* doesn't really explain it.

Unless, inside Rosa, under the surface, there were already so many fissures and crazings that she was not in the end so hard to crack open. Or, to put it another way, maybe she was fucking nuts from the beginning. Adeline's remark about the personality disorder was just a jibe but it has lodged in Luke's head.

And yet there's another way of looking at it. Sure, if you're a normal person working from normal premises, this looks senseless. But surely part of being a revolutionary is that you're not working from the same premises as everyone else. If you feel a certain way about what ends are imperative, about what means are acceptable – well, maybe this isn't irrational at all. From whatever aberrant place Rosa started, maybe a calm and pragmatic calculus could have led her to this.

As he talks to Cam, Luke doesn't even know which of those two pictures he believes in any more. After yesterday her outline is still too blurred.

'For all we know,' Cam adds, 'they could already have her.'

'The cops?'

'Or the Woolsaws.'

'Either way she wouldn't give us up.'

'You're saying that because you know her so well?'

Luke once again feels shamed by Cam's gaze. 'When I told you she was for real – obviously in hindsight that was fucking stupid – but it was also true, in a way. She's committed to this.'

'Douglas was committed too. But we know he must have told them about Rosa. Which means before they killed him they got him to talk. And whatever they did to him, they could do the same to her. That's why we have to leave.'

'Now?'

Cam shakes his head. 'When everything's ready.'

'And when's that?'

'I don't know.'

Hearing those words out of Cam's mouth is as disorienting now as it was back in Park Royal. It's like rushing for a fire extinguisher and aiming it at the blaze and seeing nothing come out but dust. Did Luke misconstrue Cam's stillness? Usually it means there's nothing Cam needs to do, but this time does it mean there's nothing he *can* do?

'There's a safe house that we would have gone to,' Cam says. 'But just now I made a call. Talked to someone I hadn't talked to in a while. And they told me that a few people have gone missing in the last few days.'

Luke goes cold. 'Oh, shit.'

'The Woolsaws are getting closer. We have to assume that whole section of the network is blown.' He gestures at the phones in front of him. 'I'm trying to sort another safe house, but it's going to take as long as it takes. We may have to get out of London.'

'So what do we do until then?'

'We stay here. It's still safer than being out in the open. People get caught when they're out in the open. No matter how clever they are.'

Chapter 36

The door of the flat opens and Rosa launches straight into her spiel. 'Hi, I'm so sorry to do this, I don't know you, but I was on a first date with the guy in number twenty-three' – she points to the floor above – 'we went for a walk, and I came up for a coffee afterwards, it was literally just going to be coffee, but things started getting really weird, and then when I said I was going to leave, he got, like, really . . .you know, and I've called an Uber but it's going to be another eight minutes and I don't want to wait in the lobby because he's . . .I just, like, I just don't know if he's . . .'

She bites her lip as if she's hanging on Jemima's response. And that's not all acting. Because she *is* hanging on Jemima's response. She's tried this routine on several other young women over the past couple of days, and those other times, when it didn't work out, she could just move on. If she got turned down, or if the woman turned out not to be alone in the flat – no problem, there were plenty more doors to knock on. But this time it actually matters.

It takes Jemima a moment to process it all, after which Rosa expects to see the customary flash of doubt on her face. But no, twenty-four-year-old Jemima Weston turns out to be the easiest mark of all. 'Oh, you poor thing,' she says, utterly without scepticism. 'Yeah, of course. You can wait in here and then I'll go down with you when the Uber comes.'

'Oh my God,' Rosa says, 'thank you. Thank you so much.' Even in London, she thinks, people can still be so trusting, it almost defies belief. The wonderful thing about women is that they really look out for one another.

Straight ahead of her is Jemima's 'gallery wall', the cluster of little framed prints that places like this always have, designed to produce an ambient impression of artiness without the threat of being confronted with any individual artwork. Rosa already knows the gallery wall, which expands every so often like a mould colony, and indeed every other detail of this very bijou starter flat, from Instagram and TikTok. Jemima posts nonstop. By going back through her feed and triangulating her favourite brunch spots, it was an easy task to work out what neighbourhood she lived in. Then by examining the view out of the living room window, visible over Jemima's shoulder in various clips, and comparing that against Google Street View, it was only slightly more laborious to determine what building she lived in and on what floor.

The flat is a one-bedroom. No flatmates. Up until about three months ago, there was a boyfriend who appeared constantly on Instagram. But then the boyfriend vanished and has not yet been replaced on the feed. Also, the camerawork has noticeably suffered as a result of this film-crew shortage. Which isn't to say that Jemima is celibate, but if there were anyone embedded deeply enough in her life that you could expect to find him lounging around her place at 3 p.m. on a Monday, then he would certainly have shown up by now.

Sure enough, there's nobody else here. So Rosa neglects to close the front door behind her as she comes in, obliging Jemima to turn and do it herself. Whereupon Rosa takes the spanner out of her bag and hits Jemima over the back of the head.

Without a sound Jemima crumples to the floor. Rosa squats down and tweaks her face, checking she's really out cold. Then she takes a roll of duct tape and some zip ties out of the bag. Covers Jemima's mouth. Ties her wrists and ankles.

In the day-in-the-life video that Jemima uploaded last week, she showed herself dropping her keys in the vintage Moroccan bowl on the side table every time she came in through the door, but evidently she isn't quite as dependable in reality, because when Rosa goes to look, they aren't there. So Rosa props the door open with the bowl itself as she goes back out to the stairs where she left her rucksack and the baby in its pram. Then she wheels in the pram, which she stole on Sunday from outside a café on Westbourne Grove, and shuts the door.

After that she takes Jemima by the ankles and drags her into the bedroom. Across the carpet and into the en suite. And dumps her in the bath, first hauling her torso over the rim, then her legs. There she's less likely to hurt herself or knock anything over if she wakes up and starts to struggle.

This is the third time Rosa has done this, so it's beginning to feel smooth, mechanical. The first two times were just so that she'd have a place to hide out for twelve hours or so. She's certain she could survive on the streets if she really had to. After all, in the cover story she told everyone at the Nail, she'd done that for months at a time. And she's lived so long as that character, filled in so many of the details – getting your period, she once told Luke, is the single worst thing about sleeping rough in the countryside, and now she can't even remember if she read that somewhere or just improvised it – that her training feels utterly real.

All the same, life's a lot smoother if she can charge her phone and clean her wound and change the baby's nappies and not have to push the pram around all the time. So she's been doing this instead.

She gives the women sips of water so they don't get dehydrated, and right before she leaves she presses into their bound hands a pair of scissors taped shut with several dozen layers of duct tape. In an hour or so a determined thumbnail can pick all the tape off the blades, but that's enough of a buffer to make sure Rosa is long gone by the time they cut the zip ties. Yes, maybe they'll piss their jeans a few times during the whole ordeal – and in fact the smell of piss has been a running theme these last three days, because Rosa cannot motivate herself to change the baby until the stench is absolutely unendurable – but there's no permanent damage. It's not like they have to go through what she's been through. It's not like they have to lose their parents. See their defiled bodies. See their open throats.

If they understood all that, these complacent women with their nice west London flats – if they understood the stakes, if they understood that there was war raging around them – they'd understand why she was doing this. They would not only forgive her but they would apologise for not doing their part sooner.

Luke would never have had the stomach for it. That's why she didn't bother to ask him. Even Cam might be too soft these days. It would probably be all massages and birthday cakes and apologies, like it was with Adeline.

She knows she can't keep it up forever. She forces the women to unlock their phones so that she can reply to text messages, fobbing off anyone who wants to know *Why aren't you here?* or *Why aren't you picking up?* And as she leaves she promises that if they ever breathe a word to anyone about what happened she'll come back and kill them. Soon enough the police will find out that this is happening, see a pattern, start issuing warnings. There will be a description of her on the news. But she doesn't need to keep it up forever. Because this is what it's all been leading up to. Her other two hosts were picked at random, but Jemima Weston is a VIP.

She hears the baby mewing. For its last few feeds, she's given the baby oat milk with a few drops of gin mixed in – all these girls have oat milk and gin; indeed, one of them didn't have much else – and it's been sleeping pretty well. She's put the T-shirt she took from Adeline's room under its head as a pillow, so it can enjoy the smell, and when it gets especially grouchy, she plays it Adeline's video, the one where she talks about how evil her parents are, so it can hear its mother's voice. That seems to help a bit, although she sometimes wonders if she ought to do the reverse: play the video only when the baby's well behaved, training it with treats like an animal. Well, she hasn't read any baby books, and even if she had, it's possible they wouldn't have much to say on this question.

On the way back through the bedroom to mix the baby another cocktail, Rosa sees that the doors of Jemima's wardrobe are wide open. She doesn't need her costume change yet, but she may as well take a look now. Jemima is stick-thin, but Rosa ought to be able to fit into at least some of her clothes. The outfit needs to be something reasonably glamorous that will cover up the bandage on her shoulder and ideally also her tattoos.

She gets so absorbed leafing through the rails that she decides this time she'll just let the baby tire itself out for a while. Jemima has a lot of beautiful stuff. Prada and Loewe and Dries. Apart from her parents, obviously, and her friends, the thing Rosa has missed most since joining the Nail is wearing clothes that she loves, and it's been such a long time that just running her hand over good silk or cashmere makes her feel like some awestruck medieval peasant. Each time she has walked alone through these women's homes – and now, in Jemima's flat, most intensely of all – she has imagined other possible lives for herself, now foreclosed. She tells herself that a revolutionary shouldn't be so covetous and shallow, but self-reproach does little to suppress the feeling. A more effective remedy is to remind herself that even if she *had* lived the life that was expected of her, she never would have had any of this, because her parents aren't as rich as Jemima's. A nice one-bedroom in Notting Hill, full of designer clothes, in her twenties, on a journalist's salary? Forget it.

She's slipping one arm into a Burberry trench coat when she hears a key turning in the front door lock.

Chapter 31

A male voice. 'Sorry I was so long, the first place I tried didn't have any.' And then: 'Are you in the bedroom?'

Which tells Rosa that he's about to find her no matter what, and she wants to keep him as far away as possible from the bathroom, so she drops the coat and comes out into the living room. A man in his forties stands there with a plastic shopping bag in one hand. Handsome and broad-shouldered even if he does look like a bit of a dad.

It's like that moment in her parents' house all over again. Each of them is looking at the other and thinking, You're not supposed to be here. Except the polarity is reversed. She was here first. This guy looks bewildered. Why shouldn't she be the Detective Inspector John Deakin this time? Fennig nearly had Luke fooled, and all it took was confidence and calm.

She smiles. 'Oh, hi.'

'Hi . . .'

He's taking in the pram beside the kitchen island. While Rosa is taking in the wedding ring on the hand holding the plastic bag. And all at once she puts it together.

Jemima does have a new man in her life, but he's married, which is why he hasn't shown up on her Instagram. He was over at hers, maybe while he was meant to be at work, judging from his crisp white shirt and suit trousers. She sent him out with her keys to buy smoked salmon or prosecco or condoms. And now he's back, expecting to find his bit on the side but instead finding a completely different girl. Bad luck for Rosa – and for him too, because now he won't get his mid-afternoon shag – but she was well aware that something like this could happen. Doesn't mean the operation is blown.

'I'm Sophie,' she says.

Instead of taking the obvious cue to reciprocate, he just hesitates and then says 'Hi' a second time. With a squirrelly look. As if he's very conscious that officially he isn't here. Mustn't be here. Which should make this easier.

'You're Jem's friend?' she says brightly.

As much as he might want to, he can't really offer a 'No comment' when he's just let himself into Jemima's flat with Jemima's keys, so the guy gives a reluctant nod. 'Is she, um . . .'

'She had to go over to her mate's place. There was some emergency? She looked pretty worried. I'm Sophie, by the way. I live in fifteen. We don't have any water in our flat at the moment, our stop tap is completely fucked, so she's been letting me come over to shower and stuff. Complete lifesaver, what with the little one and everything.' She gestures towards the pram.

The guy is looking puzzled. Understandably so, because Rosa knows her story doesn't add up, not really. She sees him reach into his pocket. Probably going for his phone.

She absolutely does not want him calling Jemima from here in the flat. Because she doesn't know where Jemima's phone is right now. And it might start ringing.

'Have we met before?' she says.

The hand falters.

'Or at least I've seen you in the lobby, maybe? You've been over here a few times, right?' There isn't the slightest accusatory note in her voice, in fact she says it like someone completely unfamiliar with the concepts of fornication or infidelity, just innocently alluding to a fact that might destroy this man's life if it got out.

He smiles uncomfortably. 'All right, well, I'll just give Jemima a call,' he says, turning to leave like he can't get out of here fast enough. 'Nice to meet you.'

Rosa rejoices. She fooled him. All she has to do is respond to his missed call with a text from Jemima's phone: *so so sorry I disappeared like that – Alice is having another crisis and it was scaring me a bit the way she sounded so I just had to get over there. I'll probably be with her the rest of the day but let me know when I can make it up to you. sorry again!!! x x x.* Alice will be a cameo from one of Jemima's real-life brunch friends, chosen on the physiognomic grounds that, as Rosa remembers it, she looks the most fragile of all of them. A guy his age shagging a girl Jemima's age must surely tolerate a certain amount of chaos as the price of admission. Of course, when the price gets significantly steeper – when it also involves comforting her after her ordeal and getting questioned as a police witness about a case of assault and imprisonment – at that point Rosa can see him cutting the painter. But he has no idea that's on the way.

His hand is on the door handle when a sound comes from the bathroom.

The groaning hum of someone trying to cry out with her mouth taped shut.

Chapter 38

The philanderer turns back.

Rosa smiles. 'Ah, that's my other kid. She's five.'

But the groaning gets louder. More insistent. Rosa left the bathroom door open so she would be able to hear if Jemima was getting up to anything she shouldn't, but the result now is that the sound is very audible.

The guy looks at Rosa again, reassessing her. Then quickly he moves past her towards the bedroom.

Rosa has no time at all to decide what to do.

Cam would tell her to run. But she can't run. Jemima Weston is the only candidate who fits all the criteria. Rosa doesn't have a backup. Leaving this flat would mean abandoning the whole venture. And it's not as if she has anything go back to afterwards. She gave up everything she had for the Nail and then she gave up the Nail for this. And now she's so close to her goal. Just hours away.

She could hit him over the head with the wrench, just like she did Jemima. Tie him up right beside his lover. They would get a bit of horizontal time together after all.

But what if he didn't go down on the first blow? He's a lot bigger than she is, and also she got shot in the shoulder two days ago. If he managed to pull the wrench out of her hand she'd be fucked. She had planned to bring a can of pepper spray with her from the school, which would have been perfect for this, but at some point on Saturday night – after she made off with the pistol which Luke then graciously gifted to Fennig – Cam put all that stuff under lock and key.

Over on the kitchen island, beside a grapefruit half on a chopping board, there is an eight-inch knife.

'Oh my God,' the guy says from the bathroom.

❧

Sometimes after you ring a doorbell you hear so much mysterious thumping around that you wonder if the person inside has not only had to descend the stairs but also clear the hall of various armoires and harpsichords before they can reach you. Such is the case with Gerald Weston, who takes considerably longer to get to the door than his daughter did a few hours ago. But then again his home is considerably bigger. Over his shoulder there is no gallery wall, just a boring old oil painting in a gilt frame.

'Er, hello?' he says.

Rosa presses play on a video and holds the phone up for him to see. 'This is your daughter.'

The video shows Jemima bound and gagged in her flat, with dried blood on her face and hair. The blood actually isn't Jemima's, it's her older lover's. But Gerald Weston isn't to know that.

Aghast, he looks from the phone to Rosa. 'Who are you? What is this?'

The funny thing is – and this is certainly one of the wilder coincidences of her life – she's met Gerald Weston before. He came to give a guest lecture to the journalism course she was on when she was twenty-two. They talked for only a moment afterwards so there's no reason why he'd remember. Still, he's now the only person on Earth who's met her in both of her two lives. And this made the result feel almost predestined when she narrowed down the list of candidates to just him and his daughter.

It wasn't as if she could just download a guest list for the

Woolsaw summer party. Instead, she had to piece together a list of probable invitees based on who'd been documented as attending in previous years.

Gerald Weston is a political columnist of the old-fashioned type, meaning he doesn't tweet and he makes erudite classical references and he is unapologetically chummy with politicians, presenting his closeness to them as an asset and a virtue. He wrote a piece in 2015 reporting on certain noteworthy goings-on he'd witnessed at the Woolsaw summer party – well, noteworthy if you find that stuff interesting rather than repellent – and a similar one in 2019. So it seems a pretty safe bet he'll be going this year.

And another article, not by him but about him, revealed that he has separated from his extremely wealthy wife. She now lives in a manor in Dorset, while for the time being he has held on to the townhouse in Kensington. In other words, he lives alone, and works from home. Just like his daughter – well, insofar as she works at all, a hazy subject in her case. All of this was very convenient for Rosa's operation.

'Is there anyone in the house with you now?' Rosa says. She wonders if he'll notice that she's wearing Jemima's clothes. A button-up jacket and a matching long skirt by some Korean designer she'd never heard of, in two layers of silk-polyester blend, sheer olive green on the outside and pale grey on the inside; probably too cool for the Woolsaw party, but it alludes in some distant way to a Chanel suit, and anyway she looks good in it.

'What is this?' he says.

'If you want to know what's happened to your daughter, tell me if there's anyone in the house with you now.'

'No, there's no one. What's going on?'

'I'm a member of the Nail,' Rosa says. 'The same organisation that is holding Adeline Woolsaw. We have your daughter Jemima.' She doesn't want to sound like a kidnapper in a film, so she tries to summon a bit of the good solid clarity she learned on that journalism course, laying out the facts as straightforwardly as possible.

'Listen carefully. Every fifteen minutes, I send a text with a code. The codes are different every time. If the text doesn't arrive, or if the code is off by a single digit, my friends will strangle your daughter to death with a steel wire. Do you understand?'

His mouth gapes.

'I said, do you understand?' In one sense she has him in the palm of her hand, but in another she's as powerless as any salesman making a cold call. One of his hands is still gripping the door. All he'd need to do is shut it on her and call the police. Or ask her to prove that Jemima is alive. Jemima *is* alive, but she's also on her own in the flat, so there's no feasible way for Rosa to do that.

But instead he says, 'Yes, I understand.' Rosa hides her relief. What she was counting on was that no normal person's mind goes straight to 'Well, how do I know she's not already dead?' It's only cops and security consultants who think that way.

'Are you going to the Woolsaw party tonight?' she says.

'Yes. I mean, I was, I—'

'Good. You're going to bring me with you.'

He blinks at her. Then he seems to steel himself. 'No. Even if I was willing to do that – they have searches, they have X-ray machines. This year there'll be even more security than usual. If you think you're going to smuggle in a bomb or something . . .well, you're not. This is pointless.'

'They can search me. That's fine. I'm not bringing in any weapons. I'm not planning to hurt anyone.'

'I don't believe you. Why would you be doing this if . . .'

'It doesn't matter if you believe me. If you get me into that party, your daughter will be released unharmed at nine o'clock tonight. If you don't, she'll be killed. There's no other way out. This isn't a game.' Maybe this last remark *does* sound like a kidnapper in a film, but with Gerald Weston it has a special relevance, because the most odious quality of his writing is that he treats politics as just gossip, sport, showbiz, rather than something that actually affects people's lives. Guys like him are insulated. They never have to feel the effects.

Well, now he finally knows what it's like to have something at stake.

'I'm sorry, you can't ask me to take part in a . . .No. No. It's just not possible. But we can come to some other arrangement. I'll have my editor print your manifesto on the front page. Or whatever else you can think of. But I can't get you into that party.' He glances back into the house, like maybe he's thinking about how far away his phone is. He isn't scared enough. She has to close the deal.

'No negotiation. Either Jemima lives or Jemima dies.' She hits play on the video again and holds the phone up even closer to his face. 'She has been informed of exactly what we're doing. So when she feels that wire around her neck, she'll know that you chose not to save her.'

He swallows. Then at last his shoulders go slack and she knows she has him.

'Good. Now help me with the pram.'

He stares at her, baffled. 'Help you with the what?'

Chapter 39

'We don't know for sure that's where she's going.'

Adeline gives Luke an impatient look. Most of the time, because of all that black privacy film, the common room is as good as windowless, but it's such a beautiful day outside that you can almost feel the late-afternoon sunshine ripping its way through. 'Yes, we do. She took Percy yesterday and the party's tonight. That's not a coincidence. And we already know she had ambitions on that score. You told me as much.'

'But your parents won't even be there,' Luke says.

'No, but all their accomplices will be. Everyone who helped them get to the top and everyone who helps them stay there. If she thinks she can make Park Royal happen again – well, where better?'

'She'd be out of her mind.'

'We already know she's out of her mind.'

'But I mean it's impossible. The security. She'd never get near it.'

'Just like kidnapping the Woolsaws' daughter was impossible?'

If Luke is being stubborn, it's not because he doesn't agree with Adeline. The truth is, he does. It's because of the consequences that follow from agreeing with her.

'Adeline. Come on. This is different from meeting Hattie. You have to see that. For exactly the same reason that Rosa will never get into that party, we'd be insane to go anywhere near it. *You* would, especially. It's too much of a risk.'

'Too much of a risk? What exactly would I be risking? What do I have to lose now, Luke?'

'At least you're free,' Luke says feebly.

Adeline wheels around, throwing her hands up at the four walls of the common room, their blacked-out windows and peeling institutional paint. 'Free? Here? Maybe I felt free for a little while. But look at the situation I'm in. I can't just run off to South America. Not without my children. I can't even leave this school, in case someone sees me. So I'm not free. I'm trapped here just as much as I was at Cyneburne. Except my bed here isn't as comfortable. Luke, if worst comes to worst – if I get picked up outside that party – what will happen to me? I won't go to prison for stealing that painting – my parents would never allow that. I'll probably just end up back at Cyneburne. Exactly where I would have been if none of this had ever happened. And maybe they'll let me see Mia again. Am I really supposed to be so afraid of that?'

'But you can't let that happen. You can't go back.'

'No, Luke, what I can't do is sit around here just hoping for the best while both my children are still out there. So don't ask me to.'

She holds his gaze for a long moment. Until Cam appears in the doorway. Gestures with his head for Luke to come out into the corridor for a word.

'One hour,' Cam says when they're alone together. 'Make sure she's ready to go. It's all set up now.'

'Where are we going?' Luke says.

'You'll find out when we get there.'

Though the baby was here only a few days, you can feel his absence, just as much as Rosa's, and Luke has a fresh sense of the school's bereftness as they stand here in this long corridor that leads to nothing but empty rooms. It's as if the withdrawal they're talking about has already happened and they're just the leftovers. 'Is it a long way?'

Cam nods. 'There's nowhere left in London that I can be sure is safe.'

'Adeline wants to stake out her parents' party tonight. To find Rosa and the baby.' Right up until this moment, Luke has been feeling like he isn't sure about it yet. But he realises now that he *is* sure. In fact, not only sure but apparently dead set, all in, gritted teeth, because how else could he possibly have the nerve to say what he says next to Cam? 'I'm going with her.'

'No, you're not.'

'If we can catch Rosa and bring her back, then we're out of danger. We don't have to leave.'

'What's a lot more likely is that all three of you get picked up at once.'

'Well, Adeline's going to go no matter what, so—'

'No matter what? She was a hostage before, Luke. She can be a hostage again.'

'We're past that.'

'That's not for you to decide.' The adjustment that Cam makes to his posture could hardly be subtler and yet now he seems to loom twice as high over Luke. 'The Nail is bigger than you or me or her. You know that.'

Luke never imagined it might come to this. He never imagined he'd be standing in front of Cam, making a very physical calculation.

Cam, if he wanted, could choke Luke out just like he did that security guard. Do the same to Adeline. Throw them both in the back of the van. Drive up to the new hideout. Call in some other comrades, from some other cell, and just reset. Luke's acutely aware of all that, and there's a part of him that would prefer to apologise, bow his head, and shuffle off.

But he can't do that to Adeline. 'I'm going with her,' he says again. Cam's regard at this moment is so dire that Luke must overcome a bodily instinct to turn his face away, as you would from a hurricane wind or a thrown brick. But he just about manages to stand his ground. Until finally Cam's posture shifts again. And Luke can breathe out.

'You understand if you don't come with me now, that's it,' Cam says. 'You aren't part of the Nail any more. We never see each other again.'

Luke's heart is still pounding. 'Yeah. I understand.'

'You got into this for Holly. Because the Woolsaws murdered her. And now you're quitting it for a Woolsaw.' He nods towards the common room.

'The Woolsaws have a lot of victims. She's one of them.'

'Right. She's *one* of them. The point is to do something for *all* of them.' He sighs. 'I'm so fucking tired of this. Time after time, for thirty fucking years. And I don't know how many more rounds of it I've got left in me. You know, this is why we never win. They have patience. They have discipline. We don't.'

He turns and walks away. Luke calls after him. 'Cam.'

Cam turns back.

'If we get away,' Luke says, 'we'll have to change cars on the way home. Is there anything we can use?'

He's pushing his luck. And he expects Cam to say no. But Cam thinks it over for a moment. And then, with sadness in his voice: 'There's a van in Wembley. You can take that. I've got no use for it any more.'

Chapter 40

Standing on the platform where he'll deliver his speech, Jasper Brownlow scans the crowd. He spent the whole afternoon researching the guest list to make his networking more efficient. In some cases, of course, no cramming was necessary, because of the exalted positions these people hold. The prime minister is here. The leader of the Opposition. Most of the Cabinet and most of the Shadow Cabinet too. The mayor of London. The governor of the Bank of England. The editors of three daily newspapers.

And in others cases no cramming was necessary because he's already met them socially. For instance, the Marquess of Carisbrooke, who owns practically all of Hampshire: Jasper went out with his daughter for a while at university. Or Cecilia Ossory-West, who is seventeenth in line to the throne: Jasper got to know the whole family the last time he went skiing in Klosters.

But there are also a lot of grey suits whom Jasper would not have recognised without a bit of swotting up. All the Woolsaw Group's senior management and corporate board. But also the company's bankers. Its auditors. Its consultants. Its lobbyists.

In time, Jasper could be more powerful than any of them, assuming he plays his cards right with the family. But that's all the more reason to start building relationships now. Things will run smoother if these people already know and like him when he's telling them what to do.

Although there are a few TV presenters and eligible young aristos here, it is hardly the most attractive or glamorous crowd he's ever seen. However, anyone who's ever actually been to a party full of very beautiful people knows that the best thing about it (apart from the possibility that you might fuck one of them) is the exhilarating sense that you are in the *right place*, that you are where everyone else wants to be. And in that regard, nothing can beat the Woolsaw summer party.

From this platform, just in front of the Triton Fountain, he can look out across the terrace where about three hundred of them are drinking champagne. This is the only night of the year that Queen Mary's Gardens – the most beautiful part of Regent's Park, nestled within the aptly named Inner Circle, just east of the boating lake – is closed to the public. At the other end of the lawn a large marquee has been set up, in deference to a weather forecast that did predict some rain but has now been thoroughly refuted by the harmless streaks of cirrus up above.

As his gaze passes across the Downing Street press secretary chatting to the director of the Institute of Economic Affairs, he notices, beside the hedge that curves around the bottom of the terrace, a young woman with a pram. Rather extraordinary to bring a baby to a party like this instead of leaving it at home with the nanny. But perhaps she sees it as some sort of feminist gesture. Well, it had better not start crying during his speech.

There's a man with her, who Jasper now realises is Gerald Weston, the political columnist. Quite an age difference between them. Is that his daughter, and the baby a grandchild? No, he met Jemima Weston at a wedding last year, and this isn't her. A younger girlfriend, then? Didn't he separate from his wife recently? So could that be Weston's love child? Weston does have a grim look on his face. As if he feels a bit trapped. Well, you *would* feel trapped if you'd knocked up your rebound fling by accident and then she insisted on wheeling the result into the Woolsaw summer party to make a statement.

The woman who's running the party – he keeps forgetting her name – comes up to join him on the platform. It's time. She taps on her wine glass next to the microphone, to spare him the indignity of doing it himself, then once the crowd has quieted she yields to him without a word.

'Good evening, everyone.' A bit too close to the mic, so he pulls back an inch. 'My name is Jasper Brownlow. As most of you will know, I am Adeline's husband. We were married early last year. This past week has been the hardest of my entire life, as indeed it has been for everyone in the Woolsaw family. I can understand if many people were surprised to learn that this event would be going ahead. But what my mother-in-law and father-in-law wanted me to emphasise to you all is that they never want to be without their friends.'

While he's talking he becomes aware that the woman with the pram is doing something absolutely inexplicable. She has taken out a cigarette lighter and – unless his eyes are deceiving him – she is holding one of the baby's hands over the flame of the lighter. Not unreasonably, the baby has begun to squeal. It very much seems as if he's witnessing an act of child abuse.

But this is his big moment. Everyone's eyes are on him. If you break off in the middle of a speech like this, you can never properly get your momentum back. So he decides that someone else will have to deal with it. He looks away from the woman and raises his voice slightly to drown out the baby.

'It is with the support of their friends that they've accomplished so much over the past twenty years. It is with the support of their friends that they will weather this crisis. And it is with the support of their friends that the Woolsaws will heal afterwards.'

The sky, he senses, is darkening. And there's a feeling on his skin as if one of those abrupt summer storms is gathering. Maybe that baleful weather forecast was right after all. He curses internally. If they'd had just a couple of minutes' warning they could have moved the platform into the marquee where the rain couldn't dampen his speech.

'So that's why Conrad and Silvia didn't want to call this off. Even if, for obvious reasons, they couldn't be here themselves – even if there is a very grave shadow over the proceedings – even if we all have Adeline in our minds at every moment.' He pauses solemnly. 'The point is, we keep going. Our friends are still our friends. Those bonds will stay as strong as ever, so that we can all get through this, shoulder to shoulder. We will not allow the people who took away Adeline to take away the source of our resilience.'

There is a smattering of applause. But it's spoiled by the baby screaming, louder and louder. People are starting to look over, probably wondering why that woman doesn't wheel it out of here until it calms down. And there are murmurs of shock and disbelief as they, too, see that she's torturing the baby with the lighter.

Meanwhile, something is drifting down out of the sky that was so recently clear. But it's not rain.

It's softer, floatier, grey tinged with dying orange. Embers. Still gently warm as they brush his forehead. As if carried on the breeze from a bonfire.

Maybe someone is burning garden debris elsewhere in the park. It would have to be an awful lot of debris, though, because there are an awful lot of embers.

He keeps fighting for the attention of the crowd even as he's losing that battle on multiple fronts. 'As many of you will know, Adeline has a passion for the arts. So that's why we are asking you tonight to donate—'

Something drops out of the sky.

It makes no sound but for the faintest whoosh of displaced air, yet it's so fiery it leaves a streak on the retina. It might be four or five feet in diameter, but there isn't time to judge for sure, because when it lands it bursts apart like an enormous drop of liquid.

Drenching the crowd in flames.

The people who were right underneath it are on the ground now, knocked off their feet by the force of the impact, their bodies completely engulfed in fire, as if they've been hosed down with napalm. The people nearby are screaming, their clothes alight, and after an instant of complete bafflement and disorientation, the screaming spreads throughout the Woolsaw summer party, as if that baby's wail has fractured into a hundred shards.

Another fireball plummets to Earth. Straight into the densest part of the throng. As Jasper stands there on the platform, frozen, he can see the ripple effect of the impact, as everybody lurches backwards from the heat. But already another is landing, and another, and another, so that your lurch away from the last fireball has every chance of bringing you closer to the next. Without meaning to he lets out a small, frightened sound, which the speakers carry across the lawn in a way that might be embarrassing if it weren't completely drowned out by the pandemonium. This is a terrorist attack. It must be.

He sees that the only person in the crowd who doesn't seem at all perturbed is the woman with the pram. She's just standing there calmly. In fact he thinks he can make out a smile on her face.

Jasper knows he ought to get under cover. Nearly everyone else is running for the marquee. The instinct is understandable. It's the closest thing in sight to a roof. But Jasper is already wondering whether it's really such a good idea.

A fireball hits the marquee roof with a drum-skin thump. Flames splash across the canvas. Another hits the corner. The support pole tips sideways, and the entire roof starts to slide along with it, breaking apart as it does so. More of the support poles topple, and now, as Jasper watches, the burning roof flops like a blanket over the dozens of people sheltering inside. Jesus Christ, he thinks, aren't those things supposed to be flame-retardant? He wouldn't have thought the screaming could get any louder, but it does.

A man still recognisable as the secretary of state for work and pensions crawls from beneath the fallen roof, half of his body consumed by flames. He stretches out his hand as if reaching for something and then slumps sideways into the blackened grass.

Jasper can smell burning plastic and burning flesh.

People are looking for other exits. But the fiery ruin of the marquee is blocking the north-south path that everyone walked up to get here. There are no walls, only hedges – *hedges*, Jasper's thinking, how hard can it possibly be to get over, or through, a fucking hedge? – yet it *is* hard, evidently; harder than these panicked people were expecting. Jasper sees one woman in a fascinator who's still scrabbling away at the purple beech when a fireball blasts straight into her, turning the hedge into a pyre. Considering the density of expert security staff at this party, you'd expect this to be an absolute masterclass of an evacuation, a Bolshoi Ballet of high-stakes crowd management, but so far Jasper has noticed one earpiece bloke shouting impotently as not a single person listens and another earpiece bloke who stands frozen with his arms up, shielding his face as if that could possibly make a difference.

Jasper tells himself to think rationally. Yes, he could die on this platform, but he could just as well die running away. The hedges may have a rampart-like quality, widening towards the bottom, but he's certain they don't form an unbroken wall around the gardens. There must be plenty of other ways out. For instance, how were all the waiters moving back and forth between the terrace and that little building where the canapés were being prepared? If he just takes a few seconds to look around –

Adeline.

His 'wife.'

That's her. He is absolutely sure of it. In the photo from the heist her hair was down, but today it's in the same low ponytail her mother made a sniffy remark about when Jasper came for tea at Cyneburne.

She's approaching from the north end of the terrace. Despite the inferno around her, her attention seems to be fixed on the woman with the pram. It looks almost as if she's trying to sneak up behind her.

Her presence here must be connected to the terrorist attack.

Obviously the rabble who kidnapped her are behind this, and once again she has volunteered as their accomplice.

Except how can a bunch of sewer-dwelling Maoists be capable of making fire rain from the sky? There are certain weapons you hear about on the news as being especially malign but you don't really have any mental image of them – depleted uranium, white phosphorus, thermobaric whatever-it-is – could this be one of those? Could they have raided an MOD depot somewhere?

Regardless, Jasper knows that if *he* is the one to bring Adeline back to the Woolsaws – to carry his bride over the threshold, as it were – that will guarantee his future with them. He's perfectly aware that his position with the family is still provisional, a question of immediate usefulness in unsettled circumstances. His initial courtship of Adeline went nowhere and if he has once again been called on stage it is only because he can be relied upon to pull off the part. But this is a chance to earn their undying gratitude. He will be the heir. The prince. Important people are dying all around him and that is going to complicate the future in ways there simply isn't time to think about, but no matter what happens, the Woolsaws' power will only grow – perhaps even faster because of this – and he will share in that power.

The thought of that takes hold of him, all through his body, every bit as visceral as the fear he feels.

As the comets continue to fall, he steps down off the platform. Jogs towards Adeline and quickly circles around her. She hasn't seen him. So before she can reach the woman with the pram, he runs up behind his wife and grabs her from behind.

Chapter 41

Their assumption was that Rosa would be loitering around on the periphery of the event, just like them. She would be trying to find a way inside and they could catch her before she did.

They never imagined they would see her just stroll in.

Luke and Adeline are sitting on the green across the road from the rose gardens, peeking through a gap in the hedge. She's in the same oversized sunglasses she wore to McDonald's, and from a distance they should look like no more than a young couple who've found a quiet corner to snog or roll a joint, but here they're positioned about eighty feet from the gilded ornamental gates that serve tonight as the entrance to the party. Most of the cars they've seen so far have deposited their passengers outside these gates to be checked against a list and scanned with an X-ray wand, but once in a while – presumably when it's an extra-high-security guest – the car is allowed to roll farther up the path before its passengers leave the safety of the back seat. With eight o'clock approaching, there's still no sign of Rosa, and when the black cab pulls up, Adeline's in the middle of persuading Luke that it's time to move on. Circle the gardens. See where else she might be lurking.

But then Rosa gets out of the cab.

The first thing Luke notices is that she's wearing clothes he's never seen before, fashionable and expensive-looking, plus she's got dark lipstick on. Of all the times in his life he's turned up to a party and seen an ex there looking disconcertingly good, this one is certainly the most intense. In the seven months he knew Rosa as part of the Nail, she cycled through only about four different outfits, and never wore makeup. He's been trying to hold together an image in his mind of this woman he loved but it just keeps breaking into more and more fragments.

An older man gets out too. And helps her lift a pram out of the cab. Luke is hardly entitled to see Percy as his ward – it's only been a week – but he still feels a twinge of anger at the sight. I built a fucking bassinet for that baby, he thinks. He doesn't belong to you.

Luke and Adeline watch in astonishment as Rosa and the older man present themselves at the gate just like everybody else. One of the security guys gives Rosa an apologetic smile before waving the X-ray wand over the pram. And clearly it doesn't find anything because after that the whole family is ushered inside.

'What the fuck do we do now?' Luke says. The same ring of security that's protecting all those VIPs inside is now also protecting Rosa.

'We warn them,' Adeline says. 'Make an anonymous call. I know you're not very fondly disposed to the people in there but they don't deserve what she's planning. Anyway, if they evacuate, then Rosa will have to leave too, and then we'll have another chance to catch her.'

But as Luke explains to Adeline, it's not as simple as that. Obviously they can't tell the truth about Percy, so they would have to make up a story about a nonexistent bomb that was set to go off in five minutes. But when it comes to nonexistent bombs, the cops have heard it all before. Nine out of ten bomb threats are hoaxes, so unless this one was judged credible it might lead to a search but it probably wouldn't lead to an evacuation. The police can be pretty certain that nobody at that party is wearing a suicide vest under their linen suit, and the idea of an IRA-style squib on a timer preceded by a tip-off is a relic of another era.

Of course, Luke could call with a description of Rosa, warning that she was planning some sort of attack. That might lead to Rosa getting taken quietly aside. And under questioning it would soon become clear that she wasn't supposed to be there . . .

'But if we do that,' Adeline says, 'they'll take her, and they'll take Percy. And he'll end up back at Cyneburne. Which is what my parents want most of all.'

'Yeah, so—'

'We still have to do something! There are a very large number of people who are invested in the prime minister's personal safety and you and I know that at this moment he is not safe so you cannot be telling me there is no feasible way to . . .For goodness' sake, Luke, if I go up to the gate right now and tell them there's a bomb—'

'No, Adeline—'

'If I go up there, they'll know who I am, they'll know this isn't a hoax, they'll have to take it seriously—'

'Then we lose Percy and Rosa *and* you—' Luke says 'we' when really he means 'I'.

But then they hear a voice from the direction of the party, amplified but still too distant to make out the words.

'That's the speech,' Adeline says. 'If I was her, this is when I'd do it.' She tosses away her sunglasses. 'I won't have people dying because I didn't intervene.' She starts to get to her feet, but Luke grabs her hand.

'You can't!'

Adeline pulls her hand free. 'You've forgotten I'm not your hostage any more.'

She strides a few paces towards the road. And then stops. Because another voice is carrying on the evening air, this one an unassisted cry from smaller lungs, yet to Luke it's ten times as piercing, because just as he did outside the garden shed, he feels an immediate recognition, a sickly attunement in his bones. Most of the time that baby makes a racket, he tells himself, that's all it is, a racket, it's not Park Royal again . . .

But then he looks up, because the light is dimming. And what he sees overhead doesn't look like a clouding-over so much as an impurity bubbling to the surface, a poison leaching from behind the sky. Yet the speech is still droning on. If there were ever any hope of preventing this, it's too late now.

From above, a swirl of glowing dots. Like cinders shedding from a kiln.

Followed by a huge glob of flame.

Adeline gasps as it drops through the air. At the last moment they lose sight of it behind the trees that ring Queen Mary's Gardens.

Then they hear screaming.

Luke glances through the gap in the hedge again. All the police and security people around the ornamental gate are shouting and running.

'Come on,' Adeline says, as another fireball sails downward. She doesn't even hesitate, unlike Luke, who very much does. He's about as eager to run into that blast zone as he would have been to picnic under the ice at Park Royal.

But this could be their chance.

They come out onto Inner Circle and sprint clockwise along the road, past the park offices on their right, until they're as close as they can get to the party itself. When they scoped out the gardens earlier there were security guys posted along the wrought-iron fence, but now there's nobody to stop them from climbing over. The fence isn't that high but they still have to give each other a bit of help to vault over without getting speared. Then they push through the foliage and all of a sudden they're in hell.

This is so much worse than Park Royal. Yes, the hail was all-pervasive, inescapable, but at least there weren't that many people out in the open, whereas here there are hundreds of party guests and every single fireball seems to have smashed straight into a knot of them. Where once you would have crossed this upper terrace by threading your way between the flowerbeds, now you'd have to thread your way between multiple human bonfires, enough that the air is not only hot but also turbid with little shreds of blackened fabric. Luke watches in horror as a man with his whole torso alight hurls himself into the pool of the ornamental fountain; the bronze fish are still spraying water from their mouths but it's too dainty a volume to be of any use. A hundred yards away what must have been the marquee is now collapsed in flaming rags. And still the sky is vomiting these impossible coals.

'There she is,' Adeline says.

Rosa. The pram beside her. A smile on her face.

They agreed that when they found Rosa it would better if she saw Luke first rather than Adeline. Of course, they had very different circumstances in mind, but the point still holds.

'You go straight for her,' Adeline says. 'I'll loop around behind.'

Luke nods. Clearly she can see the fear on his face, because she touches his hand and says, 'The closer we get to her, the safer we are. Percy isn't going to bomb *himself*.'

So he moves past the benches and the fountain towards Rosa, and he gets within a few strides of her before she clocks him.

Shock on her face, replaced quickly with an even bigger grin. 'We did it, Luke. We finally fucking did it.'

Luke can see Adeline moving up behind Rosa, low to the ground like an athlete, ready to dodge anyone who might careen blindly into her path. The idea is to distract Rosa, keep her talking, until Adeline can yank away the pram. And the best tactic to do that, they agreed, is for Luke to pretend that he's come here because he's on her side and he wants to run away with her.

But now that he's face-to-face with Rosa, trying to con her like that feels . . . impossible. Pointless. Totally incommensurate with the situation they're in. So he says, 'Rosa, I'm just here for the baby.'

'Oh come on. Look around, Luke. This is it. This is revenge for Holly. Finally. Aren't you excited?'

And the truth is, a tiny part of him *is* excited. If the Woolsaws murdered Holly, then these party guests are their accomplices – blithe, detached, complicit. Every year they get together to raise their champagne glasses and toast what a brilliant job they've done of trampling everybody else. Except this year *they're* the ones howling in pain, begging for mercy that will not arrive. And even the survivors will be scarred. Chastened. They'll know that judgement can come for them too.

The Nail has never accomplished anything like this, not in all those months of planning and training and hiding away at the school. And not before that either. Cam might act so dedicated and war-weary and seen-it-all-before but the truth is he couldn't manage in thirty years what Rosa improvised in a couple of days. This is historic.

And yet Luke still wants it to stop.

Partly it's because of the collateral damage, the waiters and security staff who are caught up in this. But it's because of the guests too, even the cabinet ministers in their evening wear, reptiles fattened on power and complacency and Woolsaw Group banquets. Yes, if he had the chance, he'd lock them up naked in cages and hang them off Westminster Bridge. But that doesn't mean he wants to see them burned alive. Not even the lowest of them, not even as revenge for Holly. Maybe that confirms the accusation Rosa used to make, that he never really had the stomach to be a revolutionary. Well, so be it.

'Rosa . . .' he begins. But he doesn't know what he's going to say to her, and there won't be time to say much, anyway, because Adeline is almost at the pram—

Except that before Adeline can get to it, Luke sees that someone is coming up behind *her*—

It's that guy from the Woolsaw press conference. The guy who pretended to be Adeline's husband. He grabs her torso, locking her arms against her sides.

Rosa has noticed that Luke is staring past her. So she glances back. And scowls when she sees Adeline. 'Luke, look at me,' she says.

Luke starts forward. He has to rescue Adeline.

But Rosa reaches into the pram and snatches up Percy, who still wears the floral babygrow Luke bought for him, now pretty grimy. She holds him up in front of her like an object, a very smashable vase, even as he continues to wail. 'I said look at me. Not her. This is between *us*.'

Luke stops. 'You can't kill him,' he says. 'Then you'll have nothing.'

'I don't have to kill it,' Rosa says. 'I can just twist its little arm off. I wonder what it'll do then?' She nods skyward. 'Might be interesting.'

By now Adeline is on the ground and her 'husband' is on top of her, holding her down as she struggles. Luke wants to help her – he *has* to help her – but he can tell Rosa is serious about hurting the baby.

'You and me are going to leave together, okay?' Rosa says. 'This' – and she gestures at the horror around them – 'is just the start.'

Luke sees something land on Rosa's skirt. One of those wind-blown bits of debris. Maybe a little bit of cocktail napkin. Still glowing at the edges.

She doesn't notice. And for an instant, nothing happens. The glow fades. 'We go after the Woolsaws next,' she says. 'And then their whole fucking breed.'

But then the glow winks back to life. With just the tiniest whisp of smoke rising from the swishy sheer material of Rosa's skirt.

Luke points. 'Rosa—'

She looks down. Sees that her skirt is on fire. And tries to pat it down.

But there isn't time. Because the fire is already spreading, so unbelievably fast, faster than Luke can even follow.

As it reaches the bottom hem of the jacket, Rosa screams, and the baby drops to the grass.

Luke runs forward. Both for Rosa and for the baby—

But instead of letting him knock her down and roll her on the ground, Rosa, panicked, takes off running herself. Towards the fountain. But the rush of air as she moves only spreads the fire farther, up to her shoulders, up to her hair, until she's wrapped in flame, a shroud that clings to her body and billows in her wake.

When she's still a few yards from the stone lip of the fountain, she trips. Falls headlong.

And even though the baby is still just lying there on the ground—

Even though Adeline is still wrestling with her 'husband'—

Luke goes for Rosa. There might still be time to put the fire out.

By now she's completely wreathed in it. Rolling her on the ground won't be enough. He has to get her into the water.

He grabs her under the armpits. Which means plunging his hands into the flames devouring her jacket. He cries out in pain, but still hangs on long enough to haul her up and over the lip of the fountain. Almost into the water—

When, in the same split second that he registers a surge of furnace heat from above, the air itself seems to brighten and then ignite – and he's hurled backward by a shattering blast of fire and steam.

He lands, dazed, on the gravel. A fireball must have come down right in the fountain.

His eyes, his cheeks, and most of all his hands feel scoured by flame. Everything else is far away. He tries to get up, but he can't. It just won't happen.

A hand on his shoulder. 'Are you okay?' Luke blinks. Adeline is crouching beside him, with the baby in the crook of her arm. Percy isn't even crying any more.

'Rosa—' he starts to say. 'She's – we have to—'

Adeline has a cut on her lip. 'Luke, I'm sorry, I think . . .'

He looks over to where Rosa lies sprawled across the lip of the fountain, face down and motionless. Apart from the left cuff of her jacket, which is still smouldering, she isn't on fire any more. But most of the hair is gone from the back of her head and the skin is a ghastly dark red verging on black.

Nonetheless, he starts crawling towards her. He wants to reach out and shake her awake.

But when he gets close enough to smell the char of her flesh, his stomach turns, and his movement falters. Either she's dead, he realises, or she's so far gone he can't possibly help. All the same, shouldn't he stay with her? Doesn't he owe her that much, after everything?

But then, for the first time, he registers the sound of sirens in the distance. 'Luke, we've got to go,' Adeline says.

Chapter 42

Don't put off until tomorrow what you can do today, Shirley always tells his patients, like that woman the other week who just could not seem to understand how irrational it was to delay the operation on her collapsing spinal canal because she didn't want to take the time off work. Unfortunately, he's no good at taking his own advice, because at this point his iPhone battery only lasts a few hours and yet he's been too busy juggling his day job as a hospital doctor and night job as personal physician to the Nail to get it replaced, even though the ever-present back-of-mind anxiety that his phone's about to die only intensifies the stress of that predicament, which was bad enough already and has certainly contributed to his shitty bedside manner with patients like that spinal stenosis woman.

Towards the end of today's shift, his phone is where it spends most of its time, charging at the nurses' station. So he doesn't learn what's happened until another doctor asks him if he's heard about the thing in Regent's Park.

'What thing?'

A terrorist attack, the other doctor says. Some swanky party got bombed. Lots of VIPs. Politicians. Apparently there are so many casualties headed to the emergency wards in central London that it will have knock-on effects all the way up here in Barnet.

Shirley would love it, absolutely love it, if he had no personal connection with these events. But he suspects that he probably does. So he gets his phone back from the nurses' station. Checks Telegram.

Sure enough, he has a message. But not from Cam. From Luke. He's sent the code that means 'Come to the school' and the code that means 'There are injuries.'

This last week has been relentless. Because he hasn't just been on call as a doctor for the Nail, he's been on call as a babysitter as well, which frankly does not feel like the fullest use of his abilities. The last time he spoke to Cam, Cam intimated that after all the recent mayhem they might be lying low for a while. Which Shirley was very happy about. It would be so relaxing and restorative to put aside his Nail work for a bit, leaving him with no care in the world but the trifling demands of twelve-hour shifts as a junior doctor at a crumbling and understaffed north London hospital. He even thought he might be able to get his battery replaced.

And now *another* emergency. An emergency presumably connected to this attack on the Woolsaw party, which, based on the headlines he's now scanning on his phone, looks like by far the messiest thing the Nail has ever been involved in. He wishes he could just ignore the message.

But if he were capable of saying no to outrageous claims on his time from people who barely appreciate him, he would have quit the NHS years ago, wouldn't he?

He's run out of excuses to give the charge nurse for leaving early, and with the overflow that's probably coming they wouldn't cut it anyway. So he just slips out when nobody's paying attention. On the way to Northolt he keeps the radio on, and whenever he's stuck at a red light he refreshes the news on his phone. But it's all pretty garbled still. No death toll yet. They've confirmed that the prime minister got out alive – presumably they put that out up front for the sake of the financial markets – but a lot of powerful people are still unaccounted for. What could have possessed Cam to do this?

he wonders. After all that creeping around, all those very meticulous and targeted ops, he suddenly decided fuck it, we're going full Gunpowder Plot?

And then, as he's waiting to turn onto Old Ruislip Road, a new headline pops up.

Someone at the party was filming one of the speeches on their phone, and now the video is on Sky News. Once the attack starts, the image is so shaky you can't make out much. Then the phone gets dropped in the grass, and from that angle you can't make out much either. Except that later on, a female figure looms into view for a few frames.

And this person looks very much like Adeline Woolsaw.

The lights change. He's coming around the curve, heading for the turn-off that leads to the school, when he sees two police vans parked up ahead, with several cops standing around beside them.

And it strikes him these aren't the first he's seen in the neighbourhood. There were a couple of others up at the roundabout. He didn't think anything of it at the time. But this can't be a coincidence, can it? Tonight of all nights, a quarter mile from the school?

Something is happening

Or has already happened.

He's longing to make a U-turn. But that would just make him look suspicious. So he keeps driving. Hoping they'll wave him past.

Instead, they wave him down.

He stops. Lowers the window as a policewoman comes over.

'Good evening, sir. Do you mind if I ask where you're on your way to tonight?'

'My girlfriend's.' He has a detailed biography of this fictional girlfriend in his head, just in case he ever needs it, mostly drawn from a real ex of his except that this version of her lives in Hayes. 'Why?'

'So you don't live on this road?'

'No, I live in Finchley, but I came from work.'

'Why were you driving this way?'

It's a reasonable question. Old Ruislip Road loops off the main road. It's not a shortcut to anywhere except itself – and the school. That's probably why they stopped him.

'The app told me to,' he says. 'Traffic on the main road, I guess?' Don't look away when you lie, he reminds himself, but don't make *too much* eye contact either, not like you're forcing it.

'At this time of night?'

He shrugs. 'I don't know – ask the app!'

'What kind of work do you do?'

'I'm a doctor at Barnet Hospital and actually I've just come off a twelve-hour shift, so . . .' He gives her a tight smile to finish the sentence: can we get this over with?

'Do you have any ID?'

He takes his NHS ID card out of his wallet and shows it to her. That little card let him drive wherever he wanted during the Covid lockdown and it should have the same effect here. Nobody's going to think a doctor could be a terrorist in his time off. How would he have the energy?

'All right. Have a very good evening, sir.'

'What's this about? Is something going on?'

But she doesn't answer. Just waves him on.

When he gets out onto the main road, he calls Cam.

Number not in service. What the hell?

So he tries Luke. Wondering if he'll get the same result. But Luke answers.

'Where are you?' Shirley says.

'At the school.'

'All of you?'

'It's just me and Adeline and the baby.'

'Go. Now. There are police on Old Ruislip Road. They're stopping people. Something's going on.'

'Shit. Shit. Okay. Where are you? Are you close?'

'Yeah, I just passed the turn-off.'

'Can you pick us up?'

Can he?

There are two possibilities forming in Shirley's mind.

One is that the police know only that the Nail are hiding out somewhere in this area. But they don't know exactly where. They're still just casting a net. Stopping drivers on the off chance. They have no idea yet that Ruislip School for Blind and Partially Sighted Children – a derelict building with no lights in the windows – is even inhabited. In which case Luke and Adeline might have a chance of escaping on foot, north across the fields, out of the search zone.

The other is that they know all about the school. They already have it encircled. In fact, they have one of those drones overhead with a thermal imaging camera that can see warm bodies. If Luke and Adeline try to run, the police can choose whether to pounce on them right away, or wait and see where they go. And if Shirley stops to let Luke and Adeline into his car, then he's just as fucked as they are.

There's no way to know. So wouldn't it be safest to just hang up on Luke? Drive away? Make a clean break? Even supposing the police scoop up the rest of the network, Cam would never give him up. And Luke and Adeline might cooperate – he doesn't trust them nearly as much as he does Cam – but they don't know his real name. They don't know which hospital he works at. They don't know anything about his life. He's always been careful about that. And there are twenty thousand doctors in London . . .

Except he just showed his ID to that policewoman.

Suppose there's no drone. Suppose the police are just groping in the dark. But then somebody recognises Adeline when she's skulking around the adventure golf course looking for somewhere to hide. She gets caught, and maybe under interrogation she mentions a doctor. And his name is already in someone's notebook.

If he abandons them, they're fucked, and maybe so is he. Whereas if he helps them run far away from here, never to be seen again, there's no better clean break than that.

Plus there's the whole bloody moral issue. His commitment to the cause. All that palaver.

'Shirley?' Luke says. 'Are you still there?'

Chapter 43

They loop around the left side of the lorry-hire place so they'll be farther from the lights of Western Avenue. It's dark out here, with wild grass and hogweed up to their waists, and she very nearly blunders into a ditch before Luke grabs her by the arm.

Shirley's car is parked in a lay-by on Sharvel Lane, lights and engine off. And this time it's Adeline's turn to stop Luke. Because if the police *are* watching Shirley, this is it. This is where she'll end up kneeling on the ground with a submachine gun in her face while Percy is plucked from her arms.

But what else are they going to do? Hide in that ditch until everything blows over? So Luke takes her hand and together they run out of the long grass and across the road to the car. They get into the back, and before he starts the engine, Shirley, too, seems to pause for a moment, as if he's waiting for catastrophe. But no police materialise out of the gloom. Instead he just pulls the car out of the lay-by and they're away. 'What the fuck is going on?' he says.

As concisely as possible, they explain what happened at the party. And then they work their way down the hierarchy of injuries.

First, Luke's burned hands, from trying to drag Rosa into the fountain. They're now a nasty salmon colour, and back at the school Adeline wrapped them in cling film.

Second, Percy's burned right hand, from when Rosa tortured

all that doom out of him. Cling-filmed too. She won't ever know where he was, what he might have been enduring, between Sunday morning and Monday night. He can't tell her, and now Rosa can't either.

Third, the bruise on Percy's bottom, from when he was dropped. Not too florid.

And last, Adeline's broken finger, from her fight with Jasper. She'd never been in a fight like that, and she got the sense that maybe neither had he. He seems like the type who might have held down a few women before. But if really he'd known what he was doing, then he wouldn't have left that opening for her to knee him in the groin and then smash a champagne glass in his face, would he?

'If he's bruised on his arse,' Shirley says, regarding Percy, 'that means he didn't get dropped on his head. So he's probably fine. I'll dress all those burns, but you could have found out how to do that on the internet. You didn't need to call me down here for this.'

'We didn't realise we'd be asking you to evacuate us as well,' Adeline says. She's sitting in the middle seat, wearing a hoodie with the hood up, to reduce the chances that a CCTV camera will get a lucky angle on her. They must be passing the air force base on the left because past the yellow fence she gets a glimpse of what looks like runway.

'I don't understand it,' Luke says. 'We got away from the school. Which means the cops weren't watching it. But how would they have found out the area we're in but not the actual location? Did they pick up one of the cars on CCTV but they couldn't track it all the way back?'

'I think I know,' Adeline says. She takes a deep breath, wishing she didn't have to say this. 'When I escaped from the school, that first night, I went into a woman's house. She was nice to me but she called the police before I could stop her and I had to run off again. Before I left I made her promise she'd never, ever tell anyone about me and I honestly thought she really meant it. But after tonight . . .'

'She sees on the news that the Nail has killed half the Cabinet,'

Shirley says. 'She sees your picture so she knows you're involved. And she rethinks her promise.'

'It would have been obvious that I'd come from somewhere pretty close by. So if she told the police that . . .'

'Why didn't you say anything before?' Luke says. It's the first time she's heard him sound angry with her. 'If Cam had known we had a breach that serious, we would have cut the painter days ago.'

'That's exactly why. My position seemed rather delicate and I didn't want to get locked up again.'

'We were supposed to trust each other. If that woman had changed her mind sooner – or if Shirley hadn't been coming over here right when he did—'

'I know. I'm sorry.'

'You can lecture her all you like about operational security,' Shirley says, 'but last week when I warned Cam that Rosa was lying to you all, I assumed there would be some kind of response. And instead you did – what? Absolutely zilch?'

'She wasn't working for the cops,' Luke says defensively.

'Right, no, she was just a galloping liability in various other ways. And now here we are. So where am I taking you?'

Neither of them answers, because neither of them knows. Adeline finds herself thinking about *Hampstead*, still sitting there in the common room. Presumably the police will be searching the school before too long, and she hopes they handle it gently.

'Why don't you just go wherever Cam is?' Shirley says.

'Because we don't know where he is,' Luke says. 'We're split up now. I mean for real. All we know is he was on his way out of London.'

'Well, I can't just keep driving forever.'

'Where do you live?' Adeline says.

Shirley audibly scoffs. 'No. Absolutely not.'

'We don't have any other options.'

'You may not have been aware of this, but from the very beginning I've had an understanding with Cam, okay? I'm not all in like you lot are. I'm an accessory. I aid and abet. That's all. I have a life of my own and it's separate and I have no intention of giving it up. Which means I'm not sheltering two terrorists in my fucking home. Because I know how that's going to end. They'll be looking for you even harder now, and without Cam – without his network – you don't have a chance. If he were here he'd be telling me not to do this.'

'Just for a night,' Luke says.

'I have a *flatmate*.'

'Where else can we go?'

'Maybe you and the baby can find a barn.'

'Please,' Adeline says.

There's a long silence. From what Adeline can see of Shirley's eyes in the rearview mirror, she can tell that he's fuming. Finally he swears under his breath and whacks the steering wheel with his fist. 'Fine. One night. *One*. If I can convince my flatmate to get out of the flat.'

'What will you say to him?' Luke says.

'I don't know, something to do with the hospital . . .I'll say – I'll say you and her are coming off heroin for the sake of the baby and you needed somewhere to go. All three of you are going to spend the night screaming and shitting so I'll put him up in a reasonably nice hotel and I'll do all the chores for the rest of the month to say thank you. He ought to believe all that, because I'm such a wonderful altruistic person.'

'Adeline,' Luke says. 'Look.' This whole time Luke has been sporadically refreshing the headlines on his phone, and aside from that picture of Adeline pulled from the mobile phone video, there hasn't been much new for him to tell her. But now he shows her the screen.

Her parents have released a video statement.

Adeline's grasp of the modern media landscape is just about firm enough to understand that this doesn't fit. A video statement is something that social media influencers put out when they've accidentally said something racist. It is not something the Woolsaw family puts out in the immediate aftermath of an atrocity. Why would they have done this?

But as soon as the video starts playing on Luke's phone, she lets out a gasp. Because she understands.

Instead of filming the video in a study or a drawing room, they've chosen to film it in a corridor on the ground floor, just in front of the lift down to the basement. Her mother is sitting in a Victorian carved wooden chair that certainly doesn't live there the rest of the time and must have been brought out specially. Standing in the background of the shot, next to the lift doors, are Mia and a man whose hand is on Mia's shoulder and whose head is cut off by the top of the frame – but from his suit and his build she can easily recognise him as Fennig.

When Adeline's mother speaks, she doesn't use one of her public voices. She uses a voice that she uses only for Adeline. A cold, disappointed, disciplinary voice. 'Like everyone else in this country,' Silvia Woolsaw says, 'we are horrified and saddened by tonight's terrible events. But for my husband and I, they are all the more painful because of our daughter's apparent involvement. We pray she will come to her senses before there is any further violence, and we will make any sacrifices we have to in order to bring her home.' That's it. The video ends there.

'She can't do this!' Adeline says through tears. 'She can't do this!'

'What's wrong?' Shirley says from the front seat. 'That all sounded pretty anodyne to me.'

'A long time ago I made my mother promise that Fennig would never be in the same room as Mia if it could possibly be avoided. She's just a child and she doesn't deserve to have nightmares about him the way I did. It's the only promise to me my mother has ever kept. But there he was with his hand on her shoulder.'

'So it's a threat?' Luke says.

'Of course it's a threat! Why do you think she was talking about praying and sacrifices? Why do you think they filmed it right in front of the lift that goes down to the basement? Because the chapel down there is where my parents kill people on the altar!'

'Where they what?' Shirley blurts, and Adeline realises that although he was present for Percy's birth, he still hasn't been told the rest of it.

'My mother is talking to me,' she goes on. 'Me alone. Nobody outside Cyneburne even knows who Mia is. And the message is that if I don't bring them the baby, they're going to do something to her. Their own granddaughter.'

Chapter 44

They arrive in Finchley close to midnight. Shirley's flat is one of those terraced houses that have been converted into four flats, meaning it's not exactly the most discreet or impregnable hideout – all the flats except the basement share one front door, plus Percy is wailing as they get him inside, meaning that, if questioned, any number of Shirley's neighbours might remember an unfamiliar baby arriving at an odd time. Shirley takes the cling film off all three burned hands, only to redress them with fresh cling film. A couple of paracetamol tablets for Luke and a crumb of it dissolved in a tea spoon of breast milk for the baby. Then he shows Adeline into his flatmate's room, while Luke gets a duvet on the sofa.

'Should we sleep in shifts?' Luke says. 'Keep watch?'

'For what?' Shirley says.

'The police.'

'And if you see them coming, what will you do? Go out the back window? If they've tracked you all the way here, it's already over. For you and for me. As far as I'm concerned, it's out of my hands at this point, and anyway it's been a very long day so personally I'd sooner just get some kip. If you need anything in the night I'm sure you can work it out for yourselves. And remember – tomorrow you're out of here.'

As Shirley closes his bedroom door, Luke kicks off his shoes. But when he looks up, he sees Adeline still standing in the doorway of the other bedroom, and she gestures with her head for him to come in. He goes in and sits down on the bed, and she closes the door before sitting down next to him. It's a spartan room, with so many sacks of protein powder piled on top of the chest of drawers that they look like livestock feed at a farm. They speak in low voices so Shirley won't hear through the wall.

'I just can't stop thinking about the video,' she says.

'Do you think she'd really do it? Hurt Mia?'

'Hattie told me how angry she was after we stole the Auerbach. That was a public humiliation for her. But also it was just a painting, and she's got a lot of paintings. There was only her pride at stake, really. But what Rosa did tonight...My parents don't have friends – if you asked them, they'd say they did, but they don't, not really. All those people who died, they don't care about them as *people* – but if you think of them as parts of this machine they've spent their lives building, they do care about that, a great deal. Now Rosa has smashed up the machine – probably not beyond repair, but pretty badly all the same – and as far as my mother knows, I helped. I can't even imagine how furious she is. In the past I never really worried about her doing anything to Mia, because I could tell my parents felt some regret about what they did to Alston. But these are special circumstances, and anyway my mother's never been all that fond of Mia. She was a "mistake." A waste of effort. Because they needed a boy. I really think she could go through with it. Oh, Jesus, Luke, what are we going to do?'

'We can still get Mia back.'

'How? We're just *this* now.' She gestures with her hand, taking in the two of them, the bedroom, the baby sleeping in a little burrow she's made for him in Shirley's flatmate's underwear drawer.

He lowers his eyes, acknowledging the point. 'Well, we can try. We can still try.'

'I really am sorry about what happened with that woman near the school. I mean, I'm not sorry about trying to save myself, but I'm sorry about not telling you sooner. Maybe if I had, Cam would have moved us to another safe house, and now we'd still have somewhere to lie low, instead of . . .'

'It's all right. You just did what you had to.'

He's surprised when she leans towards him and kisses him. But he doesn't want it to stop – until she tries to take his cling-filmed hands in hers, and he jerks away because of the pain.

'Oh my goodness, I forgot.'

'Don't worry.' He wishes he could put his hands on her, but as they continue to kiss, all he can do is enfold her in his arms, hands hovering awkwardly at her back. After a while he swings his legs up onto the bed and she does the same, shrugging off her hoodie before moving on top of him. The next time they break off she makes a bashful face.

'You know that I've never . . .'

'What?'

'Don't make me say it. I've never done anything past kissing before. I'm twenty-three and I've had two kids and I've never done anything past kissing.'

'Well, you've been so picky,' Luke says. 'Your parents had that nice guy lined up for you and you turned him down.'

She laughs. 'You're right. I only have myself to blame, really.'

After that she grows a little bit more assertive, her tongue sliding over his, her body sliding over his, although she's still nowhere near as forceful as—

All of a sudden Luke becomes horribly conscious that only a few days have passed since the last time he did this with somebody and now that person is dead. Burned alive in front of him. If she were here, he can imagine what she'd say. 'Wow, you moved fast, Luke. I'm practically still sizzling. Couldn't even wait a whole night before you moved on?' All the urgency of the escape, and now the happiness of finally being together with Adeline in a way that always seemed impossible at the school, did push Rosa out of his mind for a while. Maybe that's inexcusable. Maybe he ought to be grieving

Rosa. And for that matter, maybe Adeline ought to be grieving Mia. After all, she's right. They don't seem to have much hope any more.

But whatever else they *ought* to be doing, right now they have no appetite to think about anything but each other.

'Will you sleep in here tonight?' she says after a while. The two of them are lying on their sides, face-to-face, feet and ankles intertwined because at least neither of them has any sore places below the knee.

'Definitely,' he says.

'Percy will be waking us up all night.'

'Yeah, well, I only would have been on the other side of the door. I think I was in for that either way.'

'And you wouldn't believe how much I sweat. It was the same after I had Mia.'

'I don't mind.'

'I *have* shared a bed before, but only with other girls on sleepovers, back when I was still allowed to do that. My parents have slept in separate bedrooms for years, and I never used to understand it – even if you haven't really been getting on with someone, why would you ever give up the chance to have someone there with you after a bad day?' She strokes his cheek. 'Not that today has been *all* bad. Not *quite* all bad.'

Chapter 45

Even in the early years of their marriage, Silvia Woolsaw's husband was prone to nightmares. Perhaps that should have been a warning to her that he wouldn't, ultimately, be strong enough for the vocation they'd chosen. Back then, when he was still much more experienced than she was, there were certain rituals he wouldn't allow her to participate in – to protect her, ostensibly, but afterwards he would whimper and convulse as he lay beside her in bed, so which of them was really the delicate one needing protection? At any rate, she soon learned to sleep through almost anything, even his fiercest nocturnal terrors. But it's been so long now since they've regularly shared a bed that she is out of practice, and on the rare occasions that she allows another person to spend the night with her – let alone two other people – it tends to be a rather fitful one.

So when she wakes in the small hours, that's what she blames it on. Yet when she regards her two naked bedmates in the dim light coming through the open door, they both appear perfectly still. The Brownlow boy, on her left, sleeps like an infant, mouth wide open, softly huffing. Whereas Fennig, on her right, looks as if he's only shut his eyes to listen better. This is the first time she's let either of them into her own bed. With Fennig it always felt unseemly. Her grandmother often used to tell gossipy stories from the '40s and

'50s, stories the young Silvia probably shouldn't have overheard, and one moral she absorbed was that when you start letting the servant stay overnight you have abandoned all dignity. Even after all that he's done for them, Fennig is still a servant, and what happens between them happens in other rooms.

Meanwhile, Jasper, for all his good looks, is sufficiently callow and nervous around her to smother all erotic interest, or at least that's how she felt about him in the past. Indeed, he was a real shrinking violet about her summons tonight – partly, no doubt, because he had a freshly bandaged face; partly because she is ostensibly his mother-in-law; and partly because, it's true, Fennig can be intimidating, in this context or in any other. But she didn't allow him to plead off. After everything that had happened, she needed to lose herself in the flesh for a while, and she wasn't sure that Fennig alone would be enough.

Even if the party had gone perfectly smoothly, it would have been a frustrating day. Barred from attending her own celebration, in case it gave the impression, to a lot of people who have no right whatsoever to judge her, that she wasn't consumed enough by the theft of her daughter. She understands the strategic value in maintaining a public image, but she chafes against it, and longs for the day when it won't matter any more.

Then the attack. So many friends gone. So many invaluable relationships. So many years of courting and coaxing and bribing and bullying. So much hard work. Wiped away.

Of course it can all be rebuilt. Among the guests there were quite a few tiresome people she's happy to be rid of, and in the long term all this upheaval may even strengthen the Woolsaws' hold, since they will have so much influence over who is elevated to replace the dead.

But in the short term, what a maddening inconvenience.

As soon as she was told about the fire raining from the sky, she knew it must've had something to do with the baby. Which meant her daughter was involved. And then, on the news, that image of

Adeline in the gardens. Even after all that embarrassment with *Hampstead*, it had never crossed Silvia's mind that Adeline would have such audacity, and this was what really made her fury spill over. Adeline has dirtied the Woolsaw name. Made the whole family look fractious and feckless. *If you can't even control your own daughter* . . .

So she released the video statement. Yes, it was a decision made in anger, without her usual cool deliberation. But she doesn't regret it.

Predictably, however, her husband was indignant. He confronted her in the upper drawing room, where she was watching the coverage on television.

'You've made a very serious mistake,' he said.

She didn't look at him.

'Mia is His daughter. She may not be His heir but she is still His child. And you have threatened her life.'

'Adeline must be made to see sense.'

'I'm not talking to you about Adeline. I'm talking to you about the master we are privileged to serve.'

'How do you think He feels about what happened today?' she said. 'About His son being used as a weapon by those troglodytes? We serve Him best if we put an end to this nonsense at the earliest possible moment.'

'That doesn't mean you can go on television and threaten His daughter with harm.'

'I don't have any intention of going through with it. We'll find them first – Adeline and the baby.'

'But even to utter the idea – it's a blasphemy. A terrible one.'

'It's just words. That's all.'

'Of course it's just words, that's what "blasphemy" means! That doesn't make it all right.' He sighed. 'I never realised you'd become so . . .' He looked away from her.

'Say it. Come on.'

'So ungrateful. Complacent. About everything He's given us.

You sometimes let yourself believe – don't you? – that we could have achieved it all without Him.' Those last few words he said in a quiet voice.

'Couldn't we?' she said. 'Has it really never crossed your mind? When you consider everything we understand now about this country and the people in it and how they allow themselves to be ruled. How they *beg* to be ruled. Did we need Him? We had rich soil and plenty of rain and we still tell ourselves it's only prayer that brought us a harvest?'

Her husband looked at her, shocked. The truth was, although she didn't let him see it, she was rather shocked herself. Never in her life had she spoken a sentiment like that out loud.

'Pride,' he said ruefully. 'A sin of pride.'

'Why don't you just go back to your books, you cripple?' A day like this and still he came to her cavilling and complaining. He might be good with the business, the banalities of it, but at home he's nothing but a burden, a withered limb. That ridiculous electric cuff, to prod him awake when he's drooling on himself. She knows he's not as ashamed of it as he ought to be, because he sees himself as a wounded explorer, returned from the jungle with grand stories to tell. Well, everything he's so proud of she has done as well. Every ritual he wouldn't let her join him in back then, she eventually undertook herself, on her own. She made a point of that. And it didn't enfeeble *her*. He's always been too cautious, too well prepared, too academic. If he were an explorer, then he'd be one of those wealthy Victorian amateurs, dragged down by his own equipment, waterlogged and blistered and hunched under the weight of his pack. But if you walk naked into the unknown you can walk back out without a scratch.

'You must learn devotion again, my love,' he said to her. 'You *must*.'

'Don't talk to me about devotion. When was the last time you made a real offering? When was the last time you wet the altar?'

'Devotion is spilling blood in *His* name. Not in your own.'

He left the room, and she sat and glowered for a few minutes, before getting up and going out into the hall. She walked around, calling out as loudly as possible for Fennig and the Brownlow boy. Announcing that they were both to spend the night with her.

Then, when they were all in her bed, she left the door wide open. She'd caught him once, eavesdropping on her when she was with Fennig. Well, in case he should feel drawn to do that again, she wanted him to hear everything as clearly as possible.

Now she considers sending one or both of them away. She no longer feels the need for other bodies beside her. Their warmth will linger pleasantly and she'll sleep better.

But then something twists in her gut.

And she realises why she woke up. It wasn't a bedmate turning over in his sleep. It's something infinitely worse. Something that has happened only once before in her life.

Her gorge rises. She vomits onto her pillow. Out of pure instinct, like an animal trying to hide, she crawls to the edge of the bed and flops down onto the rug beside it. She hears Fennig say, 'Are you all right, madam?' But only faintly. Because already the bedroom is disappearing, the walls folding away to reveal infinite darkness, infinite cold, in which she spirals and plummets like a seedpod from a storm-racked tree. She is shivering so hard she might bite off her tongue.

There are no illusions here, no surfaces. Everything is flayed back to its essence, including herself. She sees so much more clearly than she ever could in waking life. Clearly enough to regret everything she has ever done. To detest and repudiate herself. She is dirty and useless and unworthy and pathetic. It feels as if she's been here a thousand years already and she would rather die than face one more second but she knows death is a mercy she doesn't deserve.

When the admonition comes, it isn't in words. Like everything else in this realm, it's just a pure understanding, which crushes her, deafens her. But if it could be translated into utterly inadequate human language:

> YOU THREATENED TO
> HARM MY DAUGHTER.

I'm sorry, she tries to say. I'm so sorry.

> AGAIN AND AGAIN I LEND YOU
> MY CHILDREN TO BRING UP. AND
> THIS IS HOW YOU REPAY ME.

I'm so sorry. I was so foolish. So, so foolish. All I have ever wanted is to serve You.

> YOU WILL MAKE AN OFFERING
> IN PENANCE. A PROMPT
> OFFERING, APPROPRIATE TO THE
> MAGNITUDE OF YOUR SIN.

Yes. Of course. Anything. Thank you. Thank you for giving me another chance. I know I don't deserve it.

> THIS IS THE LAST TIME I
> WILL BE SO FORGIVING.

And all of a sudden she is back in her bedroom. Curled up on the rug, her body still shaking and spasming, while Fennig kneels over her. She has bile running down her chin. She knows from last time that it will be hours before she can even stand unaided, and over the next few days she will lose a good part of her hair and her nails.

Regret rises within her about what she has just agreed to do. But she tamps it down. There can be no irresolution. Of all the party's aftershocks, none is more important than this. She must keep her promise. And quickly.

Chapter 46

One thing Luke has learned at the Nail is that extreme circumstances will trivialise all the other shit in your life but they can never quite erase it. In just the same way that his first sight of Rosa last night reminded him of all the other times he'd ever run across an ex at a party, when he comes out of the bedroom to find Shirley already up and making coffee, it is on some level a situation where last night Luke crashed at the flat of someone he doesn't know that well and now that person knows he spent the night with someone who isn't his girlfriend.

All the same, that is only one small part of the dismay he feels at having to face Shirley. Because of the baby, none of them got much sleep, and quite possibly the neighbours didn't either – sound carries so easily between the flats that Luke can hear the television from the floor below. All night, even through his exhaustion, and even through the narcotic effect of having Adeline so close, Luke felt growing dread. Because he knew their reprieve was running out. Now Shirley is probably pissed off to discover his houseguests were investing last night's energies in coupling up rather than in formulating a plan that would, one, get them out of here promptly by checkout time and, two, not land Shirley in a cell right next to them. And Luke has absolutely nothing to say to reassure him.

'Show me,' Shirley says, gesturing at Luke's hands. As Shirley satisfies himself that under the cling film the burns aren't any more pustulant than they're supposed to be, Luke catches the words 'nationwide manhunt' from the radio on the kitchen counter. The blinds are still down front and back. 'You'll want to change these again this evening,' Shirley says. 'Remember, not too tight, they're not a packed lunch.'

'Thanks,' Luke says, even though the mere words 'this evening' make him feel panicked.

And then Adeline appears at the bedroom door, holding his phone. 'It's ringing,' she says.

He winces as he grasps it because his hands sting even more than they did yesterday, but when he sees the screen, he's thrilled. Because it's an unknown caller. Which means it has to be Cam. Rosa's dead, Adeline and Shirley are here with him, and nobody else has the number.

Cam will have a solution. Cam will tell them what to do next.

But when he answers, it's a woman's voice on the other end. Middle-aged and posh.

'Hello?' she says. 'Who am I speaking to, please?'

It has to be a wrong number. So he almost hangs up. But what stops him is that the woman sounds unmistakably nervous.

And then she says, 'I need to speak to Adeline.'

'Who is this?'

'She'll know. She'll know who it is.'

That's when it dawns on him. When Adeline met up with Hattie at the McDonald's, she gave her a phone number. A phone number that doesn't actually connect to a phone but to a VoIP server overseas, which then makes its own call to Luke's phone, encrypted and untraceable.

He covers the mouthpiece. 'I think it's your nanny,' he says to Adeline. Her eyebrows shoot up, then she takes the phone. Goes back into Shirley's flatmate's bedroom, shutting the door behind her. Leaving Luke and Shirley to sit drinking coffee and listening to the radio. The latest death toll from the Woolsaw party is 121, with many others still in critical condition, and the police still haven't confirmed whether the attackers are among that number. Apparently COBRA is in session and the Houses of Parliament and Buckingham Palace have both been sealed off, which Luke can't help but find amusing. They're not exactly in a position go after the King next.

After about a quarter of an hour, Adeline comes back out of the bedroom, carrying Percy on her chest. She takes a deep breath. 'Hattie wants to help,' she says. 'I mean really help.'

She sits down with them to explain. 'It seems she's finally hit her breaking point. The video. I know she just looked the other way when my parents killed Alston – my younger brother,' she adds for Shirley's benefit, 'but evidently she's not willing to do that a second time. She wants to get Mia out of Cyneburne before my mother can hurt her.'

'And you believe her?' Shirley says. 'Didn't she hang you out to dry the last time?'

'If she wants to get Mia to us,' Luke says, 'all she has to do is bring her somewhere with no cameras – maybe Hampstead Heath, they could walk there from Cyneburne—'

'No, it's not that simple. Mia hasn't been officially allowed out of Cyneburne since she was a baby. She'll have to be smuggled out. And Hattie can't do that alone.'

'So who's going to help her?' Luke says. Adeline looks back at him. When he understands, he's speechless for a moment. 'No, Adeline, there's no way. I want to get Mia back too, but there's just no way—'

'Hattie says something happened last night. I mean late at night, *after* the party. My mother was already furious but by this morning she was frantic.'

'So what was it about?'

'Hattie doesn't know. But from how utterly stricken my mother looked, Hattie thinks it must have something to do with . . .Well, the thing that Hattie knows about but can never ever bring herself to say. The Long-Before. And now both my parents are leaving Cyneburne, with Fennig but without Hattie or Mia. They have to go somewhere, do something, all very mysterious, but it's apparently so important that even putting the pieces back together after the party is now secondary. They'll be gone at least a few days. Which means this is the best chance we'll ever have to get Mia. When my parents go away, they take some of the staff with them, and the ones who are left can breathe out a little bit. The tight ship isn't quite as tight.'

If Luke is softening on this obviously insane idea, he doesn't know whether it's because Adeline is really making a good case, or because in a cowardly way he's just so relieved to have something, anything, to latch on to instead of no plan and no future. 'And Hattie thinks she could get one of us in?'

'Two of us,' Adeline corrects him. 'It would be you and me.'

'I thought the whole point was to keep you as far away from that house as possible,' Shirley says.

'Yeah, Adeline, if we do this you shouldn't be anywhere near it—'

'It would be absurd to do it without me. You'll be seeing Cyneburne for the first time. I've spent twenty years there.'

Shirley gets up from the table with a sardonic little smile as if he's making an overdue exit from a lunatic scene. As he takes the mugs over to the counter he says, 'Of course you realise I'm not having anything to do with this?'

'At the very least you'll have to look after the baby,' Adeline says.

'I can't exactly take it to work,' Shirley says over his shoulder.

'You won't go to work today. You'll take Percy somewhere, and you won't tell us where you are, and you won't bring him back to us until you know for certain that everything went all right at Cyneburne. That way, if everything *doesn't* go all right at Cyneburne, my parents will have no way of finding him, no matter what they do to Luke and me.' Luke is shocked by the evenness with which she says this.

Shirley turns back. 'But say I never hear from you again, what am I supposed to do with him after that?'

'Give him a nice safe upbringing somewhere far away from here. Make sure he appreciates art and he's nice to women.'

'Oh, come on!' Shirley says, rolling not just his eyes but his whole head in a great arc of incredulity as if searching for someone, anyone, still sane. 'I told you yesterday. I'm not all in like you are. I never was. If you get caught, I'm not going to start a new life in eastern Peru as the adoptive father of your terrifying baby.'

'Mia and Percy are my children and I want them to be with me and I don't want them to be with my parents,' Adeline says. 'I don't expect you to care about that any more than I care about anyone else's kids, which is not at all. But why did you get involved in this in the first place? Because you were alarmed by my parents' power and how they were using it. Well, you didn't know the half of it. If they get this little one back' – she nods at the baby in her lap – 'then in due course his coronation will follow. And there'll be no going back after that. No resistance, no sabotage, ever again. But if we can make absolutely sure they don't find him, it doesn't matter so much what happens to me. It pains me very deeply to say this, but in the grand scheme of things, it doesn't even matter what happens to Mia. The worst will have been averted. I know you're a doctor and you must have saved hundreds of lives so you hardly need to hear a lecture on moral duty from someone who's never really done anything to help anyone. But all I can tell you is, not to sound too grandiose, the person who keeps Percy away from my parents may do more for their fellow man than any single person has ever done in all of history. And as it stands there's nobody that person can be but you.'

A silence. Then Shirley sighs, and Luke can see that he's resigned to his fate. 'Oh, yes, very shrewd. Easiest way to win over a doctor. Appeal to his fucking god complex.'

Chapter 43

Seven or eight years ago a Reg Butler sculpture was dropped on the floor as it was being moved from one floor of Cyneburne to another. The damage was so bad that even Plowden & Smith, the storied south London art-restoration firm, couldn't make the perfect and invisible repairs that Silvia Woolsaw usually relied upon from them. Cyneburne's security guys will certainly have this disaster in mind today as a Plowden & Smith van brings a Kenneth Martin back to the house after a touch-up. This piece, a small brass-and-steel mobile from 1953, may only be worth about twenty thousand pounds, but it's even more delicate than that Reg Butler, and Hattie has apprised them of the strict instructions she got from Mrs. Woolsaw before her departure: unlike most deliveries to Cyneburne, this one is not to be left at the gate but driven up as close as possible to the house to minimise the distance it will have to be carried, and none of the staff except Hattie are to lay their clumsy hands anywhere near it.

Why should the security guys think twice? After all, Hattie has been here longer than any of them. She's so deferential to the Woolsaws they make fun of her for it behind her back. They'd no more suspect her of being a traitor than they'd suspect her of having a tail under her skirt.

But that doesn't make it any less terrifying for Luke as he pulls up to Cyneburne's gatehouse.

He's shaved his hair down to a grade two, he's wearing glasses, and he's put foundation over the last faint vestiges of the caterpillar stings, but beyond that he isn't disguised. Which is rational, because nobody but Fennig knows what he looks like, and Fennig left with the Woolsaws. But it still makes him feel horribly exposed.

'Hi, I'm from Plowdon & Smith,' he says. One advantage of the sculpture story is that he has the perfect excuse for wearing white gloves, although his hands still hurt as he grips the wheel.

'Ah, yeah, all right. You'll be wanting to go all the way up the drive?'

'That's what I was told.' He tries to channel that friend of his who used to work for the fancy florist. Thank God he doesn't have too many lines to deliver in character, because for all he knows he's just a mess of obvious tells, twitching eye and flicking tongue and throbbing vein.

But then the gates swing open, and Luke drives into Cyneburne.

Maybe in the countryside these vast grounds might not be quite so remarkable. But here, a few miles from the centre of the city, they seem like a defiance of the laws of physics, a rose bush blooming at deep-ocean pressures. The best comparison might be Regent's Park – on a normal day, with no fire raining from the sky – except this isn't a public amenity or a historic monument; it's a private estate, belonging to one family. This is what the Woolsaws' work has bought them.

And then there's the house itself. In one way it's a little bit disappointing, because to Luke's eyes it doesn't look like a gilded palace or a crenellated castle so much as just a red-brick house, like those Georgian townhouses on Harley Street, that somehow never stopped growing. Still, the sheer size of it, the windows beyond counting, would astonish you even if you didn't know that half its volume was concealed below ground.

He takes the van down the drive and around the left side of the house. And there she is, Hattie, waving him down, thin-lipped and stiff. Willing her not to lose her nerve, he parks the van, gets out, and nods hello. Although he doesn't see any more security around, the two of them probably still ought to be playing their parts, just to be safe: 'Hello, you must be . . .' and 'Yes, that's right, I'm here to . . .' But there seems to be a mutual agreement between them that neither of them can really hack it.

He's parked the van against the wall at such an angle that – he hopes – anybody who could possibly be watching will have their view blocked as he goes around to the back, opens the doors, and lets out his passenger. Adeline steps down onto the gravel. She's home.

Hattie opens the side door (one of the most impressive doors Luke has ever seen but by the standards of this place probably just a mousehole for lowly staff). She steps inside and looks around. Turns back to signal that it's safe. And they follow her through. Into the house.

If Luke has ever set foot inside a place like this before, it was on some dimly remembered school trip to a museum or stately home. Dark walnut panelling and complicated woodwork that seem designed to shush and stifle any possible feeling of airiness the high ceilings and big windows might otherwise inspire. Displayed on a nearby side table he sees something that looks a bit like a bent bicycle wheel, presumably a minor treasure from Silvia Woolsaw's collection. No sound but a clock ticking and the creak of their steps on the floorboards.

Turning a corner, they reach the lift doors he recognises from last night's video. Hattie presses the burnished metal button.

The lift will take them down to the basement, where Mia is currently being confined. According to Hattie there's another nanny taking care of her down there, so all they have to do is deal with this nanny, quietly and if possible nonviolently. After that they can bring Mia up in the lift and hide her under a tarpaulin in the back of the van. Then they'll simply drive away, with Hattie on hand to smooth their departure. And afterwards she, too, will flee Cyneburne, never to be seen again.

The lift arrives, with nothing so plebeian as a ding. The doors open.

Adeline screams as Fennig steps out and strikes Luke in the face.

Chapter 48

When he wakes up, his arms are up above his head, and there's something in his mouth. Something rigid, holding his teeth apart. Eyes still half shut, he tries to push it out with his tongue, but it won't move. He can feel a tightness around his cheeks and the back of his head, like straps pressing into him.

Now he rouses enough to open his eyes fully. And the first thing he sees is Cam.

Across the room, Cam is lying naked on a black slab. He's been gagged with what looks like a horse's bridle, which must be what Luke is wearing as well. His wrists are fastened to the top of the slab and his ankles to the bottom.

The whole room is clad in what looks like rusted metal, and the reflected candlelight casts everything in a dried-blood colour, albeit gloomy enough that you can't really get a sense of how high the ceiling vaults overhead. Fennig is here. So is Silvia Woolsaw. This is the first time he's seen her in person, and she's naked too. The two of them stand chanting beside the ancient-looking black object that dominates the entire room like the furnace in a stokehold.

If this is the chapel, that must be the altar.

And even when you're not looking at the altar, you're still conscious of it, as if you were in a room with a gaping hole in the floor. It gives him a feeling in his gut that's alien, exogenous, unwavering. A demand. An appetite.

Movement in the periphery of his vision. He turns his head.

Adeline, too, is fixed to the wall, her wrists roped through a snap hook above her head. She looks back at him, eyes wide with terror.

He tries desperately to make sense of it all. Hattie must have betrayed them, bringing them straight to Fennig. And Cam must have got caught while he was on the run. But why is Adeline down here too? Whatever ending the Woolsaws have in mind for the Nail, that can't be what they want for their daughter. Shouldn't she be safely locked up in her bedroom by now?

Fennig passes a dagger to Adeline's mother. Seeing it, Cam starts writhing on the slab. But Fennig holds him down.

Silvia Woolsaw plunges the dagger into Cam's stomach.

Luke's yell of horror can't get past the bridle in his mouth.

Cam's whole body stiffens as blood spills down his side and onto the black stone. Instead of withdrawing the dagger, Silvia pulls it sideways, then up, to make an L-shaped cut. She peels back a flap of Cam's skin. Adjusts her grip on the dagger to guide the tip more precisely, then pushes it into his chest cavity. What she does with it in there Luke can't really see, but every move she makes is slow, graceful, rhythmic, practised.

She reaches in with her free hand. And pulls out what must be Cam's heart. Cam's eyes are still open but he isn't moving any more. Luke fights the urge to vomit.

Her forearm slick with blood almost to the elbow, Silvia passes the heart to Fennig, who places it in a bowl on a ledge on the altar. And after that she cuts out a second organ, which goes in a second bowl. Then a third. By now a terrible abattoir smell of steaming offal has reached Luke's nostrils.

Fennig unfastens Cam's wrists and ankles, and then – the only gesture of this entire ritual that feels truly peremptory – he just rolls him off the side of the altar. Cam's body thumps onto the floor.

When Silvia looks up from the altar, she sees Luke and Adeline watching. She walks over to them. 'I'm afraid he didn't get very far,' she says to Luke. She has the same upturned grey eyes as her daughter. 'We scooped him up in Birmingham a few hours ago. I suppose you're absolutely on tenterhooks wondering if he told us anything important before he died. Well, I'd better break it to you that it doesn't make any difference. Anything we need to know we can find out from his liver. I'm quite sure we will shortly be on our way to finding our grandson.'

She reaches out to stroke her daughter's cheek. Adeline tries to turn her face away, but she can't evade her mother's hand, which leaves behind a trail of Cam's blood. 'I'm so sorry about this, darling. Sorrier than I can say. I never dreamed it would come to this. But it's such a terribly difficult position we've found ourselves in. You see, I have to give Him what He's owed. He just won't accept anything less. If only you had come home . . .But it will be over soon, and I promise, no matter what happens, Mia and the baby will be safe. Safe and happy. I know you weren't always very happy here, and I will do everything I can to make sure things are easier for them.'

Even as Luke is still in shock that – if he understood that right – Silvia Woolsaw has just preemptively apologised for murdering her own daughter, she looks over to Fennig and points at Luke.

He's next.

Fennig produces a pair of shears, and Luke thinks, Jesus Christ, they already have the dagger, so what are those for? But Fennig uses them on Luke's white shirt, cutting it cleanly off him while his hands are still tied above his head – that is, the cut is clean, but Fennig hasn't so much as wiped his hands, so Luke gets a smear of Cam's blood on his bare chest. Next, Fennig unbuckles Luke's belt –

But then an electronic beep – a wildly incongruous sound down here in this dungeon – starts ringing out from the direction of the door. All four of them look over to see a red LED flashing on a touchscreen panel.

Now Fennig does wipe his hands on a silk handkerchief, then goes over to the door and types a code into the panel. He turns back to Silvia. 'It's Hattie,' he says.

'Oh, for goodness' sake,' she says. 'All right. Go.'

Fennig leaves the chapel, shutting the door behind him.

Silvia grabs Luke around his throat and at the same time reaches behind his head to unbuckle his bridle.

'Who else is here?' she says, letting the bridle drop out of his mouth so he can answer. But Luke doesn't even understand what she's asking.

'Hattie has just pressed her panic button. That means something's going on upstairs. You must have got someone else onto the grounds. Who is it? Tell me now or Fennig will skin you alive and salt your flesh before I open you up.'

Chapter 49

Hattie was awoken at five in the morning by a knock that she recognised as Fennig's. She had only a moment to compose herself before he opened the door and looked in. 'You're to see Mrs. Woolsaw at once.'

'All right, all right. I'll be straight up.'

'I'm to bring you.'

Hattie lifted one nightshirted arm. 'Well I can't go like this.'

It would have taken too long to pick out new clothes so after Fennig closed the door she changed hurriedly into yesterday's. He led her up to the dressing room that adjoined Mrs. Woolsaw's bedroom, where Hattie found her employer curled up in an armchair she never normally used, clammy and shivery and deathbed-pale.

'My goodness, Mrs. Woolsaw, are you all right?'

'Late last night the police finally found out where Adeline was being hidden. But she wasn't there any more. They've scattered like rats. You know Adeline better than anyone. Where would you go, if you were her? Is there anyone who would shelter her?'

Hattie shook her head. 'It's been years since she really had a friend.'

Mrs. Woolsaw's withered condition was no handicap here, because even in full health it was with small gestures, low tones, that she laid you open. 'Don't just stand there with that mousy expression on your face – I need you to think! You love my child just as if she were yours, don't you? I know you do, because you never had one of your own. Well, for her sake, this can't go on any longer. This isn't a jolly adventure any more. Adeline has murdered people.'

'I'm not sure about that,' Hattie said timidly.

'What do you mean you aren't sure? Adeline brought the baby to the party and she let one of her comrades torture it so it would wreak havoc on our guests. Jasper saw that with his own eyes.'

'Maybe it wasn't exactly what it looked like. I know Adeline wouldn't kill people. And I know she wouldn't let anyone hurt the baby.'

'Do I have to remind you that only a few months ago she made a serious endeavour to have it sucked out of her womb? The fact is she doesn't care whom she hurts or what she wrecks.'

Hattie wanted to retort that this was a bit rich coming from Mrs. Woolsaw, who only last night had broadcast herself threatening a six-year-old girl. She thought of the expression on Adeline's face after Hattie had suggested giving up Percy in exchange for Mia and her freedom. 'But she cherishes that little boy now. She does. I know she'd never put in harm's way.'

Mrs. Woolsaw narrowed her eyes. And immediately Hattie knew that she had made a very grave mistake.

'What makes you say that with such certainty?'

Hattie told herself she mustn't panic, because if she panicked it would be obvious to both of them. 'I remember how she was with Mia—'

'When Mia was born Adeline only doted on her to spite us. So what makes you think she would take any special interest in the new one?'

'Because she's a good girl and she . . .'

No matter how drained Mrs. Woolsaw's gaze was, it still had Hattie pinned like a butterfly.

'Have you spoken to her?' Mrs. Woolsaw said.

'No! Of course not. Of course not. If I had I would only have said – I would only have told her to come home . . .' She was babbling now.

'You've spoken to her.'

'No, I wish – I wish I had because—'

Mrs. Woolsaw called Fennig over.

With Mrs. Woolsaw staring into her soul, and Fennig standing over her shoulder, was it any wonder that Hattie's will broke? She was terrified of both of them, but in different ways. After twenty years Fennig seemed to her something less than human, Mrs. Woolsaw something more. Fennig was just an avatar, a purpose condensed into an instrument, a hunting dog with blood on its fangs. Whereas Mrs. Woolsaw – well, as the fear she felt around Mrs. Woolsaw had grown and grown, so too had the respect. The awe, really. Even after all their disagreements, even after all the harsh words she had endured from Mrs. Woolsaw, and small acts of cruelty, and occasionally quite large, even devastating acts of cruelty – might she be married to Stephen by now, if Mrs. Woolsaw had not stepped in? – even after all of that, she still admired her more than anyone she had ever known.

By the time she had finished confessing and explaining and apologising, she was a mess. But Mrs. Woolsaw was much nicer, much more understanding, than she had expected.

'This is a wonderful opportunity to correct your mistake,' she told Hattie. 'A gift, really. Life doesn't always offer us such opportunities.'

So, with Fennig and Mrs. Woolsaw watching, Hattie called the number that Adeline had given her. Said everything that Mrs. Woolsaw had instructed her to say.

She hoped she might feel relief afterwards. But she didn't. Even coming back from her illicit meeting with Adeline, that mad risk, she hadn't felt as jittery as she did now.

'Very well done, Hattie, you didn't put a foot wrong,' Mrs. Woolsaw said, but then dismissed her almost at once, while Hattie was still longing for someone to reassure her, really reassure her, that she'd done the right thing. All Hattie could tell herself was that by nightfall Adeline would be back here, safe, with her children. And one day might forgive her.

❖

It was the flowers that made Hattie worry.

Three times that afternoon she went up to Adeline's room to look it over. The first time was to make sure it was neat and lovely and just how Adeline liked it. The second time was to double-check, because she was agitated and had to occupy herself somehow. Everything was fine, of course. Except there were no flowers.

So she went up there a third time, only half an hour before Adeline was due to arrive. And still there was nothing in the vase.

Mrs. Woolsaw always made sure there were fresh flowers in Adeline's bedroom to welcome her back. Always. Even when she was furious with her daughter. In Hattie's mind, this was Mrs. Woolsaw's way of saying 'No matter what happens, no matter what you might do, no matter what we might say to each other, this is your home, and I am your mother, and I love you.'

And so today, when Adeline was finally returning after such a long time away, after getting swept up in such a regrettable business, meaning that relations between mother and daughter would inevitably be quite complicated for some time to come – surely the gesture was more important than ever. In fact, it was the thought of the flowers that had helped convince Hattie to make that phone call.

Adeline probably wouldn't want to admit that the flowers meant anything to her, but Hattie knew she'd notice if they weren't there this time, and deep down she'd be sad.

So Hattie worked up the courage to go back to Mrs. Woolsaw's dressing room and remind her. 'The flowers for Adeline, Mrs. Woolsaw. Would you like me to do them, or . . . ?'

'What flowers?' said Mrs. Woolsaw, who was looking stronger already, if still rather drawn. 'What are you talking about?'

'For her room. She'll be expecting them.'

A flash of scorn across Mrs. Woolsaw's face. 'You can do whatever you want with her room, just make sure you're out there in time to welcome them in.'

As she went downstairs to pick the flowers herself from Alston's Garden – sweet peas, because she hadn't brought gloves for the roses – Hattie told herself that circumstances were simply too fraught for Mrs. Woolsaw to observe every little tradition. And yet she couldn't stop thinking about that look on Mrs. Woolsaw's face. There had been amusement in it, as well as contempt. As if in some way Hattie had drastically missed the point.

❖

Bill at the front gate hasn't even been told what's going on, since Mrs. Woolsaw wants him to behave perfectly naturally when the van arrives. And Hattie envies him. Because she has to usher Adeline and Luke – who in fact would never have passed for Plowden & Smith, you can see at a glance he doesn't carry himself like someone who does delicate work in wealthy people's homes – into the house knowing exactly what's about to happen and suppressing the urge to blurt out the truth. Fortunately, as with the phone call this morning, she doesn't have to pretend not to be nervous. That she really couldn't manage.

Then she watches as Fennig knocks Luke out cold and two more security men materialise to overpower Adeline too.

She wants to comfort Adeline, tell her that this is for the best. But Adeline is struggling too hard, screaming, thrashing, spitting. Hattie assumes that Adeline can be given a sedative and taken up to her bedroom while Luke . . .Well, it isn't very pleasant to think about what will happen to Luke, but the fact is, no matter that Adeline talked about him like a friend, he did kidnap her, and he must have known when he chose this path what fate might be at the end of it.

But Luke and Adeline aren't separated. In fact they're both carried into the lift, as Hattie trails along behind, helpless and confused.

'Why is she going to the basement?' Hattie says to Mrs.

Woolsaw. They can't possibly be taking her to the chapel. For everyone involved in Adeline's care, it has always been the cardinal rule that she shouldn't be allowed anywhere near the chapel. Even Hattie herself has never so much as laid eyes on the chapel door. For that matter, where is Mr. Woolsaw? Shouldn't he be here to welcome his daughter home?

Once again that flash of scorn from Mrs. Woolsaw. 'Why don't you go upstairs and look in on Mia?'

'Adeline should be going straight to her room. She needs rest.'

'We've got it in hand,' Mrs. Woolsaws snaps. 'You aren't needed any more.'

Instead of going to see Mia, Hattie finds herself going up to Adeline's bedroom. She stands there, staring at the sweet peas she picked. Of course Mrs. Woolsaw will need to ask Adeline some firm questions about the baby's whereabouts, that's perfectly reasonable, but why should it have to happen down in the basement? Unless perhaps Mrs. Woolsaw wants to teach Adeline a very harsh lesson by showing her Luke's comeuppance.

Either that, or . . .

Or . . .

She could go down to the chapel. Make absolutely sure that Adeline is going to be all right.

But she knows Fennig will be down there. He'll never let her through the door.

All this time, as she stands there consumed by worry, she has been absently pinching the skin of her left forearm with her right hand. And now her fingers find the panic button dangling from her GPS bracelet.

She goes to the window and opens it. Then she takes off her bracelet, places it on the window ledge, and presses the button.

Chapter 50

When the door of the chapel opens, Luke is expecting Fennig to come back in. Surely their brief reprieve is over.

But it's Hattie.

Silvia Woolsaw strides across the metal floor to meet her at the doorway, blocking her from coming in any farther. Hattie's eyes widen as she takes in the altar, Luke and Adeline strung up against the wall.

'What on earth is going on?' Silvia says. 'Fennig's just gone to look for you.' She glances down at Hattie's wrist. 'You're not even wearing your bracelet!'

'I'm sorry, Mrs. Woolsaw, but you mustn't do this. You aren't thinking clearly.'

'Get out. This has nothing to do with you.'

Hattie pushes past her, heading for Luke and Adeline. 'Wouldn't it be better if – if we all just—'

Silvia grabs Hattie's arm. And Hattie lashes out, smacking her employer in the face with the back of her hand.

Silvia reels backward. And it's hard to say which woman looks more astonished afterwards.

But if Hattie's just crossed a line she can't uncross, perhaps it strengthens her resolve. She hurries the rest of the way over to Adeline, and stretches up on tiptoe to free her bound wrists from the snap hook. 'Mia is up on the third floor.' She goes for the knot that binds Adeline's wrists, but she hasn't even started on it before Silvia catches up with her, the candlelight etching deep black lines of rage into her face. Silvia grabs Hattie by the hair and drags her away.

Adeline's still gagged. But Luke isn't. 'Adeline!' he shouts.

She shuffles over to him and holds her wrists up to his face. Behind her, Hattie and Silvia are grappling. His teeth find the loop that Hattie has already loosened. Bites down and tugs. Loosens it a bit more – and a bit more – and a bit more – grunting with frustration because how can something so important be so fucking fiddly? – until there's just enough give in the knot for Adeline to pull one hand out.

Now she can do the rest herself. But before she unbuckles her gag, she unhooks Luke's wrists and unpicks his knot.

Luke and Adeline are both bending to untie their ankles when the door opens again. Fennig surveys the room. Though he is by all accounts an implacable guy, it's still extraordinary how calmly he takes in the sight of Hattie kneeling on top of Silvia, each of them clawing at the other's face. Everyone is tinted in this light but Hattie is about as red as Luke's ever seen a person. 'You impudent bitch!' Silvia screams, before Hattie bats her hands out of the way just long enough to land a closed fist on her throat.

Fennig darts towards the altar. Grabs the dagger. And then, before Luke and Adeline even have time to react, he plunges it into Hattie's back.

As he pulls it out, and she topples sideways off Silvia, a wave of emotion moves through Luke – but it's a wave that comes from outside, not inside – a snarl of frustration, like a dog on a chain scrabbling toward food it can't quite reach. The altar must feel cheated.

Adeline still hasn't got her ankles free when Fennig rushes at Luke with the dagger. But she's close enough to grab for his tie. He turns his head—

Maybe it's because Luke has mentally replayed so many times

that disastrous moment at Rosa's parents' house when Fennig grabbed his wrist to make him drop the gun – but now, without so much as a conscious thought, he grabs *Fennig's* wrist and twists it around. But the goal isn't to make him drop the dagger. Instead, Luke shoves with his whole body, shoves hard enough to push it between Fennig's ribs, this weapon that killed Rosa's parents and Cam and maybe Douglas and who knows how many other people—

Hard enough. But not fast enough. Because Fennig turns his wrist so it's only the hilt of the dagger that bumps against his chest. At the same time, he jabs an elbow at Adeline, who is still hanging on to his tie, and she falls with a clatter onto the steel floor.

Except, no, it wasn't Adeline who made the clatter, it was those shears – the ones Fennig used to cut Luke's shirt off him. They've slipped out of his jacket.

Adeline's ankles are still bound. But from where she is now, everything she needs is in reach: the shears, which she snatches up, and Fennig, who she drives them into, right above his hip bone, all the way up to the handle.

Fennig doesn't make a sound. But he does stumble away a few paces.

Luke picks Adeline up, taking her whole weight in his arms, bride-across-the-threshold-style, for the first time since the kidnapping. Carries her out through the door and puts her down in the corridor outside. The last thing he sees before he slams the chapel door shut is Silvia in pursuit. All that flailing around under Hattie has smeared a mask of blood across her face.

The door hinges inwards, which means he has to hang on to the handle with both hands to stop Silvia pulling it open. That's not a long-term solution, though. Especially once Fennig starts hauling on it too.

But Adeline, who has finally got one foot out of its binding, now reaches for the drop bolt that Luke hadn't even noticed – a heavy one, in fact incongruously heavy for a door this size, more like something you'd see on a warehouse or a barn – and pushes it down into the strike hole. Cautiously Luke releases his grip on the handle. And although you can still see the handle trembling as Silvia pulls on it, the door itself doesn't budge.

'Why is there a bolt on the *outside*?' he says to Adeline, who is only now unbuckling her bridle.

Before she answers she pauses to gurn some feeling back into her mouth. 'I think it's in case things go really wrong during a ritual.'

'What do you mean, really wrong?'

'I mean so wrong that something crosses over.'

Chapter 51

There's a part of Adeline that isn't surprised that her mother was about to slit her open on an altar. After all, she's always known that if her parents killed Alston, they could kill her too. 'He won't accept anything less,' her mother said, and after all these years, Adeline still has no more than the murkiest outline of who 'He' is – this force that has shaped all their lives – but clearly, when 'He' demanded Alston, the *carissimum sacrificium*, that wasn't a one-time fee.

But there's also a part of her that still doesn't believe it was real. Her inner five-year-old, the same one who was upset to hear from Hattie that her parents were arguing, is now saying 'Mummy wouldn't do that to me.'

But even as those two sides of her struggle against each other – the cold cynical side and the blind childish side – what has her really shaken is Hattie. Her nanny has been a steady and predictable constant of the universe for Adeline's entire life up until last week. Yet she struck Adeline's mother in the face, which feels like a breach of the laws of nature just as much as icicles falling from the sky – and now she's dead.

The fire stairs bring them up to the hall between the two ground-floor dining rooms. Adeline is about to lead Luke down this hall when she hears a voice and hurriedly drags him through the nearest set of doors. They wait there as they hear footsteps go by outside, along with a one-sided conversation, presumably over an earpiece. Then they creep back out, heading for one of the four staircases that take you up through this enormous house.

Anywhere else this might be an impossible gauntlet to run. But at Cyneburne, Adeline finds it almost trivially easy. She's lived here for twenty-three years. Was a prisoner for the last seven. From childhood games of hide-and-seek, to eavesdropping on her parents, to avoiding Hattie when Hattie had been sent to fetch her, to stalking the handsomer male employees around the house out of sheer boredom . . . She knows every inch of Cyneburne – every banister and every mullion, every rug and every floorboard, every doorknob and every light switch – and she can haunt it like a ghost. And yes, there's a small army of staff to avoid, but the thing about a house with over a hundred rooms is that even that small army gets spread pretty thin. The only real challenge is having Luke by her side. That makes it into a little bit of a three-legged race.

However, when they get up to the third floor, Adeline does have a new revelation about this very familiar place, which is that even up here you can feel the altar's pull. In fact, she understands now that she's always been able to feel it, all through Cyneburne. It was just that, until she went into the chapel, she'd never quite *known* she was feeling it, like a faint background stench you're so accustomed to that you don't even register it until you're confronted with the source.

They've got all the way up here without being seen, but when they come to the carved mahogany double doors leading through to the south corridor, they find them locked. 'Damn it!' Adeline says. Since this floor is back in use she hoped that maybe these doors wouldn't be kept locked any more.

It's possible that if they took the main staircase, and went round from that side, they'd have better luck. But on the main staircase they'd almost certainly be spotted.

'Can we break them down?' Luke says, prodding the door to test the lock.

'Maybe with an axe.'

'Can we get an axe?'

'Even if we could, people would hear. What we need is a key.'

'So where do we get a key?' Luke says.

Adeline can think of one person with a key who is no more than fifty feet from them right now.

It may be that her mother didn't warn her father what was supposed to happen today. But Adeline cannot believe that he is completely oblivious to everything that's been going on in his house. So if he never came downstairs, that means he didn't want to participate, but he also didn't want to intervene.

And at times like these – when her father is doing his very best to ignore something he'd rather not face – he has a fixed habit. He sits in his study with Elgar on the stereo, either paging through one of his texts on the occult or working on its binding. Even more than his watches, this collection is his pride and joy, much of it sourced at enormous expense from the obscurest corners of the world. Although he's quite skilful at those binding repairs, many of the older scrolls, manuscripts, and prayer books have to be stored inside cardboard file boxes, so where an amateur's collection of leather-bound Victorian grimoires might look very impressive on the shelf, her father's peerless hoard has, paradoxically, the banal appearance of a solicitor's archive. He learned Latin and Greek at school from age six, and that covers a good chunk of the texts, although he's taught himself various other dead languages and writing systems to read the rest. A few still remain undeciphered even by the Woolsaws' hired scholars.

When Adeline was much younger, too young to understand how sinister all this stuff was, she would sometimes try to peek over her father's shoulder, and he would keep her from seeing – but in a teasing way which in hindsight must have been designed to foster some curiosity. It chills her now to realise that he wanted to hook her. Well, she did once sneak in when he forgot to lock the door, but although she's sure there must be some unspeakable images festering on those shelves, the books she happened to pick out that day had nothing but page after page of unintelligible gothic script, and she soon lost interest.

'We'll get the key from my father,' she tells Luke.

'Your father?'

'I know it sounds absurd but if he's close by I think it's our best option. We just have to make sure he doesn't call for help.'

'Does he have a panic button like Hattie?'

'He never wears it in the house.'

So they go back down the stairs to the second floor. Along the hall, past her father's bedroom. And through the door of the study, she can already hear the *Dream of Gerontius*.

Chapter 52

Luke's first sight of Conrad Woolsaw in the flesh is considerably less dramatic than his first sight of Silvia Woolsaw. Conrad is just sitting there in an armchair by the window with a book in his lap, wearing what Luke at first takes for two pairs of glasses on top of each other but then surmises must be reading glasses with some sort of clip-on magnifying attachment.

'Adeline!' Conrad puts the book to one side and gets up from the chair. 'What are you – what are you doing here? I mean, it's wonderful to see you, my darling, of course it is, but how can you be . . .' He blinks. 'And who is this?'

'We've come to get Mia,' Adeline says as Luke shuts the door. 'We need you to give us a key to the third floor and tell us which room she's in.'

'Does your mother know you're up here?'

'She was going to kill me, Dad.'

'I'm sure that's not true.' He glances towards a nearby footstool. Following his gaze, Luke sees an iPhone lying on the tufted leather. And Conrad is now looking at Luke again, very obviously calculating whether he can get to the phone quick enough.

He makes an attempt. But Luke darts forward and sweeps the phone off the footstool, out of his reach, then grabs Conrad Woolsaw by the shoulders and forces him back down into his chair. He's not that hard to push around, this billionaire empire-builder. Luke has never thought of himself as particularly intimidating but maybe it helps that he still has no shirt and an indeterminate amount of blood on him.

When he looks into the other man's eyes, there's only one thing he can think about. Silvia Woolsaw is an expert in power and influence, but Conrad Woolsaw is an expert in numbers. Yields. Efficiencies. Like all that money they saved at the Hazelwood mental health unit.

Adeline goes to the stereo and turns the choral music up higher. 'Where are your keys?'

'I'm not going to help you kidnap Mia.'

In the pocket of her hoodie Adeline still has the length of cord she slipped off her ankles, and now she passes it to Luke. 'Tie him up.'

This might sound like a reasonable request on the basis of Luke's recent track record, but the reality is that the Nail always used plastic zip ties and he doesn't really know any knots. All the same, he goes around behind the chair, whose back is so broad he has to pull Conrad's arms up over the top instead of around the sides. At this, Conrad finally starts shouting. 'Help! Fennig! Fennig! Help!' So Adeline claps her hand over her father's mouth. Luke ends up tying about three and a half improvised knots on top of one another, which seem sturdy enough when he tests them.

'Check his pockets,' Adeline says.

Luke pats Conrad down. And he doesn't find a set of keys. But he does find a black plastic box. It snags when he takes it out of the trouser pocket, and he sees there's a wire attached to it, snaking up over the waistband and then back down inside towards the thigh. 'What the fuck is this?' he asks Adeline, thinking that it looks a bit like a microphone pack, except Conrad Woolsaw is probably not sitting around in his own house with his leg hair miked up.

'It's his electric-shock thing,' Adeline explains.

'His what?'

'It stops him from zoning out.'

Examining the device, Luke sees three dials labelled intensity, frequency, and pulse width and a switch labelled randomizer.

'How high does it go?' he says.

It takes Adeline a second to understand what he's suggesting. 'Oh God Dad, this is so unseemly. I don't want to do this. Just tell us where your keys are.' She takes her hand away from his mouth, but he just gives a brisk shake of the head. Adeline sighs. 'Okay, I'll look around,' she says to Luke. 'You do what you have to. We'll see which one of us gets somewhere first.'

She goes over to check the drawers of the desk, leaving Luke to put his gloved hand over Conrad's mouth as he switches randomizer to off, turns frequency and pulse width all the way up, and slowly cranks intensity. When the dial is about halfway to the top, he can feel Conrad Woolsaw's jaw tense. When it's about three-quarters of the way to the top, Conrad starts groaning and squirming, his bound hands knocking spasmodically against the back of the armchair. Luke leaves it there for a few more seconds and then turns it back down. 'Where are your keys?' he says, unsealing Conrad's mouth.

'Adeline, will you look at what you're doing?' Conrad says, his voice hoarse. 'Will you look at what's happening in this room? This isn't who we brought you up to be. This can't be what you really want.'

'Why are you being so stubborn?' To Luke: 'I'll check next door. Keep trying.' She goes through the doorway into the adjoining section of the study. Leaving Luke alone with Conrad Woolsaw.

He knows he's supposed to be interrogating him about the third floor. But instead he finds himself saying: 'When people die because of you – do you even hear about it?'

'You'll have to explain what you're referring to,' Conrad says, condescension in his voice even though he's still breathing heavily.

'I don't mean in the basement. I mean out there. Someone dies because the Woolsaw Group decided to trim their overheads – does anyone ever mention their name? Like in a meeting or in a report or something?'

'This is what people of your political persuasion can't seem to understand. Tens of millions of people use Woolsaw Group services every year. So, by pure statistical inevitability, tens of thousands of those people will die for one reason or another. No, of course I don't hear about every one of them.'

Luke wants to ask him about Holly.

Whether he's ever heard of her. Whether her death intruded into his life for even an instant.

But Luke knows he can't do that. Because that would be tantamount to identifying himself by name. Which would probably result in the Woolsaws going after everyone he's ever been close to.

Of course, he knows what Rosa would exhort him to do if she were here. 'Tell this prick Holly's name. Tell him exactly how she died. And then kill him. That way, your sister will be the last thought he ever has, and you don't have to worry about any consequences.'

Adeline comes back into the room, dangling a set of keys for Luke to see. 'They were in your Barbour, Dad. We were going to find them anyway. Why did you make us go through that?'

'I love you, Adeline, and that's why I will not be a willing accomplice to this ghastly error that you've fallen into.'

'I got these as well,' she says to Luke, lifting up her other hand, in which she holds about half a dozen watches by the straps like a gardener with a bunch of radishes.

'Why do we need watches?'

'Because I remember him saying once that one of his Patek Philippes was worth over a million. But I can't remember which one it was so I just took a few of them. They might come in useful later. I imagine these are easier to sell than Auerbachs.'

'You won't even get a fraction of what they're worth,' Conrad says.

'That's fine. Tell me where Mia is.'

'Adeline—'

'Shock him again.'

Luke reaches for the box.

'No!' Conrad blurts. 'No. Don't. For goodness' sake, she's in Alston's old room.'

Adeline regards her father. 'Mum's right, you know. You're weak.' To Luke: 'Let's go. Make sure he can't call for help.'

Luke takes off Conrad's shoes and socks and stuffs both socks in his mouth, then looks around for a way to keep them in there. On a desk nearby is a book so old it's nearly disintegrating, surrounded by what must be bookbinding tools, rulers and brushes and awls and scalpels and most usefully a role of linen tape, a length of which Luke puts over Conrad's mouth. Meanwhile, Adeline pockets the longest knife on the desk, then cracks open the study door and checks the corridor outside. 'Come on,' she says.

But Luke hesitates. Because this doesn't feel finished.

Adeline sees his hesitation. And seems to understand. 'We really don't have long.'

He could send her out of the room. Take a bulldog clip from the desk, put it on Conrad Woolsaw's nose, and leave him here to suffocate with the socks in his mouth. Then this fuck will never do any more damage again. If Holly's death had any purpose, it was for Luke to make sure there will never be another Holly. So why doesn't he just end it here? He knows that's what Rosa would demand of him.

But he doesn't know what Holly would demand of him. What kind of revenge she would actually wish for. What kind of person she would want her brother to be.

He imagines her here. 'I killed him,' he'd say to her. 'For you.'

'*For me?*' She'd give him one of her incredulous looks – wildly exaggerated, almost clownish – a treat to witness when they weren't directed at you and still quite funny even when they were. 'What do you mean, for me? Fuck's sake, Luke. You fucking muppet.'

He fetches a glass carafe of water from the desk, brings it over to the armchair, and empties it over Conrad's leg. Because wet skin conducts better. Then he picks up the plastic box and turns intensity all the way to the top. As Adeline turns away, Conrad's eyes widen and his toes curl. Though muffled by the socks, a keening can be heard. A second wet patch appears on his trousers, this time at the groin.

Holly was screaming for four hours in her room. Luke isn't sure how much juice is in the battery, or whether Conrad will be found by the staff before it runs out, but either way this probably won't last as long. He just hopes it will feel like longer.

Chapter 53

Before they go to find Mia, they slip into another bedroom so Luke can arm himself with a fireplace poker. All fourteen rooms on the third floor still get aired and dusted twice a week, so you wouldn't even know they haven't been used in years. Many of them are connected by little passages, which is how guests staying at Cyneburne back in the old days could have adjoining bedrooms without actually having to share a door as if they were in a hotel. This makes the whole floor sufficiently mazelike that even before it was closed up during Adeline's childhood, hide-and-seek and other such games were forbidden up here in case they dragged on the entire day. So the plan is for Luke to draw away any security guys guarding Mia, and keep the chase going for as long as possible, while Adeline deals with the nanny.

Yet when Adeline peeks around the corner at the door of Alston's room, there's nobody posted outside.

While Luke keeps a lookout, Adeline tiptoes to the door. She kneels down to look through the keyhole, but it's blocked, so she puts her ear to it instead. And at first she hears nothing – but then, when she holds her breath and listens even harder, she makes out the faint but unmistakable sound of Mia burbling on as she plays with her toys. Instantly her eyes fill up with tears. This is the first time she's heard her daughter's voice in almost six months.

She opens the door. Mia looks up from where she's sitting on the carpet with her little animals. 'Mummy!' she exclaims. Adeline rushes across the room to her, so overwhelmed by the sight of her daughter that it hardly occurs to her to wonder how Mia could have been left all on her own up here—

Until she hears the door shut behind her. And she looks back to see her mother.

Now fully dressed, face and hands clean, Silvia Woolsaw turns the key in the lock. 'I want to have a conversation with you, Adeline,' she says. 'A proper conversation. And it was silly of me to think that would be possible downstairs with all those other people around. So I thought I'd just wait for you up here.'

Adeline can hear Luke rattling the handle from outside. She raises the leather-paring knife she took from her father's study. 'Close your eyes,' she says to Mia, who only widens them in puzzlement. She always used to cut Mia's sandy fringe herself but at some point in the last six months her mother has achieved her dream of excising it entirely.

'Don't be ridiculous,' Silvia says. 'You won't touch me with that. I'm your mother.'

'You were going to . . .' But she doesn't want to say 'kill me' when Mia is listening. 'You were going to put me on the altar.'

'That's exactly what I want to talk to you about. Just put that thing down.'

Adeline tells herself she's going to puncture her mother the same way she did Fennig. Leave her bleeding on the floor while she takes Mia away. Even Hattie took her shot, didn't she? Craven, submissive Hattie. And just because her mother has a gaze that can cow prime ministers, that doesn't mean it can cow *her*. After all, prime ministers are easy marks, but she knows all her mother's tricks, always has . . .

And yet the truth is that it feels absolutely impossible. Maybe back in the chapel, amidst the fray, if she didn't have a chance to think, she could have done it. But not now. God, she's feeble. That must be why her mother came up here to wait for her without a single security guy. Because she knew she wouldn't need them.

'Come out onto the balcony with me,' Silvia says, gesturing towards the French doors.

'Not a chance.'

'Come out onto the balcony with me, and I'll tell you exactly what happened to Alston.'

'I'm not interested in your lies.'

'I'm not going to lie to you. I'll answer any question you have. I want you to know the truth, Adeline, because it's the only way I have of making you understand, I mean really understand, everything that's been happening today.'

Adeline feels her heart pounding. The rational part of her is well aware that she shouldn't listen to a single word that comes out of her mother's mouth, and yet she so furiously, irresistibly, desperately does want to know.

How could you do this to him? And how could you do this to me?

When her mother reaches out for the paring knife, she ought to pull away. Yet somehow she doesn't. Her hand does close tighter around the handle, but only weakly, as if already prepared to relinquish it. As her mother takes it from her, it might as well be a crayon gently plucked from Mia's grip. She just watches as her mother tosses it onto the armoire, out of Mia's reach, then takes her firmly by the arm and guides her to towards the French doors.

'We knew these balconies were dangerous,' her mother says, undoing the catch top and bottom. 'The doors were supposed to be kept locked, and neither of you were ever supposed to come out here without a grown-up holding your hand. But Hattie was distracted and you seized the moment. No, Mia, darling, stay in here.'

'What are you talking about?'

'We were so relieved, afterwards, when you seemed confused about what had happened. That was the only silver lining. And we did everything we could to help the memory fade.'

Just now, as her mother opened the French doors, Adeline noticed that several of her fingertips were bandaged, and now in the sunlight her hairline is looking patchy, a bit like how Adeline's did for a few months after her first pregnancy. Is all this from the scuffle with Hattie? The balcony looks out to the west, and the houses past the garden wall are some of the most expensive in London but they're still basically shacks compared to Cyneburne, which means there's nothing but oak trees to obstruct the view of Hampstead Heath, and beyond that the suburbs, with Ruislip and the school somewhere over the horizon. 'What memory?' Adeline says. 'What do you mean?' She glances back at Mia, who is contentedly twirling a plush giraffe.

'Perhaps I'd better start from the beginning. If there's one thing I want you to understand, it's that none of this was ever supposed to happen. I mean making you have children so young. It shouldn't have been your duty to bear His son, it should only ever have been mine. I'll spare you the details – of course you were only two when all this happened – but back when we had Alston it was all a great deal messier. There was certainly no possibility of artificial insemination. These days, after a great deal of research, we've mastered certain methods of obtaining His seed, but twenty years ago we didn't have the know-how yet. So the only way to do it was for Him to visit me Himself. The old-fashioned way. I promise you, Adeline, it was much, much, much more gruelling than anything you've ever gone through.

'Afterwards, I was pregnant, but I was also in shambles. Medically, I mean. Because of all the rigours of His visit. Really, darling, you'd shudder to hear about it. I shouldn't even have been able to carry a baby to term but of course you know as well as I do that His sons are very tenacious even in utero – Alston never weakened, thank goodness. And once he was born the doctors insisted that I have various ruined parts cut out of me. Very much overdue, they said. So there was no possibility of my ever having another child.

'But that was all right. Because our family was complete. Your father, and I credit him to this day for his foresight, was adamant that we should have our *own* child before I had the other kind. So we already had you – our natural child, his and mine, the product of our love. And now we had Alston, your half-brother – my son, but not your father's son – to sit at the head of our empire when he grew up. And you loved him. But you also sensed something in him, I think. You were only as old as Mia is now, but somehow you did. You sensed his origins. You sensed his purpose. And you didn't like it. And in some childish instinctive way you must have decided that he couldn't be allowed to live. And so you killed him.'

Adeline stares at her mother in incredulity. All that wind-up just for a ridiculous lie. 'I didn't kill him. *You* killed him. You sacrificed him.'

'No, Adeline, we didn't. Why on earth would we have sacrificed His heir, the culmination of everything we'd been working towards? It was you.' The railings beside them are wrought iron, waist-high, with cross braces meeting in a fleur-de-lis, and now her mother stoops to put a hand through the gap in the cross braces. 'You managed to push Alston through these and off the balcony. And afterwards you protected yourself by not remembering, as children sometimes can. But that's why Alston's Garden is where it is. So flowers will bloom where our little angel fell. And that's why we locked up the third floor afterwards. Because it was so painful for us to come up here.

'The trouble was, we still needed an heir to sit on the throne, but as I said, I couldn't have any more children myself. So we really had no choice but to use your womb as soon as you were old enough. And then of course there was the enormous frustration of Mia turning out to be a girl. So we had to wait a few more years until we could obtain another bounty of His seed, and then do it again.

'Since I was about your age, Adeline, I've had only one aim. His kingdom on Earth. And almost as long as you've been alive you've been trying to thwart that aim, knowingly or otherwise. And, as your mother, it was maddening. But at the same time, as your mother, I'm glad you're as determined as I am. You showed that with Alston. That's why I used to bring you flowers from Alston's Garden every time you strayed. Because I was happy for your own sake that you'd drawn a veil over what you did, but I also never wanted it to leave you entirely. The understanding, deep down, of who you are and what you're capable of. Yes, I was about to put you on the altar. But it was precisely *because* I love you so much that I had to do it.' She touches Adeline's arm. 'I made a mistake, you see, and now I have to make amends, and He knows how much you mean to me. As I said, He simply won't accept anything less. And I know that if our roles were reversed, you'd do the same. In a sense, you already have. You killed someone you loved because you had no other choice.'

Adeline is thinking about those nightmares she has. Alston falling away from her. She always thought that was merely one of the dreaming brain's unsubtle metaphors. A symbol, not a memory. And yet her mother's story has made something flicker on inside her, like an old wiring system buried under the plasterboard – every confusing little moment or puzzling little interaction, going back years and years, finally connecting up, if indeed this was what the adults were trying to hide from her – and all of it is converging here, on this balcony, where she's realising, yes, this *is* where those dreams are situated, this *is* where something awful took place. Her mother was clever to bring her out here, maybe otherwise she could still have denied it to herself, but to be physically back here at the scene, where she hasn't set foot since it happened...As much as she longs to, she can't tell herself it's not true. It has a grim familiarity, a grim correctness.

She killed her brother, whom she loved.

Adeline looks back at her mother, fresh tears in her eyes. And in her mother's expression, she detects some satisfaction. Because the plan worked. Adeline has been humbled. But she detects some sympathy too. Real sympathy. Against all odds, it seems her mother is still capable of that. Seeing her daughter's pain and feeling pain herself.

'I never wanted to burden you with all this, Adeline. And if I have, I promise that it's only so that we can understand each other just a bit better. And I hope now we do.'

Adeline nods, 'I think I do understand better now. Whatever you're capable of, I'm capable of too. I always have been.'

'That's right. And I'm sure Mia will be just the same. Because she's your daughter. And you're mine.'

She reaches out to embrace Adeline. So Adeline reaches out too.

And shoves her over the railings.

Chapter 54

Adeline is probably right that you'd need an axe to smash through one of these doors. So Luke's been trying to come up with some ingenious way of forcing the lock open with the fireplace poker. In terms of the right tools for the job, this probably isn't any better than when Adeline was trying to escape from her cell with that cheap aluminium wardrobe handle. But he has to find a way to save her. They've come so far, it can't all fall apart now—

But then he hears the latch turn on the other side. And the door swings open to reveal Adeline standing there holding the hand of a little girl in a blue dress.

'What happened?' he says. As Mia stares up at him with great curiosity he belatedly tries to wipe some more of the blood off himself.

'Rather a lot. Mia, say hello to our friend Luke. Come on, we'd better be quick. I think everyone downstairs will be distracted for the time being.'

'Distracted by . . .?' But that's when he makes out the distant sound of screaming. 'Is that your mother?'

'Lucky for her she landed in some rose bushes.'

Luke scoops up Mia and holds her against his shoulder as they make a run for it. Down to the first floor they take the same staircase they took before, but then on the landing they hear multiple sets of footsteps approaching. Adeline has to clamp down on the watches in her hoodie pocket to stop them from jingling as they dash down the corridor and out of sight.

'What now?' he whispers to Adeline, out of breath from hefting Mia.

'The main staircase is just over there.'

'I thought we were trying to avoid that.'

'We were. But from here it's the fastest way out.'

Their luck holds. They meet nobody on the staircase, which leads down to Cyneburne's vast entrance hall. Fluted wooden columns support a gallery along the rear wall, and high above that is the famous glass dome, which means that in contrast to all those dusky corridors upstairs the whole space is bathed in sunlight, though Luke is in no state of mind to appreciate it. He's already thinking about what they'll do if they can get out of the building unnoticed: find a vehicle, maybe even the same van they arrived in, and then—

Before he knows what's happening, he's been pushed to the ground, and Mia has been ripped from his grasp.

Fennig must have been behind one of those columns, and now he's backing away with Mia bundled under one arm and the dagger held against her throat. Blood has soaked through his untucked shirttail and the upper thigh of his trousers, but maybe he found time to bandage himself underneath, because he's not moving like a man with an open stab wound.

When he's put enough distance between himself and the people he's just ambushed, he lowers Mia until her bare feet meet the parquet and they're in the same position from the video, her head at his waist. If she's frozen in his grip, then it's more from sheer surprise than anything else. She probably has no idea what that cool pressure is under her chin.

'If you take one more step, Miss Woolsaw, I shall cut your daughter's throat.'

But Mia must have understood *that*, because now her brow crumples in fear, and she looks to her mother for help. And her mother is looking back and forth between her and Luke, begging him every bit as desperately to do something.

But he can't think what to do. No matter how afraid he is of Fennig, no matter that he'd lose the fight, he'd willingly take a run at him if he thought he could save Mia. But there's just no overcoming the fact of that dagger.

And Adeline seems to accept that well before Luke. Because with terrible speed, terrible certainty, even as Luke's mind is still helplessly racing, she discards everything but the one possibility she can still see in front of her.

'Her for me,' she says to Fennig, face set. 'You've only got two hands, you can't take all of us. So let Mia go and you can have me.'

'Several more men will be here momentarily,' Fennig says, his tone perfectly polite. 'Not one of you is leaving this house.'

Adeline holds the blade of the paring knife against her own stomach. 'Right now you have Mia. But Mia isn't any use to my mother. Only I am. She needs to sacrifice me to make amends. And if I kill myself before she can feed me to the altar, then it'll be like a waiter dropping a plate. Dinner will be ruined.'

Luke can't stop himself from blurting out: 'Adeline, no—'

She ignores him. 'I swear to God – or actually I swear to *your* filthy greedy boss, wherever he is' – Luke sees Fennig wince at this blasphemy – 'I'll put this knife right through something crucial before you or anyone else can lay their hands on me. If possible I'll get my liver so you won't have the chance to rummage through it afterwards. And my mother will be sunk. But if you let Mia and Luke go, I promise I'll make it easy for you. I'll climb on that slab myself.'

'If I let them go now, it won't make any difference,' Fennig says. 'They'll never make it off the grounds.'

'Then you don't have anything to lose. And at this point neither do I,' she adds, tightening her grip on the knife handle.

Fennig nods. 'Very well, Miss Woolsaw.'

Adeline looks at Luke. 'If you're quick, you can still get out. Just make sure they never find Mia or Percy.'

Luke wants this to be a trick. A brilliant gambit to outwit Fennig. Because he doesn't think it's very likely that he *can* get out of Cyneburne without Adeline's help. And because he can't lose her like this. He can't

But this doesn't feel like trick. When he looks at Adeline all he sees is resignation. Luke himself isn't resigned to this. He refuses to be. But he can't think what to do.

'I'd like to hug her before I go,' Adeline says.

'No, Miss Woolsaw, I'm afraid that's not how we'll do it.'

Adeline's expression doesn't waver. 'All right, then you'll send her over here—'

'No, Miss Woolsaw, that's not how we'll do it either. Be so good as to stand just there, please,' Fennig says, pointing to the middle of the entrance hall. 'Mia will stay where she is, and I'll come to you.' Luke realises how shrewd this is: if the exchange involved Adeline and Mia crossing the hall in opposite directions, then one of them could suddenly veer off course and dash towards the other. But this way, Fennig and his dagger will be in between them the whole time.

'Mummy?' Mia calls out, imploringly, almost impatiently, an urgent reminder to put things right, because that's her mother's job.

But Adeline can't put things right. 'Do exactly as he says, angel. You mustn't run to me. You must stay where you are, and then when I go off with Fennig you must go with Luke.'

Fennig repositions Mia so she's seated on the floor with her legs folded under her. As he walks away from her, though the dagger is no longer at her throat, she only looks more distraught, her face collapsing into sobs. Adeline gives Luke one last look before she turns to Fennig. A little nod, emphatic. Telling him again he must save Mia if he can. Beyond that, all he can see in her face is the strain of this moment, so whatever else there might be to communicate – from her to him, or from him to her – there just isn't any space to do it.

This is really happening. He never thought there would ever

come another time in his life as crushing as when he found out Holly was dead.

As Fennig reaches Adeline, Luke hears footsteps, and looks up to see that two security guys have emerged onto the gallery. Maybe they heard Mia sobbing. Any hope of escaping unnoticed with her, scant as it was already, has just fully evaporated.

Fennig steps behind Adeline, and now it's her throat the dagger is pressed against. 'I love you, angel,' Adeline calls to Mia. 'I love you so much.'

Mia's sobbing has turned to bawling. 'Mummy,' she's saying, 'Mummy, Mummy, Mummy,' over and over again until the word tears apart into a scream.

And in this scream there's a vibration like a bone drill going right through your marrow, an unearthly vibration that Luke has heard before. At Park Royal and in Queen Mary's Gardens.

From high above, a sound like a thousand windows breaking at once. Luke looks straight up. The glass dome. It's falling in. Yet even as it falls, the sound stretches on, a staticky chittering, as if in flight the broken pieces are somehow continuing to subdivide. Sure enough, by the time the glass has fallen almost to eye level, it's a jumble of different sizes, from shards the size of snowflakes to shards the size of that paring knife. And the reason Luke has time to make this out – the reason the glass isn't already upon him before the thought can even form in his head – is that at this point it *changes direction*, swerving in mid air like a flock of birds. He hears a shout of 'Fuck! Run!', which must be one of the security guys, while Mia continues to wail, and the shattering sound has now given way to the clicking of stray fragments hitting walls or floor. Glittering in the sunlight, the dervish tightens, twists, turns back on itself, and heads straight for Fennig and Adeline, speeding towards them like a train.

Luke himself shouts wordlessly in horror as it hits them. They are both swallowed up by the glass. Which then, with the suddenness of a cut string, clatters all at once to the floor. So that the hall is silent but for the final waning sobs from Mia – whose eyes are squeezed so tightly shut that Luke doesn't know if she saw it, any of it, what just happened or what now remains:

Her mother, still standing there, corpse-pale and covered in little nicks and grazes, but otherwise **unhurt**.

And nothing of Fennig but blood on the shining ground.

Chapter 55

Early this morning, after what she went through in her bedroom, Silvia Woolsaw felt so weak that she asked for a wheelchair to be readied. How convenient that it should still be waiting a few hours later, when her need for it was considerably more acute. Her doctor said that with her legs so smashed up it would be weeks before even the wheelchair would be feasible, but she simply refuses to be invalided at a time like this. Whenever she has to spend any time at all confined to bed she begins to feel that everything important is happening downstairs out of her earshot. In the end her doctor reluctantly admitted that the wheelchair wouldn't actually kill her. So here she is, sitting in the ground-floor drawing room with her right leg elevated, looking exactly like her grandmother did when she used to get those swellings, even down to the glass of Madeira.

'My love.'

She looks up. Her husband stands in the doorway.

'Conrad.' For once she is glad to see him. He looks rather better now than he did after they found him tied up in the study. From the direction of the entrance hall she can hear the maids still gathering the last fragments of glass like gleaners in a field. For the sake of the parquet she won't let them use brooms – her face will heal from the rose-bush scratches, but it's hell to buff palisander – so they've been at it for hours.

'I'm so sorry, sweetheart. What an abominable day.'

'He won't wait much longer, you know.'

'Why don't we go down to the chapel? We can pray to Him together.'

'We can, but that doesn't mean He'll take any notice. Our master isn't merciful.'

'No, He isn't, but all the same—'

'All right. All right, I'd like that.'

She's quite capable of wheeling herself around, but nevertheless she lets him push her to the lift. She used to like it when they were courting and he would do silly chivalrous things for her. Such a long time ago.

Fortunately the lift was designed so that if necessary it could fit not just a wheelchair but even a medical trolley. They always planned to grow old in this house, and they wanted to make sure that nothing would ever keep them from visiting the chapel, even if it was literally their dying day.

'I know we've had some very serious setbacks,' her husband says as the lift descends, 'but if there is any silver lining to today...Perhaps it's a chance to start afresh. You know, sweetheart, everything of any importance that we ever accomplished, we accomplished *together*. Don't you think so? And we've been so at odds lately, and where has that got us?'

'You're right.'

'For richer, for poorer and all that. We should never have let a few differences of outlook drive such a wedge between us. Next time we'll just talk it out, with none of this ill feeling.'

'That's very sweet, Conrad. But if He takes me away, then there won't *be* a next time, will there?'

'Well, all we can do is throw ourselves at His feet. We have been faithful servants. I do believe that.'

Fennig never had a chance to go back to the chapel, which means the aftermath is untouched: Hattie's body and the terrorist ringleader's lying there in pools of clotted blood; cold organs in the bowls on the altar; a rope, a bridle, and a pair of shears scattered on the ground. As Conrad drags the ringleader's corpse out of the way, Silvia rolls her wheelchair to the credence table where the paraphernalia of the unfinished ritual is still laid out.

'Will you come over here and kiss me, Conrad?' she says.

He kneels down beside her. It starts as just a peck on the lips but she opens her mouth and makes it a long, almost teenage, kiss.

'You're right,' she says afterwards, one hand fondly holding his cheek. 'No matter what, we still have our bond. There have been times when I told myself I hated you, but all this time, darling, I've loved you. And I still do love you.'

She picks up a chalcedony dagger from the credence table and slashes her husband's throat.

Then she holds him steady so he won't slump across her and drench her lap with blood, though he's still close enough that she can caress him as she murmurs the prayer, the prayer of the *carissimum sacrificium*, the same prayer she would have said over Adeline if it hadn't all gone wrong. She can feel the reredos stretching out to reach him, and the reredos isn't particularly happy about it, but in her condition allowances must be made, and in the end it drinks its fill as usual. When it's finished, she strokes Conrad's hair one last time and then shoves him away so that he topples sideways onto the floor.

Her wheels leave blood trails along the corridor and into the lift and back to the drawing room and across the rug. A maid, who must have seen the trails, comes in looking worried, and when she sees the blood on Silvia's nightdress – inevitably some did get on her – she stammers in alarm. 'Madam—'

'It's perfectly all right. Just leave me, please. I'll shout if I need you.'

She wishes Fennig were here to clean up all this mess. She wishes he were here to bathe her and dress her and take her to the lavatory until her legs heal – she knows that in his devoted, imperturbable way he would've made the whole business seem not at all degrading for either of them. She needs a new Fennig, but how will she ever replace him? A new chairman of the Woolsaw Group's board as well. A new nightdress. A new chancellor of the exchequer. New glass for the dome, and perhaps new floors beneath, if they do turn out to be scarred beyond repair. These choices crowd upon her in such disorder she can hardly sort through which are important and which are not. And that's quite apart from finding Adeline and the baby, which trumps it all. She drinks another glass of Madeira, feeling very lonely indeed.

If he hadn't insisted on Adeline going to that bloody obstetrician . . .

'Darling?' The voice is just a wet whisper.

She looks up. Her husband stands in the doorway. He's hunched over but she can still see the gash in his neck, red against his blanched skin.

The glass falls from her hand. 'Conrad?'

'He sent me back, darling. He wouldn't take me. He said . . .He said I was no offering at all. An insult, He said. Not even fit for the altar. Just a broken thing, no longer wanted.'

It takes her a moment to understand the implications.

Then – for the very first time since all of this started – Silvia Woolsaw truly panics.

From her wheelchair she can't reach up to any of the paintings on the wall. So she has to chivvy her revenant husband into doing it.

'Conrad, take down the Hockney! Quick! As quick as you can!'

'Darling?'

'Take it down and put it in the fireplace!' She looks around. There's a Denis Mitchell sculpture on a side table, low enough for her to reach. A mother and child, in carved wood, so it should burn pretty well. Pumping her tired arms, she rolls herself across to it, cursing as one wheel snags on the rug. 'Take everything down. Both the Auerbachs. Get the Freud from the other room. And start a fire. Use the firelighters. Hurry!'

'I don't understand, sweetheart.'

'I have to give Him what I love! He'll only spare me if I give Him what I really love!'

She lobs the Mitchell into the fireplace.

But then the geometry of the room begins to unweave, and she realises it's already too late.

'No!' she wails. 'Please! No! Not yet!'

The void gapes beneath her like the greatest leviathan in the ocean swallowing up a single microscopic krill. And she tumbles down into it, a fall with no end.

Chapter 56

The rain seems to be holding off so after lunch they decide to go down to the beach. 'Beach' might be a strong word – it's really just an edge of sand beneath the dark knuckly cliffs. But there's not much else to do around here. And at least by now nearly all the bones are gone.

A fortnight ago Mia had a fever so bad they had to send for the GP from the village. Inviting an outsider was the biggest risk they'd taken since they got here, but it was still better than bringing Mia to the surgery, with its forms and its databases and its cameras, so they were lucky Luke's mum knew the doctor well enough that he was happy to make a house call.

Because Luke had only ever talked about his mum in the context of Holly's death, Adeline had formed an image of her as a hermit shuffling around in her mourning veil, but the truth is she's a cheerful and vigorous woman, so talkative in fact that Adeline wonders how on earth she managed when she was living here all on her own. And that has its uses, because as soon as it was established for the doctor's benefit that these were Luke's girlfriend's children and the girlfriend herself was temporarily absent but rushing home as fast as she could, Luke's mum swept away any further enquiries with a torrent of her own questions about various village goings-on. Most of these the doctor was forbidden from answering for reasons of professional ethics, yet somehow the precise tone and phrasing of his demurral always seemed to resolve them to her full satisfaction. Which left Luke free to just hover nervously, having called Adeline on his mobile and left the line open so she could eavesdrop from out in the field behind the house.

Luke wasn't nervous only about the doctor. He was also nervous about Percy, who was screaming so hard that Adeline had to strain to make anything out. And this wasn't the harmless kind of crying, this was the ruinous kind, the kind that most of the time ends with people dead on the ground. Luke found himself glancing out of the window at the sky, he told her afterwards, wondering what kind of plague Percy was going to call down upon them.

But the doctor did his work, and nothing seemed to happen. Until the next day, when Luke's mum coaxed Adeline into going out again. 'Just for a bit. I know you want to stay with her every minute, but trust me, darling, you'll go mad if you do.' So Adeline took the dog down to the beach. And there she found the bones.

So many bones that from a distance she mistook them for some strange white sargassum left behind by a night tide. But as she drew closer she made out skulls, femurs, ribs, like a mass grave dumped in piles on the sand, as high as your knee in places and stretching on at least a quarter of a mile. She hurried to put Teddy back on the leash in case he thought he'd hit the jackpot – last month he found what must have been a sheep's jaw and they had to chase him round and round before they could get it off him – but in fact he refused to go anywhere near the reef of bones. She went home and told Luke, and they were both worried, because anyone else who saw it might post pictures on the internet, and that would attract outside attention, journalists, police. But they were grateful, this time, that their 'beach' is so mediocre, because that means it's generally deserted. And over the next several days, the tide dragged the bones away again. So that by now there are only a handful left, and Teddy makes no further objection.

Luke is nervous about how often things like that will happen.

They already know that the everyday miseries and indignities of being a baby are not enough to set Percy off. Certainly he will cry himself raw, but he won't work his terrible magic. That seems to come only when he feels under threat. Luke points out that he wasn't under threat when that GP was tending to his sister, but Adeline thinks he just has a special loathing for doctors. After all, when has he met them before? The abortion clinic, where he was almost vacuumed up. Harley Street, where his mother was poked and prodded like a prize mare. And the school, where he was delivered in a cell by a man in a mask. It's quite understandable, really. So if they can just keep him out of the way of the medical profession, at least until he's old enough to bribe into acquiescence, like she used to bribe his sister to open wide for the dentist – well, there's nothing else to threaten him, not out here in the back of beyond.

As for Mia . . .Adeline is still hoping what she did at Cyneburne was an aberration, never to be repeated. Saints have to perform two verifiable miracles before they can be canonised. Well, maybe Mia will be satisfied with just one. In the past, it was easy enough to put Mia's origins out of her mind. Because Adeline's parents regarded Mia so much as a failed experiment, a factory reject, she almost convinced herself that Mia was all Adeline and none of the other thing. That doesn't stand up any more. Mia has proven she has the other thing in her, just as Percy does.

But a lot of people come from a bad line and turn out all right. After all, Luke's dad was apparently pretty rotten as well.

If it's strange to move in with your boyfriend's mother after knowing him only a couple of weeks, it's even stranger when you bring along two kids, and he's not the father, and you can't offer a satisfactory explanation of who the father is. But Luke's mum has taken it more or less in stride. She recognised Adeline from the news, and at the start she asked a lot of questions, but she soon accepted that she'd have to manage without proper answers. She understands, though, that the father is beneath any mention. Anyway, in this case Adeline doesn't even like to say 'father.' She prefers to say 'sperm donor.'

Those antique Patek Philippes were their ticket out of England. Sure enough, the auction value of the six watches was at least three million pounds between them. Shirley managed to fence them to the cousin of one of his patients for twenty-five thousand pounds in Bitcoin. And then he managed to convert the Bitcoin to fifteen thousand pounds in cash. A little bit of a loss, yes, but it tickles Adeline to think about how livid that would make her father, and anyway, it was enough to get them smuggled across the Irish Sea in a fishing boat, then down here to the southwest edge of the country, seventy miles from Cork, where Luke's mother grew up and where she returned after Holly's death. It's the most beautiful place Adeline has ever been. Also the windiest.

They don't know how long they'll stay. They're still waiting to see how it all shakes out at home. Her parents haven't been seen since that day at Cyneburne. Which means, Adeline is almost sure, that whatever fate her mother was so worried about must have claimed her after all. The Woolsaw Group keeps grinding along all the same, but these days, without all those dear friends at the summer party to help keep it out of the news, there's more scandal, more anger, more resistance. People know the name now. Her parents would be livid about that too.

Unless – until – their bodies are found, they can't be declared dead. But when they are, there will be an inheritance waiting for Adeline. She's discussed many times with Luke whether one day it might be possible to reclaim it, and then do some good with it. Adeline Woolsaw is wanted on various criminal charges, but with the right lawyers, couldn't she talk her way into a suspended sentence? After all, she was kidnapped. She was coerced. She was brainwashed. Everyone knows that.

In the meantime, they wait, and they hide. It's a cosy kind of hiding. Cosy, but not always easy. That small, draughty, isolated house, with two children, and Luke's mum. She frequently reminds herself that this is the way that normal people have lived since the beginning of time. Nobody needs sixty-five rooms. Still, a couple more wouldn't hurt.

For the most part, though, her old life feels not just remote but absurd. Luke's mum teases her about her airs and graces – the other day she called her 'duchess,' and both Luke and Adeline grew sombre for a moment because it reminded them of Rosa – but here there's none of Rosa's venom, only running jokes, and Adeline enjoys those, because nothing makes her feel more normal than being made fun of for how abnormal she is. The truth is, there are only two things she deeply misses from before.

One is the art. Most of it should be in museums, but there are just a handful of things she would keep if she were allowed to. Keep, and cherish, and look at with her children.

And the other is a feeling. A feeling she was only acquainted with for about a week, when she was with the Nail. Filming the video. Stealing the Auerbach. Mounting the raid on Cyneburne. The feeling of fighting back. She wonders sometimes if she will ever have a chance to feel that again.

As Mia chases Teddy down the beach, she looks out to sea, and finds herself thinking about Alston again. Luke keeps telling her she should forgive herself for what she did to him. But what preoccupies her is how utterly unnecessary it was. Yes, he was supposed to sit on her parents' throne. But if Percy can turn out all right (and she knows he will) and Mia can turn out all right (and she knows she will) and Adeline herself can turn out all right (and she hopes she has) – well, then surely Alston could have turned out all right too. His fate wasn't sealed until Adeline herself sealed it. All she can do now is hold on to his memory. Out behind the house, they have started a garden, which is to say a wildflower patch that they try to keep the birds off. Not only for him, but for Holly too.

She feels Luke's hand on her back. She kisses Percy, whom Luke carries in a sling, then Luke himself. 'Uh-oh,' he says, looking past her, and she turns. Mia has fallen down on the sand. She gets ready to hurry over, because lately Mia has been displaying a rather toddler-ish tendency to burst into tears over even the smallest bumps and scrapes. But then she sees that Mia isn't crying, she's laughing. Teddy starts climbing on Mia's head. And Adeline feels the beginnings of rain on her cheek, just an autumn rain, clear and cool.

THE END

ABOUT THE AUTHOR

T.k.

For more fantastic fiction, author events,
exclusive excerpts, competitions, limited editions and more

VISIT OUR WEBSITE
titanbooks.com

LIKE US ON FACEBOOK
facebook.com/titanbooks

FOLLOW US ON TWITTER AND INSTAGRAM
@TitanBooks

EMAIL US
readerfeedback@titanemail.com